The Blue Heron

Gene Farrington

"NOMU - a great place to write."

"we are products of our language"

Published by Water Street Press

Healdsburg, California

Water Street Press paperback edition published April 2014

Cover art by Sally Eckhoff

Interior design by Typeflow

Author photo by Ann Grillo

Produced in the USA

ISBN 978-1-62134-170-3

In the tradition of the
"novelist" Paul Michel,
I dedicate *The Blue Heron* to
my own reader:
Marian Copeland.

Prologue

IN CYBERSPACE *– a chat room*

dsharpe: In the beginning was the word and the word was ****.

themoll: What kind of word is ****?

dsharpe: A shag.

themoll: A what?

dsharpe: Boinking. Brit for ****.

themoll: A ball. A bang.

dsharpe: Ah...drum the bang slowly.

themoll: Too graphic.

dsharpe: A verb transitive or intransitive. To have sexual intercourse with.

themoll: To victimize.

dsharpe: Used in the imperative as a signal of angry dismissal.

themoll: To act wastefully or foolishly.

dsharpe: A noun: An act of sexual intercourse.

themoll: A noun: A despised person.

dsharpe: An interjection: Used to express extreme displeasure.

themoll: From the Middle English fucken.

I

dsharpe: A Germanic verb meaning to strike, move quickly, penetrate.

themoll: And?

dsharpe: Borrowed from the Dutch fokken.

themoll: I've never found it in the OED. Yet it is in the AHD. New College -

dsharpe: AHD. New College?

themoll: I forgot you're British. The American Heritage Dictionary. Why the beginning?

dsharpe: I hang by Oxford. There was only ******* and talking about it.

themoll: ">->"

dsharpe: Seriously. There could be no creation until a discussion of it could be conducted. Illumination. Light. It is about words. Creation is not about God. It is about words. In the beginning was the word.

themoll: What is this fascination with "word"?

dsharpe: I'm about words. I'm writing a novel. Attempting to write a novel. As I say, in the beginning was the word.

themoll: There are beginnings. And there are beginnings. In the beginning was Jamestown.

dsharpe: What is Jamestown?

themoll: It was the beginning of this country.

opech: There was a country here long before Jamestown.

dsharpe: Who the fuck are you?

opech: Don't you mean "who the **** are you?"

dsharpe: No, I mean who the fuck are you?

opech: I am someone interested in beginnings. Particularly Jamestown.

dsharpe: We're having a private chat here, mate. Do you mind?

opech: The heron, as if carved from the blue rock, *The Blue Heron (title)* protruded from the marsh. It remained motionless. I, Opechancanough, stood watching it as if expecting some sign, some warning of danger, from the bird, but the blue heron remained silent and immobile. It stood a mystery, its plumed head and needle beak pointing toward the Bay.

themoll: Opechancanough?

opech: Yes.

dsharpe: You know Opechancanough?

themoll: American history. He was the brother of Powhatan.

dsharpe: Means nothing to me.

themoll: Pocahontas's uncle.

dsharpe: Cinema...Disney...

themoll: Not exactly, but you have the idea.

opech: By then I was not a young man. By the reckoning of the *Españoles* I had *66 años*, but I still moved with great speed and agility avoiding the marshes; I wore no mantle, only a cloth tied about my midsection. I towered with long stretches of legs. My head was shaved on one side and on the other my hair hung long, draped with a turkey feather and a line of pearls. My face was painted with marks of red and black dye.

themoll: I've got the picture and that's all very nice. But who are *you*?

opech: Opechancanough was not my real name of course. That name was a secret, but it was what I was called among The People. It meant 'soul of the Whiteman,' and perhaps there was truth to it. I

3

sometimes thought as the Whiteman, or at least understood the thinking of the Whiteman. I was a werowance, the leader of the Pamkunkey. Not so exalted as my brother who was werowance of all The Powhatan, but I understood better than my brother the danger the Whiteman posed.

dsharpe: Let me get this straight. You're telling us that you are this whatever you are that lived in the...

themoll: Late sixteenth and early seventeenth century.

opech: The BiTan had spoken, their words confirmed in the entrails of an eagle; the invader would come from the sea and The People would be destroyed.

dsharpe: Would you stick it?

themoll: I'm rather fascinated by this.

dsharpe: Why? He is either putting us on or needs to be in hospital.

opech: The Pamkunkey believed it; all the other tribes believed it. I, too, accepted that the invader would come, but I could not accept that The People must be destroyed. Destiny was the way of the gods - of Okeus, he that brought evil - of Ahone, the beneficent sun. But the *Dios del Españoles* was merciful as well as wrathful and the paradox was that I was a product of both cultures, an outgrowth of my youthful education among the *Españoles*, and while I could accept the oracles, the prophecies of the BiTan, I could not stand idly by and accept the consequences.

themoll: Carl Bridenbaugh's theory.

dsharpe: What do you mean?

themoll: I told you I was a grad student. My discipline is history, American history. Jamestown most particularly and I am doing my thesis on the first women in America -

opech: Not the first women!

themoll: OK. The first White women. Anyway, Bridenbaugh has this theory that long before the English came to Jamestown, Opechancanough was taken back to Spain when he was only fifteen years old by Spanish explorers.

opech: That is true. I had not always painted my face. In my youth I had been Don Luis and my face was scrubbed and I wore the constrictive dress of the Whiteman. It was the constriction I feared most for The People. The Whiteman closed himself in, in his clothes, in his solid wall dwellings, and in his cities where bodies massed with room to neither stretch, nor breathe. It was the cities which frightened me, pushed together places with throngs of moving flesh, moving and never going anywhere. It was no wonder they wanted our land, the K'tchisipik. Their land was overflowing.

dsharpe: Spare us. themoll, where exactly is this Jamestown?

themoll: Virginia. We're talking 1607.

dsharpe: Jacobean period.

themoll: Yes, the Virginia company. The founding of America.

opech: It wasn't lost. There was nothing to find.

dsharpe: East coast of the States, kinda midway down on the map, right?

themoll: Chesapeake Bay.

opech: K'tchisipik.

dsharpe: He's crackers.

opech: The real history.

dsharpe: Yes, like you were there.

opech: It is all a matter of perspective.

themoll: Subjective you mean. History is subjective.

opech: I was an eyewitness.

dsharpe: Like you expect us to believe that bloody dribble.

opech: But it is the truth. My truth. My history. Not the White chief's, your Anglish King James history, David.

dsharpe: It's dsharpe to you. AND HOW THE HELL DO YOU KNOW MY NAME?

themoll: dsharpe, you are shouting.

dsharpe: I won't shout. How do you know my name, opech?

opech: You are writing a novel, David, of Jacobean England but -

dsharpe: Don't call me David. And HOW DO YOU KNOW about the novel? You're a hacker. You're not simply an intruder. No one knows about the novel. You've hacked into my computer.

themoll: Shouting again.

opech: Fiction. What you write is fiction. I am speaking of reality.

themoll: I do know America of the same period and opech seems to know his stuff. But then...maybe he just knows Bridenbaugh's stuff.

opech: I am here. You talk about me as if I weren't here.

dsharpe: "Weren't all there" is more like it. He's annoying me with his Rousseauian glorious-native crap. He couldn't be on the Internet now if this land of yours had been left to the damned Injuns as you call 'em. I get sick of civilization bashing.

themoll: I'd never call them Injuns, let alone damned Injuns.

6

opech: Are we the better for all your civilization?

dsharpe: I'm not interested in your viewpoint of history.

opech: Here's some history for you. I kept watch, kept vigilant. *Los Ingles* had come. They built a square mound on an island among the Roanoke. It was a five-day walk in the direction of the midday sun beyond the great and dismal swamp. But *Los Ingles* had come to stay and proclaimed it and I knew the encroachment would spread like a fire set at the edge of the forest and in that I was proven right. They had killed the Wereowance Wingena. And word came; they were looking for a place of deeper water on which to settle, a great bay. At the worst time, the freezing time, I wrapped myself in furs and with warriors journeyed to the Roanoke. By the Secotan, I was guided to the place where the English huddled in their wooden houses. I eradicated the spark before it could spread its lethal flame. But for a few babies and children taken as captives, there was not a voice left to tell the tale. The bodies were burned and the ashes dumped in the sea. Not a hair remained. *Los Ingles* vanished without a trace.

themoll: Are you telling me Opechancanough was responsible for what happened at Roanoke?

dsharpe: What happened at Roanoke?

themoll: The settlers at Raleigh's Colony at Roanoke vanished without a trace.

dsharpe: This was the seventeenth century, right?

themoll: Roanoke was the late sixteenth.

dsharpe: And you don't think he's putting us on?

opech: And David Sharpe or is it David Ersby? I must ask after Vere.

dsharpe: ENOUGH!

7

themoll: What's going on?

dsharpe: This hacker is aware that the protagonist in my novel is a David Sharpe. That's why I use dsharpe as my cyber name. Vere is an image, an important character.

themoll: So, opech. You're pulling dsharpe's leg. You know him.

opech: I knew David Sharpe.

dsharpe: David Sharpe is fiction, asshole. And there is only one way you could know about David Sharpe. You've hacked into my computer. I haven't shown any of the manuscript to anyone yet. I don't talk to people about my writing. Never specifics. You are fucking frightening, dangerous.

opech: It was the Whiteman who was dangerous. The Whiteman owned. It was not the land of people, but the land of a man. It was a concept The People could not grasp, particularly the Great Powhatan. The People could not see how the common earth could be part of a man. But I knew. I understood that the Whiteman would come and bit by bit claim the earth as his.

dsharpe: I think I'd better get out of here before I completely lose my temper.

themoll: HOAS. The women, one woman in particular I will be writing about has her beginnings in England in the period of your novel. If you are writing historical fiction of the period, I am really interested. Can we keep in touch? My e-mail address is themoll@wm.edu.

dsharpe: Yes. I suppose. I'm angry and unnerved right at the moment. Cheers.

themoll: TTYL.

[dsharpe name disappears]

themoll: opech, do you mind telling me now who you really are and what the basis is for your theory that Opechancanough was responsible for the disappearance or destruction of the colony at Roanoke?

opech: I am who I say I am, Opechancanough the werowance of the Pamunkey. I could not allow the Whiteman to take the land of The People. The Whiteman had to be stopped before he began and so I watched and waited, seeking ships on the horizon, questioning travelers from the Susquehannocks, or even the enemy the Monocan for news of the Whiteman and I sent warriors among the Accomac.

themoll: You're sticking with your story?

opech: You're part of my story, Molly. It is Molly Sharpe, is it not?

themoll: I am not frightened like David that you know that. I am interested in your story. My ancestors were part of the founding of the Jamestown colony.

opech: Molly and David Sharpe. That is why you responded to a request to chat from a dsharpe. That is why you are interested in his novel, is it not?

themoll: Yes.

opech: I waited there by the *Mar Magnifica*. I reached the Point from where I could see the K'tchisipik as it met the great waters. The sky touched the sea unbroken by any sail. Not yet. The Whiteman had not come yet.

themoll: But they would come in those three ships.

...

themoll: opech, are you still there?

...

themoll: Opechancanough...

David

LINCOLNSHIRE

—the present—

DAVID D'ERSBY WENT onto Google.uk and started to type in o-p-e-c-h-. How the fuck had he spelled it? But it didn't matter; the search engine found it with those few letters: Opechancanough. From there he went into Wikipedia: "It is speculated by some historians, including Carl Bridenbaugh..." That was the scholar Molly had mentioned. "...that Opechancanough was the Native American youth, son of a chief, transported voluntarily from the village of Kiskiack in Virginia to Spain in the 16th century at age of 17 and educated." He read on to the end of the article.

Bullshit! This online intruder, this hacker was creating his persona, making himself up from Wikipedia. But that was no worry; what was of concern is how the hacker knew about his novel and the characters in it. He could buy a new computer. It wasn't the money, it was the annoyance.

All his documents, software. He would think about it. He needed some air. He needed to think about his writing, his characters. He needed to drive out onto the Wolds.

The Wolds of his imagination were not the Wolds in his vision. Centuries had plowed and furrowed the chalky past into hedgerowed quilts of light and darker tan. A pattering of trees scratched the grey sky on the distant rise. At the juncture, David pulled the Mercedes, almost the same color as the soil, off the narrow road and got out. Lanky, his mother called him, but he was more slight than tall. In tight blue jeans and the hand-knitted white wool jumper, he perhaps appeared taller than his six feet. From a mound of bits of solid hard chalk, turned out of the field by a plow, he picked a jagged-edged piece up and rubbed it between his finger and his thumb. A pheasant — haughty, almost indifferent — crossed the road. David stood alone. He felt alone. Separated from humanity. And in the wolds of his imagination, in the wolds of his fiction, a wilder beauty rolled barren and uninterrupted. And he could hear his novel: "Words filled the emptiness…"

The Novel

—1605—

Words filled the emptiness. David Sharpe stood on the vast stretch of emptiness and yelled from the full depth of his lung capacity. "I is alone in the world. There be no one else." He looked up at the grey sky, a swirling thick gruel. "And there ain't no God, neither." God's wrath reigned in Lincolnshire in the Wesleyan year of the Lord 1605. A jagged cut of lightning tore the sky. A sharp crack of thunder followed. He flung himself to the ground, burying his face. As he got to his feet, a raven pecked past him. Agnes Strawberry of Magna Muckton, a witch, was said to go about in the guise of a raven. "A day to you, Agnes." He had already offended God; there was no sense in offending the devil as well.

The smell of the not-too-distant, but not visible, sea brined the air like a wet seine. He wondered what was at the ends of the sea. The master said the world was round.

12

Anybody could see it was flat. If it weren't, the sea would all run off and how was anyone to stand on the upside downside. He didn't learn much of value at the grammar—*amicus, amici, amico, amicum, amice, amicorum*—but the Latin was of no use to a son of a husbandman. The boys at the grammar were gentry or yeomen's brats and he was made to wait on them, except on the Sabbath when he walked home to see his mam. He shared a bed in a small room with one of the young masters, Weston Winterwell, a scholar from Cambridge, who taught David of distant places, of kings and queens. And London, where people were as thick as sheep on the moor.

David was alone. Taunted. He served boys at table or in their lodging in the sooted grey-stone grammar with its dark musty rooms, a gift of the great Lord Willoughby, who came to the school and the boys would line up. The great Lord Willoughby, who was not a bit old, with dark hair and penetrating dark eyes, would single David out and ask, "What's your name, lad?"

"David Sharpe, my Lord."

"And do you learn your declensions and your sums, David Sharpe?"

"I do, my Lord."

"It is imperative," the tall man would say, ending the brief inquisition. He never asked another boy a question. And each time it was the same. After, the boys would squeal at him. "What is the sum of all the dirt 'neath your nails?"… "My name is David Sheepdung, my Lord."… "It is impigative." David escaped within himself. *Perhaps there is only I. The rest will vanish.* He wouldn't stay except for his mam. "You're bred to it," she would say, but he didn't know what that meant. His mam was sickly, with little enough to eat, his pap drinking every pence away, and she, always with a babe to the tit. They died, those babes. Maybe ten in all. There was only David and the new one left and him nigh a fortnight old, but not named as yet lest he die and the name be wasted. David had been the first born. He was fourteen.

The raven hopped ahead of him, eyeing back occasionally. The sky opened and the rain poured out like a stave being emptied. He ran the course of the narrow road, the jagged sharp rock biting his feet through the soft foot bindings; he owned no real shoes. As quickly as it came, the rain quit. His coarse tunic was soaked and clammy against his skin. He picked up a stone and careened it across an open field. And another in the direction of a pile of sheepskin. It hit the pile with a hard thump.

The pile rose up from the earth. "AARRRH," it screeched out. A figure in sheepskin, having pushed aside the other skins under which it had been buried, stood, a giant, twenty hands at least tall, a terrible bearded creature with snarls of craggy hair and poxed skin, loused and scabby. It was the shepherd of Grimwoldby Wold. "You're a bastard, David Sharpe."

"I is not."

"You're a bastard. No right to be called Sharpe."

"I is not."

"Why be the pup of Willie Sharpe a notion to take a horn and sit with him's betters in the grammar to Lough? Aha, you little turd, 'tis a bastard you be for last and always."

"You tell false."

The great creature sank back into the pile of sheepskins and made not another sound. David continued down the road, uncomfortable in the clammy garments and the hint of bastardy. Not to be the son of Willie Sharpe—that pleased David, but to be a bastard was none to his liking. He walked slowly, kicking at stones. He entered Little Muckton, a cluster of cottages about the church and its yard, some no more than hovels. There was little else to Little Muckton, save the sound of a barking dog.

"Scratch my foot like a good lad, Davey Sharpe. Does itch most fierce." Goodie Wells, her feet and arms in the stocks, looked drenched from the rain. David went over under the tree, its stretch of branches still dripping from the rain, and started to remove a shoe. "'Tis the other foot, lad."

He took off the other shoe. "What did ye do this time?" he asked.

"Me mouth. 'Tis always me mouth. A little up toward the toes there, Davey. Oh my, that do feel well. 'Tis a great Christian kindness you do Goodie Wells."

"Who'd you slander this time, Goodie Wells?"

"The parson. I said he'd swive a chicken e're it'd stand still long enough, but the part which angered him more drastic was that I said his diddling tool would probably fit the hen's hole."

"Be that a fact or conjecture, Goodie. You experienced the parson?"

"Fah on you, lad. 'Twould be but disease to let that lecher touch me privates. No. 'Tis no firsthand experience. But there's little Goodie Wells don't know of about Little Muckton folk, for a fact."

"If that be so," David asked, stepping back from the dripping tree, "be I a bastard, Goodie?"

She paused and then spoke gently. "It be whispered in places."

"What places?"

"The back stairs to Ersby Hall."

"Why Ersby?"

"If a thing be worth knowin', it's found in the houses of the lordy." She attempted to readjust her body as if to find a measure of comfort in her confinement.

"Whose bastard be I?"

"Who's to say. 'Tis 'twixt your mam and God and some poker with a will to his way. And don't be tearing your good mam's soul with your probings 'bout it. Poor lass has enough to bear as 'tis."

"I won't." He walked from the stocks down the path by the dark stone church, wondering what his mam would say about his not being at the school, but Liptomb, a skinny tall lad, ugly as Miz Primby's water, had started yelling, "Winterwell's whore." And then the other boys picked it up; soon everyone seemed to be shouting, "WINTERWELL'S WHORE" until he couldn't stand it and so he had run, not to the little room in the back, but out of Lough toward home.

He saw the raven, be it Agnes Strawberry or otherwise, perched above the low entry to the dung and clay hut and David knew before he stooped and entered the wet darkness what omen the raven bore. The latticed openings that served as windows let in a trace of light that fell across his mam, a narrow woman with eyes unlike his own, enormous and never at rest. They seemed at odds with her thin body sinking in exhaustion, inquisitive, penetrating, a sharp blue. Her eyes, like her perfect white teeth, seemed parts borrowed from one of a better sort, mismatched when affixed to the grey poxed skin and the sagging tired frame. "It's dead," she said. She clung to the infant, pressing it to her breast.

"Let me take him," he said.

"Not yet." The three-legged stool creaked under her as she grasped the dead baby even tighter in her arms. "It still be warm yet. Time enough when him's grown cold. There be some gruel in the pot and a bit of beer in the corner I hid from the pap." The pap, Willie Sharpe, snored loudly from the pile of straw against the back wall that served as their communal bed. The thatch had leaked and David made his way around a small puddle of mud. The hut had no floor, only the pressed earth in which the accumulated layers of their history were imprinted, a year of footsteps atop another. He spooned gruel from the black kettle hanging over the fire, a circle of stones from which smoke drifted indifferently.

"Did the master teach it to you?" It was a weekly question, a ritual, a moment in which his mam seemed to take vicarious pride. Either she did not comprehend that it was not yet the Sabbath eve or else she simply was ignoring the fact that David had left school a day early.

"Today, the Master Durhman spoke on Zeno of Elea."

"Ah, Zeno," she responded as if he were an old intimate, "...of Elea. And what does Zeno know?"

"The best way to explain it is by example. Suppose I go to Lough—"

"But you do. Ever and a week to the grammar."

"Aye. But this is 'a suppose I go,' like the other Greeks I've told you on. However, in order to reach Lough I must first get half way there."

"Aye, that's a fact."

"But to get to half way there, I must first get to half way to half way and so on."

"The only way to get there."

"But if I always must get to just half way I can never get to Lough."

"But you do get to Lough." She leaned forward, nearly dropping the dead baby, but caught it as she held to the stool.

"I know that. But what Zeno says has the logic to it."

"Has the silliness to it. I think the Greeks must have thought the whole world a pretty silly place and we all but silly beings." She paused. "These Greeks spoke Latin, did they not?"

His head ached whenever he tried to figure it out. The world was round according to the master, but logically it was flat. According to Zeno he couldn't reach Lough, but he did. "Greek, Mam."

"Greek or Latin, that be it then. They couldn't put it in the King's own good English where it wouldn't seem so silly."

"'Tis as silly." He sipped the beer. "As silly as me sitting in the grammar with my betters."

"Why be you home today?"

"Because the name callin' is worse. I ran off. I'm sorry, but why must I go there?"

"Among the ungentle, the only hope e're is to read. It be like a key to a secret passage."

The gruel was tasteless. "Maybe for a yeoman, but not for dirt like us."

"You don't be dirt, Davey."

He pointed across with his stone cup at Willie Sharpe. "We be dirt."

She set the dead baby down on the earthen floor. "You ain't be his." She spoke in a whisper.

He looked at the tired woman. "And whose be I, Mam?"

"'Tis a vow on that. I would not say."

"But be it he who pays to the grammar?"

"Fah not. The good Lord of Willoughby was hardly more than a boy hisself when you were borned."

"How come you know so much of the Lord Willoughby?"

"As a girl I was milkmaid at Ersby there at Spilsby."

"You never said."

"'Twas long ago. You was borned there. And old Lord Willoughby, the youngin's father, he was a great girth of man. He sawed to me being married off to Willie Sharpe and all. Peregrine Bertie, as was his name, had been a general in the lowlands and he had a great booming voice what made them all to do at Ersby as they be told. They was noble, the Lord's mother being the Duchess of Suffolk and all."

"Be Ersby far off?"

"A long day to be and back." Her eyes seemed to look fondly back to Ersby.

"And you lived at such a grand place."

"Aye. I was borned there, too. Me own mam and pap were both got by the pox there. Pap was millwright to the manor and me mam, God rest her, worked to the scullery. Lord Willoughby had them buried to the yard at Spilsby church.

"Then 'twas he which sent me to the grammar?"

"Nay, that is the doin's of the young Lord, Robert."

"But what's the use of it?"

She got up from the stool, setting the dead baby on a worn wooden bench. She was short but he noticed at moments of importance she stood taller, the slump gave way, the arms reached out and up, extending her. "Lord Robert said when the time came I was to send you to Ersby and he would see to a place proper for you. Perhaps the time be come. You don't need no more silliness of the Greeks."

"I do read and write with a good hand."

"Then the sooner to Ersby. On the morrow you shall go to Ersby. It's a long walk."

He drained the beer cup. There was fright at the thought. "Maybe I should wait."

"No need. You don't belong 'neath Willie Sharpe's thatch, and since your mind be prone to that fact, it will be no easy thing, your stayin'. Your place be to Ersby."

"Why is so? I needs to know."

"You needs best not to know. The vow will be kept. You will be made welcome."

He stepped back to warm himself by the coals. "Why did you leave Ersby? Why didn't you and him"—he nodded in the direction of Willie Sharpe—"stay to there?"

"It was as the Lord would have it. He gived us some acres of ground, but Willie Sharpe, like a fool jack and it were a cow to be trod off for some colored beans, gave way the acres for a horse he was determined to go to Lincolntown upon. I much guess to be a highwayman. They would no doubt ta' hung him to now, but the horse died." His mam settled back on the stool. "Ersby be a wonderous place, and that but their little house. They has a great castle of a place called to Grimsthorpe. 'Tis a distance and a half, beyond the Fens. But I heared talk of what a fantastical place it be. And Ersby itself was grand as I had the eyes for." She wiped her mouth on the thick rough fabric of her sleeve.

"Now we must put the dead babe to rest." She reached in the pocket of her overskirt and, as if a great treasure, handed him a half dozen or so hand-forged iron nails. "Beneath the faggots out behind I hid some board. Make a box, need be but tiny, and we'll take the dead'un to the parson."

David

RAVENSBY ABBEY

—*the present*—

AND SO WORDS had filled the pages. The novel had begun here in this place, on these wolds. A world that looked like this, but centuries earlier. Yet as solitary.

A drop of rain and another fell as if trying to fill the solitariness that surrounded David d'Ersby. He slipped back in on the leather seat. Down from the rise, the narrow road twisted. White cottages crowded close on each side of the Mercedes. A few pink-petaled trees dripped rain. Spindly arms of forsythia stretched yellow in all directions. He drove through Spilsby where Ersby Hall had once stood. Not a trace left. But St. James, the Apostle and Martyr, while slightly Victorianized, held its stone ground, its more ancient spiked square tower rising over its nineteenth-century Ancaster stone parts. Within, the effigied corpses of the Berties, the Lords and Ladies Willoughby, their noses tweaked by civil war, still occupied their gated chancel.

The rain came heavier as he left Spilsby, a blur in his rearview mirror. It was a short drive over the familiar two-lane road. The great black iron, trimmed-in-gold, entrance gates were there, anchored on his right. From them, a long, grassy, unused road led up to Ravensby Abbey. A sign admonishing cars not to pull off had not stopped one from doing so and a blue Renault blocked the entrance. A hatted man dripping rain was holding a camera through the iron. It didn't matter. The gates were never opened. David turned up the side road.

Words could not describe the condition of the Abbey, Edward had said. But without words, how could one comprehend the current condition of where once stood a sprawl of medieval splendor? Rotting timber, leaking roof, crumbling stone, nesting birds, broken glass — these words along with damaged, falling, collapsing, overrun, neglected, created the picture. It resembled something unrestored in gothic fiction. But it had been restored and rebuilt several times in its history, most recently in the nineteenth century. David wasn't certain why Edward had bought it. He seldom was there, and David and his mother occupied it with too few servants to contain the rot. Edward had undertaken no restoration, though he mentioned getting to it on a few occasions. Edward was his mother's husband. He lived in London, and David's mother also had her own London house. In Bloomsbury. He saw the parked green Jaguar.

The heavy timber door scraped the stone floor as he entered through the kitchens. Martin, Edward's man, was heating something at the stove and didn't turn about. Bydie, the cook, tossed David a smile and a carrot as he went through. The hallway was dank, but the drawing room was warm and a fire burned, though it smoked slightly. His mother was perched on the arm of a flowered-fabric chair, staring out into the remnants of a garden.

"Edward is here." She looked to have been crying. "He says he's come home to die."

"Nonsense."

"He wants you to go right up. He's not taken his room. He's in the great red room." She fidgeted on her perch.

"It leaks and the fireplace doesn't work."

"I know. But he insisted."

Water puddled in the stone as he made his way up the turning of the back stairs. The electric was working in the great red room and cast gloomy shadows. Edward, buried beneath a stack of quilts, looked like he had been made up for death.

"It's all taxing." Edward's voice was barely audible. "Smile, David, that's gallows humor."

"Mother said you told her that —"

"I'm dying, David. I've been dying for months."

"You've never —"

"What was the point?" He coughed and gagged and motioned for David to hand him the towel. He spat something into it and David turned away, but not soon enough. The towel was blotched with red. Not just red, but a red-red, like stage blood. "I was never here." He coughed again. "I am sorry about the Abbey. I meant to... It could have been a monument."

"Shouldn't a doctor be here?"

"Too late. Martin will tend to me."

"What is it?"

Edward only coughed again into the towel and it seemed apparent in his face that he was fighting great pain. Yet the articulation of words did not reflect the pain.

"Can I give you anything?" There was an array of medication on a nearby chest.

"Martin will." He sighed with apparent pain. "We need to talk. You're not my son."

"I know."

"You have my name." He said nothing for a moment and then quietly added, "I can't leave it to her. None of it."

"Mother?"

"Yes."

"I...I will find a way. I'll take care of her."

"Yes. You will take care of her." There was agony in his voice. "I am leaving it to you."

"But I am not your son."

"But there is no one..." His voice drifted off. There was silence.

Martin came in the room. David moved over to the window, giving the place at the bedside to Martin. He was not an old man, but there was an old-fashioned diffidence about him and while he spooned something into Edward's mouth, it was done without intimacy, not without care, not even without affection, but without crossing the line.

"Tell him," the voice from the bed said, barely audible.

"It's hard for your father to speak," Martin said. "He asked me to explain this to you. To alleviate the heavy tax burden that would ensue were he to leave you Ravensby, he has bequeathed it to the Caring-Lessor Foundation. He has purchased Berling Hall near Lesser Steeping for you. You know it?"

The voice from bed spoke. "...once Ersby land."

"Your father's solicitors will go over all this with you. Your father wants me to only assure you that he has left you more than comfortable. I think he should rest now."

"You will see to her," the voice spoke from the covers and coughed. Martin brought a fresh towel. "And, David, I need…" He put his face into the towel and removed it. "... may need someone to go to the continent for me. Would you…?"

"Yes," David said.

"Bavaria…" The weak voice trailed off.

"*Ich sprechen Deutsch*," David responded and left the room. He hadn't the vaguest notion why Edward would need him to go to Germany. The rain was coming harder against the glass and dripping off in the corner. The wall covering was stained from previous rains.

His mother was crying openly but still sitting on the arm of the chair, staring out at the ruins of the garden. The flowers of her dress made her appear an appendage to the chair.

"I'm his heir," he said.

"He's always been good to you, David. You've never wanted." She dabbed her eyes into a handkerchief with red strawberries. David thought of Desdemona. "Eton, Cambridge."

"Yes. And he is looking out for me now."

"There's nothing left, David."

"He said Berling Hall is to be ours."

"He's delusional. Ravensby, what little upkeep there's been, the taxes and our lives have left him penniless."

"He said Ravensby was to go to Caring-Lessor."

"I would expect they would decline it."

"What will become of it?"

"Collapse into a ruin. It's not far from that now."

He put his arm around her shoulders and he, too, gazed out at the decaying garden. "What is to become of us?"

"I have a little to manage for myself. I have already spoken to, phoned…." She faltered as she softly said the next two words. "…your father." Never by name. She never spoke, never revealed his name. It added to David's isolation. "He has agreed to a regular stipend. It will be quite suitable. I want you to be able to continue your writing."

"Do you suppose Edward will want to be buried here?"

"I would think not. Poor Edward's been metaphorically buried by Ravensby as it is. Maybe Spilsby church. The Baroness would have to give her permission, if he were to be buried with the Berties." She walked to the window. "Twenty-nine years of guilt. I will be free of having to live with that." It was said more to herself than to him. "Have you eaten?"

"I had a bit of pub grub in Lough."

"Yes, then."

He left her and went to his room. A fire had been laid. He stood at the window staring down at the ruined horseless stables through the distorted streaks of water that streamed down the window from clogged eaves above.

He looked back at the blank computer screen. It was dark, almost ominous. There was a voice in there. But how did the voice know? How could the voice know if he had not hacked into the computer? How could he know Sharpe, d'Ersby and Vere? Especially Vere. Historically, the Vere surname was the correct choice. It belonged to the novel.

But he knew it was more than that. He was haunted by the name Vere. He lied to himself, denying the resemblance, but when he looked at David Aubrey Vere it was like looking at himself in a mirror as if dressed for some masquerade. He hated David Aubrey Vere. Not really because of his homosexuality, although that was his excuse. He could see his own reflection in the streaming window and he saw a Vere bastard. His mother did not need to tell him. David knew. The face in the glass distorted by streaming water; he turned from the image.

There was a coldness at Ravensby Abbey. It permeated its occupants as it did its walls. Had someone stood at this same window centuries earlier and heard the rain? Or was there no history? Was it all subjective contrivance? This was the home he had known for so much of his life and the rhythmic sound of rain was a part of it. The grey day. This was his history, his memories.

He touched the shift key. The dark screen lighted and he went online. The themoll appeared.

---

themoll: Are you OK?

dsharpe: Not really, but I'll survive.

themoll: I hate to freak you out any more than you are, but my last name is Sharpe.

dsharpe: Bloody hell, love. This is ******* weird.

themoll: Coincidence. That's all.

dsharpe: And what would opech have done with that?

themoll: I probably shouldn't tell you this, but he knew.

dsharpe: He knew your name was Sharpe. You didn't tell him?

themoll: I didn't tell him.

dsharpe: This guy is a real cyber stalker. Probably dangerous.

themoll: I don't know. He's an interesting one if he is. And knowledgeable.

dsharpe: I prefer not to hear from him again. Hey. It was because my cyber name is sharpe, dsharpe, that you asked to chat, wasn't it?

themoll: Yes. What led me to my graduate research was that I am descended from some of the earliest colonialists, David and Molly Sharpe.

dsharpe: This is a bit nuts. David Sharpe is fictional. An extension of my imagination.

themoll: But my ancestor was David Sharpe. It is simply coincidence.

dsharpe: Do you believe that?

themoll: I have to.

dsharpe: And then there's Vere...

themoll: Vere, where does Vere come in? Wasn't it a Vere that was supposed to have written all of Shakespeare?

dsharpe: Edward Vere. Earl of Oxford. But I think Shakespeare wrote all of Shakespeare.

themoll: And Vere is in your novel?

dsharpe: A character, purely fictional, important and kin to the historical Edward Vere. But I knew a bloke at school, David Aubrey Vere, probably descended from Edward Vere in a roundabout sort of way.

themoll: But your Vere is fictional.

dsharpe: Yes and what disturbs me is that this opa-whatever character knew about him. I am rattled. Baffled. The real Vere is a bit of a wanker.

themoll: Translate.

dsharpe: A poofta.

themoll: Gay.

dsharpe: He must have fancied me. He was always about.

themoll: I hadn't thought of you as a looker, strangely enough. Are you?

dsharpe: If I were a character in my novel I would describe myself "as ugly as raven's dung." I don't think the bloke had any taste. He had money though. His mum came to visit perched in the back of a Rolls, hat bigger than the late Queen Mum's. Vere introduced her to me. She wouldn't have pissed on me if I were burning to death.

themoll: And that was in your school days?

dsharpe: Except he ended up at Cambridge as well. I was at Trinity. He was at Pembroke. He's a year or something older than me. I'd be out with my mates and there would be Vere. It was as if he were following me. I yanked him aside one night and told him to get lost. Told him I preferred my bonking with women.

themoll: We always seem to get around to *******.

dsharpe: Don't we just. We veer, to coin a pun.

themoll: To go off course.

dsharpe: To shift clockwise in direction.

themoll: Tergiversate.

dsharpe: Equivocate.

themoll: Apostatize.

dsharpe: Evade.

themoll: Perhaps Re-vering.

dsharpe: Not the poofta.

themoll: The character.

dsharpe: I could change his name in the novel to Erev.

themoll: An anagram.

dsharpe: Not just an anagram, but a semordnilap.

themoll: What on earth is a semordnilap?

dsharpe: A word spelled backwards.

themoll: Palindromes spelled backward.

dsharpe: You got it. Anyway. I thank you.

themoll: For what?

dsharpe: For cheering me up. It's a bit heavy here at the old Abbey. My mother's husband is dying.

themoll: I am sorry, David. You live in an abbey?

dsharpe: The crumbling remnants of one. Ravensby is falling down...

themoll: And your stepfather?

dsharpe: Strange, I suppose I never thought of Edward as being my stepfather. Always as my mother's husband.

themoll: I take it he married your mother when you were quite grownup.

dsharpe: Actually not. They were married several years before I was born.

themoll: But he's not your father?

dsharpe: No. Edward and my mother were living in Riyadh. Edward was in the Foreign Service. Mother became pregnant with me and apparently there was no way I could be Edward's child. Mother fled Saudi. I have never been told who my father was. As I am not dark enough to be an Arab, I gather it was some other Brit. While I was raised in the d'Ersby's family home with the d'Ersby name, and later came here to the Abbey, it has always been made very clear to me that Edward was not my father. I don't know why I am telling you all this. Telling this to a stranger.

themoll: Maybe because I am a stranger. Revealing one's soul is so easy in cyperspace. The facelessness of it, I suppose. Your parents divorced?

dsharpe: Never. Nor did they ever really live together.

themoll: No brothers or sisters?

dsharpe: I was the one and only non-issue of their relationship. And you?

themoll: Only child. I'll tell you about it later. For the moment I need be off to prepare for a seminar on tobacco as currency in the seventeenth century. Anyway, I am out of here. TTYL.

dsharpe: Ta.

David signed off but as the screen went dark, he knew he would have to buy a new computer. He would load the portion of the novel that was written onto a flash drive or an external hard drive and leave this computer to the opech hacker. But for the moment he returned to the novel, to David Sharpe in the hovel: "The sun rose..."

The Novel

ERSBY HALL

—1605—

The sun rose before David, warming the day. As he left the dank, dirt-floored hovel, the sun embraced him, hugging and touching his face with fingers of heat. His mam stood, small under the timbered lintel, the sun washing over her without contrast. "Beyond Alford be Willoughby. 'Tis there you bear from the road and take to the path by the woods and o'er the wide Wold. Just beyond the Steeping you be to Spilsby and Ersby Hall." It was the sixth time she had given him the same directions.

"Mam. I'll be home afore sun let down."

"May and may not."

Certainly he would be home. The sky was blue as ribbon and gently streaked with clouds as thin as lace edging. The rocky countryside rolled in the distance. There was a contentment stretching from his torn foot bindings up to his cowlick. David sensed with limited insight the nature of freedom. Only a few sheep nibbling on a rise intruded on the vast landscape. His eyes devoured the novelty of the unfamiliar and, while it was probably little different than the landscape to the north, there was strangeness to the bend of the road or the placement of trees, enclosures, brooks and tilled fields. Beyond Greater Muckton, an old woman, shriveled but quick of fingers, sat at a spinning wheel outside the door of a cottage whose roof had sunk on one side and, from the weight, leaned so heavily that the building tilted and looked ready to collapse. The pedal foot kept pace with her one hand raised near the distaff. "I'd wager a goat's turd you be on route to Ersby."

"Yes."

"I can tell a Bertie as easy I can the plop of me own cow. Your name, lad?"

"David. David Sharpe."

"Aye. Explains it."

"Explains what?"

"The gentle quality about you. I got a nose for gentry. I can smell 'em."

"You smelled wrong. I be far from gentry. 'Tis crude folk I am."

"You be raised by Tess Beard was you not? And that no good Willie Sharpe?"

"Aye. You know me, mam?"

"I knowed Tess since she was at her old woman's tit."

"Then you know I ain't gentry folk."

"I knows the secret of Ersby Hall. And I know you ain't no child of Tess and Willie Sharpe."

David felt as if there were a hole in his innards. "I ain't no seed to Willie Sharpe, but me mam's me mam. Me mam's me mam."

"Child, you be better blood."

"There ain't no better blood than me mam." David could not constrain the pain in his stomach.

She slowed her wheel. "Your mam is a good woman, but she's mean folk like me. Breeding do tell. You can sees it in them what's born to it and, child, it flows in your veins like melted gold."

"No," he said.

"I can't says to all I know for they would cut out Githie Dornby's tongue. And it be best for you not to pry too much neither. But take whate'er they offer for it be yours by right of birth."

"It's not so. None of it's so."

"Aye. You're the secret of Ersby Hall. But you must not say to knowin' any but what they tell you at Ersby, for they will not just cut your tongue out, but will remove your pretty head, if they have a mind, and affix it to the spike at the gate."

He understood. She was old and daft, crazy as a cow bit by a mad fly.

"It's the truth. Believe what I says. I was there in Ersby Hall when you was still corded to her."

"To who?" The old crone was making him angry.

"That is the great secret of Ersby."

"You made it all up. They will tell at Ersby that you be mad, crazed as a loony-tic."

"You but breathe a word to what I say and won't be your head by itself what hits the stone, but they lop off Tess

Beard's as well. Be off now, David de Ersby. I have my spinning to be done. And ye a life to learn."

He left her, but her last words stuck in his head. 'David de Ersby.'

It was beyond Claxby on the path that edged the great woods that he met the squat man. The man straddled the path as if to prevent David from passing. David tried to move around him.

"You ain't gettin' by till you gives me the coin you cozened from me ancient pap, Vere." The voice was high-pitched and piercing.

"I know you not. And I ain't nobody called Veer. Now let me by."

The squat man stared up at him and squeaked. "I'm a troll and I can keep you from passing with me evil powers." His eyes wandered over David as if looking for some secret.

"You ain't no troll. Now let me by." David shoved him out of the way and moved on down the path.

"You ain't Vere," the voice screeched after him. "You ain't Vere…but you tell him…You tell Vere…" But the rest was lost in the wind.

David ran until he reached a stone bridge. The river water was cold and he washed his face and rinsed his mouth. Up the incline through a cluster of trees, he saw what must be Ersby. It was both wondrously magnificent and slightly awry. A configured menagerie of darkened-oak timbers and white plaster, it seemed to spread in many directions; it looked to sink under the depressing weight of its timbers and array of chimneys. The heavy oak and plaster was interrupted by endless windows, diamonds of glass in lattice. The magnificence of the Berties was apparent in the massiveness, but there was something about Ersby, as if it had been built with haste, that made it not entirely intimidating. At the front of the house were huge timbered gates in the wall, and within one was a small door. He opened it and was startled as a bell clanged. He stepped into a cobbled courtyard.

"Close the gate ahind ye." A grizzled man was up at an open upper window. "What d'ye want?"

"I've come to see his Lordship."

"He ain't here. He be to Grimesthorpe. You can go to Grimesthorpe."

"No," David said. His mother had said it was a place too far to get to.

"What be your name?"

"David Sharpe," he replied, but it wasn't really his name any longer.

"I thought such." The grizzled face smiled without teeth. "I go ask Master Peregrine be he the will to see ye." The face disappeared from the open window. Peregrine? Lord Peregrine his mother spoke on, but he was dead. A red-combed black rooster pecked between the cobble. A pig grunted and poked its snout around one of the many corners.

An oak door creaked open. It was not the grizzled face, but a boy in a dirty jerkin with sleepy eyes and a face torn by the pox. The place smelled of burnt wood, rosewater, and musty timber. David's eyes did not adjust quickly and he saw only massive shapes, some light from windowed rooms, and the silhouette of a staircase wide enough to drive an ox up. "You wait in the hall." The boy's voice was as lazy as his eyes. David followed into a room that rose the height of two churches.

"Who is Master Peregrine?" he whispered to the boy.

"His Lordship's brother. Stay to this room." The boy went out.

A few embers sent a drift of smoke upward from a massive fireplace at one end of the great hall. He peeked into an adjacent room where a table was piled with books. He had never seen more than two chairs in his whole life and here was a room with, he counted, seven. As he moved about the great hall, he caught his reflection in a lavishly gilded mirror. He had seen his own image in clear ponds and polished pots, but never so distinctly, never before in a real looking glass, and he scrutinized the face he found there. It was a small face, carved, with tiny dark eyes set apart, a large nose and a dimpled cheek. His clipped hair was dark and seemed to go off in all directions; he smoothed it down. He was preoccupied with his face when he sensed someone watching him. It was momentary; a ghostly white-faced woman appeared above on an open second level and then vanished. David hid himself around the corner of a large cupboard to watch for her. She appeared again, leaning over from the opening above. Her face was bone white with tiny red painted circles. She wore a stiff ruff about her throat, but beneath was open and her breasts were pushed up and over the fabric of the opening, exposing darted nipples in dark, almost black areolas. He was fascinated with the sight. She held a mask over her eyes, but when she moved it away as if looking for him, he caught a glimpse of the small dark eyes on the small face. He knew she was not young, but the ethereal white took away any sense of age, and she appeared as much dead as alive. She caught him watching and vanished.

David

RAVENSBY ABBEY

—the present—

DAVID D'ERSBY PUT the manuscript aside and slept fitfully. The rain had stopped in the night. In the morning he went down the stone steps to the kitchen.

Bydie set a bowl before him on the heavy wooden table. David gazed into the bowl. "These are very nice."

"What are nice?" Bydie asked.

"The cornflakes."

"How can cornflakes be nice? They are simply cornflakes."

He was only trying to make conversation. Silence, except for the urgent chopping of a knife and the burring of the tired refrigerator, sputtering and swearing death at every whirl. No still life here. Only a space empty of words — a pause, perhaps — that he had attempted to fill politely. He ate the cornflakes and did not find them nice.

Polished shoes, starched shirt, black tie and creased pants, Martin entered, taking a tray to the scullery.

"How is he?" David asked.

"Little change."

"Tea?" Bydie asked.

"Very nice." Martin sat at the table across from David.

"Toast?" Bydie set the cup and saucer before the manservant.

"Just a biscuit, perhaps."

David was surprised by the sound of a car, a big car from the engine roar. It whirled silent. Two men came in without knocking, dressed identically in black suits, pale ochre shirts and plum ties without pattern. One man towered, a spindly pole, at what must have been six and a half feet and probably weighing less than twelve stone. He had deep-set large black eyes and seemingly unmanageable coarse black hair. He looked as if he would be at ease in the conspiratorial, narrow streets of Jerusalem. The other was red — red-haired, red-skinned, red-bearded and red-nosed. A thick short man with a Celtic air, Scottish or Irish. He wore an embroidered yarmulke.

Martin rose, seemed uneasy. "McGold. Candleberg."

"You were expecting us?" the tall man asked.

"You were expecting us?" the red red-haired man repeated.

"Das Wort," the tall man said and the red red-haired man added without a break in the sentence, "Ist Jude," as if they were presenting a password. It was quite ridiculous.

"I'll take you to him." Martin led the way out of the kitchen. The two marched behind with their attaché cases, like something from Monty Python.

"Dangerous." Bydie's voice was flat and final.

"Dangerous?"

"You'll see."

He did not see. He went into the drawing room. His mother sat in the flowered arm chair in the same flowered dress. Perhaps again or perhaps yet. He did not know.

"Two men have come to see Edward."

"I'm sorry." She paused and then added, "I am going to Bloomsbury." The way she said it, Bloomsbury seemed more a state of mind than a geographical place.

"Why are you sorry? Who are they?"

"It doesn't matter who they are. Should I have George take me to the station?"

"I will," he said. "Will you be in London long?"

"I'm not certain. I will go ready myself and take the two-sixteen." She rose, tapped his hand lightly, and left a dolor-ous hole in the room. She had been sad as long as he could remember. He knew she had few friends. Society mostly ignored Margaret d'Ersby, as did her own family, the Per-fect-Lawrences, after what they called that "unseemly busi-ness in Saudi." But he suspected his mother had a new lover in London. He had first learned of an indiscretion, over-heard actually, in a Cambridge pub. Talk of a captain in the Queen's Guard and some "bit of piece," a Margaret d'Ersby. It had shaken him. And after, there had been the professor of Comparative Literature. David had dropped by unan-nounced and was unnerved to find a greasy little French-man in his mother's house. "*Comment allez-vous?*"

"Fine," David had replied with determined English, but he was not fine seeing this man at home in his mother's house. Words — were they greater weapons if they were in French rather than English? Duel was a French word and fence was etymologically linked to defence and foil, which lacked French heritage, but was derivative of the obsolete fulyie: plain and simply *shit*. And that was David's ultimate and immediate evaluation of the dark little bald man who probably gave lectures about Ionesco's *Bald Soprano* with a decidedly French distain for the English language. Words do not simply form thinking, David thought, but formed one's emotions. Or did emotions form one's words?

He left the drawing room for his own room. His own life seemed more fictional than the fiction he was constructing: a father, who-was-not-his-father, dying in a red room and being visited by two Pinteresque figures; a mother, who-was-less-than-wife to the father-who-was-not-a-father, going off to a lover. So much unstated, unpronounced, but there, glaring constantly at him. He was a bastard, but no one, not even the Perfect-Lawrences, least of all the Perfect-Lawrences, ever uttered the word. It was the silence that was telling. And now there had come that American Indian voice from the seventeenth century interjecting nonsense into his private cyber conversation with the rather pleasant American bird interested in words. He suspected she was ordinary. Perhaps she was ugly, but he could hold words to her as if holding them to a candle flame, watching them transfigure. Ordinary was only a word, but a word, which might be the construct, the defining delineation of *themoll*. Was he, himself, only a construct of words or a deconstruct?

Summary so far

Molly

WASHINGTON, D.C.

—her childhood—

THE YOUNG MOLLY Sharpe thought Ordinary was simply part of the Catholic mass. Then she overheard one of the Sisters say, "Molly is an ordinary girl." She scurried to the dictionary: *adj. a. Of no exceptional ability, degree or quality; average. b. Of inferior quality; second rate. See synonyms: common.* She had been eleven, but from that moment she chose to appear as extraordinary as possible. She knew she was not ordinary, never had been ordinary, but she felt it necessary to show the world she was not ordinary. Until she was two, her life was perhaps ordinary. She did not remember. But she remembered when she was two. Well, she didn't remember exactly, but read about it later in the newspapers and then it became a part of her tumultuous memory. She was two and riding in the back seat in a car seat facing the world as it went backward and she didn't actually remember that world because that part wasn't in the newspaper, only that she was facing backwards (which in itself was forward-looking for child car seats at the time) and she knew that her birth, itself, however ordinary the first two years of her life had been, had been extraordinary, quite spectacular. As the dim calm and darkening stillness fell on Ravenna, Ohio (Molly understood the nature of approaching tornados), pregnant Dorothy and her twenty-eight-year-old husband fled the third-floor apartment for the cellar. It was a cellar, as she was told, not a basement, never seen by Molly, but she imagined it was entered only from outside the three-story house and that it was wet stone and dank with only one window of light. Not in color. Something out of Dorothy's Kansas. And the tornado struck and she was born in the damp and dark place while violent winds tore the world above her. In the cellar, there were no other occupants of the three-story, converted-to-apartments frame house, only her mother and her father, Dr. David Dean Sharpe. Unfortunately, his doctorate was in history, bestowed by Kent State University, and so she was born in a cellar while the house, white she imagined, had been flattened above her with only her doctor father, who was not a medical doctor, attending her mother at her birth. That was extraordinary drama.

Next came Morgantown, West Virginia, an ordinary time, where David Dean Sharpe became an Assistant Professor of History and of which she had no memories, no pictures. And then the trip to Washington, D.C. It was twilight, it had to be light, after all, as the world was visibly passing her by backwards, as her printed memory would have it, and as she rested (so the article had stated; how did they know she hadn't slept through the whole event?)

in the back of the 1970 Saab as it was struck, head on, by a drunk driving on the wrong side of the divided highway. And her non-remembered remembrances had the car whirling and turning and tipping and flopping and David Dean and Dorothy Sharpe were pinned, slashed, mutilated and dead and she screamed unharmed upside down in the rear. The drunk who had hit them went to jail, probably out by now. She didn't care. She had no sorrow over the parents she never knew. She never joined MADD nor SADD, nor was particularly angry at drunks. Her grandfather, Randolph David Sharpe, died in a boating accident on the Chesapeake in 1962 and his wife of grief a year later. Dorothy had been an orphan. The Sharpes had a direct line to the founding of Jamestown, but had never been prolific in the process. There was only an uncle, young James Sharpe, Father James Sharpe of Baltimore, David Dean Sharpe's brother, and he became her guardian and she was raised by nuns in Washington, D.C. And from an ordinary day when she had learned that she was ordinary, she determined never to be ordinary again.

David

RAVENSBY ABBEY

—the present—

ANY FURTHER EXPLORATION of David's existential nature, his postmodern existence, was interrupted by Martin. "Your father asks that you come to him." He wore a dark face that matched his trousers.

"And the two men?"

"They have gone."

In the bleakness of the red room, Edward's head was slightly elevated by an array of pillows, a red-stained towel tucked beneath his chest. "Will you go to Munich for me?"

"Why?" David asked.

"Tomorrow?"

David's simple "Yes" was questioning, but indicated compliance.

Then Martin said, "You will take the zero-nine-fifteen Lufthansa flight to Flughafen München from Heathrow. In this envelope is your airline ticket, your Munich train-bus pass and a supply of Euros. Take a number three S-Bahn train from the Flughafen to Rosenheimerplatz. Take a taxi to the Blattl's Hotel, Altmunchen, Mariahilfplatz Number Four. It is a small pension. Spend the night, enjoy the evening. You will take this attaché case with you. It is empty. In the morning at zero-nine-thirty, board a number six bus for Marienplatz. Wait with the tourists in the platz. When the glockenspiel strikes ten, go to the Staatsangehörig Bank Bavaria on the south side of the platz. Ask for Herr Rolf Liebendof. He will be expecting you. Give him the attaché case. After a few moments he will return a case to you. Take a taxi to the hotel; ask the driver to wait. Check out, take your bag and take the taxi to Flughafen München. You will take the sixteen-thirty-five Lufthansa flight back to Heathrow. Never let the attaché case from your sight. Bring it back here."

"Do you understand?" Edward asked in a hoarse voice from the bed.

"I understand. But, of course, I don't understand why."

"Better left unsaid," Martin told him. His mother had forsaken the flowered dress and with it a sense of dowdiness. In her red suit and red shoes, she looked smarter, ready for combat in the city. He helped her in and then slipped in the driver's side. "Tea at the Savoy?" he jested.

"A bit red for tea at the Savoy, don't you think? Perhaps more suited, forgive the pun, for nibbling sweetbreads and pigs feet stuffed with mousse at La Tante Claire."

"You're grossing me out."

"Sometimes you sound so hideously American." As the car slipped down the drive, she added, "You must be careful, David."

"I'm always a careful driver," he said. "Or did you mean my word choice?"

"Neither. You must be careful what Edward asks of you."

"I'm going to Munich for him."

"I know," she said.

"You seem to know everything. Who were the two men that visited Edward?"

"McGold. Candleberg."

"Yes, but who are they?"

"Best not to inquire too deeply into Edward's affairs. Do you keep in touch with David Vere?" She had changed the subject without a pause.

"No." He was emphatic.

"You should."

"Mother, he's gay."

"You're not a bigot, David. You have other homosexual friends."

"But David Vere is not a friend. Why do you bring him up?" But he knew why.

"I think it would be nice if you were friends."

David changed the subject and they talked of the Pinter revival, *Betrayal.* "Nicely done." But her response had been edgy and he realized his mention of the work was inappropriate.

He spent the night amid the tropical plants and palms at the Sheraton Skyline near Heathrow, which was extravagant, as opposed to the Blattl's Hotel in Munich, which was small but clean and comfortable. It was early afternoon and he found a beer garden where a band played Dixieland with an incongruous oompah beat. He met Lise at the long wooden table. She was a charming dark-haired Slovenian with large breasts and a birthmark on her neck that resembled a sinking Titanic. Her English was better than her German, neither of which was spectacular, but they settled on it as a means of communication. "Will you take I...Lise," she added as if unsure of the correctness of the I, "to the opera?"

"What opera?"

"Der flauten something."

"The Magic Flute?"

"Yes."

"I'm leaving tomorrow."

"Tonight?"

"You want to go to the opera now?"

"Yes. At Gärtnerplatz."

"Is it far? Can we get tickets?"

"I am virgin," Lise told him on the short bus ride. He didn't respond because he didn't know how to respond.

The performance had been sold out, but they were able to get good seats in the stalls that had been returned. The production was magnificent. The Germans knew their Mozart and did it well.

"Thank you," he told her and nestled his nose near her birthmark.

"Thank you much," she responded. "Much. Much. I wanted to see the man sang Papagano. I had once the sex with him."

"With the tenor playing Papagano? I thought you were a virgin."

"I am. I gave the man some cocksucking."

"Lise, you are very strange, although quite beautiful."

"I am beautiful strange." She put her head against his shoulder as they moved through the crowd down the high wide steps. "Would you like me to give you some cocksucking?"

It would be impolite to refuse. He laughed at his thought.

"Why do you laugh? Do you not want the cocksucking?"

"Yes. I want," he said. "Should we catch the bus?"

"You said you stay at Altmunchen. We walk."

And they walked, holding hands, along Cornelius Strasse and across the stone bridge over the black night river to Mariahilfplatz. The red stone of Mariahilfkirche rose dark above the black trees in the surrounding platz. The kirche appeared so isolated, deserted in the barren platz.

He used his key and they entered the small lobby and up the equally small elevator to the second floor. Lise clung to him as if he might melt. The kissing was long and passionate. The cocksucking, short, quick and over.

"Papagano had smaller cock." And she added without breathing, "Would you me gift?" She moved in the dark like a nervous moth. The only light escaping into the room came from the bathroom.

"What would you like?" he asked, nude on the bed.

"That." She pointed to the attaché case.

"That I can't. That is my father's. I could give you a hundred euros."

"I am not whore."

"I have little else to give."

In the small bathroom, she gargled his mouthwash and spoke as she spat it out. "Then I take hundred euros. But I am not whore."

He gave her euros. She dressed, although she had only removed her clothing above the waist — a tee shirt that read "Baltimore Ravens" over which she wore a blue woolen jumper. "Thank, David." She went out without a kiss or word. He was overwhelmed with a sense of emptiness. Nothingness. He was left with an erotic memory. It was not enough. He slept fitfully.

In the morning, the figures of the glockenspiel emerged to the pleasure of the pressed throng of waiting tourists. David was jostled by a Japanese woman and her Yashica. He went into the Staatsangehörig Bank Bavaria. Herr Liebendof looked more Mediterranean than Germanic, a clean-shaven little man with crisp black hair pasted to his head. He showed David to a blue leather seat that matched the blue of the walls, the blue of the carpet, the blue of the counter where tellers toiled. David watched. A man with wide shoulders and strings of platinum hair. A woman with a nasal, piercing voice slinging her Deutsche darts in all directions. An emaciated young woman in a clinging orange dress that clashed with the blue of the bank. And a dwarfish man sitting several blue leather chairs away in a trench coat. And lingering body odor. His woolly short legs failed to reach the blue carpet. He appeared to wear neither trousers nor socks and his brown shoes were oil stained. His broken teeth grinned at David.

Herr Liebendof returned and David rose and accepted an attaché case. He nearly dropped it, so taken aback was he by the unexpected weight. And it rattled. He had a vision of coins and diamonds shaking about inside. "*Danke,*" he said.

"*Wiedersehen.*"

He took the taxi to Flughafen München, clinging to the attaché case. There was no custom difficulty in traveling within the European community, but he was concerned about the contents of the attaché case at the security gate. He had images of being dragged away by shouting German police: "*Engländer, was ist?*" And the problem was he didn't know *was ist.* It could be chunks of South African gold or human bones from some archeological dig, iron scrap or retrieved sunken treasure, an ancient artifact stolen from some Egyptian tomb, a bomb or a collection of pfennigs, pre-war sculpture stolen by the Nazis, disassembled weapons or bits of contraband ivory, remnants of the walls of ancient Troy stealthily and illegally carted out of Turkey, rocks or wreckage. It could be anything but empty. He nervously set the case on the conveyor belt and emptied his pockets, watching the case slip through the cascade of waving black canvas as it vanished inside the recess of prying exposure. He stood, waiting for a screaming, blasting alarm.

"*Bitte,*" someone behind him said.

"Sorry." He walked through the framed detector. There was nothing, only the black case resting silently and then pushed along by his other small bag on the belt.

In the waiting area, he smelled him and looked up to see the dwarf seated nearby. The short man tapped his dangling oily shoes together. German soldiers in fatigues and polished boots came down steps and mingled about where David sat clutching the case. The dwarf grinned. David's gate was called and he raced to find it. There was no sign of the little man as he rode in the comfortable first class cabin. At Heathrow he caught the Underground bound for King's Cross St.

Pancras and as he found a seat he looked across to see the dwarf, trench coat now open revealing green lederhosen. David avoided looking, riding through station after station. He caught his train. No sight of the dwarf. The towns, the English countryside moved peacefully by his window.

He tried to focus on the David of his fiction but could not leave the David of reality. What was life to be after Edward? His grandparents, the Perfect-Lawrences, were polite and coolly kind to David. They sent him expensive gifts on Boxing Day and on his birthday. They had appeared at appropriate times at school and he had spent days and once a whole weekend at Leyton-James Hall near Gainsborough, their oh-so-carefully-tended country home. As their name seemed to imply, they were perfect Lawrences without sin or blemish and they did not lavish love on the fruits of sin. Still, the Perfect-Lawrences would probably not leave him without means and found his intent to be a novelist a properly nice, properly suitable, properly acceptable pursuit for a young man, so far superior to "so many young wastrels in this day and age." Still, the Perfect-Lawrence's help was not calculable. But perhaps his mother was wrong. Perhaps she had no knowledge of Edward's financial situation. Yet, so little escaped her. Maybe his fortune rested in the attaché case.

"Let me help you, sir," Martin said, taking the case from David at the Abbey.

The "sir" jolted him. It was a new diffidence. It had been Master David and then, more recently, nothing, as if the servants and others about the Abbey didn't know what to do with him during the awkward years. "Did you have a pleasant trip, sir?"

"Without incident. How is he?" They moved across the ancient stone floor into the hall.

"Sleeping at the present. I will come for you when he awakes." Martin vanished with the case up the great staircase. David went up to his own room and picked up the manuscript. He began with: "David grimaced…"

The Novel

ERSBY HALL

—1605—

David grimaced, winked and made faces at the image in the mirror. He pushed his lips up with his finger to examine his teeth.

"David."

Startled, he swung about to face a man of middling stature. He had a slight pointed beard and wore a gold earring.

David attempted a bow. "My lord."

"I am not 'my lord'—I am Peregrine Bertie." While his small dark eyes did not seem to smile, the large resonant voice did. "Let me look at you." He held David's chin, turning his face to one side and then the other as if examining some ware he was about to purchase. "Yes. Yes," he said. "Robert is right. We can make something of you. Come." He led the way into the room with the chairs. "What do you know of your birth?"

He was uncertain what he dare reply; the warnings of the old crone may have been nothing but madness, still… "I've been told I was birthed here, my… uh, here in this place." As he turned about, he was startled by a portrait. It had not been visible to him when he had been peering into the room.

"And the circumstances?"

"The circumstances, sir?" There were four portraits, but only *one* held his attention.

"Of your birth."

"Only that me mam had me. And that Willie Sharpe not be my pap."

"Sit." The man pointed to a chair. David stared at the chair. He examined it and then gently lowered himself down on the seat, sitting first on the edge and then sliding onto the chair until his head rested against the sharp carving of the back. In all, it was an uncomfortable experience.

The man seemed to be smiling. "So if you are not Willie Sharpe's, whose be ye?"

"I don't know, sir." He turned back, peering around the chair to get a better view of the portrait. It was astounding. "That be a fact."

"Life be full of unanswerables. And oftentimes such riddles be left unresolved. Know you the myth of Pandora? She opened a sour kettle of fish, she did, think you not?""

"The Greek lass. I do, sir."

"Curiosity killed the cat. Doors be locked to keep what's in as well to keep what's out. And such like. Don't you agree?"

David did not turn from the portrait. "I do, sir."

"Then we are of one mind." The man got up. "You seem interested in our portraits."

"I was just looking at him. 'Twas all." David looked down at his hands.

"The one to the left is Lord Peregrine Willoughby, my father. He died but a few years ago. The next is Lord Willoughby, my dear brother Robert. You have seen him. And that is obviously me. You read your Greek and Latin well I am told."

The portrait Peregrine Bertie didn't mention was so like his own image in the looking glass. "Who be that picture of?"

"'Tis Vere. He be the youngest. The terror of us all. Christ College shall hopefully endure him."

"A strange name."

"A name as old as the conqueror's England. Veres since doomsday have been the Lords of Oxford. Mother be the sister of the nineteenth Earl, Edward. We Berties are of tolerable blood. Even a bit of Spanish royal blood to our veins. And whate'er your breeding, we need make a gentleman of you. A gentleman seeks to explore the cosmos, as it were, and leave it and himself slightly better than he found both." Peregrine went to a shelf and took down a book. "This is a guide to the ways of gentle living. I would have you study it."

David took the weighty tome. "Am I to take it home?"

"You are to remain here."

The suddenness alarmed him. "For how long, sir?"

"Until you are to be sent down to Cambridge."

"Dressed like this?"

"One hopes not. No, we shall dress you properly and find a proper study for you. And though, like my friend, Master Bacon, I incline toward some healthy skepticism about orthodoxy, I think the religious life be a fine calling for a young man of your sorts. Do you ride?"

"I've never been a'horse, sir."

"That can be remedied. The Lord Lincoln has a Turkman or a Greek, whatever he be, a fine trainer of horsemen. He trained Captain John Smith for us. You shall meet Captain John when you go to London."

"To London?"

"Of course. Every gentleman goes to London now and again, David Sharpe."

David edged the heavy book on to the table. "That isn't really my name, is it?"

"No. I suppose not, but what would we call you?"

David was hesitant. "I was born to this house and…"

"Yes. Yes. I think you are right. We shall call you David d'Ersby." He went to the wall of portraits and yanked a wide cord. "I think his Lordship would be pleased with that choice. Robert has been exceedingly gratified with your progress at Lough. You shall call me Peregrine. Under the circumstance, that is quite proper. And I will mold you into a gentleman, David d'Ersby."

The sleepy-eyed boy who had shown David in entered the chamber.

"Chowder, this is David d'Ersby. You will find some attire, perhaps something of Vere's will fit, and see that he is properly adorned in the fashion of a gentleman. He is to be treated as such. You will tell the others. You can lodge him in that chamber that was Master Vere's. See the bed cloth is properly aired, and that there be a sufficiency of candles. The young gentleman has a fair mind of reading to do."

To all this the servant scowled.

"After you are properly dressed, David, I will take you to meet Mother. She is to be addressed as Lady Mary. She is not well, nor has she been for a number of years, and gets readily confused. She has a new husband, but often doesn't remember where she's left him and returns to Ersby or Grimsthorpe. She may mistake you for someone else."

David followed the scowling Chowder from the room. The clothes into which David was helped smelled of another's body, another's sweat. They were weighty and confining, and yet he felt the transformation. There was an inherent need to stand just-so, to pose, brought about by the stricture of the breeches and the billowing doublet and jerkin. The colors were a brilliance of red, gold and green. There were endless small buttons, and Chowder had pulled the fabric of the shirt out through panes slashed up the sleeves. The boots didn't quite fit and pinched his toes. He was admiring himself when Peregrine Bertie entered.

"Narcissus himself?"

"I hardly recognize me. I look like Vere in the painting."

"Yes..." Peregrine paused. "In all, Vere will not like you, nor you he, I suspect. Vere is not an easy fellow to like. Were he not my brother I should loathe him." Peregrine moved to the doorway. "Come, lad, Lady Mary awaits. Answer honestly. Volunteer nothing. And if she makes little sense at times, be not alarmed."

David walked with difficulty along the heavy oak floor, his boots pounding against the planks. Lady Mary was the figure he had seen above the great hall. Her face was a true mask; he later learned it was a layer of powdered eggshell and lead which held her face in a caked, expressionless form. Each cheek was illuminated with a brilliant circle of red. The carrot hair was a wig worn slightly askew. Here and there grey strands sifted from beneath. David had a difficult time not looking at her breasts pushed up out of the neckline. "Are you one of my children?" She looked up into his face.

"No, my lady," he replied

"I sometimes lose touch. I have four boys. There is Vere and Robert and… who's the other one?"

"Me, Mother, Peregrine."

"Ah, yes, Peregrine, my favorite. Could always gavotte better than the others. Did you know my brother Edward once tried to shove a dead linnet up my privates? Edward is obdurate. The Queen hated him; the Queen loved him. I always loved him, even when he had a dead linnet. He ran through all his fortune and then his wife's. She was such a sparrow, but that daughter of theirs…what is her name?"

"Elizabeth," Peregrine said.

"Yes that's the one, a glorious thing with breasts like pomegranates. A Vere, through and through. We could marry her to you. What's your name?"

"David."

"David what?" She extended out a hand. It dripped rings and fell before it reached his own.

"David d'Ersby," Peregrine told her.

"Ah, yes. I remember you as a child. You've grown. I have two husbands. One's dead, but I can't recall which. When Peregrine and I were first wed, the old Duchess, a beast of a woman—all prayers and airs—that sanctimonious dollop with her sweet vindictiveness would hardly let me near Grimsthorpe, a civilized place, if such can be said to exist in Lincolnshire, and bestead she trucked me off to Ersby, which is so close to the end of the earth one durst not stumble lest one fall off. Ersby's such a place of unchastity, but you know that. The Duchess once told the Queen that she was far much given to masses and trappings and the Queen near took the old Baroness-Bitch's head. But, alas, she lived long enough to be the bane of sweet Mary Vere, whose brother was the greatest poet ever to live. Sir Nicholas Bacon said I was the loveliest of all the court ladies, but he died, so I lost my beauty. It is always the way. So you are David d'Ersby? Publius has spake that it is sometimes expedient to forget who we are. Bear always Publius in mind. It is more easy to get a favor from fortune than to keep it. 'Tis the truest of maxims. Look to the Lady of Scotland. Merry, she was twice queen, would be thrice. That's what killed her. Still in all, time gets 'em and Bess as well is dead. All the queens are dead, save James." She giggled.

"Dangerous talk, Lady. Madness to speak thus."

"Whom fortune wishes to destroy, she first makes mad. Still, David d'Ersby, I could tell you things on the King 'twould be well to heed."

"We must go now, Mother," Peregrine Bertie said, attempting to lead David out.

"No!" she ordered, her voice strong with finality. "You must know this, David d'Ersby. What is past is not present." She looked over at her son. "Don't fret so, Perri. I will say no more of the King's inclinations. Whatever else your mother be, she is the heart of discretion. These years,

David, I have been the paragon of discretion. You know, I hated Lord Peregrine Bertie when first I was made to wed him, but after the old she-bitch went to her death, I learned to have grave affection for him. He was a goodly man of honorable ways, kind even when a great trust had been breached. It is more difficult to endure forgiveness and kindness than it is pain. Perhaps that is Peregrine's revenge. I oft do not remember things for it is easier to forget. But I would recall this: it seems better to marry for love and passion. It be a safer retreat; for when all else fails, there is still the bed for comfort, if it be but a moment's respite. How old be you, David d'Ersby?"

"Fourteen."

"Fourteen years longer is a time, and more time to be without passion." She fingered one of the exposed nipples. "I am weary. You must go now."

Molly

— growing up —

MOLLY WAS NOT ordinary and she had not been left without resources. A house, said to have been lived in by Pocahontas and John Rolfe, was hers, left her by her grandfather. There was money, old money, enough money, tobacco money accumulated through generations, never disseminated by an overabundance of progeny, only diminished by inheritance taxes, and carefully tended between generations of death. There was the Bible with entries of birth and begetting in the safe deposit box in the bank in Richmond. And in the Bible was the beginning and in the beginning was the word. The word of the first begats. David and Molly begat a son, David Dean Sharpe, in 1607. And then David Dean Sharpe begat Dean Opechancanough Sharpe in 1632 and he with his Indian wife, Otocotah, begat Dean Benjamin Sharpe in 1662, who begat David John Smith

Sharpe in 1690, who begat Dean d'Ersby Sharpe in 1715, who begat David de Vere Sharpe in 1750, who begat Robert Gosnold Sharpe in 1780, who begat Dean Archer Randolph Sharpe in 1815, who begat Robert Dean Peregrine Sharpe in 1850, who begat David Robert Edward Sharpe in 1882, who begat Randolph David Sharpe in 1919 who begat David Dean Sharpe in 1947 and James Peregrine Sharpe in 1948.

Molly first visited the Bible with Uncle James. She was seven or eight and still ordinary when he entered her begetting. In the large safe deposit box there were ancient Indian copper ellipses, tobacco seeds in a yellowed envelope, old coins, land plots, sketches of cabins and boats and mailing tubes in which there were rolls of very old paper, ragged at the edges. Father James unrolled the frail pages with delicacy. "The journal," he said and let her examine the writing, which she could not read as it seemed a scrawl. "Someday," he told her, "you can come and read the story of Molly Dean Sharpe. What's here in this box is now yours."

Father James took her to lots of "national" places in Washington, in Maryland and in Virginia. But mostly she was in the care of the Sisters of Visitation at the school in Georgetown. Her reading skills had been quite ordinary, but the day she changed, she became a determined, exceptional learner. Books became her world, the school library her domain. She read more, multiplied faster, sang louder, leapt further, spoke more often, raised her hand constantly. She became an extraordinary sponge soaking up the taught-world around her. She was the goalie on the lacrosse team. She was the lead in Sister Martha

Mary Berner's *Camelot*. She was also independent and willful. She wore her uniform to classes, but having learned to sew under the careful eye of Sister Mary Jordan, she made almost all her other clothes, strange as they were. At thirteen, she began wearing period clothes, first Edwardian gowns of her own creation with slight trains that collected dust as she rustled through the room. Then the progression of phases: Jane Austen, the medieval, the kimono, the Victorian, the Russian peasant, the native Nigerian, Arabic, Tyrolean, and Dutch girl. Sometimes the clothes didn't last well; sometimes the phase didn't either; sometimes the appropriate fabric was hard to find or emulate. But Uncle James found the idea "fantastically amazing" as he smiled and spoke to the nuns about it. "Creative," he reminded them. "She is intensely interested in history."

"The child," Sister Anthony Turner said, "is extraordinary, but peculiar."

Peculiar she didn't mind. At fifteen, she was determined to have sex. It was appropriately her flapper period and she wore hats down over her simulated marcelled hair. Her goal was to do the entire football team of one of Washington's best prep schools. Only slightly into the project, she gave it up, not only out of non-interest, but she read that sexually-overactive women were called common. And common was ordinary. She would not be ordinary.

Father James allowed her to buy a car when she was sixteen and, on weekends, she explored the geography and accompanying history of the James River, Williamsburg and the art galleries of Washington, Baltimore and Richmond. And when in Richmond, if the Bank was open, she

visited the rolled journal of Molly Dean Sharpe. She loved
the galleries and was particularly intrigued with the Pre-
Raphaelites and the Bloomsbury artists. But she loved all
art because it was visual history; it captured and reflected
the simple daily events of time — as did fashion — in a way
that written records of political upheaval, war and turbulence of major happenings did not. She left the school in
Georgetown as valedictorian of her class and, beneath
the cap and gown on graduation day, she wore a symbolic
hide dress to emulate her Powhatan ancestors. This was
her silent tribute to Otocotah of the begotten Bible. In
her valedictory, she spoke not about the horizons open to
her fellow young women graduates as they went forth and
all that "garbage," but rather about how women defined
the world in which they lived, and how what they wore in
this day and age established their equality as women and
bespoke their freedom. The mothers and fathers of the
other graduates applauded politely, obviously thinking her
more peculiar than extraordinary.

At the oldest Catholic women's college in the United
States, she majored and excelled in history; she played
lacrosse and dressed frequently in the fashionable clothes
of 1940s movie stars, shoulder-padded and brimmed-hat-
ted. She wore bright red lipstick, pageboy haircuts, dif-
ficult-to-find shoes, and equally-hard-to-find seamed
stockings purchased by mail from a Hollywood costume
shop. She scrunched into classroom chairs surrounded by
young women in Levis and Nikes. She stood out, but she
was not a loner. She had some good friends who adored her
"eccentricity."

"She's a bit peculiar," some said. But peculiar was perhaps an essential part of maintaining a 4.0 grade-point average. And the School Sisters of Notre Dame did nothing to discourage peculiarity and certainly encouraged the extraordinary. She also put on weight. She wasn't obese, nor even fat, perhaps, but she was adding pounds and losing a slender look that befit the dresses of the '40s.

From the oldest Catholic women's college, it was most natural to select the oldest college in the country, William and Mary, for graduate school. But she had not chosen it for its age alone. She wanted to focus on history, as her father had, specifically the history of women, the women of the first settlement of Jamestown, one of whom was Molly Dean Sharpe, the author of the journal in the safe deposit, and for whom she had been named. She had taken the journal out briefly, long enough to Xerox the fragile pages. These she was transcribing into contemporary English as part of her graduate work.

Molly was encompassed by Williamsburg, so real, so fake. It kept her focused: there was no capturing truth. Williamsburg was an illusion, a recreation, a re-creation, a cleansed version of history and, aside from the occasional plop of horse shit, was void of the pungent smells of unwashed bodies and musky attire. At the end of the workday, the shop folk, free from the gaze of indentured tourists, took off their laundered eighteenth-century costumes worn over deodoranted bodies. Even while in costume, like minions in Pirandello's *Henry IV*, they occasionally snuck out for a cigarette or spoke with fellow actors on this simulated real stage of history, without the simulated language of pre-revolutionary America. As she wandered the campus or the village or went to the Rockefeller Library, only the most astute noted that her attire was of an earlier period than that worn by those hired to impersonate the eighteenth-century villagers. She dressed now almost entirely as Molly Dean Sharpe would have dressed in Jamestown a hundred years earlier than Williamsburg. The remembered/disremembered events of her life at two were indicative of the unreliable nature of mnemonics. But wasn't that what all history was, simply an accumulation of memories? And she always kept this mnemonic unreliability in mind as she read and reread Molly Dean Sharpe's journal.

She drove to Richmond to inspect the Bible. Strange, she thought as she lifted the Bible from the box, she had never really looked at the book beyond the begats and yet, because of its age, it was probably the most valuable item in the box, even more so than the journal. But there in the begats were the names she was seeking: there in clearly defined hand were the names "Dean d'Ersby Sharpe" and "David de Vere Sharpe."

She did not live full-time in her old house further up the James River, but rented a tiny cottage in Jamestown, closer to the college. There at her computer, she went online searching to see if David d'Ersby was on Facebook. He was not, but he had a web page. There was an exhibitionist nature she sensed about some people who created personal web pages and she felt that about David in their limited chats. She looked at his picture. He was much better looking than she had expected. Perhaps it was only a flattering picture. He seemed to be wiry with small, dark, almost brooding eyes. He had rather unruly dark hair and he lacked the coarse masculinity so common to American men. He noted his Cambridge degree, his interests as writing, literature, history, sailing and skiing. He stated that he lived in Lincolnshire but was often in London and on the continent. He liked to travel and spoke French, German, and Dutch. He had yet to publish a novel but had one in progress, while several of his short stories had appeared in minor literary periodicals. He stated that he lived in a ruined abbey and was an only child. He liked to go drinking with his mates. His ideal woman was tall, blonde, liked to ski, hike, sail, and was not afraid of sex. His e-mail address was posted at the bottom of the page: dsharpe@ britread.com.uk. There had been 1,373 hits to his web site. Hers made 1,374. She printed out his page and logged off.

She had to admit his looks were appealing. But she was hardly his ideal woman, perhaps no one's. She faced the reality: she might be extraordinary, but she was unattractive. She could not resist looking in the mirror. She was decidedly not attractive. But destiny was created from beyond appearance and the coincidence of names could not be disregarded. She was beginning to see an idea of a patterned life existence. She put his page aside and turned off the computer. She picked up the photocopied first pages of the journal and began to reread them: "Writ about events…"

The Diary

LONDONTOWN

—1606—

Writ about events of Londontown the 10 &
6 day of May in year of our Lord sixteen one
hundred & 6. What once writ was lost. And
I begin anew after days at Bridewell & do call
so upon my memory to suit these recollec-
tions. Benjamin Joseph begun me keeping this
accounting, but he be now gone as I will relate.
I write of good hand & make record here now
of that what had befell me. I was found, not
born. Mary Fleet Dean, Benj. Jsph. had me so
christened, 'twas as I were found by Dean of
St. Paul's into wee hours near to south door,
my cord but newly cut. The Dean sent me to
the wet nurse w/ one breast a' Fleet Street, in
turn give me to the legless beggar from where-
upon Benj. Jsph. paid three shillings-two. "Better ta name ye Mary Fleet Dean than Three
Shillings-Two," he did say.

On day of me thirteenth natal, or upon
the day whch Benj. Jsph. gave me to call such,
I begin this record. A day like to others in
Londontown, I moved mid mill of merchants
& beggars, hucksters & thieves up Cheap-
side toward St. Paul's w/ urgent message fer
Benj. Jsph. He usually be taken for Jew. He
did accept such abuse more than let be known
who he be actual. As being attuned to such
secrecy of his life, I did bear clandestine writs
to great houses, oft opened night door to
shrouded visitors w/ Spanish speech, served
beer to strange travelers, took cloaked figures
to waterman at Billingsgate, and oft led dark
bearded men of Irish brogue above in the narrow house where Benj. Jsph reside, & I as well,
w/in shadow of St. Olave's church.

Benj. Jsph were to take me cross river to
see the players come past noon. In the great
church I did move among whores, cutpurses,
money lenders, murderers, traders, hirers,
brawlers, job seekers, & spies all what were
conducting commerce in great middle aisle. I
found Benj Jsph. amid them. He be of great
girth w/ unruly red hair, habited in rich scarlet & black merchant attire. Bushy brows,
kind eyes, & thick full beard in converse in
French. I knew he did see me & I stood apart.
I did understand French as Benj. Jsph. had
taught me & Spanish, a bit of Italian & Irish
& German. But most to read & write English

& Latin. I told Benj. Jsph of my message, how the toothless man to Westminster said I must tell "that Andrew be known & how there be danger." I did make inquiry if that would mean there wld be no players seen upon the day. He did reply 'twas my day & we would go Southwark.

That day were one of heat & the theatre had a press of bodies & the smell of humanity greater than rosewater & lavender attempting to suppress it. Mr. Henslowe be near the entrance picking his teeth w/ his finger. He did own the house wherein I lived w/ Benj Jsph. He knew the goings of the house, but more determined by purse than by the King's church. He said as to how he be abroad to keep an eye upon some of the players who owed money & that most were half the time to jail & other half be spent paying what they owe to him for bailing 'em out. He told of the day's play by Mr. Shakespeare & how the King did like it, but how the King was Scot after all & given to liking plays full of witches. A tall slender figure in black flowing robe come by & touch Benj. Jsph. on the shoulder, saying "Beware the Ides of March." Mr. Henslowe told that t'ere but a notice of the morrow's play, the Globe doing *Julius Caesar* again.

I loved more the pit, close to the actors where I could shout & bellow w/ the mob, but Benj. Jsph. said t'was me natal day &

so we sat among a better sort & whores w/ painted faces & painted exposed nipples. Smell of tobacco permeated the air about us. Benj. Jsph. pointed out great men sitting on stage near the actors, one Lord Southampton, another be the Earl of Northumberland's bro. George Percy. I feared the lordy. They oft appeared in disguise at the narrow house beneath the shadow of St. Olave's & usually be great trouble. MacBeth were killed & the crowd cheered, but I sat silently, thinking, & then Lord Southampton stood crying out, "Long live the King." The gallery cried back, "Long live King James." & a voice from somewhere cried, "& Prince Henry." From above, which had been partially hidden by a curtain, a boy, Henry, the Prince, appeared to yells & cheers of the crowd. He smiled, extended his arms & then vanished. We were quiet as we crossed to Billingsgate. Benj. Jsph. said he tried to be tolerant, but thought betimes Shakespeare's words spake like the anti-Christ & surely life be more than 'a tale full of sound & fury told by an idiot signifying nothing.' We arrived at the narrow house & drank beer & ate marchpane & apples slopped in cream. Benj. Jsph. gave me presents of gold piece & ivory comb.

In the night came a constant rapping at the door. I slipped from bed & went down & opt the door but a crack. The figure be

hooded, a part of the face visible was pox
marked & he pleaded to let him in. I told him
to go away. He demanded to see Father Joseph.
I told him there be no one here known as
such and this be the house of a merchant. I
tried to close the door, but the man held his
knee to. He told me was great danger & that
I must get Father Joseph. Benj. Jsph appeared
in his night shirt & bid me open the door.
The man's hood fell back & he be w/ deep
socketed eyes. He said he come from Roger
Aschem & told as how Father Andrew be
taken to the Gatehouse at Westminster on a
warrant of treason. Benj. Jsph assured the messenger Father Andrew would tell nothing. The
man told as how under torture he had told
everything; how this be the house of a priest.
Benj. Jsph told me to dress, but the man said I
was to stay & that my going would be dangerous for us both. He said Master Aschem was
specific on that. Benj. Jsph. agreed, saying he
would send for me as soon he be set & went
to dress. When back he advised me to let no
one in & when the soldiers come to go to the
secret hiding place. He blessed me, pulled up
his hood & went out. I pleaded w/ a closed
door.

On the next day I heard cries of "Jebbie"
on the street. At the door a pounding & rattle of swords. As they broke opt the door, I
slipped inside the wall through the secret

panel where I had hid before. I could hear loud voices & slashing & banging. I hurt from standing so long in the narrow space. When they be gone and I wandered the house, all of value taken & left be smashed & broken. My new ivory comb & gold piece be gone. I left the house & wandered. For four nights I slept near the garbage & dung heaps in crowded narrow spaces off the cobbled street & on the 5th day I heard cries. "Jebbie to burn at New-gate! Papist burning at sunset." I went. Amid jeering crowds, eating cakes & screaming, I stood saying nothing, neither weeping nor cry-ing out as the stench of the burning of Benj. Jsph's flesh rose in grey smoke. I knew Mac-beth was right. Life were a tale full of sound & fury, told by an idiot.

These are events as I remember & put them down after my days in Bridewell. *↑ stopped reading)*

Molly set down the photocopied pages. She decided to begin the translation of the journal into a more contempo-rary idiom. She turned her computer back on and opened up a new document in Word. "Writ about events in Lon-don from the fourth day of June in the year of our Lord six-teen hundred and six" became June 4, 1606, London. She continued typing from the journal:

I rely upon my memory to serve me as I recall that first day at Bridewell. The rain whipped unmercifully against the window as

I attempted to peer out at the Thames below, but the swipe of water smearing down the panes made the river a brown streak. The room was cold and empty, adding to my sense of aloneness. The days of wandering, of begging, of eating refuse, of sleeping in narrow spaces between buildings and of aimlessness had left me aware of my singularity, my apartness. Benjamin Joseph was no longer there to reach out to, and where my feeling for him had been there was only a painful hole. A man, dressed like a clerk, came into the room; his heels echoed in the emptiness. I gave little consideration as to what he might be. It simply did not matter. His voice had a monotonous quality as barren as the room as he asked me if I was a Papist. I responded with an indifferent no. He sat on a bench, the only piece of furniture in the room, and informed me that I had lived in the house of the Jesuit. Yes, I told him. He asked again if I was not a Papist. I told him again, no. He told me that the priest was dead and I told him I knew and that there was no God, only the sound and the fury, and he said for saying thus I would be whipped. And I told him it made no difference. He asked me how old I was. I told him I was thirteen. He knew my name was Molly Dean and called me that and asked if I was a lewd and sinful creature. I asked him of what crime I was being charged. He told me that this was no trial and I was not in prison but in Bridewell, a place of redemption. Though they never called it a prison it was the same as such, I would soon learn. He told me I would be redeemed at Bridewell where I would live in the joy of God. He left me alone, his heels echoing in the emptiness.

A woman entered, the door closing with a bang. She was fat and wore a filthy skirt hitched up, revealing an equally filthy and torn petticoat, and ordered me to take off my garments. Her voice was raw and hoarse. I removed my clothes, letting them fall to the floor, and stood naked, the flesh covering my thin frame pimpled with goose bumps. My breasts, however, were large and full for my age. The door banged again. A wizened man, looking near death in age, entered. He carried a large whip and his breathing was a loud rattle. She told me I was to be beaten. And while I told her I'd done no wrong, it seemed of little matter. I felt the cruel first cut of the whip biting my shoulder blade and across my spine and it heightened my sense of being removed from the old man and the harsh-voiced woman. I could not fathom their thinking, nor grasp why they were whipping me. They, I realized, did not feel my pain. They were remote and distant from me. And in the pain I had the sudden comprehension that every individual was remote from every other. I was alone. But there was power in that as well as pain. For no one else could really know what I was feeling inside. No one could destroy whatever that was. That gave me control over my life and, I realized, over my death as well! I could die if I wished! That gave me great power. Life *was* all sound and fury—without purpose. But I was not ready to die. Especially at this moment of realization of the power I held over my own being. Free! Isolation meant freedom. They could lock up my body, but not me, not the inner me. That was in my power, not theirs, and as the whipping continued, I felt it less and less. I realized that as long as I let no one have the slightest part of me, I was free and I near wanted to cry, not from pain, but from the joy of understanding.

The dried up old man gave a rattled breath and, dragging his whip, left the room without a word. My back was a fire of pain, but it was inconsequential; it would heal. The woman handed me a plain blue dress, made me put it on and told me I would like it in this place and that it 'twas once a king's house. I slipped the dress on, but it cut at my back. I was shown a shackle and rebelled, but was told it was the rule and the woman bent down and clasped the iron shackle around my ankle. But it didn't matter. The part of me that mattered was beyond their reach, locked within myself.

I was taught to sew caps, ugly green caps. I had not the slightest idea for what or whom they were made, a steady stream of ugly green caps. For eighty-four days I made caps, keeping to myself, hardly speaking to the other girls, girls who all made ugly green caps, dense girls weighted by their own foolishness. I slept in the long room where they crowded three and four to a bed and I smelled their bodies and listened to their snoring, but I was wrapped in a cocoon of isolation and even at the long table as they slopped the grey gruel, I ate only enough to keep the hunger from paining me and ignored the chatter and the giggles. And they left me to myself. "Daft," they said of me. Sometimes, for my reticence, I was whipped by the wizened old man, but I had learned to ignore the whip and hardly felt the pain.

And that is the recollection of events as I best have memory of them and have so set them down. Here, as I sit by Joan Alleyn's fire, I begin a reckoning from the morn I left Bridewell forward. Hoping through this accounting to charge myself to keep true to myself, to keep my own counsel and allow no man, nor woman, nor child to tread upon that part of me which is solely mine own. That these pages may be my constant reminder that I am a singular being, self within self, strong and in control of my own destiny.

It was the eighty-fifth day. I was sent into a room with a gilded bench and a tapestry of Diana and the hart. I caught a glimpse in a small gilded mirror of a gaunt-faced girl with the hollow, sunken eyes and hardly knew it to be myself. The door opened on Mr. Henslowe. He said he had been searching for me and just learned of my being in this horrid place, but that he had paid for me to leave and would see to me. He had found a few clothes of mine left in the house and had brought them. He said though I looked ill that Joan would fatten me up. I asked him who Joan was and he said his daughter, Joan Alleyn. I told him she ran a house for whores in Southwark near the bear pit and theatre. He claimed it was a house for young ladies of quality and I most assured him that I knew it to be a stew and I asked if I was to be made a whore. He assured me most emphatically I was not and that he would not bring such a dishonor upon the ward of Benjamin Joseph. He said I could earn my keep about the place lending a hand to Mistress Alleyn, but only when I was well again. The fat woman came and removed the shackles. I put on the gown brought for me, but it hung on me as if it belonged to someone else. I followed Philip Henslowe out of Bridewell. I had come to the place in June, it was now August, yet I felt years older. Whatever youthful innocence had been mine drifted up in the smoke of Benjamin Joseph's death.

I followed Henslowe through the streets and he talked back at me constantly on the wind. I caught words from the air: "rich husband," "marchpane," "fatten up." The foul air of London, its offal and decay and the stench of Fleet Ditch filled my nostrils as if it were a pleasant nosegay. Shrikes flew overhead; a baby cried in pain; a penny whore giggled from the dark space between buildings; the town was a chorale of noise. The loud clang of Bow-bell rang out. At Queenshithe, Henslowe found a waterman to take us across. Southwark is a marsh of tidewater and Mistress Alleyn's was reached by crossing a short bridge above the marsh. The sign of the cardinal's red hat hung above the door, signifying the trade of the house, and we entered beneath it into a large room, smelling of pomander and cooking, to be greeted by Joan Alleyn, a jolly woman with bright eyes accented with wide crow's feet and huge worn hands, which contrasted with the elegance of her dress. She fussed and called me a poor thing. Mr. Henslowe assured me I would be content in Joan's hands and left. Joan laid out a table of pickle souse, fritters, cold mutton, sugared and gingered apples and strong black ale. After watered porridges, stale fish, hard often moldy bread, and putrid beer as my fare, I could barely get bites of it down. Joan asked if Mr. Henslowe had told me what the house was and I assured I knew the sign and that it was a stew. Joan said Mr. Henslowe was reluctant to admit to it, but a stew it was. She said she had never been a whore herself, but it was a good living and assured me the girls were of a proper sort and not common Win-chester Geese, as the term went. She also said that the clientele for the most part were a bet-ter sort, gentlemen and a few merchants. She excused herself for going on so, saying I must have lived such a sheltered life. I assured her I knew almost every doxy, cony catcher, foin and ruffler, bawdy basket, or penny whore what worked the streets of London. She was most glad I knew the world but assured me that living with whores hadn't made one of her and wouldn't make one of me.

I asked what I needed to do for my keep; she told me after I gained some flesh I could lend a hand to the stitchery as the maids, so she called the whores, was always in need of some sewing up. She thought before long, being near fourteen, it would be a hus-band I would require and that we not let Mr. Henslowe find me some old worn piece of flesh. When she asked what I missed most about London, being locked in that terri-ble place, I told her the players, that the theatre was my most favorite thing. And she went on about Mr. Alleyn and what an actor he was and I told how I saw him as Dr. Faustus and believed all of London thought him the best actor in the Kingdom. Joan Alleyn said she would send me off to the theatre on the morrow.

As I sit here at the trestle entering these words, two of the whores sit at the other end playing at hazards. I met them all earlier. They are Winchester Geese as common as any I had seen, despite Mrs. Alleyn's view to the contrary. With painted faces and painted nipples and the orange wigs, they are friendly, if loud, a dozen in all. They all look the same and I cannot remember which whore is attached to which name. These are the events of my first day at the household of Joan Alleyn.

David

He had never associated Martin with written words, but there he was in his room off the hall leading to the back stairs, typing at a keyboard, paper grinding out from a printer. David went up and found Edward asleep in the red room. He was about to slip out when he saw the attaché case. He picked it up but realized there was little point in opening it. The heavy contents of the case were gone. So he set it down and went out.

On the stairs he met Martin coming up. "He's sleeping."

"That is good. I was about to look in on him, sir."

The "sir" again. "What does he do?" David asked.

"He mostly just sleeps."

"I don't mean that. I mean, what does he do professionally?"

"He is an important man."

"That doesn't tell me much."

"Much is better left unsaid. There is some I can tell you. Walk with me in the garden, sir." His voice was conspiratorial. Martin in his crisp style looked out of place in the mangled, unkempt surroundings. "For many years your father was part of the Foreign Service but not really a diplomat."

"A spy."

"Part of MI Six — I suppose you could call him that. He had close links to the Israeli Mossad. When he left the Foreign Service, he became an important executive with Hussad Bel Geneve, which later became Tonsi a'proc ni eveneg, which is essentially the most powerful financial institution in the world, but few have heard of it and fewer know anything about it. It is a powerful private company, perhaps Swiss-based, but primarily a holding institution, with heavy shares in many of the giants of American, Japanese, European, Southern Asian and, of course, British corporations. As you realize, capitalist institutions run the world and Tonsi a'proc ni eveneg is among the most powerful of these."

"And who runs this giant power? What man controls the world?"

"That's the amazing thing about giants like Tonsi a'proc ni eveneg. No one, actually. They exist with a chairman, who may or may not have great power, a board and a CEO. These roles often change and shift. They are in many ways self-operative. I have a theory that the world is a ship without a captain at the helm, kept afloat by a crew of capitalists, of course, who know the sea, to complete my metaphor."

"And Edward's role in this?"

"He has been the chief executive of innovative services."

"And what does that mean?"

"He heads the espionage section."

"And the Staatsangehörig Bank Bavaria?"

"A totally-owned subsidiary of Tonsi a'proc ni eveneg."

"I don't imagine you can tell me what was in the attaché case."

"I must get back to Edward."

David went to his own room and logged on. He had an e-mail from opech@earthgo.com. His first impulse was to delete it without opening it. A copy had been sent to the-moll@wm.edu. The message was brief: "For you." There was an attachment, truehistory1.doc, which he also opened with reluctance.

Opecancanough

FLANKED BY THIRTY warriors I moved beneath the pillars of cedar piercing the blue. Sunlight shone through the needles as if from color-leaded windows. I thought of the immense Cathedral of Seville and my youth. Such as this I found impossible to describe to The People, so I kept the cathedral locked within and spoke little of these things except to the child Matoaka, who had great curiosity for the world beyond. How remote it seemed, not just in time, or in distance across the months bridging the great sea, but in the reality of it; for despite the years of my captivity, as I had come to think of it, it seemed a mere hallucination. I had gone of my own will, or at least that of my father's, the Werowance of the Powhatan. The Whiteman, with hair on pale faces, had come during *cattapeuk*, the planting season. We thought them gods, came to accept them as men. Admiral Pedro Menendez de Aviles promised that were the son of the great Werowance to sail to España he would be returned, well and with much wealth. On the great water

I learned the language of the Whiteman and of his God. I had not distrusted the Whiteman then, but in the years in Spain and later in New Spain, where the Nahuatl were treated as slaves, I came to understand their greed. I knew if they came to the K'tchisipik they would take away the land and enslave The People. Still, I admired the ingenious nature of the Whiteman, his skills, his intelligence, his ability to learn from books and retain such vast knowledge.

I was kept in Spain for five years until, with the help of Admiral Menendez de Aviles, I was able to convince the friars that I should return to my own people, offering assurance that I would bring them the true teachings of Christ. I sailed from Sevilla but was taken to Mexico. The Viceroy Don Luis de Velasco took me into his palace. He called me son, patted my cheek, squeezed my shoulder, gave me gifts, patted my behind, became my godfather, hugged me, dressed me like a prince, kissed me and had me christened with his own name Don Luis. I was told I would stay in Mexico, for if I were to return to the Ajacans they feared I would revert to my pagan ways. The Nahuatl, the Aztec, who had been a great people, had become cowering slaves, their wealth taken, their freedom gone. The Viceroy was given to prayer. I knelt and prayed to be sent home. I thought of escape and knew the K'tchisipik could be reached by land for a Nahuatl priest told me of a Monacan who had reached Mexico, but there were great rivers to cross, many mountains to climb and many unfriendly tribes.

Then Admiral Menendez was named Conqueror of Florida by the King and issued an order that I be returned to my father as he had promised. I traveled by ship in the care of Father de Segura and the other friars. But we arrived at a time of sorrow. The People had endured a rainless summer and a bad winter and there was hunger and illness like never before. My father had died and my brother Wahunsonocock was the Powhatan. He thought I had come from the land of the dead in the sky and he said I must be the Powhatan, but I told him no, that I would be his trusted brother and teach him new ways. But neither he nor The People could comprehend the wonders of which I spoke. Dressed as a Whiteman, I lived among the friars though I was not really one of them and I was not really one of The People. The friars treated The People as if they were children and ordered them about. It was the way the Spaniards had treated the Nahuatl and I saw what would become of The People, so I went to live at Werowocomoco, took wives and lived as my brothers lived. The friars asked me to return and reminded me of my promise to bring their God to The People. So I returned, but when I came back with Opitchapan and other warriors, Father de Segura humiliated me in front of them, dishonoring me with names, demanding I admit that the god Okeus was a devil, calling me a liar and ordering me to kneel and confess my sins, shouting at me that I would go to hell. I was in a great rage at such humiliation and I took a club and battered de Segura's head open. Opitchapan and the warriors attacked the other friars and killed them all. That event was long past.

Now in this brighter time, my warriors and I left the pine forest and came to Werowocomoco, the place of the Powhatan. The women were working in the planting field which encircled the stretch of long houses, arbors of bent saplings covered with bark; the bark coverings on many of the houses were rolled up on one side and the only fires the outside cooking fires. Opitchapan, my brother and a werowance as well, greeted me by my secret name, Apachisto. Opitchapan and I were born of the same womb, rare among sons of a werowance, and there was a special bond between us. I followed him into the *yehaukan*, the long house. It was a family gathering. Everyone seemed to talk at once in the slow deliberate Algonquian language. In the enclosure was my brother Kecatough, my brother the Powhatan, two of his wives, his sons, Pochins and Parahunt, two priests with black-painted bodies and hair dressed with dyed deer hair and gathered in topknots crowned with feathers, and Powhatan's girl child Mataoka, whom we called Pocahontas. I had brought her *attaup, attonce,* a finely-made bow and quivered arrows, and my brother the Powhatan questioned why I would bring a squa child such a gift and then laughed for he knew she could hunt as well as his sons.

We had gathered to discuss what the priests had read in the entrails of the eagle: the coming of the Whiteman. The Powhatan was worried about the Kecoughtan, who did not provide the tribute demanded.

"The Kecoughtan sit like our guard at the gate of K'tchisipik. We can't afford traitors." I reminded them: "When the Whiteman comes…"

"As the eagle has spoken," the priest Towantow interrupted in a deep melodic voice.

"*Cassacunnakack, peya guagh aquinton uttasantasough?*" Opitchapan asked. How long before the English ships would come?

"Who can say?" I answered my brother. "But they will come."

"Can we stop the power of the great thundersticks?" the Powhatan asked.

"We must try. The Kecoughtans must not seek the help of the Whiteman when he comes to bring evil against us. Invite the Werowance of the Kecoughtan to come to Werowocomoco and gather the warriors of Appamatuck, of Pamunkey, of Mattapoini, of Youghtanund and Powhatan. We will hold the ceremony of the stake for this Werowance and his Kecoughtan warriors who will join him in having their flesh picked away. And for the few we can trust, we will put a head to the stone for them." It was a ritual: to vouch for another's life, a man laid his own head upon the stone and the victim was spared.

"Great warriors who are trusted should not be wasted at the stake," Powhatan said.

"I should lay my head to the stone for the greatest warrior." Pocahontas proclaimed.

"Do you know such a warrior?" I asked.

"You, Uncle, Werowance of the Pamunkey."

I spent the night in a *yehauken* which I shared with Opitchapan. A woman came to my bed, but I sent her away. Toatoka was my young squa and by consensus the most beautiful of women. I had a great fear of losing her, and, at her insistence, renounced sexual pleasure with other women, which was against custom. In the morning I joined the others in the river to bathe. Matoaka glided through the water with the sleekness of an otter and dried herself with a blanket of feathers. "I should like to go live with the

Whiteman. I should like to see the great books speak. The pictures which talk."

"Not pictures, but more just marks, scratchings, put together into sounds. Here." I reached over and took a stick and scratched A in the dry ground. "That is 'Ah' like in *arrapeh*."

"That is *arrapeh*?"

"No only the 'Ah' sound. All of *arrapeh* would look something like this." I scratched out the word. "To understand what the scratches mean is called 'to read.'"

"I shall learn to read when the Whiteman comes."

"He will bring much evil when he comes."

"And much greatness. This will be like Sevilla where there are big houses of giant stones and men ride on animals."

"On horses," I said. She sat listening and nodding. The other bathers came from the water. The sun sifted through the lengthy trees. Matoaka took the stick and scratched A in the dirt. "It would be my joy that in your lifetime the Whiteman would not come here," I said, "but I am afraid that will not be."

"I shall be friends of the Whiteman and learn to read scratches and how to build houses of stone."

David

THE ATTACHMENT ENDED abruptly. How had this opech creature found his e-mail address? But then if he was a hacker, David realized, that would certainly be easy enough. But why was opech sending this to him? He replied, demanding an explanation, and almost immediately a beep signaled he had a message. It was his response to opech returned. No such address existed.

An hour or so later he found themoll online.

---

dsharpe: Have opened the file?

themoll: Yes.

dsharpe: Factual?

themoll: From his perspective, I expect so. Some of it can be found in Bridenbaugh.

dsharpe: I am not exactly sure how he found my e-mail address. I guess if he's a hacker...

themoll: I am not tall, nor blonde.

dsharpe: My web page.

themoll: Precisely. And by the way, I thought you were "ugly as raven's piss."

dsharpe: You don't think I am?

themoll: No.

dsharpe: Thank you. But it's unfair. You have my picture. I have none of you.

themoll: I don't have a scanner. One of these days I will send you a photo.

dsharpe: Do. What's to be done about opech?

themoll: Not much can be done. You could ignore him, but that's not easy.

dsharpe: I sent him a reply demanding an explanation. It was undeliverable.

themoll: I tried that as well.

dsharpe: How does he do it?

themoll: I suspect with expertise in computers. Hackers can manage. If that's what he is.

dsharpe: Hacker. A guy who mutilates or chops up unsuspecting victims.

themoll: Frightening thought. Hacker. A guy who drives a cab.

dsharpe: Hacker. One who botches the job.

themoll: One who cuts the budget. Better government.

dsharpe: Hack. A tool made for hacking.

themoll: To hack. To cough.

dsharpe: Hack, a horse used to pull hackneys.

themoll: Hack, a sloppy job.

dsharpe: Me, a bad writer.

themoll: The novel not going well?

dsharpe: I'm not entirely happy with it. It needs pruning.

themoll: Hack, to cut away. Does your novel need hacking?

dsharpe: Perhaps. To hack. To cut, to penetrate.

themoll: We always end up there, don't we?

dsharpe: *******. Yes. Are we ended?

themoll: I have to go.

dsharpe: Send me your picture. You can go to one of those places that will scan it.

themoll: Yes, I suppose so. OK soon. Keep me posted if you hear from opech again. TTYL.

dsharpe: Cheers.

He would hack the hell out of the next chapter. Words, he was using far too many words and he needed to start tossing them away. The art of poetry was brevity. He was no poet, but he could be more precise in his prose. He picked up the chapter and began hacking: "David was..."

The Novel

LONDON

—1606—

David was on the road to London. As the gentle rain sifted down, he rested the horse at the top of the rise. The view seemed vast. The world was large and much of it, he was discovering, an accumulating mass of the incomprehensible. He had become a voracious reader, and though becoming aware that there were no certainties, he found doubt a difficult concept to accept. He had gone back to Little Munkton three times to see his mam and she had seemed ill at ease with him, reticent, diffident, and he urged her to let him take her away, but she would not hear of it. On the fourth trip he found the hovel empty.

Peregrine approached on a grey mount and, at some distance behind, the irregular train of coaches, carts and wagons of the Berties followed. "You may be disappointed with London." Peregrine seemed oblivious to the gentle rain. "It's a bed of merchants. Even the King is at their mercy."

David would not let his enthusiasm be dampened. "The nobles, the poets, the players, the philosophers...you said I would meet Bacon."

"Aye, you shall. But you must not expect too much. He will be enamored of a mind so ready for ideas. But you must not confuse his writings, his ideas, with the man himself. In all truth, he's an opportunist. I'm only trying to caution you. I think you may be expecting too much of the city."

The first cart approached, bouncing and tossing a carved and canopied bed, followed by a coach bearing Robert, Lord Willoughby, his Lady and his chaplain, Generous Brown. Robert Bertie stuck his head out, adjusting his brimmed, red hat. "Be on the watch. This area is notorious for highwaymen."

Parson Brown stuck his enormous-eared head out. "And Jesuits. They go about disguised as swineherds."

"Cut down a boxwood and you will find a Papist," Peregrine said after the coach had moved on.

"It's his ears," David said. "He can hear rosary beads rattle clear across a moor."

The fourth coach stopped and a footman in haste helped a young lady out. She ran to the edge of the road and began retching. A second lady alighted. The ailing maid, a fair-skinned creature with eyes the blue of robins' eggs, was Alice Wingfield, a cousin of the Berties. David had danced with her at Grimesthorpe, but he had been as awkward in his speech as he was with his feet. She had skin like the light of a soft white candle and when he touched her hand, it had been like fire.

"Too much coach?" Peregrine asked.

"I suspect too much belly." Mistress Montague, Lady Willoughby's younger sister, made a gesture to indicate an expanding stomach.

David was certain she was mistaken. He got down off his horse to help Mistress Wingfield as she came back toward the coach. She had spewn vomit down the front of her cloak.

"Oh, leave me be," she said and freed herself from his attentions.

David rode off ahead, more angry at his own stupidity than at her rebuff.

Peregrine caught up with him. "You've all the markings of a gentleman."

No. David knew otherwise. He had the veneer, but something was lacking at the core.

A hawk swooped in the sky overhead. "Ironic, isn't," Peregrine said. "I loathe hawking. I could not bring myself to teach you. But then Percy did a fair enough job, I suspect." The Percys were cousins of the Berties on the Vere side. "In George's case what passes for gentility is sheer laziness. I suspect if there were not a servant about to undo him, Percy would piss his breeches e'er he'd undo himself. You will be seeing him on Wednesday at Southampton House. There will be many influential men there, some with the Virginia Company. What think you of Virginia?"

"I had not thought on it at all."

"I'd think you intrigued by the vast unknown."

"I have enough struggle accepting that there is an underside to the world without wanting to go there."

"Our cousin, Thomas Smythe, has invested heavily in the venture. Captain Smith, of whom I spoke, be a party to it.

Sir Edward Wingfield is planning to go on the first voyage, along with another kinsman, Captain Bartholmew Gosnold."

"Sometimes, I believe you are kin to all of England." The sun had come out and it rode like duck down at the back of David's neck, warm and soft.

In London David walked amid a mass of pressing flesh, merchants with their elegant cloaks dragging in the slop of garbage and excrement, gangs of brawling street boys, gilded-gowned dowagers weighting the shoulders of slender sedan bearers, hucksters slapping fish toward his face, kites screeching above roofs, handless beggars demanding alms, preachers threatening damnation, doxies in doorways offering dirty bodies for pennies, men of substance hurrying as if constantly tardy, and David sensed that the earth moved from London. In its contagion, David was flush with its vibrancy. He found fall flowers yet blooming and wives spreading their laundry upon the green. He found stalls of booksellers, saw puppeteers, a peacock—its feathers fanned, witnessed a man being hung, his bowels turned out, crossed on to the great bridge with its piked heads like sucklet sweets on sticks, its toll merchants and endless shops. At Billingsgate, he ate wondrous fish in a tavern where everyone seemed to be talking at once, and he stood by the Thames at the end of the day watching the mass of moving boats. He wished never to leave London.

Peregrine and he walked, hurriedly as if Londoners, to Holborne. Southampton House was massive blocks of stone. Entering through huge doors, they were escorted by a blue-clad footman into an immense hall of splendor. Peregrine excused himself and David stood, feeling like a weed in a formal garden. Men bedecked and bejeweled were arranged in symmetrical clusters in the mirrored hall as if placed to be suitable accoutrements of the decor. A middle-aged man with small dark eyes and a pointed black beard giving his elongated face the thrust of a dagger stood with two crimson-attired men. He spoke in a grating, high-pitched voice. "… the great crime is not in its sinfulness, but in the hideous product of such." He glared at David with total disdain.

"That cyster-faced laystow staring ugly at you be Sir Edward Marie Wingfield."

David turned, surprised by the deep Lincolnshire voice of a stocky man, hardly taller than himself. A rough beard encircled his pleasant mouth and he had dark friendly eyes. "He enters a room like a bad fart, unpleasant to be around and not much to him but air."

"But why such a look for me? I've never met him."

"But he knows of ye, David."

"You know my name?"

"David, who looks enough like shittle-brained young Vere to be his looking glass."

"You have me at a disadvantage. I know by your voice you be of Lincolnshire."

"Of Lincolnshire, Davey, but of the world as well. When I be but bare older than you, I served the fighting Veres. We won the war and then, through the graces of the Humes, you've no doubt heard of them, great Scots, half of which live in Paris, cuz Scotland's such a horrid place—well, I was on my way to Scotland to visit some more Humes, when the ship did wreck and I was stranded on an isle. 'Twas when the pilgrims threw me over—"

"You're Captain John Smith," David interrupted.

"Captain Jack I be. I've had adventures, lad. Why, Henry, the young Prince, be my dearest friend. I've traveled the earth. I've saved kings and great ladies, killed more enemies than most men can accumulate in their dreary lives. And now I be off to seek the short route to Cathay and bring England to the savages. Many that be here are bound for Virginia or investing in it. The tall man, there, with the hook where his hand should be, he be the Admiral of our party, Captain Christopher Newport. He'll tell you, were a fact that the crocodiles et his hand, but the story has no truth to it. Captain lost his hand fighting the Spaniards. And the man there with cheeks like markings on a sea chart be Sir Thomas Smythe, a prime investor in Virginia. That he be talking to is Sir Edwin Sandys, who would have the savages to the baptismal font."

"Are the savages terrifying?"

"They be intriguing. I've been learning their language. Wingfield and most others don't concern themselves about such details as the savages, but if this trip is to be successful, understanding them and the lay of the land be crucial. Surveys and maps. Success depends on knowing the little things."

Peregrine Bertie came up to them accompanied by a tall man with long narrow stretches of leg, sumptuously dressed. He had a trimmed beard that extended his narrow angular face. His hair fell long and off his shoulders. "So this is your David." The voice was like soft honey.

"David," Peregrine said, "this is our host, Lord Southampton."

"My Lord." David bowed slightly.

The man took David's face between his boney long hands. "You are prettier than Vere, and he won't like you for it. But the resemblance..."

"I have yet to meet him, your Lordship."

"Well, you shall meet him soon," the Earl of Southampton said. "For he is here in my house."

Peregrine turned to Smith and was not smiling. "He has killed a man in a duel. The King be hard set against dueling."

"I will see what my Lord of Salisbury can do about it," the Earl said, touching David's face. The underside of a ring scratched his cheek gently. "I have noted that beauty, great physical beauty, has our forgiveness as its reward." He looked pensively toward the ceiling where cupids encircled a woman suckling a wolf. "Are you forgiven all your transgressions, David?"

"I have little beauty, my Lord, so I must be careful not to transgress."

"A beauty who does not recognize his beauty is the more enchanting." His long tongue wet his upper lip. "I will show you a miniature of great beauty. You will swear it is of you." The Earl started to walk away. He turned back. "Come, David." With Peregrine's prodding, David followed the Earl through corridors into a peculiar room with animal heads, armor, and paintings hanging in spaces between shelves of books and narrow windows. On a rug-draped table sat a casket with enameled paintings and stones set in silver leaves. The Earl withdrew a key from his cinch and opened a chest filled with papers. He dug into the papers and handed to David an oval miniature on a chain. "Think you not it is beautiful?"

David studied the tiny portrait. It was beautiful and, while it looked like his reflection in the mirrors of the great hall, he knew he was not beautiful and he spoke softly. "Perhaps it is that a painting captures but a moment that makes that which it holds beautiful."

"A painting captures the soul and were I to have a miniature made of you it would be, I am certain, more beautiful than this of Vere. For your soul is yet unsoiled. I think—"

He was interrupted as the heavy door to the room opened. A man came in, a bit of a man, barely five foot, old, with a hump back. The Lord Southampton shut the lid of the chest quickly and turned the key in the lock. David still held the portrait in his hand. The small man moved with a limp and was dressed all in black, trimmed in fur despite the heat. "I'm sorry, Henry," he said. "I was told you wished a word and didn't know you were in private with young Bertie." He gave David a look of disdain.

"Despite the resemblance, Robert, this is not young Bertie. Rather David d'Ersby." He took the miniature from David. "Find you the way to the hall, David. I need an urgent word with his Lordship."

David went through different doors and found himself near Sir Edwin Sandys and Sir Thomas Smythe, still engrossed in conversation. "... we fetched him," Sir Edwin was saying. "We gave him his authority." He lowered his voice. "Prince Henry supports the view that no man has the right to command a nation without the approval of its people." His voice dropped to a whisper. "My Lord Southampton holds a confidential document in which the Prince has put this in writing."

David knew he should not be listening and pretended all his attention was elsewhere as he moved off toward Peregrine, who asked, "Where is his Lordship?"

"With some little man, a hunchback."

"That little hunchback be Robert Cecil, Lord Salisbury."

"He who rules the King rules …" and David let the rest of the line drift off.

"Precisely," Peregrine told him.

Sir Thomas and Sir Edwin came over to them, scrutinizing David. "Be you a Vere, boy? You look much like Edward de Vere. Those same beady little eyes."

"This be David d'Ersby." Peregrine's voice indicated there would be no further explanation.

Sir Thomas smiled. "Perri, they do tell this story of your Uncle Edward, as to how he farted one day in the presence of the great Queen and it was why he had spent seven years in Italy. And finally when he returned to England and was admitted to the presence, the Queen says to him, "I have forgot the fart, Edward." Sir Thomas roared with laughter and then his manner became grave. "But Edward was a wastrel and the present Oxford, poor Lord Henry, is left to borrowing from the likes of me. Know this, young David, it is not near so much what you gain, as what you don't spend that makes you wealthy."

There was an interruption as the Earl of Southampton entered the hall accompanied by the Earl of Salisbury. And despite the lameness of the small dark man, they swept grandly through the room, clusters of men parting like waves before great vessels. A poxed, chinless man with eyes in deep black sockets plucked the sleeve of Lord Salisbury as they passed. For a moment David thought the Earl might explode in anger, but the fury dissipated as suddenly as it had appeared and the Earl stood calmly, the man whispering in his ear.

"Not the most subtle of Cecil's spies," Sir Thomas said. "The Virginia-bound voyagers will regret having him along."

"Captain Kendall knows armaments and proper defense. A brilliant strategist," Peregrine said.

"He thrives on dissension and disruption—"

Sir Thomas was interrupted by a pleasant looking man with a deep bass voice who joined them. "You must be David. We are kin."

"You mean you and I are kin," Peregrine spoke sharply.

"Yes. That is what I meant."

"David, this is Captain Bartholomew Gosnold." Peregrine turned to Gosnold. "We were discussing Kendall. I'm afraid you are not all the most congenial of bedfellows. I hope you do not quarrel all the way to Virginia, or half will be overboard afore you arrive."

"We have seen that they won't," Sir Thomas told him. "It was at my Lord Southampton's suggestion that the council to manage in Virginia will not be known until they arrive. They are under sealed orders and, until they reach land, Admiral Newport is in authority. Of course, with Captain Gosnold here of his own ship and Captain Ratcliff of his."

As the Earl of Salisbury, accompanied by Captain Kendall, approached, the group diffidently stepped back. The Earl stared at David and said, "Edward Vere killed my sister."

"He certainly did her no great kindness," Peregrine answered, obviously trying to pacify him.

The Earl never took his eyes from David. "Hariot believes inbreeding causes madness. There is too much inbreeding among the Veres." The gaze was intense and threatening. David shuffled uneasily. And then the Earl looked at Peregrine. "I shall tell your lord brother that I will see to the matter of Vere. But the youth must be bridled." With that, the Earl walked off, followed by Captain Kendall.

"Robert Cecil is tired." Peregrine spoke in a near whisper.

"Tired of the King spending it faster than he can find it," Sir Thomas said not too softly.

Later, filled from the heavy food and fighting drowsiness from the wine, David stood alone again with Captain Smith. "I have watched you," Smith said. "You be wise and not poke too deeply into your lineage. There are two things bring a man closer to death, and one be an abundance of curiosity."

"And what be the other?" David asked.

"'Tis the seeping of the sap of life. The old 'halek.'" Smith sensed he was not reaching David. "Swiving, lad. Each time a man do swive, his strength be drained off and he never gets it back. And when he's swived too much, it kills him."

"But everybody does it."

"Aye and they all die. It makes goodly sense, Davey. A man only has so much of life in him. And each time a little of that life be drained off, it weakens him."

Gosnold and another man came over to them. It was the other man who spoke to David with a smile. "If Jack Smith has been filling you with wild tales how he is the most wondrous creature in the Kingdom, he lies. For I am. I have more to my head and my parts. I am the better educated, the better born, the better soldier, the better—"

"Liar, Captain Archer. Far the better liar," John Smith told him.

But at that moment the banter ceased. The doors at the far end opened with a flourish and there, posed and framed as if in a picture, stood a young man, all in white with a dash of gold trim. There was something almost ethereal in his dazzling appearance. David knew instantly who he was, for despite the splendor, it was as if he had conjured himself. The young man walked straight to David and embraced him. "I am Narcissus," he said.

Molly

VIRGINIA

—the present—

SYRIL LOVELL'S NOTE was not from Syril Lovell, as Molly well knew, but from Syril Lovell's social secretary. Syril Lovell was terribly rich, terribly Black, terribly important, and the notepaper looked terribly expensive. Inez Lovell, Syril's daughter, had been one of Molly's good friends at college and on occasion Molly went home with Inez to the sprawling edifice on Massachusetts in D.C. Syril Lovell, despite her exceedingly dark skin, was exceedingly white in most other ways. Her straight hair was pulled into a social-ite's chignon. "I wouldn't be caught buried in a hat," she told Molly after a few moments of acquaintance, as if to estab-lish firmly that she was not one of "those" Black women. Syril Lovell had a pampered, exercised body, which she carefully dressed in starkly tailored ensembles from the most renowned Japanese and/or Italian designers. Inez's father seemed to spend most of his time in Europe, as the

North American Vice President of some nearly unpronounceable multi-international of which Molly had never heard, Tonsi a'proc ni eveneg.

The note previous to this one from Syril had been in Syril's own hand, hastily written, but still on the same embossed ivory paper stock. "Come at once. Panic with Inez. Only you can help, my darling Molly. Syril."

Molly had arrived to find Syril in a striking yellow Nidaba suit, not looking the least panic-enveloped. In her distinctly peculiar syntax she declared at the door, "Inez, not that in principle I have anything against lesbians, has announced she is a lesbian."

"I am, Mother."

"You aren't," Molly told her. "It's only a phase." She knew Inez.

"You think so?" Syril spoke as if Inez was not present.

"I am sure of it," Molly assured her

"I am in love with Little Ice." Inez was emphatic.

"She's an Eskimo." Syril rolled her eyes in a what's-a-mother-to-do manner.

"She's an Aleut."

"I've always known," Syril said, "that trouble would come from naming her Inez."

"So Sartrean," Molly said, "but it will pass."

"You really think so?"

"Yes."

"Hey, I'm here," Inez said and added, "We don't have sex. We rub noses."

The latest note read: Darling Molly, I know you are fond of the Bloomsbury artists. Ticket left in your name at the side-east entrance of the National. Exhibit's only in town for a month and a bit. But no waiting line for my dear Molly. Do enjoy. Syril Lovell. P.S. The phase has ended. Little Ice has melted away.

But Molly, who was often in contact with Inez, already knew that. Inez was in another phase; she was dating a professional wrestler, whom Molly had seen flinging bodies across the TV screen. If the Desirable Grynch, as he was known, with his bulbous nose and skin that looked as if it had been charred in patches, was not the ugliest man Molly had ever seen, he certainly was the runner-up. Molly assumed the phase would end. Yet despite Inez's phases, there was stability about the Lovells that drew Molly to them. They represented "the family" for Molly. While the father was never physically there when Molly visited, he existed. He was real and provided for them extremely well. Whenever Molly thought about marriage it was in terms of the Lovells. With no actual evidence, she saw it as a loving, ordered unit of husband, wife and daughter.

David

DAVID WAS IN his thinking mode of writing rather than keyboarding mode. His protagonist was about to go off on his own to the Old Globe in seventeenth-century Southwark and David was attempting to keep him in check. Thinking, feeling for words, turning ideas through his mind, he wandered through desolate rooms, damaged further from recent rains, puddles still on stone floors. He went back to the library. The books had no special arrangement, but he knew where to find *Mrs. Dalloway* and took her from between *Tom Jones* and *Finnegan's Wake*. Wouldn't Virginia Woolf have been appalled by that placement? He backed into a comfortable chair, threw his Levi-ed leg over the chair arm, and buried himself in Woolf's words. The reason he had chosen *Mrs. Dalloway* was that Woolf appeared to have such complete control over her characters. He read for hours, focusing, however, not so much on character as originally intended — on Clarissa, on Septimus — but on the connections. He rested the book in his lap and gazed at the dreary landscape.

In this existential world, where we float like isolated molecules, it is the colliding into one another, the connections we make that create the lives we lead. Because it is stronger than truth, fiction allows connections that often seem incongruous, though Woolf made them seamlessly. The phone call from his mother broke his thoughts. She wanted him to come to London that afternoon.

"Edward is unchanged," he said.

"Yes," she replied.

He packed a few things. Maybe he would be back in the evening; maybe he would not. She didn't explain why she wanted him in London. He never asked on these occasions; she never called for him without reason. He took an appropriate companion, *Mrs. Dalloway*, to accompany him on the train.

Molly

MOLLY HAD TAKEN the train from Richmond to D.C. She wore a new floor-length skirt of crude linen woven by a Jamestown weaver who lived amid a yard of junked cars in a mobile home along the James. Molly had hand-stitched the linen to assure the authentic seventeenth-century look. Voices reverberated above as she lifted her skirt and climbed the marble stairs to the Bloomsbury exhibit.

She had expected only paintings and was surprised to see the pottery of Quentin Bell — the blue bowls and plates, each with an image representing themes in the works of Quentin's aunt Virginia Woolf. For *Mrs. Dalloway*, the face of a clock, the hours. Molly thought of Clarissa and Septimus. Was life but six degrees of separation? Coincidence was the matrix of connection. She moved on to examine a ceramic and a sketch by Dora Carrington, who, like Virginia, had ended her own creative existence, only not so cleanly with a few stones in the pocket, but by blasting herself through the mouth with a rifle. Or was it a shotgun? The bulk of the exhibition was the works of Vanessa Bell and Duncan Grant. There between the wars while Septimus leaped to his death, they painted and, as if children of the yet-to-be '60s, made love as if it were a natural function and extension of life, having little to do with marriages and children, but perhaps having to do with art. There was an incestuous nature about the works: Vanessa by Grant, Grant by Vanessa, Virginia by Vanessa, Leonard Woolf by Vanessa, Vanessa's self-portrait. And there was Grant's portrait of Virginia — a white-faced, gaunt, but young Virginia of 1912, waiting in that large black hat as if for the madness that was bound to come. The face so white, a mad white, an inscrutable white, a mask white. The eyes peering from out of the white frightened Molly and she felt a closeness in her chest that brought tears to her eyes. She walked from the portrait and tried to immerse herself and be drawn into the red and green of Grant's "The Tub" and its fantastic image of Vanessa, looking like some handled water vessel. But she was drawn back to the Woolf portrait and wondered how long she would have been mesmerized by the painting had she not seen, from the corner of her eye, the young man, so recognizable, unruly dark hair and small dark eyes. He was standing before a pair of Duncan Grant paintings: "Bathers by the Pond" and "Reclining Nude." She was startled by his being there.

David

LONDON

—the present—

DAVID GOT OFF the train. Having stayed with Clarissa
and Septimus through the journey, he took a slightly longer
way to Bedford Square. He had a writer's need to connect.
Evening was settling and there was a rush of pedestrians
along Euston Road. Busy people swinging umbrellas and
brief cases, oblivious, he suspected, to the Bloomsbury past.
Toting his laptop, his Woolf and his bag, he turned down
Upper Woburn place to Tavistock Square. He meandered
through the Woolf past, most of the buildings now occupied by University College. The Woolfs' home at number
52 was no more, bombed away, but across Gordon Square,
number 46 was still intact. Behind a wrought iron rail rose
four stories of stone topped with brick, windows facing out
on the square. Here the Bloomsbury group had gathered
on Thursday evenings. Here Leonard had first met Virginia. What words must be contained in those stone walls.

The geography of the square was like an entwining blossom-laden vine that linked them all, the flowering Blooms-burys. He detected a residue of energy, as if something of the Woolfs remained. He felt renewed, able to write. He went to his mother's house in Bedford Square, reinvigorated.

"I was worried about you." She looked vibrant, was wearing red.

"I walked from the station."

"A nice evening for it." She stood in the hall blocking the closed sliding doors to the drawing room. "I think it is time you met your father."

"Why? Edward has made more than adequate provisions for me."

"I told you Edward has nothing to leave."

"I think you are wrong. He's an important executive with Tonsi a'proc ni eveneg."

"Who told you that? And what is Tonsi a'proc…?"

"Martin."

"Martin has a wild imagination. Tonsi a'proc… whatever is probably some figment of his mind. Martin's writing a spy thriller."

"Martin is writing a novel?"

"You aren't the only wordsmith at the Abbey. But I suspect Martin's prose is less literary."

"Was Edward in MI Six?"

"Of course not. Edward was in the Foreign Service. It is time to meet your father." She opened the doors. David was more dismayed at the idea than surprised by the individual.

Aubrey Vere, Baron of Denchfield, force behind an empire of publishing, television and cinema, staunch ally of the Prince of Wales, entrepreneur and philanthropist, whose lineage occupied an unusual amount of space in Burke's Peerage, stood, posed at the mantle. David would have expected him to be exceedingly uncomfortable, wishing perhaps that he had not been called here; it did not seem the case. He exuded charm. He was a tall, handsome, dark-haired man with small eyes like David's own. His extended hand was not simply a polite offering and for a moment David was afraid he was about to be embraced. But the Baron let go the hand. "You much resemble my other David." He said it so naturally, David was taken aback. David wanted to say, I may look like him, but I do not resemble him. David Aubrey Vere was his half-brother and, while that was disconcerting, knowing that he, too, was descended from the Veres, one of the oldest families in England, was empowering.

Molly

"DAVID," MOLLY SAID to the lanky young man in black who was staring rather intently at Duncan Grant's male nudes. The Edwardian cut of his suit, the grey shirt, the black tie, all seemed so London.

"Yes." His accent was British. "I'm David, but I am rather certain I do not know who you are."

"I'm Molly Dean. Online...themoll. Of course you wouldn't recognize me."

"I think you've mistaken me for someone else. Sorry."

"I identified you from the picture on your web page."

"I don't have a web page."

"Oh, I'm sorry. I mistook you for someone else, another David actually: David d'Ersby."

"Ah, David d'Ersby. My brother. Half-brother, really."

"A brother? And you are both named David?"

"Disconcerting, I suppose. Excuse my manners, Molly, is it? I'm David Vere."

She remembered Vere...gay, but brother? "David never mentioned a brother, but I suppose — "

"I don't think he knows. He's my father's bastard. Frankly, David doesn't much care for me. We were at school together."

"Are you particularly interested in the Bloomsbury Art?"

"Yes. These two border on the homoerotic, don't they? Cocks and admirable in proportion."

"But these are the only two. There is much here that's not erotic. I am intrigued by the use of color. The reds and green there in that painting."

"That's Gerald Shove on the Norfolk broads. Even his pose is sensual."

She went to examine. She hadn't noticed the figure in the painting from a distance.

"But back to genitals for a moment. I think that is the only time I've seen Christ with a dick." He pointed across the gallery to Grant's "Baptism of Christ". "And look at the size of the balls on Apollo."

"Did you come to see sex or art?" she asked.

"Both. I've seen most of this work before. I am intrigued with the Bloomsbury Group's free expression as it relates to sex. The writers as well as the painters. There is an androgyny in all, most all, of Woolf. David d'Ersby is a writer, by the way."

"I know," she said.

He moved over to Grant's unerotic nude back view of David Garnet. "There is a mural in Lincoln Cathedral. A biblical scene, two actually, on opposite walls in one of the chantries, painted by Duncan Grant. He used Virginia, Vanessa and the Bell children as models. There are some implied homosexual elements in the murals and there was talk of removing them at one point, but art prevailed over morals even in the great house of worship. What do you do?"

"What do you mean?"

"What do you do professionally?"

"I'm a grad student. American history at William and Mary."

"In Virginia, isn't it? I'm thinking of going to Virginia while I'm here. Perhaps you could guide me a bit."

"I'm afraid you will find Williamsburg's recreated history uneventfully modern after the centuries upon centuries of Britain surrounding you at home."

"It is not Williamsburg that interests me. It's the history of Native Americans. Do you want to have dinner with me? I'm traveling per diem and could take you to a really expensive place. This is not a romantic overture, obviously. I'm gay."

"I don't think it is so obvious you're gay, except perhaps your interest in the erotic nature of Grant's paintings."

"Homoerotic."

"Homoerotic. And I'd settle for a good rather than expensive dinner. Perhaps you would like something near the Circle with a gay ambience. But I came up on the train, so it will have to be early for me to get the train back to Richmond."

"I've a driver. We can go at our leisure. An embassy staff car. I'm an underling in the Cabinet — for the Exchequer.

Here for meetings on regulatory principles of mergers of multinationals. Doesn't that sound exciting?"

"Multinationals. Companies like Tonsi a'proc ni eveneg?"

"The less said of Tonsi a'proc ni eveneg the better."

They toured the remainder of the exhibit together. Molly looking for color and suspecting David Vere of looking for the erotic, the homoerotic.

David

LONDON

—*the present*—

AUBREY VERE SEEMED to sit quite comfortably in an uncomfortable period chair. "Your mother and I have decided on an income for you. An annuity of a hundred and fifty thousand pounds. If that becomes insufficient for your needs, we can always rethink the amount."

"As I have expected nothing, that seems exceedingly generous, Lord Denchfield."

"Do you call Edward d'Ersby father?"

"No, sir. I call him Edward."

"Then I see no reason why you can't address me as father."

"Yes, sir." But David was uncomfortable with the idea.

"But probably not in front of the Baroness." He crossed his legs. "You don't like my son, my other son, do you?"

"It isn't that, sir. We just have little in common. We travel, well… in different circles."

"Your polite way of addressing his homosexuality. I wish he weren't, perhaps, but he is. And we, not so much the Baroness, but Jane and I love David as he is. I have arranged a London flat for you. Fitzroy Square. A crumbling abbey must get depressing."

"Here in Bloomsbury. I have an affinity for this area."

"I would suspect so. You write. I imagine it is genetic. I am working with his Royal Highness on a committee exploring standards of English lexicology. You have not met Jane, have you?"

"Jane?"

"Your sister. You will like Jane. Her cause is the disturbing deterioration of the English language. She's a bit of a fanatic about it. And after all, the language has been evolving since Chaucer. But you will like Jane. I wish you could like David. He has an important position with the Exchequer in international finance. He has a way of understanding global economics that I would not have expected him to have. At the moment he is in Washington on some economic mission."

Molly

WASHINGTON, D.C.

—the present—

MOLLY DEAN AND David Aubrey Vere sat in the Blue Grouse on Connecticut Avenue. A baby grand occupied the center of the dining room where the owner, Teddy Valdez-Jones, rendered Mozart, sometimes *pianissimo*, but often *forte* to the detriment of conversation. The crowd was mixed, while later, in the bar, the clientele would be almost entirely male and gay.

"So, you're a capitalist," Molly said, spooning into the cold peanut soup.

"Actually, no. I am a radical socialist in principle. I am not simply opposed to capitalism, but probably to civilization generally. Do you know Edward Bond?"

"The playwright?"

"Yes. Underlying his plays is the philosophic ideal that, as a species we are not meant for nine-to-five containment in the work place, that it is antithetical to our nature."

"And if we didn't work, where would civilization be?"

"Bond's point. Civilization is numbing, destructive to our basic nature as humans."

"So we should go back to living off the soil, a commune perhaps."

"Whatever works, I suppose. Disencumber ourselves from the clutter of civilization, but mostly not working within a system that simply seems nothing more than the perpetuation of a system. When you think of it, money has no intrinsic value beyond the worth of a scrap of paper. Society, according to Bond, is a slave to a system that is entirely unnatural to the innate nature of the species Homo sapiens."

"So we should give up all the advances civilization has wrought? Say in medicine, whereby we can live longer."

"For what purpose are we living longer, except to live longer?"

"And what of the blender, the thermos bottle, the vacuum cleaner —"

"The Hoover."

"Yes, the hairdryer, the Cuisinart? But seriously, what of the airplane, the computer, satellite communication, and, for God's sake, the printing press, the dissemination of thought?"

"I'm not saying Bond is entirely right, but his thinking certainly deserves examination. It's why I am interested in the Native American culture."

"It was not all glorious. I will have to introduce you to Opechancanough."

"A friend?"

"You might say so. A seventeenth-century Powhatan chief." Molly did not mention the online voice of Opechacannough, but talked in general about the Powhatans over a pork tenderloin and some sort of purple-colored rice.

"You'd be quite beautiful," David told her, between bites of pork and in the middle of her discourse on Powhatan religious practices, "if you'd lose some weight."

"You're rather blunt, aren't you?"

"I think we are becoming friends. I didn't mean to be rude."

"You're right, of course. I intend to, I really do. Obviously pork is not the most direct route to weight loss. And you've said nothing about the way I'm dressed. Most find that disturbing."

"I figured it had to do with your research."

"It does. But, after today, I was thinking of going Bloomsbury for a while. Although I will have to lose some weight to look right."

"You'll have trouble finding the hats," he said.

The dessert cart came. Molly refrained, settling for an espresso.

David excused himself for a "loo trip." Molly decided she liked David. And she was fat. And she was glad David d'Ersby had no knowledge she was fat. She watched Vere as he stopped or was stopped on his return through the bar and was talking with an equally handsome, equally impeccably dressed man.

"I've met someone," he said as he came back and motioned to the waiter for the bill.

"How gay." She smiled. "Are you dumping me?"

"May I?"

"Yes. A handsome man for a fat broad any day."

"I will have the driver take you to the train station. May I come visit you in Virginia? It will be a few weeks. After I finish up this Treasury business."

They exchanged telephone numbers and e-mail addresses, and, accepting a kiss on the cheek, she left him in the Blue Grouse.

David

LONDON

—*the present*—

IN LONDON, DAVID was alone, awake into the night within the flowered walls of the third-floor room in his mother's Bedford Square house. He had the urge to share his news and he connected his laptop hoping to find the-moll. How strange this cyberspace world was that allowed sharing of intimate details with strangers. But she was not online, so he turned to his novel and let the David of fiction do as he pleased: "At Willoughby House…"

The Novel

LONDON

—1606—

At Willoughby House Vere would not let David from his sight. Vere was older by almost a year, but despite that year there was scant difference between them, the same height and build, the same features, the same colouring. Vere told him, "Tomorrow will be the Globe. A play special for us. We will dress alike."

Peregrine lowered his voice. "You raped a daughter and sodomized a son. You killed a man."

"It was a duel. I was called out. I am a Vere."

David peered up. Tiers of posts framed and separated pox-faced women from owl-eyed ancients, buxom wenches from ruffed gentlemen sniffing pomanders, merchants from pimpled, scratching doxies, and the smell of sweat hung over the whole Globe like a saturated bedsheet. They were dressed alike. Brilliant scarlet. David had a sense of posturing, the unreality of it.

Vere led the way to the second tier through a maze and crush of bodies. The exposed nipple of a woman, most certainly a whore, brushed David's arm and he was burnt with the flame of the touching. They reached benches in a place that hung over the stage. The play began. The actors were elegantly regaled and had voluminous voices and David's eyes were held to the stage. No doubt his mam would have seen the silliness of these supposed Greeks, yet David was drawn in by the poor merchant who was condemned to die while searching for his wife and boy child lost to sea.

"You are the one called Antipholus of Syracuse." Vere took a clay pipe from a satchel and put it to his mouth. A serving boy came with a coal and lit it. Vere spewed smoke and handed the pipe to David. "You try." David tried, coughed, was coached by Vere, coughed again and handed it back. He understood why Vere had insisted they dress alike. "And you are Antipholus of Ephesus." He did not like the tobacco.

"We are like long lost brothers come to a happy ending."

David reached out and touched the arm of the man he knew had to be his brother.

Vere took his hand, kissed the nails and then bit into them. "We are of blood."

When Vere released his hand, David's eyes drifted down to a girl who stood in the pit, back far enough so he could see her face, but only occasionally, as a man in a brimmed hat of feathers would lean forward and block his view, or a woman as wide as a great cooper of pickling would lean back doing the same. The girl had a sense of frailty about her, as if she needed tending. She did not notice him. He watched her and, even at the distance, he saw sadness in her eyes. There was something misplaced about her attire; she certainly wasn't one of the merchant class, but her clothes didn't seem to fit those of a servant either, and they hung loosely on her, except tightly over her large breasts, as if the clothes were not her own. David, now so frequently in someone's used attire, felt a kinship with her. The man with the brimmed hat again blocked his view and David gave his full attention to the young actors, whose voices were beginning to change, as they bantered in the women's garb of Adriana and Luciana. But he did not forget the girl in the crowd below. The man with the hat shifted just enough so that David could glimpse the girl's arm and hand; he wondered what it might be like to gently run his finger over the back of her hand and along her arm.

"Something more interesting than the play?" Vere asked.

"No," David told him and turned his attention back to the stage. "Maybe," he added and smiled sheepishly. A few moments later when he looked back in the direction of the girl, she was fully visible. Her hair was brown, straight, and clipped until it barely reached her shoulders. Her features were soft, gently carved, and he so wanted to hear her voice.

"You are watching the wench with hair like chopped dead weeds," Vere said. "A whore."

"No."

"A wager on it? The loser to provide a surprise gift for the winner."

"Yes." David looked at the girl. "She's no whore."

"I'll find out," Vere told him. "And you shall have her, though you'll pay me the wager."

David looked at the stage, but his mind was not on the play. "I never have, you know."

"Never have what?"

"Swived," he whispered.

"Jesu," Vere swore. "I've had boys and women, men and girls, a Papist Cardinal, a duchess, no sheep and probably not because they haven't admired me, a cripple, a blind woman, a quarter-gross of earls, I suspect, if there are that many, an Italian, a dwarf, a blackamoor, a crone without teeth, and once on a dare, a corpse. I be but a year senior to you. If you haven't made use of your organ you've already lost good use of its value."

"I want to." David looked down at the girl.

"And you shall."

He watched as she bit into an apple. At Dormio's "God-damn" pun, the girl, apple in her hand, laughed, and David laughed. Whether she sensed his eyes on her or simply turned in his direction, he was uncertain, but she looked directly up at him. He was flustered, but did not turn away. She smiled. Yet in the warm smile there was something almost painful. Rather than have her sexually, he wanted to reach down and comfort her, gently touch the skin glazed by the sun. Their eyes held one another. Then as the Lady Abbess came on stage, the girl turned her attention to the middle-aged man with the falsetto voice.

"I'll get her for you," Vere told him.

"No. It's all right."

"My wager," Vere insisted.

But when David looked back down, the play was ending. She was gone. While he was happy the merchant was not going to die and that the pairs of brothers had found one another, he felt a loss at the girl's disappearance. Vere started moving off. "I will find her," he said. "Meet me by the big oak just beyond the entrance. And mind your purse in this crowd."

David pushed through the throng of bodies flowing like Lincolnshire creeks into ever larger streams until it gushed out the portals like a great river finding the sea. He waited beneath the spread of the ancient oak. The crowd moved about him. He watched and listened without concentration, his mind attempting to re-create a portrait of the girl. From somewhere the sound of music drifted on the air, faint sounds of lute and horn. He listened, only peripherally.

Vere appeared. "Follow me." They moved around the building. A scatter of houses and marsh stretched to the river. "Do you know the sign of the red hat?" He pointed toward the sign above a door.

"Nay."

"A house of whores. She went within. Have you coin?"

"Aye...but..."

"Then, go to her, David. 'Tis time you were rid your pesky virginity."

"I want no whore." He walked in the direction of the boat landing.

"David!"

"I want no whore," he repeated.

David

DAVID COULD NOT sleep. He tried online again but was still unable to locate themoll. He was annoyed and yet she was nothing to him, a stranger with whom he had passed a few clever moments with clever words. A disembodied stream of words. Still, he had this need to tell her his news, to write words about his father. She might not even be who she said she was. Could be a woman of sixty who kept yappy dogs and nipped cooking sherry the day through or a man, perhaps transsexual with boobs, waiting to get his wong whacked. Forget her, him, it. He opened up the novel and gave his mind over to the fictional David. He began typing: "Like a cobweb..."

The Novel

LONDON

— 1 6 0 6 —

Like a cobweb spread across the door, his spirit was wrapped
from the brighter joy of the London day. He plodded,
morose and silent, toward the Mermaid. He had barely
slept; the image of the girl occupied his head like a gale,
tearing and tormenting. She was a whore; he had come to
London to be with whores, to rid himself of his virginity.
But *she* could not be the whore. The smile and the sadness
he had seen there. He wished to ease her pain, to touch her
hand, her cheek, her breast—to hear her voice, imagined
as soft—SLAM! He collided with a cloaked figure where a
mews spilled into the street, and would have fallen had not
the stocky man grabbed him. Out of wind, David gasped,
"Beg pardon, Sir." He looked into wide eyes and a bearded
ruddy face.

"Careful, lad, had I been a horse, and there be some claim
I have the manners of such, ye would be trampled down."

The man's voice, like his torso, seemed oversized compared with his stature.

"I was payin' no mind."

"Are you all right then, young sir?"

"Aye." David caught a flashing glimpse of a criminal's brand on the man's hand.

The stocky fellow tossed his cloak back from both shoulders and, with an air of insolent assurance, swaggered along the cobble. David stood for a moment, watching as the man leaped back to avoid a carter and, without a pause in his movement, flung a pence high in the air to a barefoot beggar with wild hair and eyes of a madman. But as the cloaked figure bounded along, the feigned wildness vanished from the beggar's eyes as he bit the coin before stuffing it into a heavy purse withdrawn from his ragged jerkin. The stocky man entered beneath the sign of the Mermaid tavern.

David ignored the pleading beggar and moved along, stepping into the smell of fish, bodies, stale brew and grease that was the Mermaid. Each voice rose louder than any other, forming a yelling chorus. David searched the room until he spotted John Smith's bearded face washed in light from one of the few windows. He was at a table with Gosnold, Archer, and men who looked to be laborers. Smith got up, but it was not David he had apparently seen, rather the stocky figure. "Ben!" Smith went over, grabbed the man's shoulders and led him to the table.

Captain Archer shouted, "d'Ersby, would you swive a dead dog?"

"I think not." David moved in the direction of the table. Vere had told him it was Archer who had made Alice Wingfield pregnant. David wondered if it were true.

"Then be welcome, for none of us be of the dog-swiving religion here—"

"Archer has been ranting," Gosnold motioned David to sit, "that there be a religion for every course in England these days."

"Moderation be the key," Archer said. "Nothing to excess gets one through. Lookee Ben with Smith. Lives on the brink. The point be to get from the cutting of the cord to the end without being hung."

"Then why Virginia?" Gosnold asked.

"You got to have a wee bit of adventure in that long journey toward death."

"And the gold!" another man at the table interjected.

"It is there, no doubt," Gosnold assured him. "But as Captain Archer will attest, it not be all ease and comfort. The weather can be fierce and there be bugs thick as net at times. But it is a beautiful land. The place which we name a 'vineyard' after my Martha was plentished enough to last through eternity."

"And there be land, men, for all to become free holders of great estates," Archer added. "And that be greater wealth than any gold."

Captain Smith returned. "David, lad. I did not forget thee." He turned to the stocky man. "Ben, this be a fine Lincolnshire lad, David d'Ersby. And Davey, this be the King's own poet, Ben Jonson."

"We've bumped into one another afore." Jonson winked at David.

Smith moved to the place at the table. "I would a word or two with these good men yet. Ben, take Davey above to meet our friend. We will join you but shortly."

David followed Jonson through the push of bodies. "That beggar..."

"You mean Old Abraham. He's a fake."

"Why did you give him money then?"

"It's how he makes his livin'. He be better than many a stage actor."

David followed Jonson up the narrow stairs to a chamber. A lad, auburn-haired with a narrow face, sat reading. Even sitting, he appeared tall for the youthful face. Jonson bowed. "My Lord Prince, this be David d'Ersby." David was startled. He had known the Prince to be a boy, already highly respected, but was still taken aback by the actuality of his youthfulness, perhaps no more than twelve or thirteen. David bowed deeply, nearly losing his balance.

The Prince stood up. He was, indeed, tall. "The Lord Southampton spoke of David d'Ersby, but then he is inclined to speak of a pretty lad. Me, I prefer the ladies to laddies. How of you, David d'Ersby?"

"The maids, my Lord." The sad eyes of the girl at the theatre filled his thoughts.

The Prince brushed lint from his brilliant green sleeve with a long narrow finger. "I be known for being the antithesis of my Father-King. He is wanton with lads, gossips during prayer, has a vulgar tongue, disdains the parliament and drinks excessively." This speech David accepted partially as youthful fervor, but he wondered if anyone else in the Kingdoms of England or Scotland would have dared such words. "Ben, here, takes to vices because it is dangerous. He thrives on tempting fate. When I am King, in my due time, there shall be a toleration of the Papists and Ben, finding no more danger to it, shall return to the Book of

Common Prayer. And though Parliament do so oppose any toleration, I would hope to convince them that toleration makes fewer martyrs and fewer martyrs makes fewer followers. Sir Walter taught me that. And Parliament does become ever more powerful. As my tutor has pointed out, power rests with the purse and the purse is now in the hands of the merchants and their voice be Parliament."

David wondered if the boy were naïve, or immensely astute for his limited years. He was certainly serious. The heir to England's throne did not fit the image of the court's wantonness, of which David had heard much.

The three Captains, Smith, Gosnold and Archer, entered the chamber and acknowledged their respects to the young Prince, who, standing, was taller than any man in the room.

"Well, Jack," the Prince asked, "have you a few more Virginians?"

"Laborers, Prince Henry. Would we had more and less of gentlemen."

"And you, David," the Prince asked, "are you bound for the new land?"

"No, my Lord. I be for Cambridge."

"And what will you gain in the ferment of Puritan pedantry?" Archer asked.

"The Berties would have me made a cleric, but I have hope for entry to the Inns."

"Careful, David," Jonson cautioned. "Men of the law oft have twisted bitter ways to match their twisted little minds, by which to gather twisted money for their tight little purses."

"You and I were at the Inns; have we twisted minds, Ben?" Archer asked.

"Not me; perhaps thou."

"There is great need for good men of law," the Prince said.

"I'd drink to that," Gosnold said, "were there something to drink."

"I forgot my manners," Smith said. "My temperance oft makes me a poor host. I'll send down for some beer and a bit of dinner as well." He called for the host.

"Captain Smith will provide you cheap armies, Lord Prince," Captain Archer said. "He will victual them with neither food, nor drink and save you great expense."

Smith turned to Jonson. "The Host says Philip Henslowe be below in search of ye, Ben."

"I owe him," Jonson said. "He bailed me out of jail last."

The Prince spoke. "Go down and see him, Ben. Say the Prince will see to your debt."

"And how will I repay you, my Lord...for such a kindness."

"In rimes, Master Poet, in song."

"Ben," Smith took Jonson's wide shoulder in his hand, "introduce our David to Henslowe. If he's really bent to the law, men of purses like Henslowe's will be his keep."

"Aye. Come, David. I shall make you acquainted with the mighty man who controls the boards of London. There not be a theatre in all London what Henslowe's hand and purse not be in."

They went down. The room was yet more congested and, despite the throng, David's gaze was drawn immediately to the far side of the room. She sat there! By the table near the open fire was the girl— she who had stood in the the-atre pit, she with the sad eyes, she whom he must accept as being a whore, she who filled his mind. She was with a man of middling age, a merchant, by his dress, and no doubt she was here in his pay. But whore or no whore, David wanted gently to press her hand resting on the table. She turned, apparently startled for a moment at seeing David, and smiled warmly.

To David's shock, Jonson moved to the table where the girl and man were sitting. Her blue eyes seemed to dance with the reflection of the fire. Her hair was the colour of hemp. David wanted nothing more in all the world but her. Yet she was a whore.

The man had a heavy, jocular voice. "Well, Jonson, are you well? Did jail suit you?"

"It never suits me, Henslowe, but I am accustomed. Indeed. And I always find a new face, a new character in the Clink to make an illustrious hero of the stage."

"Be this one of your bedfellows of the Clink?"

"I think not. No, this be David d'Ersby, in the care of the Berties."

"Are you Bertie kin?"

"In a manner of non-speaking, sir."

"I like your wit." Henslowe smiled. He was missing teeth. He turned to Jonson. "This is my charge. Mistress Alleyn's care, actually, but then I suspect you've met. She was the child of Benjamin Joseph's house. God rest his soul."

"Molly Dean? Is it Molly?" Jonson examined her. "We miss Benjamin Joseph." It seemed to David the sadness hung even heavier in her eyes. "You are no longer the child."

"No, no longer a child." David looked at her hands as her fists tightened. "I, too, have been locked up. 'Twas Bridewell. Mister Henslowe took me out and to live at Mistress Alleyn's."

"'Tis a whorehouse," Jonson said.

"Aye, sir. It be a stew."

"Not a stew, really, no…" Henslowe hemmed.

"'Tis a stew," Molly said flatly.

"One of the best stews in Southwark," Jonson said. "Don't be lettin' them make a whore of you."

"Joan would ne'er do so. Nor I allow it." Henslowe appeared affronted by the suggestion. "We are taken to Molly. But we don't seem the only ones." He looked directly at David, but with more amusement than maliciousness.

"As to the matter of my debt—"

"I was thinking a new play, Ben," Henslowe interrupted.

"Your offer is kind, but I have a benefactor who will settle the debt."

"A benefactor? And who be this benefactor, Ben? Who can afford such friendship?"

"Prince Henry."

"The young heir? Would I could but meet the likes of the Prince on a day. Would be—"

"Would you like to now?" Jonson interrupted.

"Where?"

"Here. He is above."

"But that I could. Would be worth a debt well charged… well, perhaps not quite that, but akin to it, least, and I would be in your debt."

"That would be a pleasant change."

"But Molly—"

"David will attend her, Henslowe. Will you not, lad?"

When alone with her, David looked into the sad eyes. "I mistook you for a whore."

"I know. You followed me."

"No. That was Vere." He reached down and touched her hand.

"He is your twin?"

"No, a year older."

"You look much alike, you and your brother."

"Even of that I am uncertain." He pushed the hair back from her forehead. "You are so beautiful."

"No, but you are kind. I can see it in your eyes. I've known great kindness and much unkindness. I have learned to see the difference."

"I so want to know you."

"No one can ever know another. We are all beings apart. In locked boxes without keys."

"I don't believe that."

"It is true."

"Love reaches…" David was surprised at his own words.

"Is dangerous. It draws us in, a deception, and is taken from us, leaving emptiness."

"It need not be. I want to show you otherwise."

"We are of different parts of a small world. I am of a meaner sort, you are gentry—"

"Not at the core. I am schooled to gentle ways. I was reared to a far meaner place than you. The only thing that set me apart from the rest of that low sort was that I was taught to read and write."

"Then you are not all you appear?"

"I am a sham."

She smiled. "I doubt a sham."

"By some quirk of birth, of which I have yet no real understanding, I've been taken into the household of a great lord and am being taught how to be what I am not."

"You at least have some inkling of lineage, it seems. I don't even know what creature bore me, let alone who conceived me. I am a foundling, birthed in some dark space barely off the street, most likely. I was raised by a Roman priest."

"It is not so different with me. I thought I knew my mam, but even of that I have little certainty. We are two of a pod, Molly Dean…I like to say your name. Molly Dean…Molly Dean…" He stared into the blue eyes. They did not seem as sad as he had found them. "When can I see you?"

"I go to the theatre."

"Do you go tomorrow?"

"Yes. To the Globe."

"Will you share the bench with me?"

"Aye."

"And afterwards?"

"We could walk. The country is near about."

"I love London and would be nowhere else, but sometimes I miss the open country."

"You come from far in the country?"

"Yes. Lincolnshire."

"I've always lived to the city. The loneliness be greater in the city, methinks."

"Aye, but it seems strange it should be thus." He paused, uncertain whether he should ask the next question. "What is it like being in a house of whores?"

"Lots of noise. What is it like living in a palace? I've seen the house of Lord Willoughby."

"Noisy, as well. The noise is simply more elegant, I suspect. Great lords and ladies piss and fart as does anyone. They simply do it with more attending on them."

Molly Dean laughed.

"I like to see you happy."

"It's hard sometimes to be happy. I feel the most vulnerable when I am happy. I understand life better when I am sad."

"Tomorrow you shall be happy and vulnerable."

"You must not forget what I have said about people being in locked boxes. We are, in the end, isolated and alone. Nothing can change that."

"Love."

"No. Least of all love."

David

LONDON

—the present—

AND DAVID RAN out of words. He was getting ready to put his laptop to sleep when a dinging chord announced a message from themoll.

---

themoll: Are you anywhere about?

dsharpe: I am. And I've had the most amazing day.

themoll: Perhaps not as amazing as mine. I couldn't wait to get home to tell you.

dsharpe: And I've been dying to tell someone. I met my father, my real father.

themoll: And I met your brother.

dsharpe: I have no brother. Wait, I do have a brother.

themoll: Yes. I met David Vere in Washington today. He's a very handsome man, this brother who looks like you. Don't you think it's the most amazing coincidence?

David reached up and snapped off the wireless modem device. He gave no reason. Let her think he had been booted. It was not a coincidence. It was the real Vere interfering in his life like the fictional Vere interfering in the fictional David's life. He was angry. And angry at himself for being angry. He did not log back on. From the moment he first saw David Vere, he had guessed who his father might be. He didn't give a shit that David was a fairy. That was an excuse. David Vere was the legitimate son, who would have it all, someday be the Baron of Denchfield. And themoll was something private, in a sense his, the private voice he could share secrets with, and now she belonged as much to David Vere and he resented that, hated that. He hated Vere, the fictional character, who somehow had become David Vere the reality. He turned off his computer and lay down on the bed.

He had written about love, as he imagined love must be for, in honesty with himself, despite the occasional infatuation and the frequent fuck, he had not as yet experienced love. But it must be what David felt for the Molly of his novel. There was love and it was real and he was writing about it. He went back to his computer. He stared at it. In that computer was his novel. Now a story of love. He had planned on buying a new computer. He hadn't even looked for one. Was there even a need? There had been no further word from the hacker, the opech-whatever-person. He should get a portable hard drive at least. Back up all his writing, including the novel. Just in case. Before he left London he would look. And maybe a new computer as well. For the moment he would concentrate on the novel. He flipped open the lid and turned it on and typed: "Overnight the cold struck…"

The Novel

Overnight the cold struck. The pleasant warmth of the day before had been driven out by harsh north winds. David stood at a window masked with frost and looked out at blowing snow. The theatres would not open; nonetheless, David intended on going to the Globe and if he didn't find her there he would go to the house of the red hat. The previous evening, chambered alone with Vere, he had told him of the unexpected meeting. "Her name is Molly Dean."

"She is but a whore."

"No, she is not." And David explained.

Vere was morose and David could see rage drawn on his face. "A whore. Or will be." There seemed an edge of panic in his voice. "She will take you from me."

"Are you mad?"

"You are all I have."

"Don't be stupid."

Vere's voice became more desperate. "We are to each other as few others be."

"Because we happen to look alike?"

"We share a bond. We are castouts."

"You, a castout? You, the brother of the Lord Willoughby, a Bertie, raised wanting for nothing."

"Are you so blind that you realize nothing?"

"Realize what?"

"That you are my brother more than they are to us. That we are born of the same horrible sin."

"What sin?"

Vere made no response.

"What sin, Vere?"

"Better you remain in peace in your ignorance. It's less painful." He left the chamber.

Midmorning, David sat reading. An old servant, nearly deaf and with an enormous welt on the back of her crooked hand, came, and screamed in his ear. "Master Peregrine would see you."

David found Peregrine at a writing table in the east drawing room. A candle burned that he might better see in the dim light. "Vere has spoken with me, David. Sit."

David sat.

"He informs me you have an infatuation of some whore."

"She be not a whore, Perri. She resides in the house of Mistress Alleyn, who they say runs a house of whores. But she be no whore."

Behind Peregrine hung a portrait of the dead Duchess of Suffolk, unsmiling and looking as if to recite a sermon.

"David, as a gentleman, there is a certain standard to which you are committed. A girl..."

"She be no whore. She is a foundling under the wardship of Mister Henslowe."

"Henslowe is not a gentleman. He probably has wealth, but accumulated in various unsavory ways, and his own daughter runs a common stew—no ward of such be fit company."

"But—"

"You are young and a long way from marriage, but let me state some guidelines for you now which may be precepts to direct you. You will attend University?"

"Aye."

"And join the ranks of clerics?"

"No. The Inns. I should like—"

"Yes. Yes, a reasonable choice. And so back to the subject at hand. Passion must be bridled. Lust, so called love, has nothing at all to do with your choice of a bride. Position, the portion you will be granted, what you are liable to gain through any inheritance, her demeanor and how she is perceived by others are far more enduring than any immediate infatuation. I tell you this now, so you may recall in the years ahead, when you think back—"

"But I must see her today," David interrupted. "A matter of honor. I promised." And then he told what was not quite a lie. "The Prince approves."

"The Prince?"

"Yes. Prince Henry was with Smith yesterday and it was there in the Mermaid that I was presented to Mister Henslowe and his ward. And Prince Henry approved of her." What the Prince had actually said when David went back up to the chamber was that he "looked a bit like a man who had been left a fortune by a deceased uncle he didn't even know." "A young lady," he had whispered to Prince Henry. "I approve. The ladies, I always approve."

"And how found you our serious young prince?"

"Wise beyond his years, Perri. At one point in our talk he said that toleration rids us martyrs and martyrs breed followers."

"Perhaps it's sage advice, even in this case. My disapproval of the wench will only make her seem the more desirable. Keep your meeting. See for yourself how she be not fit for a David d'Ersby."

And so bundled in a warm cloak trimmed at the neck with fur, David made his way, the snow blowing in his face. As he moved from the bridge, the wind began to ebb and the snow became weighted and fell in large great flakes like white blossoms, drifting down and tasting wet upon his lips. He moved toward the theatre in the path of new-made footsteps, and as he looked toward the Globe he saw the green-cloaked figure of Molly walking, her cloak brushing the snow.

"I did think you would not come." Her breath was visible as if warmed in her breast.

"Why think you that I would not come?"

"Because of the weather…because of who you are."

"I wish at times I knew who I was." He looked into her eyes and saw what appeared almost terror.

"There is nothing to fear."

"I am afraid of happiness," she said.

"The past is done." Ben Jonson had told him in detail of Benjamin Joseph's death. He looked up at the silent structure; icicles dangled from the overhead, and snow clung to the reaches of dark wood stretching the daubing. "Think you we should wait here 'til the play begins?"

"And be deader than Romeo and Juliet come the spring?"

"The play?"

"The tragedy of love."

"Love need be no tragedy, Molly."

"I almost didn't come."

"I would have gone to Mistress Alleyn's in search of you."

"There is a warm fire at Joan Alleyn's."

"Is there a tavern about?" he asked as she started to move off toward the stew.

"The Blue Boar." She stopped.

"It might be easier to be alone among strangers. Not that I'd mind Mistress Alleyn's."

"You are right. The fire will be crowded with whores. The Boar be on the road to St. Thomas-a-Watering, a bit of a walk, though."

"Are you up to it?"

"Aye." She began to run but was slowed by the growing depth of the snow.

He plowed after her. She fell. He picked her up and carried her, struggling, but finding himself excited as he held her in his arms, her face pressed against his shoulder. He stumbled and dropped her in the snow. They laughed and attempted to run, their cloak seams weighted with ice. Pushing into the warmth, they stepped dripping wet to the hearth.

The host, a skinny fellow with warts, handed them hot spiced ale. His hands were black with soot.

"Molly," a high-pitched voice shrieked across the room.

"We came to see you today," Molly told a skinny boy, his features delicate and frail.

"I did not die, today." He affected death by choking himself.

"Alexie is Juliet," Molly told David.

"I am." He crossed his feet and stood demurely in a highly effeminate stance. "You must meet my Romeo, who truly is." He led them to a table near the rear wall.

Four youths sprawled or sat on the benches on each side of the trestle. Three were young and effeminate. They all talked at once. The fourth was older, dark-haired, appeared brooding, and had a deep musical voice. Alexie introduced him as 'my dearest Romeo.' More hot ale was ordered, and David would have enjoyed himself, but he wanted dearly to be alone with Molly.

"My mother, bless her whorish soul, works in Joan Alleyn's stable," Alexie told David, and then without pause added, "You are a gentleman, but not of these parts."

"Lincolnshire."

"As am I," said the brooding Romeo. And David heard it in his voice. "Me old pap was a curate in Alfordtown, but he caught me bungholing me Cousin Arthur and would have me do public penance wearing a dirty yoke about me neck. I told him 'a shit in a dustbin' and runned off to London where I bunghole as much as I like. Where you from?"

"Ersby Hall."

"Bertie. You're a Bertie. I can see it now in your black little eyes. In fact, you're like the one called Vere. He caught me on the Lough road once and tried to rape me, but I fought like hell and woulda beat the piss out of him, but they would've caught me and strung me up, so I runned off and left him with his britches down." He took a slug of ale. "'Tis 'parent you rather be alone. What be the likes of you here with us Globe fairies?"

Molly answered, "Where else can we be? We came to see you today and so we do."

"Alexie and I as much as live here. There's a room above we share. I swive the host's wife, pig that she is, once a week to help pay the rent. It saves the host the bother. You be welcome up there."

"I don't know if it's fitting," David told him.

Molly stood up. "It's fitting."

The room was small, without a fire, but it had a real bed with a mattress rather than straw and there was a stack of coverlets. Alexie had showed off the homey touches he had added—a rug on the table, three books, a bit of needlepoint framed on a wall, a stack of candles and a brass chamber pot.

Molly removed her cloak, went over to the bed and covered herself with the coverlets.

"I am a virgin," David told her and took another gulp of ale. "Molly, I want to protect you from the bad things, from whatever brings the sadness to your eyes, but I can't marry you yet."

"It is not to be expected. Ever."

"Yes. That must be part of it." He sat down on the edge of the bed. "From the beginning it must be understood we are for each other and forever. But I must go away to Cambridge and then to one of the Inns. All this so that our fortune be assured. I have been trained for the gentle life and need to find income to exist as such on my own. I offer you a promise and waiting."

"I am young, David. I can wait. You have brought me peace. I have known no peace until now. Not since they burned Benjamin Joseph. I find peace in your eyes, David."

"In my beady black eyes." He started to remove a boot with the toe against the heel of the other. "I will be stupid. I know I will be dumb, stupid and clumsy as a drowning bear."

"Nothing matters, but you being here with me."

Boots removed, he crawled beneath the covers and kissed her and it was wonderful. And they continued to hold, to kiss, to fondle and touch and eventually, in the warmth of passion, most of the clothing fell out from under the coverlet and David proceeded to find a part of himself within her and it was all he had ever hoped it would be, but he knew he had been rough and inept. "I am so dumb," he said.

"You care and that matters more, and you have years to practice all the rest."

Molly

JAMESTOWN

—the present—

MOLLY WAITED FOR David to come back online. She assumed his immediate failure to return was because his computer had crashed. Her day had been such an exciting one. She liked David Vere and wanted to talk to David d'Ersby about him. After a few minutes, though she stayed online, she picked up the printout of the journal and began to transcribe a particular section that was of interest because it was that long-ago-Molly's feelings about Vere. She liked David Vere, but the Vere of the journal was not as liked by her ancestor.

The Diary

LONDONTOWN

— *1606* —

The days warmed; by matin's bell ice upon the marshy waters of Bankside had crinkled to water; by midday the big room at Joan Alleyn's remained comfortable although the fire barely flamed. Near the glowing embers I sat on the bench, David across from me. His hands looked large in proportion to his slight frame. I did not trust happiness. I knew that the hurt would come; that he would be taken from me. I knew that small part of me which I had held back would help me survive.

Edward Alleyn was expecting Mr. Henslowe, but Agnes Henslowe reminded him that the Rector of Lindfield was in town. Agnes was a slight woman, older than her husband. Philip Henslowe was Joan's stepfather, having been apprenticed to Joan's father and, upon the man's death, having wed the widow and gained a business. Joan asked if something was amiss with Mistress Maggie. Edward told her not to be so hopeful. Whoever this Maggie was she seemed much disliked by Joan. But Agnes assured them that Joan's father's dear sister was well. Agnes explained that Reverend Prine was seeking private advice and then explained to David that Lord Montague's family name was Browne, and digressed about the Brownes and Papist leanings and Guy Fawkes and trying to bring the pope back to Avignon, which she had no idea where that was, but the point of the matter, when she got back to it, was that Lord Montague was urging the Reverend to marry, and that Rector Prine had no wish to marry. Edward stated that was because of Mr. Farin Browne. Joan asked if Farin Browne was the handsome man, the Lord's nephew of Chelswood, given to the writing of poesy, and Edward told her indeed it was and that Master Prine was not only enraptured by the Viscount's kin, but, as he had it from Henslowe, Farin Browne was equally taken with Master Prine. I was reminded of Alexie and his Romeo.

[Here Molly typed what Molly Dean had written in the margin. "At the time I did not realize the significance this conversation would hold for me. Only later did I see its importance."]

David asked me where I might like to go on such a fine warm day. He had stretched his legs out in my direction and wore soft leather boots that he told me had been cobbled for him at great cost to Vere. David spoke often of Vere's wit and brilliance. I saw only an under-lying meanness. I suggested on such a fine day we should go to Moor Field. As we read-ied, Joan told David that Master Peregrine Bertie had come to the house the day before when we had been out. David became angry and asked her what Perri had wanted. She told him that he just wanted to see the house and hear of Molly. David said it was not Pere-grine's business, but I reminded him that the Berties were his benefactors and, in the end, it would be their will which prevailed, and as we went out David said that the Berties would not stop him from being with me. I did not wish to argue, but I knew the Berties would prevail.

We were over an hour reaching Moor Fields, dawdling on the streets of the city, but we reached the open space of the field. Beyond, windmills with their swooping pad-dles turned, nearly sweeping the tall dead grass. The land was marshy, but I led David along a dry path. I pointed out a small stream called Dame Annis Cleare Spring and that it invoked a very sad tale of Dame Annis, who was married to a rich alderman of London and then he died and left her a very rich widow. When David said that was not very sad, I told him the sad was yet to come and that she married again to a courtier, riotous and a notorious lecher. He spent all of her wealth and then left her. So she drowned herself here in this spring. David hoped there had been more water then and noted a flea couldn't drown in the present trickle. I berated him for not finding my tale more sad. He told me it was very sad and wanted to know if when he died and left me a rich widow, would I marry a disreputable courtier.

It was then I told him that if something should happen to me while he was at Cambridge, he must promise to marry, as it was proper of him to do so. He said he would never marry anyone but me, assured me nothing was going to happen to me, that he would finish Cambridge, the Inns and that we would wed and I would be as wealthy as, he called her, "Dame whatever-Cleare."

David

LONDON

—the present—

DAVID WAS EXCITED as he left the house in Bedford Square and walked, nearly ran, key in hand. He had always lived with someone and now he was to have a place of his own. A room of his own, as Virginia might say. He bounded up past the first floor to the second and, struggling with the lock, opened the door. Except for the tiny kitchen, bookshelves occupied all the walls of every room. White bookshelves from floor to ceiling. There was not even a wall to shove a bed against, hang a painting. Empty white shelving surrounded him.

The bell rang. What? "Yes," he said into the tiny speaker near the door.

"It's Jane," the voice squawked back.

"Jane, who?"

"Jane, your sister."

"I don't — ah, Jane Vere."

"I've come to help. Will you buzz me in?"

"Of course."

She looked like him — the same small dark eyes, the dark hair, unruly and not much longer than his own. She wore brownish jeans and a tight yellow top that more than revealed exorbitant breasts. Should one stare at one's sister's tits, even on a first meeting? He looked away, tried to look away. They were quite astounding.

"How do you like them?" she asked.

"Them?"

"The bookshelves. I suggested them."

"Interesting. But they are going to pose a slight decorating problem, I imagine."

"Why I've come. Men, except gay men, know nothing of decorating."

"It's very nice, but this is my first look at the place."

"I know. But I not only bring you decorating expertise. Perhaps not expertise, but an eye and some experience. And better, I bring the wherewithal."

"The wherewithal?"

"Pounds from dearest Daddy in the form of a credit card. Daddy has provided. Daddy is a dear. Mother can be a shit, but Daddy is a dear. Mamá has ice water in her veins, which accounts for the fact that she is as frigid as a Canadian trapper. No wonder father took up with your mother. How do you like Edward d'Ersby?" she added without breath.

"He is dying."

"A notorious spy, I'm given to understand. What colours do you like?"

"I'm partial to blues, greens, purples."

"Was thinking of something more masculine. Brown tones, coppers, oranges, golds." Jane rattled her words like an old movie spitfire chasing a Messerschmitt.

"I've always loved blue."

"Then blue it shall be. Restful for writing. And some green. Something hotter for the bedroom perhaps. Are you into hot and wild sex?"

"Is that a question for a sister to ask a brother?"

"Certainly one I would ask my other brother. But then, his situation is different."

"Slightly." He changed the subject. "Where do you live?"

"Nearby in Bloomsbury. Graduate study in language history at University."

"Sanskrit, that sort of thing?"

"Yes, but I am also interested in verborrhea and the misuse of the English language. From the time we were small children words were the games David and I played, doublets, five by five, hear-here, panagrams, and Walt Whitman."

"What is Walt Whitman?"

"A game Whitman used to play, at least that's the story, in which you ask the other player a question and the answer must be more than one word and not contain the forbidden vowel. That being established at the beginning of each game. Do you think our love of words is inherited? You interested in words?"

"Of course. I'm a writer."

"Beyond simply that?"

"I question whether we can exist. Is there an existence outside of the word?"

"Yes. How can we even begin on this place without the word?"

"This Earth."

"Of course, but this place, this flat. The word 'blue.'" From a bag which was blue, she took a bottle of wine and two stem glasses. "I thought we might begin with this."

"It's ten o'clock in the morning."

"What the fuck? Somewhere in the world, it's five o'clock." She took out a corkscrew. And that was his introduction to Jane. They arranged to meet during the week, but in the meantime, he needed to go home to Ravensby and talk to Edward about this change in his situation. He wrote on the train going north out of King's Cross. Beyond the city and its seemingly endless suburbs, David stopped writing and stared out at the familiar passing village and square stone rise of the church above the trees. There was a sameness about these villages, the quietness that he knew was there, though unheard within the rail car. Was it hatred of David Vere that made him write Vere with such villainy? The writing was the release, the venting of his hatred. He went back to typing. "It was another evening…"

The Novel

LONDON

—1606—

It was another evening at Southampton House. Chairs were in rows; musicians played under the light, but not quite under the possible drip of candled chandeliers. Then the music ended. Polite applause followed. Chairs scratched the parquet. The smell of sweat, pomander and rose water was suddenly released in the rising of the throng.

"Horns," Gabriel Archer whispered to David as he approached, "were meant for goats' heads. And the singers were like wind breaking in great plops from a goat's other end."

David took some wine offered by a liveried man with hair the colour of manured straw. "To your health, Captain. Where is Captain Smith tonight?"

"Jack throws names like great rocks into a piss basin, but the truth be he is not invited."

"He could have my place," David said.

"Be wary what you would give away. You would be to the Inns. I was to Grays and should I wish, it would be in rooms like these, among those gathered fortune would be made."

"Why do you detach yourself then from such a lucrative occupation?"

"Lucrative, yes. Preying on the misfortunes of men. Yet, I see the future as well. For now, they but interpret the laws, but the day looms when they will make the laws, these men of the Inns."

"It is a way to fortune."

"Ah, if that what life be about, young Ersby. But I've riches enough and—"

"I don't. My state be limbo. I'm educated to better, without the means."

"It be the fate of many a second son. Entering the law, as I did."

"But you gave it up."

"A legacy from my grandmother. I determined life had to be more interesting."

"So, Virginia?"

"Aye."

"When do you sail?"

"Only the winds and Captain Newport know. Could be tomorrow, could be a month of tomorrows. What not be voiced, the spying Spanish Ambassador can't hear and run like a poked pig to Philip, and King Philip would cry to the Scot King, who might well scuttle it for the sake of peace." He added, "Be to Virginia with us."

"I will take Cambridge 'afore the wilderness."

"What you learn at Cambridge will be the thoughts of men. What you learn at the Inns will be the teachings of men. What you learn in Virginia will be straight from God. It is a land unspoiled and a people unencumbered by a need for wealth. You will miss the chance of being upon a venture that could change the course of history. The world we live in is in a state of great flux. Men of Parliament voice ideas about men's rights, which would have been treason in times not far past. Edwin Sandys proposes that all men accused of thievery or murder be entitled to representation at the bar. It is Sandys' contention that a man is not guilty until it so proven. Think you not an innocent has met the gallows?"

"I never thought on it at all."

"Well, you should. Yet such change will not come quickly to England. But in Virginia, where distance from the King and Lords be great, these new thoughts can sprout."

"One learns to come late and avoid the caterwauling." Vere's voice was loud enough to carry as he approached. "Did you hear, Captain Archer, our Cousin Alice no longer sports a belly. It dropped early and was dead. I do expect, sir, that you aren't the only gentleman relieved at her plopping being dead."

"I am indifferent to your gossip." Archer walked away.

"I am afraid you have offended Captain Archer."

"We are better left without his company." Vere led the way into a drawing room. "I have something for you. Your winnings. I wagered you the girl was a whore and she is no whore. You remember the miniature the Lord Southampton showed you of me. The painter is Master Nicholas Hilliard. I had him make one of you as well."

"How? I never sat for a painter."

"Ah, but you have. Twice, when we feasted at Sir Edwin's. Above the hall is open and Hilliard sat up there. While you ate, he painted."

"Strange. I never noticed anyone above on either day."

"He said there was bare a difference between us and he could have well painted me and given it you and scarce a man would have known the difference. Still, I see some difference in the portraits. Here let me show it you." Vere handed David the miniature.

It was identical, even to the dress. "I wore no garb this color or style."

"Nor I when he painted me. He does the head and then an apprentice paints the rest."

"I would swear it was the miniature you gave Southampton. It looks identical."

"The angle is slightly different. But I agree, there is a great similarity, as there is between us."

"Yes." David examined it more thoroughly. "Thank you, Vere. It is a lovely gift."

"I thought you might wish Molly to have it."

"May I?"

"Of course. Go now to her, if you wish. Perri won't have to know you've gone."

Bundled in his cloak, David left Southampton House and hurried to the stew and went up to the room Joan Alleyn let them keep as their own.

"I did not expect to see you until the morrow." Molly put down her sewing.

He bent down and kissed her. "I have a gift for you." There was excitement in his voice. He took out the miniature from the purse and handed it to her.

She held it delicately in her hands. "It is beautiful."

"It is for not being a whore." He told her the story of the wager.

"I will put it on a ribbon and wear it around my neck."

He touched her gently at the cleavage of her breasts. "And let it rest here where I would have my hand." He pushed her loose blouse off her shoulders. "And my lips." He kissed her and slipped the fabric of her garment down until it hung from her waist.

"I am cold." She freed herself from him, unfastened her skirt and shook loose of it. As it fell she leaped into the bed and pulled the coverlet over her. "Now I am warm."

He had both boots off but was struggling with the tiny buttons of his doublet. "No wonder the rich need help in getting undressed," he said. "It is wonder the gentry have any children at all. By the time they get ready for bed they have lost the urge." In his haste a pearl tore loose and fell to the floor.

Later, wrapped in his cloak, he rushed toward the bridge and had nearly reached it when a stocky figure coming toward him stopped and stood in his path. At first he saw only the dark shape straddling the way, but then realized it was Ben Jonson.

"Thank the blessed Lord, I reached you before they did," Jonson told him.

"Before who reached me?"

"There is a warrant for you. Come along quick."

"Wait." David didn't move. "What warrant?"

"Come. There are men on their way to Joan Alleyn's stew to arrest you."

"What for, Ben?"

"The theft of documents from my Lord Southampton's. His men will come in search of you."

"That is ludicrous. I never—"

Jonson pointed in the direction of torches approaching from the bridge. "Never mind what is. Get quickly below in the trees!" Jonson shoved him down the embankment. The brittle grasses were wet. The torchbearers cast light and deep shadows as they passed on the road above. He could hear their voices as they moved by. The deep darkness returned.

He followed Jonson up onto the road. "What is this about?"

Jonson set a fast pace and did not turn back. "A casket of the Earl's was broken open. Missing were some documents which, from what Archer told Smith and myself, could send the Earl to the Tower and would incriminate the Prince as well."

"But why am I suspected?"

"There was a miniature of Vere said to resemble you. It, too, is missing."

They reached the Mermaid, but David waited outside in the darkness. A child dragged a dead cat along the cobble and the piercing cries of a woman being beaten could be heard from the distance. Jonson returned. "Hide your face in your cloak. Go in alone and up the stairs to Smith's keeps. I will follow." Smith sat on a stool at the writing table. "Did you break open Lord Henry's casket? Did you take the miniature from it? And some papers?"

"No."

"Vere is behind this, isn't he?"

David looked at the floor. He had difficulty openly accusing his brother.

"He is, David. Tell me what you know."

"I knew of the miniature. The Earl showed it to me that first day at Southampton House."

Smith stood. He had the definitive stance of a soldier. "Do you have the miniature?"

"Vere gave me it this evening at Southampton House. He said it was not the same miniature and that this one he had painted for me by Master Hilliard. He told me I could give it to Molly if I wished and I did."

Jonson, who had come in, stood silently in the room.

"There can be no doubt, David," Smith said. "It was that miniature which had been in Southampton's possession. There was a great commotion after you left Southampton House. Vere reported to Lord Robert you showed him the miniature, saying that you said the Earl had given it to you. Vere also told Lord Robert and Perri that you planned to give it to the whore."

"She is no whore," David said softly.

Smith continued without responding. "This was told the Berties in earshot of the Earl, who said he gave you nothing and then raced off to the drawing room. Apparently his concern was not for the miniature but documents he had placed in the casket. Archer went along as the Berties followed Southampton to the drawing room. Archer said Southampton turned ashen, then livid, and raced off from the House in the company of Sir Edwin Sandys in search of Prince Henry. When he returned, he was in the company of Lord Justice Coke and they closeted with Lord Bertie.

Through stray bits of all the commotion and the gossip, Captain Archer learned of your warrant. He was certain of your innocence, but neither Lord Robert nor Peregrine would listen to him."

"But Peregrine knows what Vere is capable of," David said. "I must talk with Perri."

"Not for the present," Smith advised. "He will not believe you haven't betrayed him. He said aloud for all of the company, including Gabriel, to hear that you are not be let in his presence, but hung like the common criminal that you are. The rest is not worth repeating."

"I need to know," David said. "What else did he say?"

"I know not what he meant by it. He said a man born of such a sin is destined to evil."

Molly

JAMESTOWN

—the present—

NOT A WORD from David d'Ersby. Perhaps he was intensely engrossed in his novel. He had not contacted her since that break in their conversation when she was telling him about meeting David Vere. What was it that he had said? "I met my father, my real father." And then something about "I have no brother...I do have a brother." Did he even mean David Vere? David Vere had told her that they were brothers. She liked David Vere, but she had to admit she didn't know him that well. Maybe he simply wanted that to be the case — that they were brothers, as they seemed to look alike. Maybe he was stalking d'Ersby. But as both names, historically, were beginning to figure prominently in Molly's diary, she was interested in the connection.

And maybe it was all about another kind of connectivity, electronic connectivity. She knew nothing, she realized, about the reliability or non-reliability of British online servers. Her own server here in Jamestown was down on occasion. That could well be David's problem.

On the floor, spread out in a sequence, were the Xeroxed diary pages. She picked up the next page and begain diligently transcribing the journal's scrawling penmanship into modern language. The story at the moment was difficult for her as she felt the seventeenth-century Molly's pain. She penned: "It was the disaster..."

The Diary

LONDONTOWN

—*1606*—

It was the disaster that I knew would come. I sat in the small chamber of oak walls. Cold winter moonlight came in from a window, high, near the ceiling. I was reminded of Bridewell; it only strengthened my inward retreat. I had already closed the door on that beyond self. The power to control my being was mine alone. It had been a weakness to let David draw me out. Had I kept to my isolation, I would not now be in this room in Southampton House at the mercy of the whims of the mighty.

I sat at the fire after David had left and showed Joan the miniature. It was yet in my hands when I saw the approach of light through a window and then came the loud pounding thumps. Joan opened the door, letting in both cold and light. Shadowed shapes stood beyond the light. A large man with slits for eyes moved from the shadows. His voice was deep and ominous, demanding the one known as David d'Ersby. I clutched the miniature and, shivering in the cold from the open door, told him David be gone. He yelled be I Molly Dean and if David d'Ersby had give me a miniature painting. I made certain there was no fright in my voice and told him he had. To which he asked me if he gave me documents for his keeping. I told him no. Nothing but the miniature of himself.

He shouted that the miniature be of Master Vere Bertie and be the possession of the Lord Southampton and ordered me to fetch it. I extended the small painting in its gilded oval. The hand which took it was ungloved and like ice. And again he demanded documents. I repeated I knew nothing of any papers. But for a moment I stood as if naked to the wind, and then quickly cloaked myself in the isolation, the protective garb of Bridewell.

And so I sat there on a bench when the liveried young man entered carrying a candle in a silver holder and told me that I was summoned. My face a mask, I followed the servant from the small chamber through a wide door into a drawing room. I nearly lost my composure as the first thing I saw was David, clad in scarlet, his back to me, seemingly look-

ing out a window into the black night. He did
not turn about. I recognized the Earl of Southampton from the playhouse. He was a narrow
long man with hair that dripped to his shoulders. He was flanked by Peregrine Bertie and
another, I assumed be Lord Robert, more
ornately dressed than his brother. A fourth
gentleman, in black with a long face culmi-
nating in a pointed beard and a narrow sharp
nose, stood apart. The most elegantly clad was
a youth, hardly more than a boy. Even seated
he appeared tall. His doublet was white and
yellow striped, trimmed in white fur and dripping with gold buttons. On a chain hung a
pendant with an enormous red jewel.

The man with the pointed beard kindly
asked if I be Molly Dean, ward of Philip
Henslowe. I responded politely without emotion. Peregrine Bertie then extended the miniature and asked in a frosted voice if it was
given me by one who called himself David
d'Ersby. I told him yes.

Southampton leaned in my direction, asking if I were given certain documents to safe
keep for d'Ersby. I told him no. He said that
perhaps I would have not recognized the
importance of some papers. I told him that
I could read and was given no documents of
value or any other papers.

The man I thought David turned about,
only it was not David, it was Vere. The like-

ness was remarkable, but Vere's small eyes had meanness in them and disdain shaped his lips. He came over and looked directly at me, said that I would lie for David as well as with him and that I had bewitched David. He ranted on about me using the papers against the Prince and called me whore.

The Earl asked if I was a child of the Devil, to which I responded no. Peregrine Bertie, his dark eyes daggers of hate, scrutinized me and said I was no doubt a witch. Vere, addressing the Earl, said he could bring witnesses who would testify that I had been the cause of impotence among more than one visitor to the stew and that I caused the death of pigs in Bankside, had been known to suckle a mole, never would eat salt and had caused a cottage to burn. He was interrupted by the elegant boy, who said he had no doubt were they to put me to the rack, or pull off my fingernails, I would certain admit to all this and being a Jewess, and of having intercourse with the Devil, himself. There be no witches, he told them, but in the madness of men's minds. The boy had a strong commanding voice.

Vere told the boy, who I realized was Prince Henry, that his father the King did not believe as he did. To which the boy replied that if he believed as his father did, there would be no need for concern over the documents. He repeated that I was no witch and he doubted I was guilty of either concealing or having knowledge of the documents. David, he indicated, was another matter, being either a spy or a fool and, in either case, should be found and hung.

The Earl raised his jewel-decked hands and shook his head, saying that they must recover the documents. And then Lord Robert Bertie finally spoke, saying he was responsible, would find d'Ersby and have him tortured if necessary to regain the papers. The Earl asked what friends David might have in high places, Lord Salisbury, perhaps; but the one with the pointed beard reminded them that they were not alone. They looked at me and spoke no further of it.

The liveried young man entered and spoke softly to the Earl who then said it seemed Philip Henslowe awaited without and inquired as to the fate of his ward.

Vere persisted that I should be charged with witchery. But the Prince cautioned him that despite his youth and liberality in the judgment of men, he was still the heir to England's and Scotland's thrones and it was his royal opinion there be no witches. The Prince asked if the innocent were to continually be punished with the guilty. Peregrine said I could not be returned to the stew, where I would be taught to lead a life of whoredom, and suggested Bridewell and redemption. I thought of the rain and the beating and it only strengthened my resolve. It did not matter what they did with me. The man with the pointed beard said that Henslowe was a Sussex man and that he could have me removed to there. The Prince indicated that he had met Henslowe and could be assured that he would do their bidding.

I was delivered to a waiting Philip Henslowe with instructions that I was to be removed to Sussex. We stepped out into the darkness. I listened to the sound of his prattle but closed my mind to his words. I shut out the world. I hugged the rough-spun cloak about me as if to insulate myself. I would not again let down the barrier. I knew David would come looking for me in Sussex. He would find me and we would be discovered and killed. I must prevent that. I was half-listening as Henslowe said something of Rector Prine returning to Lindfield and that he would have him escort me. He described Roger Prine as a lovely man, but his words were mostly lost on the wind. The bell ringer called the hour and assured 'All was well' and 'God save the King.' And to that I softly added the Prince.

As I neared the bridge, I stared into the black water, frozen in white clumps near the shore. David must believe I am dead. That must be the message Joan would give him. Then he would be safe. I would find whatever peace there was in solitariness. I would be alone. Perhaps not quite alone, for I suspected David's child was growing in my belly.

David

To BE. AN infinitive forming existence. Father. One word. Sister. One word. Brother. One word. Single words that were attempting to reshape his existence. These he was becoming and seemingly without control. Was that madness? Paul Michel said all writers were mad because they do not believe in the stability of reality. But Michel is fictional; his madness defined by Foucault or more precisely by Duncker. *To be.*

The landscape sped by the train window. A sameness each time. Stability. Yet was it the same? The reflection from those windows in that factory. Not there on another trip home. And there, where a horse had stood, there in the corner of the pasture, it was now empty of horse. Had horse become not, become nothing? All words — horse, reflection, pig. Pig, a word he remanded upon the pub keeper's wife. But not the same image. Words and only words gave birth to imagination. Where was the distinction between words of fiction and words of reality? To be David. To be fictional or real. To be or not to be. Shakespeare, the eternal existentialist.

Edward was dying. Was David to be his heir or not to be his heir? There was no stability to this reality, but it was *his* reality, or at least he saw it as *a* reality. Only over the characters of his novel did he exert control, and even they were beginning to get out of hand. David, the character, was mired in events upon which David, the writer, had not planned. Although he had not contrived an outline to follow, he certainly had a general direction, an intention toward which the novel was to go. But it was tending to become something else, ill-defined. He wrote: "Roped staves swung..."

The Novel

LONDON

— 1 6 0 6 —

Roped staves swung aloft; pulleys creaked in the giant tripod of the wooden crane; seabirds cawed. Sailors of the berthed *Susan Constant* yelled to men below as the loading continued. The winter sun was not enough to warm David against the sharp gusts cutting across the Thames. He was obsessed with thoughts of Molly. Gabriel Archer appeared from the warehouse. Even his gait as he approached seemed censorious. "You should not be out here. They are searching everywhere for you." And then, as if reading his thoughts, he added, "I have learned nothing. Joan Alleyn's is being watched constantly." Archer stood, legs planted apart. "Now come inside. It is dangerous for you to stand here in the open."

"I must see Molly."

"David, if Smith or I were to approach Philip Henslowe or Edward Alleyn, let alone go to that stew, word would reach Southampton. They would come here to Brunswick Wharf and hang you without a word. And probably John Smith and me, to boot." Archer went inside.

David turned back to the water, watching it lap at the rough rocks of the bulkhead. It reeked of dead fish and human waste. As he opened the warehouse door he was hit by the smells of sour beer, dank wood, rotten meat and rancid fats. Archer was sitting at the table amid the hogsheads and bundles, bales and rigging. Light beamed through a ray of dust from a glassless window, illuminating the elegance of the Captain's garb. "John Smith has generously arranged your passage." Archer tapped the handle of his rapier, which he had removed and lay across the table in front of him.

"To where?"

"To Virginia, of course. At some sacrifice, I might add."

"I could not leave Molly…"

"There is no chance for you and Molly. Where would you go?"

"Anywhere. Together. Away from London."

"There is nowhere. The law is against you. You have no property, no money, no friends in the countryside. You would be driven out as vagrants or arrested as criminals."

"There must be somewhere."

"There is nowhere. Is that the life you want for yourself? For Molly? Give Smith's kindness your consideration. Whate'er your opinion of Virginia, it beats the gallows." Archer leaned forward, rearranging his sword. "Perhaps on Christmas they will ease the watch about the stew. Perhaps some arrangement can be made—"

"You won't be here," David said.

"What do you mean?"

"You sail in two days."

"No one knows when we sail."

"I slept in the loft above with sailors of the *Susan Constant*. You sail in two days."

"Before Christmas?" Archer stood up.

"Aye."

"I will try. At least some news of Molly. Perhaps Ben Jonson can go to the stew…looking for Henslowe. Don't depend on it. Molly's moves are certainly being watched. She is, after all, their link to finding you." Archer returned to the table and put on his rapier. "Stay inside. Hanging is irreversible."

Archer left and the man with one eye and no voice brought David lumpy barley porridge, a piece of bony fish and beer. David picked at the fish, sucking bits off the bones. There had to be an alternative to traveling to the underside of the world. And to being without Molly. That was death in itself. The beer was rotten, but he drank it and remembered the wines of Southampton House served by liveried footman. Hearing a commotion outside, he got up from the table, tipping over the stool. He opened the door, letting in the moist but more pleasant air, and through the fog he could see the *Susan Constant*, its ropes free of the dock, being towed out into the Thames.

That night he slept, or tried to sleep, alone in the straw in the loft, absent the warm breath of the four young sailors from the *Susan Constant*, his cloak wound about him to keep out what cold he could. A rat gnawed incessantly. Archer was right, of course, there was nowhere in England where he and Molly could flee. How would they survive? The only place he had roots was in Lincolnshire and that was Bertie country. The old building creaked. The wind managed to come through every crack and he could hear the Thames pounding against the rocks. Soon it would be Christmas and he remembered Christmas at Grimesthorpe, that great stone edifice, with a table so laden with food it sagged in the center, and there had been presents of books and clothes and pieces of gold. And Lady Mary, her breasts powdered and her nipples exposed, singing of dead birds and crying for her dead brother Edward, Earl of Oxford. Lord Robert and Lady Elizabeth acted as if she were not there. Finally, when both her singing and her wailing became so loud conversation was impossible, Peregrine led her away. David seldom saw her after that but, sometimes in the night, he could hear her song and her cries and once or twice he saw her briefly from a distance, walking in the garden. Shortly before leaving for London he saw her in a field beyond the great house chasing after a pig.

The pale moonlight that had cast stripes through the cracks upon the straw vanished, and in the blackness rain fell in heavy pelts. The gnawing ceased and the rat scurried away. Unable to sleep, David lay listening to the rain, remembering Lady Mary and wondering why she was in his thoughts. Mad. And yet beneath her rantings there always seemed a current of truth.

He heard the door open below. "David."

For a moment he panicked and cringed back in the straw like one of the rats.

"David." The voice was deep and full.

He realized it was Ben Jonson. David shook himself free of the straw and slid down the ladder.

"It is pouring wet. I came without a torch." Despite the blandness of his words there was anguish in Jonson's voice.

"What is wrong?"

It was a moment before the man replied. "I am uncertain how to tell you."

"Molly?" David knew. He knew. She was dead. "Molly…"

Again Jonson did not speak. When he did it was a whisper. "She is…"

"…Dead."

"Aye, David. It is so."

"They killed her."

"No." The bulky man wrapped his arm about David's shoulder. His wetness soaked into the boy's doublet. David could not remember ever crying, but the flood of tears came.

"They killed her," David said through the tears.

"No. Joan told me she drowned. At Paris Gate."

"Was it an accident?"

"Joan said so."

"But was it?"

"What man can know for certain?"

David thought of Dame Annis Cleare Spring. He slipped from Jonson's arm and went out into the rain and fog to the water's edge and stood there. Muffled sounds of ships' bells. Water slapped the rocks. The salty tears poured down his cheeks. He stood the remainder of the night, staring into the dense fog.

David

TRAIN FROM LONDON

—the present—

THERE. DAVID HAD done it. He had killed Molly off. He sat there for a moment staring at the screen. She no longer existed. From here forward the novel would shift. He had not planned on David going to Virginia, but he had blocked himself. He stared for a moment or two longer and then logged off and closed the laptop. Done and dead.

Molly

MOLLY HEARD THE car roaring up. She recognized the familiar sound of Inez's Vette. The engine died and Molly went out on the front stoop of the Jamestown cottage.

"What are you doing here?"

"That's a helluva welcome." Inez climbed out. "I was in the neighborhood."

"Nobody's in the neighborhood of Jamestown."

Inez followed her into the cottage. "I didn't start out to come here. The Desirable Grynch dumped me for another woman and I just started driving. I need a beer."

"I'm not sure I have any."

"You always have beer."

"I'm trying to lose weight."

"You look too skinny." Inez went into the kitchen and rummaged in the refrigerator.

"He was a loser."

"To the contrary, he won most of his matches. Oh good, I found a beer behind the fat-free milk. You say that about everyone I have ever dated."

"Not everyone. Last time I said, 'She was a loser.' You need to find a relatively young, handsome, successful and sane man and settle down into a proper marriage."

Inez poured beer into a glass and slumped down onto a chair. "What do I know about a proper marriage?"

"You come from a solid home. Your parents have a true marriage."

"Get real. My father is a workaholic in Europe. My mother socializes in Washington, D.C. They barely see one another."

"And they stay married. In this day and age, I call that a true marriage."

"They couldn't possibly divorce. Daddy is more Catholic than the Pope."

"Give me just a wee sip of that beer. It looks so good." Inez handed the glass to her and Molly relished the taste and handed the glass back.

"No normal guy could get near me. If he was black, Mother would find a barrage of socially unacceptable attributes about him. If he was white, Daddy would be certain he was only in for the billions. So I've never bothered with any real possibilities."

"Grynch was really ugly."

"Yeah, that got to Sybil. Big time. But he left me for a female wrestler. Green Lettuce, she's called, and she's mostly tits. I think she paints them green or something."

"Then why be upset?"

"You'd be upset, too, if you were dumped by somebody that ugly for somebody with green tits. It isn't all that great for the self-esteem."

They were quiet for a moment. Molly asked softly, "Do you believe in destiny?"

"No."

"That was a quick answer."

"There is no such thing as destiny. We go through life battered by habit and the unknown. The most we can expect is an occasional coincidence. Why destiny?"

"I have the same name as my ancestor and now I've met a man that has the same name as the man she married."

"Met? You mean the online guy?"

"Yes."

"That's not meeting, Moll. That's conversation with a faceless nonentity. Girl, the events you are relating to happened nearly four hundred years ago. They have nothing to do with your life now. You are seeking the perfect partner, for the perfect marriage —"

"Don't analyze me."

"But it's true. Let's face it; you had an unstable childhood. You're an orphan. You're after what you think you never had. But nobody comes from a perfect environment. Two parents and more money than is good for you don't bring the perfect relationship because, girl, it doesn't exist."

"Quite by accident I met his half-brother in Washington. I don't think it is simply coincidence. There are things that are meant to be."

"Christ. I'm going out to get us some more beer."

She sped off in her Vette. Molly went back to transcribing. "The following day…"

The Diary

CARRIAGE TO LINDFIELD

—1606—

The following day Joan argued with Henslowe over Lindfield. He told her if I didn't go there it was back to Bridewell. He reminded her that her Aunt Margaret was there. Joan said that was why I should not go, that the old woman was a moralistic ogre. Lindfield or not Lindfield, it didn't matter. Yet, if I carried David's child I could not retreat into total isolation and I could not long hide the fact from this Mistress Margaret. I must take care of David's child.

The awkward goodbyes behind, I sat in the coach across from Rector Roger Prine. He was a tall man, beautiful rather than handsome, with a sculptured face, the cheekbones high, the chin cut square. The torchlight reflected his clean blond hair. His near-perfect features were only marred by a deep scar

above his right eyebrow. His beauty was perhaps more striking by the contrast of his
black attire. His voice was deep and melodi-
ous, but I saw sadness, not unlike my own, in
his green eyes. Joan, tears streaming down her
face, had promised to tell David what he must
be told. As the coach rattled over the cobblestones, I clutched a pearl button I had found
on the floor near the bed. I was tossed, jerked
and pitched back and forth until the cobble
turned into dirt and rock and the ride became
the rougher. The smell of the suet pudding
Agnes had shoved into my hands at parting
combined with the turbulence—I knew I must
vomit. I put my hand to my mouth but could
not stop myself and began to retch. The Rector banged his fist against the carriage ceiling
and the horses gradually slowed and stopped,
but it was too late. I had spewed down the
front of my cloak. With the Rector's help I
got down out of the carriage and continued
to vomit at the side of the road. He helped
me into the carriage, wet a napkin with water
from a jug and wiped my cloak. Then tapped
the ceiling. We rode in silence. Dark forests
crowded the road, black shapes upon black
shapes. I heard a piercing howl, but Rector
Prine assured me that it was only a wolf. And
then no other sounds—only the blackness. My
stomach no longer churned, but I ached each
time the wheels ground across another large

rock. The forest ceased and, in the early dawn, the shapes of cottages stretched across a valley. Rector Prine's deep voice broke the silence when he asked me if I was with child. I could only look down.

He reached over and patted my hand, saying he was afraid of what Mistress Margaret would do when she learned. I told him I had worried of that and he said I should have told Joan. I tried to explain, but not well and he, in response, told me that Joan was my friend and would have kept me from being sent to Lindfield. I could not attempt to explain to the man, a stranger, that there was no help but from within, that the world was a devastating place without hope. He told me that if Mistress Margaret turned me out, I must promise to come to the rectory. I thanked him but told him I could not be such a burden upon a stranger. He said he was not a stranger but a representative of Christ, a man of God. I told him I no longer believed there could be a God. He didn't seem the least shocked and told me that was not what mattered, but that he did and I would be welcome at the rectory.

I tightened the cloak, wet from the sponging, about me and answered with deliberate care that I was a fornicatress and would no doubt be soon found out publicly as such. I told him I knew he was to wed soon and that his new bride would not want such a burden

as myself upon the rectory. He told me he
had no wish to wed. I said I understood. To
which he replied that he didn't think I did. I
told him of Alexie who shared his bed and life
with another actor. And the Rector said that
perhaps I did understand.

The silhouettes faded in morning light
into real shapes. Birds began a morning chorus and a rooster crowed. Valleys of dried
grass or tilled clumps of earth rolled between
the stands of trees. Patches of snow edged the
dead fields. The sun rose. The air warmed.
Rector Prine read; not religious writing as I
would have expected but from a book called
A *Profitable Instruction of the Perfect Ordering of
Bees.* When we stopped for a change of horses,
on his urging I took some beer and bread,
near the warmth of the fire. I sensed the Rector staring at me. He said that we would stop
at Chelswood where a friend, Master Browne,
would make us welcome. We washed at the
tub behind the tavern and climbed up into
the carriage. I was startled to see a pistol now
resting on the seat beside the Rector. He said
there was danger of highwaymen.

As the coach jerked forward he asked me
if the father of my child was the one they call
d'Ersby. I told him that he was, but that he
didn't know of the child and, for the safety
of all, he must not, for he would come looking and they would catch and hang him. The

Rector suggested he might come anyway, but I told him that Joan had promised to tell David that I had drowned in the Thames. The Rector ran his finger along the barrel of the pistol, noted that there was great finality in that and asked if I was sure I was doing the right thing. I could but answer yes.

The day warmed. The pungent smell of pig dung swept through the carriage as we left villages behind. Sheep fed on dead grass and cows stood near thatched buildings. The Rector's voice seemed hesitant and unsure as he said he would not, of course, be a proper husband to any woman, but added that if such would not disturb me, a solution to both our dilemmas would be marriage. I stared at him in disbelief. He said that he had meant no offense. I replied that I was by no means offended, that he was most kind, but I reminded him that I was a fornicatress and he a rector. He said no need for any to know the child not be his and that the bans could be posted at once. He told me his name was Roger and that he would take good care of me and the child. He said that he would wish to see Master Browne and would I find that objectionable. I assured him I would not, yet the entire idea seemed so strange. I asked if he understood that I was a person of no standing who brought nothing to a marriage. He said I brought myself, that I was bright and had a lovely heart. He said that he assumed I could manage a house. I asked him what of the people of Lindfield, and particularly what of Lord Montague? He said Lord Montague cared not whom he married, as long as he married. He reached across and took my hand and told me he would always take care of me.

David

THE TRAIN PULLED into the reality of the old frame station, its existence established in time, aged timber and
worn platform, and his Mercedes was parked where he
had left it, all giving stability to his existence. The same
two-lane road led away from the village. The same trees
arched across the road. There was stability. He thought
of Vere, both the brother and the character. He had not
intended for the character to have such villainy. And now
came these others. Names he had searched on the computer screen at the British Library. Names that appeared in
the titles of books he lugged in the canvas bag. John Smith,
Gabriel Archer and Bartholomew Gosnold were gaining
an importance he had not foreseen. Words had generated
names that took on character and became heavy characters,
weighty material. He had found books in the old shops
along St. Martin's Lane. These names, these beings who

were but words on paper, creations of biographers and historians. He thought of the opening line of the chapter he had written on the train: "As morning light approached…"

The Novel

LONDON

—1606—

As morning light approached, invisible birds cawed in the mist. As a hole in the fog opened, David could see the dark brown water hitting the black stones. He thought of Molly in the water below. Should he, too, leap into the cold darkness? The fog lifted, the birds flew overhead, and out in the Thames he could see the *Susan Constant*, the *Godspeed* and the *Discovery* at anchor. He returned to the warehouse and sat on a bale in a corner, trying to accept that Molly was dead and that he lived.

Captain Bartholomew Gosnold came in like a gust of wind. "Cousin."

"Few men would dare call me that," David said and stood up. "Molly is dead."

"I know." He reached over and took David's hand in both of his, pressed it as if warming it against the cold. "What are you to do? Be you for Virginia?"

"There is nowhere else."

"I will have a word with Newport. He must be told not only that you are with us, but of the untrue accusation against you. It is Vere's doing. Strange that he should do such to his brother, especially you."

"He is my brother, then? That is a certainty? Is Lady Mary my mother?"

"Yes, that poor creature is your mother."

"But Lord Peregrine Willoughby was not my father."

"He was not, David."

"Who was?"

"I cannot say." Captain Gosnold looked up at the glassless window. "I will have a boat take us out to the *Susan*. Captain Newport is aboard."

"I have a sword yet no clothes for a voyage."

"I have already seen to that. There is a servant at Bertie House, Chowder, who I once befriended. He has agreed to fetch some of your own clothes for me."

"Chowder hates me. He always treated me—"

"Because you resemble Vere. Vere once chained the boy up and was burning him with a candle when I heard the screams. I took Chowder away and he stayed in my house for a time."

"Vere is mad, isn't he?"

"Yes. But neither Lord Robert nor Peregrine will face that reality, nor the truth that Lord Willoughby was not Vere's father any more than he was yours. But…"

"It is because of my parents that Sir Edward Maria Wingfield hates me, is it not?"

"Aye. Sir Edward sees not shades of truth, only sin."

"And I am a child of sin?"

The Captain said nothing.

"Am I never to learn the truth?"

"I promise someday that I shall tell you. But that pain is not for the present."

"And what will Sir Edward do when he finds me among the passengers?"

"He will be aboard the *Susan* and you aboard the *God-speed* with me."

A rope ladder was lowered for them to climb aboard. David looked up at the large letters at the bow—*Susan Constant*.

"Stay on deck. I will send for you, David." Gosnold disappeared into a forward cabin.

"Be ye sailin' then with us, sir, after all?" Jeremy had a torn ear lobe and a missing front tooth.

"On the *Godspeed*."

"'Tis a small thing and haunted by a dead Muscovite, probably won't make it across, but better'n bein' on the *Discovery*. That got no chance atall— barely bigger'n a piss basin."

"You give me great confidence, Jeremy, but—" David stopped short as Captain Gosnold signaled for him. "I'm wanted." David stooped to get through the hatch and into the cabin.

Captain Newport, his good arm resting on the table, motioned to David. "Sit, lad."

David sat on the bench.

"Captain Gosnold has advised me of the situation. There is risk, of course, in offending backers of this venture, but I am a fair man and believe in the end that right does will out, and I am more than certain, given time, you will be vindicated. In the mean, we will keep you from the hangman's noose."

"Thank you, Captain." In many ways David was indifferent whether he was allowed on the voyage or not, but he nonetheless realized both captains were sticking out their necks for him, as had Gabriel Archer, John Smith and Ben Jonson.

"I think it best you have another name for the *Godspeed's* log."

"David Sharpe was my name before d'Ersby."

"Let it be then, Captain Gosnold, your charge be known as David Sharpe." He tapped his hooked arm at the table's edge. "It be done. May God grant us a safe voyage."

David stood to go. "I be in your debt, Captain."

"Pay heed to Captain Gosnold and cause no man difficulty on this long voyage and your debt be well paid, David Sharpe."

He sat in the rowboat, silent. Captain Gosnold seemed deep in thought as well. As they approached Brunswick Wharf, David was surprised to see Ben Jonson standing in the wind.

Jonson gave them a hand from the small boat. "I was feared you'd been found out and taken off. Francis Bacon would a word with you, David."

"*The* Sir Francis Bacon?"

"Do you think it wise?" Gosnold asked. "Bacon is an ambitious man."

"He is also a powerful man. Powerful men can be of great help." The writer's voice was deep and sure. "He has indicated an interest in David's plight."

"We sail soon, Ben. Do you think David should see Bacon as things are?"

"Francis is my friend, Captain. With his legal mind and ways about the court, he can clarify all this in David's absence. David will be free to return to England when he wills, his name cleared."

"I leave it to you then, Ben."

David set off in another boat up the Thames with Jonson to Twickenham.

David

—*the present*—

He PULLED UP behind the Abbey. Something was amiss, strange… out of place. The Jaguar was gone. Martin did not drive the Jaguar unless Edward was in the vehicle. Martin ran errands for Edward but always in the Ford or the Renault. Something was wrong.

Bydie was stewing in the kitchen that reeked of mutton. "He's gone." It was said with solemnity.

Gone, like in all the euphemisms, passed, slipped away. "He died? Edward died?"

"No. He's gone."

"Gone where? How, in his condition?"

"To Lourdes."

"Lourdes? Edward's not Catholic. Why would he go to Lourdes? Did Martin go? Did they say they were going to Lourdes?"

"I tried to stop them. I said anyone in Mr. Edward's state... well, they wouldn't have it." She stirred whatever was stewing in the pot that smelled of mutton.

"And they said they were going to Lourdes?"

"Not exactly. To France. They says they were going to France. But why else would they go to France in his dying way but for a miracle at Lourdes? Mrs. Mulvaney went to Lourdes when she had the gangrene in her leg and was near dying and that was in ninety-six. Course she was Irish and believed in it an' all. Still it killed her. Didn't do the least ways good. I told them. I told Martin. There's no sense in them going. But he sat there drinking his tea and said Mr. Edward would have it. They would go to France and he was carried out to his Jag-U-whar." She said it as if it were three words. "All bundled."

"But they never said Lourdes."

"Of course not. They don't have to report to me. Just France was all they said, but I knew. And then they said that thing about the Pope."

"What thing about the Pope?"

"I overheard them. They didn't know I overheard them. But Mr. Edward said that it would be all different when the Pope was back again to Avi Gone."

"Avignon."

"Yes. And those two men —"

"McGold and Candleberg?"

"Them."

"They were with Edward and Martin when they left?"

"No. They came later. They was looking as to where Mr. Edward went. I told 'em nothin'. I told 'em he was gone and that was what and I didn't know the likes of Mr. Edward's business. And they was ranting like Tweedle Dee and Dum and they left. Mutton stew?"

"No. Thank you." The mutton smell was turning his stomach.

"You'll be home then?"

"For a few days, perhaps."

He left the kitchen and went up the back stairs to his room. How could Edward have possibly traveled in his condition? He went to the red room. There was no remnant of Edward's having been there. Not a bloody towel, nor medicine bottle. And Avignon? What on earth did the thirteenth-century Avignon papacy have to do with it?

He went back to his own dark room and sat on his bed, staring at nothing until he realized how badly he had to piss and got up and went into the adjacent WC. There on the mirror over the sink, written in what looked like blood, were the words: "*Palais du papes* more to come." He fingered the set letters. It was not blood, but neither was it ink or any matter he could recognize. It had to do with Avignon. And it had to do with Tonsi a'proc ni eveneg, of that David was certain. Who could tell him about Tonsi a'proc ni eveneg? There was a key in those words that didn't seem to make much sense in any language. David Vere would know. Well, he was not about to call Vere. Why not call Vere? A thousand reasons not to call Vere. Yet Vere was the expert in business, worked for the Exchequer, would have the right words, the explanation, details. Still? Out of the question. Vere was his brother. He was not entirely comfortable with that. Still, under the guise of family, he could expect David Vere to help him. And on his own part he could be polite, properly distant. Perhaps Vere would simply tell him to piss off. That might not be a bad thing. It came back to words, though, and David Vere's words were needed.

He dialed Jane's mobile. She did not respond, but he left a message. There, nothing to do but work on his novel. And now he was going to Viriginia; that is David Sharpe was going to Virginia. He had picked up a small dictionary of Algonquian language. The Powhatans spoke a dialect of Algonquian; that he had read in his research in the British Library. That computer voice seemed to know Algonquian. Those words which were never printed on paper in their time, words which gave meaning to the construct of the Powhatan world of Virginia. Things, actions, the same as in English nouns and verbs. The phone rang, jolting David in mid-sentence.

"I was shopping." Jane's voice was rushed. "I found a lovely divan for you — blue suede that you can sink into. Very masculine and very blue. I need you to look at it."

"Something difficult has come up with Edward."

"His condition has worsened?"

"He is gone. I think I need to talk to Vere. To ask him about a Swiss company."

"I'm glad you want to talk to David. Father will be pleased. I have his number here. Just a moment. He's not at the Embassy." She was back. "It's a Washington hotel. The Mayflower. Better yet, I need to call him anyway. Let me tell him to call you."

"Thank you, Jane."

"And the lovely blue suede?"

"Buy it."

"I will call if I talk to Vere." She rang off and he picked up the little volume that he had set down to answer the phone call. Nouns and verbs, yet sounding so different. It was such a small book, red binding, and such a find in that old shop just off St. Martin's. He again set down the book and opened up the laptop and began to type: "It's Bacon's little..."

The Novel

TWICKENHAM

—1606—

"It's Bacon's little villa, given him by the Earl of Essex."

To David, it looked more to be a palace, all massive stone and red brick, a lake stretching from it. As they moved up the lawn, they were met by a girl of perhaps fourteen or fifteen attended by two dogs and four servants.

"You will find him in the brooding house, brooding over becoming solicitor general, instead of taking a picnic with me in the cheery sun." She hurried on.

"She picnics on a winter's day?" David asked.

"She only does it to annoy Francis."

"She's his daughter?"

"Alice is his wife. His very new wife. A practical marriage. Her attraction is her family's fortune, not her youthfulness. Francis has little bother with sex."

They were led into Bacon's great library. The room was all books—walls of books, stacks of books, piles of books,

books open on tables, books to step around and over, books on window sills and a book used as a doorstop.

"David d'Ersby." Bacon was a spare man, of middling height, with hazel eyes that seemed to flicker about as he spoke.

"I be known as David Sharpe for the voyage, Sir Francis." David was nervous. "I've read your *Advancement of Learning*. Peregrine Bertie had a copy."

"Yes. Peregrine has a mind open to the new thinking, except I suspect he puts far too much weight upon the role of God. Do you find God is the answer to all things, David?"

"I have difficulty with the concept of Christ, Sir Francis."

Ben Jonson sputtered and coughed.

Francis Bacon simply looked at him. "Cherish the quality of doubt. It makes the search for truth in a rational, natural world far the easier. You have read of Copernicus?"

"Aye."

"In the totality, Copernicus is proved wrong, of course, but by simple observation, he made us realize that the earth is not the center of the universe. Kepler calculates all this mathematically, proving Copernicus wrong, correcting his errors. And now comes another Italian, this one being damned by the Pope, looking through a series of lenses at the moon to reveal the spots not be stains of odious sin but mountains and valleys."

Jonson shook his head. "Does it really matter?"

"Every bit of knowledge we can obtain about the universe enables us to understand more and harness that knowledge to make it work for us. David Sharpe, you must cleanse yourself of the idols of the past. If Peregrine has been your tutor, your head will be encumbered by Aristotle,

and by the entire idea that conceives man to be the center
of the universe. But I have not brought you here to convert
you to rational thought, rather to determine how I might
proceed to find some measure of justice in this business at
Southampton's. Tell me, what do you know of these missing
documents, David?"

David told him what he knew.

"Certainly Lord Henry would not have wanted Robert
Cecil privy to the documents if they are what I believe
them to be. In the King's possession, they could send Lord
Henry to the Tower, perhaps even the Prince. He has stated
in principle, and unfortunately committed to writing, the
precept that a king holds his power by the authority of
Parliament."

"How do you know such things?" Jonson asked.

"I make a point of knowing such things, Ben."

"You could destroy the Prince with such knowledge."

"That is not my intent. I would only guide him were
I able. For a king rules by divine right. Otherwise there
would be chaos."

David could hear the barking dogs in the hall as Alice
returned from her 'picnic.'

"She brings those damn dogs in the house." Sir Francis
moved to the doorway. "Alice…Alice, turn about when I
am talking to you."

"Turning about to look at you is not a pleasant undertak-
ing, Francis."

"You will keep the dogs outside of the house." She went
off without responding as he shifted his gaze to David. "I
shall get to the bottom of this business of the miniature
and documents. I am told you are kept in a warehouse, but

tonight you shall have the comfort of a bed. Ben can take you back to London on the morrow. We will all endure a meal in the company of Alice, who will terrorize us with her tongue, and we may feel blessed that her mother isn't here to destroy the meal completely. [Marriage ages a man faster than disease."]

David spent the night in a great bed in Twickenham. The Earl of Essex himself once slept in that bed, he was told. And he slept soundly, awakened only once by a dream in which Molly cried out to him. He arose to a warm fire. His clothes had been aired; he was helped to dress by a young groom. He left the room in which the great Robert Devereaux had once lain, feeling more the gentleman than he had in days.

["One should never marry an old man,"] Alice told him as he went into breakfast.

Light poured through the diamonds of glass. "I don't suspect I will, Lady Bacon."

Her laugh was a giggle mixed with hiccups. "This day and age, a woman is never certain of what a man's preference might be, David d'Ersby. I know a young man of Kent who has an incestuous relationship with his grandmother."

Francis Bacon entered from a door at the far end of the room. "There is more to life, Alice dear, than the pleasures of the flesh."

"It is the continuum of life, Francis, my beloved. In all your philosophizing, never overlook that prime function. [Man copulates to live as much as he lives to copulate."]

They were served birds' eggs in thick cream, baked grouse, fried pork, oat bread sopped in gravy, and spiced hot Madeira. David attacked the breakfast. The conversation was as rich as the food. Before they left the warmth of the house, Bacon gave David four books: Hakluyt's *Navagations*, Machiavelli's *The Prince*, More's *Utopia* and Montaigne's *The Essays*

Back in Brunswick he went to the warehouse to find that his clothing had been sent to him. In addition to some of his own finery there was a suit of coarse wool, another of poorer cloth, several plain shirts and a green woolen cap. There was also a musket. He knew nothing of weaponry. He put on none of the finery, rather fitting himself in the crude wool pants and a plain cloth shirt. Only his boots remained remnants of his gentlemanly status. And so with his books, his clothes, his sword and his newly acquired musket all bound in canvas, he climbed into a boat and was rowed to the *Godspeed*.

At afternoon tide the ships, having hauled anchor, moved from their mooring near Brunswick Wharf—the *Susan Constant* in the lead, the *Discovery* aft. The unfurled square sails burst forth in the strong wind like the shirt breasts of boasting captains.

Molly

RICHMOND

—the present—

MOLLY WENT TO the bank while she was in Richmond. There in the begats of her Bible were the names, David John Smith Sharpe begat Dean d'Ersby Sharpe in 1715, who begat David de Vere Sharpe in 1750. All things were connected. She would not mention the names in the Bible to David Vere, who was to arrive by train in a few hours.

It was hot, but there was a breeze in the Fan, which delicately unfolded in lines away from the center of the city. Trees dispersed the slight wind with gentility along the rows of houses. Molly drove, window open, across the Fan along a narrow series of streets to Tom's, a 1940s kind of place. Not a re-creation, but the remnants of an actual '40s café, modernized but maintaining the ambience of its origins. She ordered iced tea and the souvlakia with rice, and then took out the copy of Molly Dean's diary from her orange backpack. Yes, she would have the salad with the house dressing. Sitting there in her seventeenth-century attire, Molly looked perfectly at home.

The Diary

LINDFIELD

—1606–1607—

Mistress Margaret Dowd wears her ugliness from inside out, like festering boils bubbling through the skin. She is grotesque, with a bulbous nose with visible nostrils from which hair protrudes, and an elongated chin forced forward in two clumps that create, in silhouette, the appearance of a short, rounded beard. A large woman of immense shoulders, her great melon of a right breast stretches out the fabric of her dun-colored gown in contrast to the breastless left side where the material droops. I stare at the deformity to avoid her eyes, which are as cold as rusted iron.

Inside the dismal, filthy room, cobwebs stretch across the dank corners, dirt layers the floor and oak table. The smell of rot is sickening. Dowd glares and announces in a grating voice that I would do as I was told. To which the Rector replies that I would be here but three weeks as we were to wed. The crone sputters and rants about arrangements and then suddenly preaches on the need to eradicate Gnosticism, and all who crawl about the world, like Jews and Papists.

The eve before, as we approached Chelswood, Roger Prine had told me that the Brownes have been accused of Romanish tendencies, but a strange Roman Catholicism that would move the papacy back to Avignon. He said this was not true of Farin, who seems to have no belief in God. I voiced not my own disbelief, which had haunted me since the death of Benjamin Joseph.

Roger Prine bid me goodbye. I am left in the filth and company of this grotesque woman, who announces I am to be flogged. I stare directly into the rusty iron eyes and inform her that will not be done. There had been a time when I would have withstood the lashing, removing myself from reality, but there is the baby and no harm must come to David's child. She wraps herself in a moth-eaten cloak and leaves. I find a broom and attempt to clean. The horrid smell is from dead rats whose carcasses are left to rot. Later she would tell me she kills them by beating them with a hatchet.

The Dowd cottage stands in the row of cottages facing the pond. Beyond the pond, the street meanders up the hill to the stone church rising like a citadel. Swans slip through the pond, not feeling the cold. The stocks stand open alongside a dunking stool.

It has been a week since I last made entry on these pages. And for a week I have cleaned and scrubbed. The fire smolders beneath wet wood creating smoke that hangs in the cottage. The window boards are closed; daylight sneaks in through cracks. I make meals from barley and bits of game she brings. Come Sunday I sit in the old stone Norman church, and after, eat a hearty meal at the rectory.

Eight days after, in a small, quiet wedding, I become mistress of the rectory. Mistress Prine—I wear my name like a weighty woolen shawl. I receive the gossiping townswomen, attempt to discipline an almost useless servant girl and sit stiffly in the pew while my husband delivers three-hour sermons, for Rector Prine loves God's words second only to his affection for Farin Browne. I make every effort to be the proper rector's wife, but am best when I can be just Molly, as the three of us roam the countryside under a warm sun. Spring is pushing its way through the earth.

It is our baby, Farin's, Roger's and mine, and they worry and fuss over me. Farin would have a courtier made of him and have the King fall in love with him and create the child the Duke of Lindfield. But Roger would have him a proper young man of Parliament, a follower of Sir Edwin Sandys. And I say if a boy, he be called David. I did not consult Roger on the name, but he makes no objection.

I write now by window light in the warmth of Chelswood. Farin urges us to stay supper and spend the night, but Roger is worried about vespers. Farin tells him the Curate is an ambitious man and to leave vespers to him. It is the ambitiousness of the man that worries Roger, for he says the Curate lends his ear to Mistress Dowd. Farin said we must stay, as he had a surprise for us. A man of great learning is stopping the night on his way to Lewes. We cannot guess who he be.

It is night and I am closeted above and write by candle. The learned man, no other than Sir Francis Bacon, still speaks below. His hazel eyes fluttered and he spoke rapidly, at times stuttering slightly. He noted one should give acquaintance with anything and everything to broaden, strengthen, or shape the mind. Talk moved from knowledge to science, to God, to evil, which Bacon found to be the nature of man, but through knowledge to be overcome. Evil to Bacon was 'bout us and we must recognize that fact as Machiavelli had. Farin told him of one of the most evil-minded creatures in all Christendom who walks the streets of Lindfield, ferreting out sin.

Bacon said there is no explanation for evil and spoke of a case that he had been investigating in which a young man's blood brother for no apparent reason made him appear to be a thief, laid the groundwork for him to be killed and hence drove him into hiding and flight. I could not help but think of what Vere did to David. Bacon stated that without understanding evil, virtue lies unguarded, and that the Italians have a proverb, not gracious perhaps, but telling, "*Tanto buon che val niete.*" I translated aloud as "so good that he is good for nothing." Sir Francis was startled by my knowledge of Italian and I apologized for my presumption. He said I should not apologize and asked if Rector Prince was my tutor.

I explained a martyred Jesuit had that distinction and that I was a foundling reared by a Papist priest. Bacon said that persecution of opposing religions must cease for it fomented revolution. And the discussion moved to the rights of the individual, and the inherent divine right of kings, which Bacon held as inviolable. As the talk turned and moved logically from subject to subject, I felt the weight of the child and was overcome with tiredness. I withdrew.

I sit here now writing my thoughts and memories of the day. The room is hung with the scent of lavender. Moonlight paths through the glass and covers the bed in soft light. The sounds of the men's voices drift up from below in a soft drone. My last thoughts of the day are of David. How like the case of David and Vere was that one being investigated by Sir Francis. David. How I miss his touch, the feel of his body next to me. My hands slip down between my thighs and I gently rub myself. My fingers slip in the opening. Relieved, I am ready for sleep.

Molly

RICHMOND

—*the present*—

WHEN SHE HAD first read this passage, Molly had been astounded by the revelation. It seemed such a personal moment, even for a diary. She was fully aware that masturbation was not a modern phenomenon, women and men must have been getting off on their own since Adam first had to deal with Eve's "I've got a headache" and went around behind the hazelnut bush and jerked off with visions of some big-titted angel. But writing so directly as Molly had in the journal was somehow astounding. Molly removed the souvlakia from the wooden skewers. Over generations had any of her male progenitors read the passage? Had they been moved by Molly's experience, aroused, ashamed, perhaps enraged? If so, they probably would have torn the page from the diary. Molly squished dressing from a paper cup atop the green salad. Perhaps no one — none of those many in a long continuing line of men — had ever read the diary. Perhaps it was simply there, a keepsake, nothing of utilitarian value. There was comfort in the probability that she was the first to experience Molly Dean Prine's words. She nibbled at the lamb as she returned to the pages before her.

The Diary

LINDFIELD

—1607—

It is one of my bad mornings. Only occasionally does this melancholia wrap about me like a heavy shroud. I have a deep hunger for David. I have carefully sought no word of him. Though I have writ Edward and Joan a letter, telling them of my marriage, I made no mention of my pregnancy, nor inquiries as to David. I want to sit here alone and weep. But I do not. I must set down the pen and go to breakfast.

I am now cheered as I write this later in the morning afore we depart for the rectory. Sir Francis stood alone in the hall, but for the servants who were beginning to lay breakfast. He said that my husband and Farin had gone riding. He stood at the window noting they were, however, approaching and added that my husband seemed to have a great affection for Mr. Browne. I assured him I did as well. I asked him if, in the case of the brothers he had spoken of the previous evening, there was a possibility of exonerating the good name of the one who is accused. Bacon hesitated momentarily and then said confidentially that he was awaiting an appointment to a post of great power where his findings would carry more weight in examining the circumstances, but that he knew from evidence gathered that quite clearly the young man had been wronged. I said as I had mentioned the past evening that I knew of a similar case. He said he might look into it for me and asked if they were brothers of any prominence. I told them they were Berties. Bacon stuttered slightly and said that I must be that Molly, Molly Dean, the young woman of Joan Alleyn's stew. I told him that I was. He said he was examining the case of David d'Ersby at the behest of Ben Jonson. I asked if David was well. Bacon said he had sailed for Virginia. He asked me if I knew David thought me dead and I said, yes, that it was better that way for the Berties and Molly Dean be not of the same class. He told me I would be pleased to know that in his investigation he learned through a servant in the Bertie House that the missing documents were in Vere's possession and that a servant of Southampton's actually saw Vere break open the casket.

Molly

RICHMOND

—the present—

MOLLY PUT ASIDE the journal, the remnants of the souvlakia, and left the restaurant. She drove to the train station, a sort of brick Victorian construct, in the valley that lay between the center of the city rising in modern office structures in one direction and the hill where the white steeple of St. John's peeked above the trees in the other direction. As she stood on the platform and watched him approach, she thought how different David Vere was from the villainous creature of the diary. He looked impeccable, in the black, European-cut suit, grey silk shirt and black tie.

"My God," he said and kissed her on the cheek. "You've lost weight."

"Not enough, I'm afraid."

"Anyway, you look ravishing." He handed her his bag and took her picture quickly with his phone. "I didn't even go back to the Mayflower." He took off his coat and tie and laid them out in her back seat with care. "Had the bag in the car when I went to Treasury this morning and came straightway to the train. I am finished with this business and when I go back it will be home to London. Have you heard from d'Ersby?"

"Not a word."

"I'm not one to figure him out. Never could. Not sure how he'll react now that he's learned we are brothers. In honesty, we've always looked enough alike to be twins, despite the fact that we have different mothers."

South toward Jamestown, they entered the darkness of dense trees. It became cool, almost chilly. "Beautiful country."

"I like to think it was like this when my ancestors first arrived. The river is just off in that direction. And there are some grand old plantations along the James. Nothing old as in England, but some of the oldest in this country. And your interest in the Indians... mostly gone now, a few Chickahominy left. Jamestown, the actual site, is simply foundations and the docents there tend toward a right-wing Christian bent that I find annoying. Jamestown was not founded to bring Christ to the Indians, but that seems to be their take. It was about money, greed, economics and a quick route to China. There is Festival Park, which is a re-creation, including the three ships in which the first settlers arrived. Unreal, of course, but there's an accompanying fake Indian village you might find of some interest."

"Your e-mail said you have a cottage."

"Yes, but we won't go there. I own a small house. It's south at a place called Smith's Fort. The house is empty most of the time, so we'll have to air it out. You said you were interested in the American Indians and the house is said to have once been lived in by Pocahontas and John Rolfe. After, we can go to the cottage, which is on the river."

"The river?"

"The James. The cottage is in Jamestown."

"And how did you come by the house?"

"It's been in my family, apparently, since the Rolfes left for England."

"You're an heiress then?"

"A damn poor one. My uncle tells me we struggle to keep the taxes paid."

"Do you want to hear from d'Ersby?"

Molly nodded. "I would like to. There is such a connection between the fiction he is writing and the diary, this journal, which is the basis of my master's work."

"And he is an attractive man. He looks like me."

"And, like you, not in the least vain, I imagine."

"I have no vanity whatsoever." He leaned across and touched her hand.

David

RAVENSBY ABBEY

—the present—

DAVID PEERED OUT the wavy glassed window and looked down into the open courtyard. Only a dog. One of Edward's hounds stretched lazily on the stone walk. Ravensby was like a morgue without a corpse. How did it operate; where did the funds come from to buy food and necessities with both Edward and his mother gone? Perhaps he should ask. He certainly didn't want to be on a diet of mutton. He opted for tea and biscuits.

He needed to find out about Tonsi a'proc ni eveneg. He needed to write.

The bed was piled with open books. Words in those books had taken him where he had no intention of going. David Sharpe was bound for America. It was no longer just a matter of writing. The characters in his head and those already committed to paper were taking over by virtue of their historical reality. The books now determined much of what the historical Smith, Newport, Archer, Wingfield and the others did. He looked at the pile of notes. More words, his own words, reinterpreting someone else's idea of reality, which in itself might bear no relationship to truth.

He sat down at the laptop, turned it on, faced the blank screen for several moments and then his fingers moved in response to something in his brain: "Wind tore…"

The Novel

AT SEA

— 1607 —

Wind tore at the *Godspeed* and pounded it upon the gully of waves, lifting and slapping it against the white-foamed peaks of the angry sea. Timbers groaned as if the vessel were some helpless animal to be ripped in pieces and devoured by a ravenous beast. David retched rotten beer and maggot-infested biscuits into the wind. But the melancholic shroud that weighted him was neither from the storm, which might bring the relief of death, nor from the constant sickness. Rather, it was the eternal press of human mass endured through the endless months. He had lived with the same faces, arms, legs, hands, eyes, ears, knees, elbows, shoulders, in a monotony of unending tedium, cramped and pushed into a smell of unwashed flesh. All remained the same and the sea was infinite. There was no escape, save death.

The storm was little different than the one they had faced as they left the River Thames. Beyond the headlands at Thanet, the ships were rocked by gale winds and freezing rains. Most aboard were ill, save the seasoned men. The *Susan Constant* gave signal and the three vessels turned back to the Downs off the Kentish Coast to wait out the winds. Captain Smith, seeming not the least affected by the turbulent sea, came aboard from the *Susan Constant* in a small tossing vessel. The message he brought from Captain Newport: it would not be the northern route, but south to the Indee.

"But it is so much the farther," Captain Gosnold said. "You and I have traveled the northerly sea and know it to be a safe lane and good winds."

"But Wingfield, the fool, will be the undoing of us all. The Admiral would a list of provisions used. He thinks, if needs be, to make four rations do for six. In the Indee he says we will find fowl, eggs, fruit, fish and fresh game aplenty."

"I will have the storer make a record for him." Gosnold went off to his cabin.

Smith slapped David across the back. "Be ye well, lad?"

"Sick as a shit boar at butchering," David told him. "I long for the land."

"You'll be fit in no time. The sea grows on ye." Captain Smith added a whisper, "Who be that fat man so intent on our conversation? He looks to explode of obesity."

"That be Edward Brookes, Captain John."

"Well, he looks to take up all the air for breathing."

"He do take his fair share of space on this ship, I'll tell you that."

A month passed and they still waited for a change in the winds. As he sat near the penned pigs, David read Hakluyt's account of the Lost Colony. Disturbed by some of what he read, he told Archer, "I should resent someone taking over my land. What right do we have to their lands?"

"They own no land, actually, hold no title to land. They simply share it."

"But they have towns."

"They are not towns. What pass for houses are poles covered with mats and bark and when they get tired of a place they simply abandon it. They know not ways of civilized men. We will teach them to read and write and, in time, they will build houses and work."

"Yet Hariot says they are happy and live long lives." Later he talked to Gosnold about the Indians Wanchese and Manteo, who had come back to England and returned to Roanoke with the colonists. "Why did Wanchese, who had been to England and knew our ways, turn against the colonists?"

"Because Lane stupidly allowed the killing of the Werowance Wingina."

"The Werowance is like a king," David said to insure to Gosnold that he understood.

The voyage on the endless sea was even more dull than the waiting. Only occasionally was land visible; otherwise, it was all the sea and the other two ships. The cross of Saint George flew from the masts and above the *Susan Constant* the armorial banners of the houses of Percy and Wingfield tossed in the wind. Mariners in distinctive red and blue shirts and blue caps were visible in the rigging. David sat amidst the pigs, reading.

One day a dead white rat with pink eyes was found.

"Someone will die," Mister Brookes declared. "It is the surest omen."

The number of animals in the pens diminished as the pigs were slaughtered and eaten. The days, the weeks droned on. David scraped his peeling skin with his nails. The sun, reflecting off the sea, had turned his skin a fiery red from his shirtless days consuming Machiavelli.

"The Fortune Islands be ahead." Captain Gosnold leaned over the edge of the pigpen. "We'll get water and supplies. But when we go to shore in Santa Cruz, you must take care, David, not to be seen by Sir Edward. Nor George Percy," he cautioned. "Mostly these are called the Canary Islands now. And you must drink the wine; the best in the world. Flowers and birds the likes of which you have never seen."

David moved to the bow and watched as the orange ball of sun slipped into the sea, the last arc of it gulped up in one bite by the hungry water. A spherical Earth still perplexed him. Darkness crawled out of the east, bringing a lace shawl of stars. And then in the sky came what looked like fire. As the ship rose and fell, the fire grew until the sky was illuminated and David could see billowing smoke spreading above the flames. The eeriness of the sight left him uneasy. The rails became crowded, most of the viewers saying nothing, just looking at the inferno in the sky.

"It is called *Montanas del Fuego* by the Spanish—Mountains of Fire." Archer stood behind him in the darkness. "The Earth runs out from the inside of the peak like a scalding pudding. A boiling mass of melted rock devouring all in its path."

"Sin," Mister Brookes grunted. "'Tis the wages of sin. Vanity."

A day later the ship's anchor fell in the harbor of the island called Tenerife, which swept up from the sea like a great quilt of flowers. Blossoms of every bright colour covered the rising land, dwarfing trees, climbing over buildings and dripping from cliffs on the hillside. David slipped down the ladder behind Captain Archer into the small boat that had been lowered into the calm waters.

David was glad of the coarse loose shirt and pants. Wingfield would never give a second look to a man dressed so commonly. And he was far more comfortable than Archer could be in his layers of finery, or the obese Master Brookes, puffing and sweating in his black Puritan garb, waiting on deck for the next run of the boat.

The air ashore was a blend of smells: the mercantile odors of bales and casks, the stench of fish and the sea, the rank of sweating, shirtless men and old women in heavy skirts, the malodor of overripe fruit rotting in baskets, the fragrance of wine and wood, and the dominant perfume of the flowers. David made his way through the activity of the waterfront. He nearly ran head-on into Sir Edward Wingfield and George Percy, but he quickly retreated behind a stack of bales. Both men were flanked by servants and soldiers, and in their company was Brookes, who obviously had made it ashore. As David stood pressed against some bales of dried fish, a white cat with a black tail pounced up on a bale above and sat examining him. Catching snatches of the conversation, David heard Brookes speaking of Captain Smith's visit to the *Godspeed* back in the Downs and saying that Smith planned to take over the *Susan Constant*, kill Wingfield and Percy, as well as Newport, sail the northern route and make himself King of Virginia. David could not bear to hear more and moved off. The cat followed him.

He found Archer and Smith together. Archer was bartering for some eggs with a sinister looking man with a large lump on his arm. "We have been looking for you, David," Archer said. "I know where there be the finest wine in all Christendom."

"I needs tell you something I overheard told to Wingfield," David said.

"You can tell us all about it when we get in the cool out of this sun." Archer took long strides as he led the way to a house that dripped with vines of flowers. As they moved through the doorway, David looked back to see Brookes waddling behind them, followed by the cat. Archer called for vino as Brookes entered and took a stool in the corner.

"We could be in Newfoundland by now," Smith said.

"And freezing off our hind ends," Archer said. A Spaniard brought the cups of wine. "*Aqua para el,*" Archer said, pointing to Smith.

"But not rotting from monotony." Smith stared to where Brookes billowed in his black clothing. "Get you bored, Davey?"

"I have Hariot, Bacon, Machiavelli and More for company." David sipped the wine. It had a nutty creamy taste. The cat rubbed against David's leg.

"And the pigs," Archer added.

"Better company than some on the *Susan*," Smith said. "Wingfield could be tossed overboard, but he'd make poor feed for the fish."

Brookes, who was sipping from a cup, started choking and coughing. David had been holding back what he had overheard, but he felt Smith should be warned. He whispered what had been said, and when he finished, Smith got up, put his hand to his rapier and walked over to Brookes. "Fat man, I ought to run you through for your slander, but I'll bide my time and bring you before the bench." Leaving him sputtering, Smith and Archer and David went out the door.

They spent the afternoon together eating, drinking, and bartering along the waterfront. Smith decided he would take David to the hills on the morrow; Archer declined. Smith's parting words were carried across the water. "Early morn, David. I will meet you by the great dragon tree yonder."

The morning was sunny bright and David leaned against the trunk of the mammoth dragon tree, said to be thousands of years old, with its twisting knots of limbs forming mushroom-shaped foliage. He waited as the morning stretched toward noon. Finally Captain Gosnold moved toward him. "Captain John won't be coming. Sir Edward is bringing him before Admiral Newport on charges of plotting a mutiny. It's John's loose tongue. There's 'testing against him from the *Godspeed.*"

And so the voyage returned to tedium.

David

THERE WAS A commotion in the yard below. David stopped typing. The dog was yapping and the sound of a vehicle sputtered and went dead. He got up and peered out. It was "Message at Once," a courier, as announced on the panel of the small lorry.

David went down. George had gone out to the van and Bydie stood in the doorway. The driver, a young man with orange hair sticking out in many directions from beneath a blue cap, handed a large manila envelope to George, who handed it to Bydie, who handed it to David. "It's for you, sir," she said. The driver returned to his van and, after several attempts, started it and drove away. He had taken a signature from George, but had spoken not a solitary word. Perhaps he had nothing to say.

Only his name David d'Ersby and Ravensby were on the otherwise blank envelope, but he knew without opening it that it was from Edward. He went back up the steps, took his time opening it up with care, using a letter opener, and was not surprised to find an Air France ticket folder among its other contents. He set that aside and opened the note first. Euros fell to the floor. He read the note before retrieving them.

David, I need you to come to Paris on Tuesday of next week. There is a special job I need you to do for us. When you arrive at Charles de Gaulle take a taxicab to the Hotel Notre Dame, near St. Michel. Instructions will be left for you there. I am somewhere in France and will have you brought to me. See you shortly. Edward.

There was no explanation, nor indication of whether Edward was dying or had recovered. David picked up the money. Inside the ticket folder was a flight itinerary. He didn't want to go and his impulse was to chuck the whole packet, but he knew he couldn't. He would do as Edward asked. But he definitely needed to learn something about Tonsi a'proc ni eveneg.

He rang up Jane. "Did you get my message to David?"

"I left it for him. Hasn't he called you?"

"No."

"Let me call him again and see if he picked up the message. I'll call you back."

David examined the contents of the packet again and simply waited for Jane to call. It was less than ten minutes, but seemed much longer until the phone rang.

"He didn't go back to the Mayflower and hasn't retrieved his messages, including mine. He hasn't checked out, however."

"Damn."

"He probably met someone."

"A man you mean?"

"I doubt he would have gone off with a woman. I'll call you if I hear anything."

"Thanks, Jane. It is important."

"Ta."

Well, he was saved the embarrassment of how Vere might respond to a sudden request for help from one who had treated him so badly. He began typing again: "It was yet February…"

The Novel

AT SEA

—1607—

It was yet February; they left the Canaries. Clouds never shut out the sun. There was no rain. Water from the Canaries had gone bad, the beer soured, and the grain was infested with maggots. One lean pig remained in the pen. Gabriel Archer, dressed as if for an audience at court, sat on the deck and talked to David of food, of feasts and great wine, banquets, tavern food and food to be found in Virginia.

But David kept mostly to himself. Once, Brookes attempted conversation. David cut him short. "Jump overboard, you fat sack of shit, and save me the trouble of shoving you over." Brookes retreated.

It was afternoon on the twenty-third of March when he heard shouting from a mariner in the rigging. "Land! LAND!"

David crowded with the others at the railing peering out at the growing speck on the horizon. His first glimpse of the new world. On the following day they dropped anchor near an island. Like a swarm of insects the distant silhouettes skimmed across the water toward the ship. As they approached, David could see the narrow boats that Archer told him were 'canoes' and the creatures with painted skin, striped but cut with pictures, and long black braids of hair. They climbed up lowered rope ladders and over the rails, grinning as they offered gifts of fruit and boiled roots. The place, he learned, had been named Dominque by the Spanish. A sailor handed David a piece of yellow, juicy fruit and David devoured it. Captain Gosnold gave them gifts of knives and glass beads, hatchets and bits of copper and then the savages departed with the same swiftness with which they came.

The anchor was raised and the three ships sailed past other islands. On a day following, they anchored near to shore of the island named Guadeloupe. No savages approached as they went in small boats to a beach. David ran from the boat, feeling the earth beneath him, and sank to his knees; he picked up a handful of sand and let it trickle out from his fingers. He grabbed some tuffs of grass, pulling them out by the roots, got up and ran, touching the leaves of shrubs, and clung to the trunk of a tree as if it was his very anchor. Finally he closed his eyes and sank again to the ground.

"Are you David Sharpe?"

He opened his eyes warily to face a very pale, thin man wearing the drab dress of a cleric. "Yes," David answered.

"I am Robert Hunt."

"Master Hunt, Captain John has spoke of you."

"I bring you word from Captain Smith. He is well but angered."

"Is he shackled?"

"The Admiral would not have it, but he is confined below." Master Hunt coughed and spat thick phlegm. "My humors are imbalanced. I expect I was not meant for the sea. You read, I understand."

"O'er and o'er. I have only five books and it's been a long voyage."

"Then I must lend you some. I have a whole library with me."

After Master Hunt had left, David sat down on a grassy edge overhanging the sand. He dozed and dreamt that he and Molly stood together at the edge of the sea and Molly handed him an infant. "Your child," she said and waded off beyond the breakers. He called and called, but was helpless to follow for he had the baby in his arms. "MOLLY!"

"David."

He stared up at Captain Gosnold. "You were dreaming, Davey. Come, cousin, time we were to sea."

David slept the night on deck and in the morning when he awoke they had anchored off another island. "Nevis," Gosnold told him. "We will rest here a week. It be known game and fowl to be had."

On the sand Master Hunt led them in prayers. Archer came bearing a breastplate and helmet. "Here," he said "'tis time you become a soldier." The helmet was heavy on David's head. Archer handed him a musket. "It's a matchlock, not worth a damn. With it you can't hit the broadside of the *Godspeed* were you standing 'neath it. A wheellock is needed if you want to kill anything."

"I don't want to kill anything."

"You may have to." Archer put the barrel of the musket in the forked tip of an iron rod he had planted in the ground and instructed David. The smell of burning powder was noxious, but contrary to Archer's evaluation, before day's end he had shot a large bird, attracting the attention of Henry Percy.

"David, me boy, in hell's name be you doing here? You are lost if looking for Bertie house."

"I am in hiding, Henry. You must not tell Wingfield you've met me."

"I am the soul of discretion, d'Ersby. Are you aboard the *Godspeed?*"

"Aye. I be David Sharpe now. With Captain Bart. Be Captain John well?"

"He seems not bothered that his head might be loosed from his body. They bring him to shore."

"Could I see him?"

"You should choose your friends with more care, David. Mister Brookes says he would have all our necks and take over the ships."

"Bosh. Brookes be a liar. I was there when he overheard Smith talking."

"You may have to testify for him when we reach Virginia then."

A short time later, Percy's servant came to fetch him and brought him to where John Smith sat guarded by four soldiers.

"Davey, me boy. You look a real soldier in your armor."

"It's not the best disguise, Henry found me out." David played in the sandy soil with a stick. "Anyway, it allowed me the chance to talk with you. What is to become of all this business anyway?"

"Not much, I'd wager. When we reach Virginia I will be brought to trial, which will be most awkward as the secret box will be opened naming the council. I am certain to be among those named. In the end it be only Brookes' word against mine."

"And mine and Archer's."

"I not depend much on Gabriel. And you have Wingfield to think on."

"I can't hide from him forever. When we reach Virginia, he is bound to know."

They spent six days on the island. David shot rabbits and birds and caught fish. They made stops at several islands, catching great tasty tortoises, and arrived in a place called Puerto Rico for fresh water. Here a boar was killed and up in the sharp rocks there were eggs of so many birds they could not walk for stepping on them. It was while seeking eggs in the heat that Mister Brookes was overtaken with an attack.

"The bile and the choler are much out of balance." The surgeon stood above the pile of Brookes' sweating mound of flesh. David listened to the man's rasping breath until it became a death rattle. Mister Brookes would not testify against John Smith after all.

They sailed north, lighter, David thought, for the absence of Mister Brookes. The skies became overcast, the setting sun not visible, and then from nowhere came a great roaring gale that threw the *Godspeed* across the water like a toy boat. Thunder and lightening slashed open the sky, ripping the sea. Wind tore and pounded and beat the vessel upon the gully of waves and lifted and slapped it against the white-foamed peaks that rose from the anger of the sea. Timbers groaned as if the *Godspeed* were to be torn to pieces. David retched and clung to the rail. In the black night there was only the howl of the sky and the cries of Captain Gosnold to the crew. David, defeated, sprawled, clinging for life, heavy waves washing over him until the grey morning arose. The storm ebbed. Miraculously the sails of the *Susan* and *Discovery* appeared. They sounded for land, but the sounding proved useless. And they sounded the next day and the next, and the next to no avail.

It was the twenty-sixth of April at four in the morning when David was awakened by the yelling. Ahead loomed land. Captain Gosnold was almost reverent as he spoke. "There," he said, "between those points of land it lies. It is the Chesapeake Bay."

The three ships, continually sounding, moved into the bay. The morning sun behind them lifted out of the water. Flowers blossomed from trees and the air carried the sweet fragrance of the spring earth. Sea birds rested on hunks of logs at water's edge or wandered along white sand. The ship, alive with the voices of men, edged the shore. Toward dusk Captain Gosnold and Gabriel Archer went ashore, joining Captain Newport and a small party. In the dim light of day's end, David could make out the men as they beached the small boats and disappeared among the trees.

As darkness seeped in David perceived the silhouette of a heron standing on one foot at water's edge. It let out a piercing cry, then another, followed by a third. From the trees, a blast of gunfire shook the evening and the heron flew into the air. Shapes of men came running from the trees. A man was dragged between two others, a silhouette.

Another, David was certain by the stocky stance and dress, must be Gabriel Archer, leaning on a man and helped into the small boat that moved toward the ships.

"Gabriel Archer," Gosnold reported, "be shot by arrows in both hands. He is in the care of the surgeon aboard the *Susan*, but seems not too badly injured. One of Captain Newport's crew be barely alive. He took an arrow in the chest. No more than six savages came crawling out of the trees, bows between their teeth, and let fly a barrage of arrows. Captain Newport shot his blunderbuss and the savages went flying like a pack of crows back into the forest."

That night Gosnold and a group that included David bundled into the small boat and crossed to the *Susan Constant*. The secret boxes were to be opened.

"Davey, I'm pissed on Canary wine," Archer slurred from the bunk and held up both hands for David to see. He had been shot clean through the center of both palms. "Pissed to the gills. Looks like the stigmata. You suppose I'll be sainthooded? And me with not a teeny belief to the papistry. Saint Gabriel."

David laughed at him. "Maybe you'll go to hell for blasphemy."

"Canonized." Archer rolled over and passed out.

David sat next to the bunk listening to Archer breathe and Master Hunt on deck imploring God's blessings on the proceedings. The secret box was opened and Newport read out the first name chosen to be councilor. It was his own. A cheer went up. "I shall be on the council only for the time I am with you. After, you will be guided by the next six names I read and they shall choose a President who shall have two voices. Each of the other shall have one vote.

The next called be Sir Edward Marie Wingfield." A slight cheer from a few men. "The third is Captain Bartholome Gosnold." The response was loud and long. The fourth name was Captain Ratcliffe's, which surprised David slightly, but the man had piloted the small *Discovery* across the treacherous sea. Newport announced, "John Martin." David was more disappointed than surprised, for he was certain the last two names on the list be Percy and Archer, meaning Captain John was to be slighted. Admiral Newport spoke above the din. "The sixth name be George Kendall." There was near total silence as if everyone was stunned by the Virginia Company's choice. If the last name on the list was Percy's, David realized, then Gabriel Archer had been passed over. "The seventh and final name is Captain John Smith." There was an uproarious yell. A chant went up. "Captain John! Captain John!" David thought of John Smith, down in the hold while the rest were on deck, and could visualize the glee on Smith's face. Archer was wrong about Smith. The men of the Virginia Company who had invested their money knew Smith's worth and respected his practical nature.

The next day the men assembled the shallop, a twenty-five-foot-long sailing vessel which could be rowed and was to be used for exploration. David finally put his feet on the solid earth of this new land. He picked up a handful of white sand and let it filter through his fingers. He saw more clearly a blue heron. It stood one-legged at the shore, then it set the other leg into the shallow water, and in silence pushed itself gracefully into the air. The council had met. Sir Edward had been named president and had two votes, and with Kendall and John Martin that was enough to keep Smith from being given his seat. There was only one man who had studied the language of the savages and that was Smith, and he was kept in the hold.

Newport sat in his cabin as the ship creaked gently at anchor. "David, you will have to speak in Smith's behalf. I told Sir Edward today I would be holding a hearing on the charges against Smith. He reminded me that he was President of the council, but I informed him that it was not a council matter, that the charges were of mutiny and brought at sea and consequently a business that would be determined by maritime custom by the Captain of this voyage."

"And Cousin Edward sputtered," Gosnold added.

"Not as much as he sputtered when I told him that one David d'Ersby was among the colonists and would be testifying in this matter." The admiral stuffed another bite of fish in his mouth. "I told him that Sir Francis was being named the King's Solicitor General and he himself would be proving the charges against David falsely made."

David slipped down the ladder into the hold of the *Susan Constant*. There was the smell of horse, and although he had been told about the stallion and the mare, he was amazed to see them, healthy after the long and terrible voyage. A boy, perhaps no more than twelve or thirteen, with liquid green eyes and knotted red hair, was brushing the white stallion.

"He is a beautiful horse," David said.

"He is a god." The boy spoke in a heavy Irish brogue.

John Smith gave David a shoulder swat.

"The black mare will soon foal," the boy said, continuing to brush the stallion.

"How will they get the horses out of the hold?" David asked.

"Harness, pulleys and rope," Smith said. "That's the way Wingfield would have me out of the hold—on a rope without the pulleys."

"Soon it will end and they will give you your rightful place on the council."

"Yes. You come to testify for me, David?"

"Aye. And I am certain Captain Archer will as well."

"I would not depend on that, lad."

"I was surprised that he was not chosen. And George as well."

Smith sat down an on empty keg. "I was not. Sir Edwin Sandys had told me who was on the list 'afore we sailed as to be forewarned that I might be forearmed against the wiles of Sir Edward Wingfield. As for Percy, the council thought him too much a wastrel. Kendall is obviously in Robert Cecil's pay and Martin has had immense experience. He traveled with the great Drake, knows weaponry and ordnance. As for Archer, he would serve the council well, but he had no supporters among the London Company."

The lanterns had been lighted and the deck seemed subdued. David bent and went into the small cabin. "I am to testify for Captain John," he told Archer. "You will speak in Captain's Smith behalf?"

Archer put his legs up and lay back on the bunk. "No. I am not up to it. John will survive. After all, he is one of the council now." Archer turned and faced the bulkhead, his back to David.

But Archer's testimony was not needed immediately as Wingfield informed Newport that he would need much time to prepare. There was to be an expedition of some twenty-five men led by Gosnold up the river which they had promptly named the James. The shallop was made ready. David strapped on the heavy armor and donned the helmet. Gosnold spoke to the seated men. "We think what the Werowance Pochins told us is that there is a town of the Paspahegh upriver where the river Chickahominy joins."

David sat in the bow. Archer sat aft with Percy, who was regaled in white satin and wore what David thought a perfect target—a tall scarlet hat plumed with purple feathers. Mid-boat, George Kendall sat silent, apart, his deep-set eyes staring out from his chinless, pox-gouged face. The river was wide and moved swiftly against them. They rowed up river some distance and made landing after rounding a bend. A clearing of new grass and low brush covered many acres. David found a fresh water spring and drank his fill. Gosnold declared the soil rich and Archer named it ideal for a fort with no trees to hide attackers. They explored the afternoon away and made camp. Though a watch was set there was no sign of Indians. Come morning they feasted on roasted fish and boiled turkey eggs.

Percy drank the water. "I'd give my right testicle for a good glass of beer."

"No, you wouldn't," Archer told him.

"No, I wouldn't," he agreed.

They loaded the gear in the shallop. "So we leave Archer's Hope," Gosnold said.

As they moved upriver, heavy woods edged the shore. Vines strung down from overhead, rippling the water. To David it seemed sinister. "I keep feeling we are being watched."

"I am certain we are," Gosnold told him.

It was hot. The men did not speak. There was only the slap of paddles. "That must be the Chickahominy." Gosnold pointed to a stream feeding into the river; they rowed into it and pulled the boat to the west bank. There was not even the sound of a bird, and in the peculiar silence nothing moved. It was sudden, as if magic. At least forty Indians appeared from the trees. David stared. They stood, nearly naked, their bodies swiped with color—red, white and black, their heads shaved on one side and the hair on the other dripping with shells, birds' feet, bits of metal and pearls. They held their bows, arrows ready to fly. Gosnold struck his chest with his right hand. An Indian did the same and spouted incomprehensible sounds; he motioned for the English to follow. The bows were lowered. Gosnold followed the Indians, and the others followed Gosnold.

The woods opened into a small clearing. In the distance was a palisaded village, but they were not brought to it. The Indian leading motioned for them to halt. A stocky, elderly Indian adorned in copper and pearls was escorted with ceremony to an elevated mat. He waved his arms in the air, yelled "Wowinchopunk," pointed at himself and boomed again, "Wowinchopunk."

"Captain Gosnold." From a sea chest, Gosnold withdrew beads and metal trinkets that were handed to Wowinchopunk, who said nothing but examined the gifts, then passed them about. Mats were set and he motioned all to sit; they were fed roasted deer and boiled roots. David ate, but his eye caught an elderly savage, extremely tall, standing with a girl child in the brush. The savage took no part and David sensed his disdain.

Wowinchopunk arose and began a tirade which, from the venomous tone, did not seem to indicate approval. He pointed and screamed. The tirade seemed endless. His voice cracked and yet he screamed. All the while the old Indian and the child stood in the bushes, watching. Wowinchopunk had all the trinkets gathered and returned to Gosnold, then turned his back and walked toward the palisaded village. The others followed. Only the old man in the bushes and the young girl remained.

"I think we've been snubbed," Percy said. He took out his diary and wrote.

"He preached longer than a Puritan," Archer said.

"But made more sense," Percy told him.

Walking away, David looked back and saw that the old man and child were still standing there.

David

RAVENSBY ABBEY

—the present—

HE FINISHED THE chapter, exhausted. Burned out. But he stayed at the computer to check his e-mail. And there it was. NO! NO! Goddamn it! He had forgotten the stalking hacker. But he was back. Another e-mail from opech@ earthgo.com. A copy had been sent to themoll@wm.edu. The message itself was brief and exactly like the first. "For you." There was an attachment, truehistory2.doc. No! By God he would not open it. He stared at the screen. He would not open it.

He had to know. He opened it.

"The *shu-shu-gah...*"

Opecancanough

E · MAIL   ATTACHMENT

THE *SHU-SHU-GAH* WADED in the shallow water at the river's edge and then stopped. It stood immobile like a carved god, the tidewater gently lapping at its spindly legs. I, the Werowance Opechancanough, was alone. I crouched back in the dense grove of pines, watching the bird.

In the five seasons, the cycle of the new leaves had ended and the Cattapeuk, the corn planting season had begun. The *shu-shu-gah* screeched, its caw the sound of a wounded child. If the blue heron cawed three times it was a portent of danger. And there was danger. The Monacans above the Falls, where the great river foamed over the rocks, were preparing to attack. The blue heron jabbed the mud with its needle beak and waggled loose a crustacean. The People were strong and would repulse the Monacan, but many warriors would be killed. I stroked the stubble of my head where it had been shaved by my new sqau. She had cut me, but I had not bothered to beat her.

My woman Toatoka, the most beautiful woman of all the Powhatan, had gone off with a young warrior of the Nansemond. I felt old, and I had come here to this private place on the Pamunkey to bear my sorrow, sharing the space with none but the heron. It was not good for a man, a werowance, to have such feelings for a squa. I knew this but could not forget Toatoka, who I had never dared to strike, nor even raise a voice to. The blue heron screeched again. Toatoka, in a mantle of red feathers, haughty, had walked from the village behind the tall young Nansemond warrior. She made no farewell, and the warrior moved as if oblivious to her presence. Her mantle was as smooth as the velvet of a Spanish doña. I had stood watching her leave, my face a mask. "You are too old, Opechancanough." She gathered some beads and cooking bowls into a bundle. "I need a man of hot blood — a young man."

I made no challenge to the Nansemond warrior. Toatoka had chosen. If I had killed the warrior it would not keep Toatoka; she would go off with the next strong warrior.

The blue heron cried again. The third cry. There was danger upon the wind! "Opechancanough!" a voice called out to me. I peered into the dense pines, but saw no one. My eyes were growing weaker with age. I hated getting old. I hid the pain that running after a stag brought. "Opechancanough!" The warrior Aputonok came out from the pines. "Word has come from Pochins." Pochins, Powhatan's youngest son, was Werowance of the Kecoughtan. "The Whiteman." I moved toward Aputonok, careful not to step on the strawberries stretched along the ground. I would send the woman to gather them. "Three floating islands have entered the K'tchispik."

Not the Monacan. This was the danger for which the heron had cawed.

I hurried in the direction of the village. The women continued planting the *pagatowr*, the corn. Children played a game of ball with their feet. Inside the palisade the warriors stood. The older men had gathered in my yehaukan and sat with the messenger around the embers of a dead fire. A side of the long house had been rolled up, letting in the sun. I moved to my place on the raised matting. The messenger said, "Pochins says his uncle must live for many winters in health."

"And Pochins must remain forever brave and grow wise as the *pagatowr* grows."

A squa came in with baked oysters in shells and strawberries in a weave of twigs. I took a strawberry and signaled the guest to eat. The messenger had the wide mouth and broad nose of The People. "Three islands that move came into the waters. The K'tchisipik warriors watched from the trees. Creatures came from the floating islands to the land. They wore iron coats and iron hats. Some thought them gods, but The Werowance of the K'tchisipik reminded them they were men dressed in iron as Opechancanough said they would be. When the sun moved down from the sky, he ordered his warriors to draw their bows against the Whiteman. One of the Whiteman fell under the arrow and another drew the arrow through his hand, but the Whiteman took their thundersticks and the sky was filled with great claps of thunder and smoke, and the warriors fled."

"Did the Whiteman follow them?" I asked.

"No, the Whiteman returned to the floating islands."

"Words have been sent to The Powhatan?"

"Yes, Opechancanough."

There was silence. I took the pipe and a burning stick and I lit the tobacco, inhaling until the stone bowl of the pipe seemed well ignited, and then passed it to the visitor. "We will go to our brother the Powhatan and to our nephew Pochins." The old men puffed on the pipe and it was handed to the younger warriors who waited outside. The women packed the dugout canoes with supplies for the journey.

The Powhatan looked tired as he greeted me and led me into the yehaukan, motioning the others, even the priests to stay without. I helped my brother to his mat. "I had a dream, Apachisto." He called me by my private name. The fire coals were dead. A cold breeze of night caught me and I shivered. "It was a dream of terror. Three white monster birds swooped down from the sky, spitting fire from their beaks that killed The People. And the white birds nested upon the land, they ate the corn from the fields and The People had no land upon which to live, nor food upon which to feed and they perished in pain."

"The Whiteman must be driven off," I said.

"What the gods say will be, will be. The dream has told me what is to be."

"We can make our destiny, Wahunsonocock. The gods do not own us."

"That is the thinking of the Whiteman. Okesus will punish us for your words."

"How can the gods punish us any more than by bringing the pain of the Whiteman, of which you dream, upon us? If we are all to die anyway, Wahunsonocock, what are we to lose by trying?"

The Powhatan took a stick and stirred the dead ashes. "My pain in the great sky may be great and long for failing to hear the words of the gods."

"You are a great Werowance, the Powhatan. You will return only the greater."

"Like these ashes, perhaps neither I, nor The People, will rise again."

I took the flint stones and rubbed them until a spark caught a bit of dried grass and I blew the ember until it flamed and caught a chip of bark, and the fire began to flame. "We must try, Wahunsonocock. Perhaps as it is said in dreams and the eagle's entrails, we will fail. But we must try."

"But with care, my brother-who-thinks-as-the-Whiteman. We must do all with care. The Monocan must be led to believe that the Whiteman with their thundersticks are our friends." The Powhatan stirred the flames.

"Where is your daughter? I have a gift for her."

"She will go with you, Opechancanough," the Powhatan said.

"It will be dangerous."

"I have promised her. You have spoken of the Whiteman and she would see."

"Her curiosity about the Whiteman might not always be a good thing."

At dawn we set out down the river. Pocahontas sat near me in silence as was expected of her. The paddles dipped the water in rhythmic unison; the river opened into the bay and the canoes rose and fell over the rough waves. We hugged the jagged shoreline strewn with broken tree limbs, seaweed and debris, remnants of a recent storm. The paddlers moved the dugouts with speed and we reached Kecoughtan. Pochins stood at the shore. My nephew was a muscular young man with bold arms, a carved face, warm eyes and the blackest of hair. His beauty was flawed only by chest nipples, long and pointed as a nursing mother's.

"Uncle who has seen many places, you are welcome to this humble spot." He smiled at his sister Pocahontas but did not address her.

Approaching him I stretched out my arms and I, too, spoke in a ceremonial voice. "Nephew who is brave among men and has the wisdom already of age, it is the joy of this old warrior to be in your sight." The ritual over, I whispered in his ear. "Have you seen the Whiteman yet?"

"They have been here." Pochins led the way into the long house. His warriors followed. Young men, for the treacherous Kecoughtan warriors had been clubbed to death a year earlier.

"You saw the ships, the floating islands?"

"Yes, Uncle."

"Describe the skin which flies from the top of the tallest tree on the islands."

"White with red marks like this." He drew cross marks in the earthen floor with his finger.

The Cross of St. George. "Los Ingleses," I said in Spanish as I knew no Indian words to distinguish between the Englishmen and the Spaniards.

"My warriors saw the floating islands come round the point in a wide canoe. The Whiteman came upon the sand led by a werowance with grey hairs upon his face and only one arm. He put his one hand to his chest to tell us he wished to be a friend. Eat, Uncle."

"I eat little." But I took a root and chewed on it.

"Has the Powhatan, my father decided? We will do his bidding. If he wants the Whiteman killed, then we shall kill them."

"You should not kill the Whiteman," Pocahontas said.

"Hush, child," I ordered. "It is not your place to speak here. You will be sent out."

"Yes," Pochins agreed. "Remain silent." He broke a piece of fish from the bone and ate it. "We feasted the Whiteman and then danced the good and evil, which should show them we will defend ourselves against any intruder. Perhaps they will go away."

I knew the Whiteman had understood nothing of the dance, nor would they go.

"They gave us these." Pochins reached into a basket and held up beads and strips of copper. He extended a string of clear blue beads toward Pocahontas. "It is like the heron. As if he captured the sky. They are for you," he told her, adding softly, "You must not speak out among the warriors here as you do at home." Pochins held up pans and a saw. "The Whiteman had many gifts."

I took the saw, took a fire branch and sawed it in two. The warriors tried the saw, giggling in delight as they cut all the firewood in the yehauken, and sent for the squas to fetch more.

In the night I could see the moon through the opening in the roof. The night was luminous, a night to fly into the sky. I remembered *el caballo*. Flying on the white stallion — I, Don Luis, astride the white horse, speeding across the arid plains of New Spain. The Aztec name was Mexico, the place of the prophecy where an eagle held a serpent in its claws. My memory of the Aztec was painful, but not all my memories of New Spain hurt to think upon. There were the fields of wheat, the olive trees and vegetables growing in rows. Uprooted papaya and mango trees were replanted under the Mexican sun. I lay, tasting in my imagination the fruit, and that of the sweet cane sugar, and the pungent ripe banana, and my favorite, the warmed cacao drink ceremoniously consumed from golden goblets. I cared so little for food now, it seemed strange to me that I could not forget the foods of my youth. But nothing dominated my thinking of the past as did the horses. The horse was a god, imbued with strength and wisdom, only bearing man at its own whim, always the master. So much power could not be subjugated against its will. The greatness of the horse was the greatness of the gods. The great white stallion.

In the morning, after the bathing, Pochins came in alone to where I sat. "The Whiteman's floating islands are at rest just at the mouth of the Great River. But like the hare, they seem to multiply. There is a small floating island with only one cloth and loaded with many Whiteman it moves up the Great River."

"I will go to see Wowinchopunk," I told him.

"You look tired, Uncle. I will go."

"I am not tired, I am old. I have lived long enough to see the Whiteman come again, as I knew he would. That makes me realize the length of my long life."

"Do you believe, Uncle, in what is foretold, that they will destroy us?"

"It is not what has been read in the entrails of an eagle which bothers me, but the inability of The People to keep the Whiteman from these lands."

"You think I should have killed the Whiteman."

"No. Their guns are powerful. And it is not what your father would have had you do."

"You think The Powhatan wrong."

"I am called Opechancanough."

I took only ten warriors and Pocahontas in one dugout. I wanted to see the ships, not confront them. The blue beads hung long about the young girl's neck. I saw the blue heron standing as if frozen in the shallow mud. The bird did not move as we paddled by, around the point. There was no talk, only the rhythmic slap of the paddles. Then as we came round to where the Great River fed into the bay, we saw the three ships. There was no doubt, *Los Ingleses*. The Cross of St. George flew from all three masts.

"Look!" Pocahontas pointed toward them.

I cautioned her to be quiet. We drifted beneath the hanging branches of the willows. There was anger in my chest and foreboding. Seeing the ships brought back a hatred I felt deep inside. I could hear the voice of Father Segura berating me in front of the warriors. We came around the bend in the river. In the cove, where a stream emptied into the Great River, a boat, the fourth floating island that Pochins' warriors had reported, was at anchor. Men in armor, bearing guns, wandered about the clearing. I motioned my paddlers toward the south shore of the river into the shadows of the trees. We continued upriver to the mouth of the Chickahominy to the palisaded village of the Paspahegh. Met by six warriors, we were led to Wowinchopunk. The Werowance of the Paspahegh was not family. There was no cordiality, only formality. Wowinchopunk, who was a short man with a large head, indicated he was aware of the three floating islands. He had blotchy cheeks and six feathers, hung from the plait of hair.

"Come," Wowinchopunk ordered. As we moved into the dark of the woven hut, one of the women kept Pocahontas from going in. Wowinchopunk motioned us to sit. "Who is the girl child?"

"The favorite daughter of The Powhatan."

"I have too many wives already." The Werowance spoke without emotion.

"She does not come as a wife; she is not yet of age."

"She should not be with warriors. Eat," he said.

"What will you do when the Whiteman comes, Wowinchopunk?"

"Feed them and send them away." We talked of the Monocan. If there were not danger from the Monocan the Paspaheghs would not accept the dominance of The Powhatan without a battle.

"The Whiteman pose an even greater danger," I cautioned.

"The Whiteman will go away. The priests have spoken in the house of dead." Wowinchopunk arose, indicating he had entertained his guests all he was going to. We left the yehauken.

Word came that the boat of the Whiteman was seen at the Chickahominy. Wowinchopunk sent forty of his men into the trees. I took Pocahontas and moved into the bramble where we had a clear view. There were twenty or so Whiteman in armor carrying guns. The Paspahegh appeared in a body from the trees. "You are not welcome here," Wowinchopunk declared in a loud voice and folded his arms in defiance across his chest. His warriors stood, their bows drawn. "Go away!"

The leader of the Whiteman, not the one-armed man that Pochins had described, placed his hand on his heart and spoke, but his words were foreign. Wowinchopunk stood coldly. The Whiteman-leader opened a chest and took out colored beads, knives and an iron hatchet. Wowinchopunk accepted these and motioned to the women among the trees to bring out food. Mats were spread on the ground and Wowinchopunk pointed at himself and screamed "Wowinchopunk." The Whiteman-leader did the same saying, "Captain Gosnold." I understood *capitan*. The Paspahegh performed a dance indicating that the Whiteman should leave their country and never return again and Wowinchopunk arose and explained again and again how they were not wanted. I knew they understood none of it. He had the gifts of the Whiteman gathered up and returned to them and screamed, "Go away." His warriors raised bows.

David

RAVENSBY ABBEY

—*the present*—

"NO!" DAVID KNEW he had screamed aloud and feared one of servants would run up to see what had happed. He covered his mouth as if to put the scream back in. His next muffled "No" was almost a cry. He was angry but equally confused. How was the hacker able to do this? Here on his own computer, where his novel, the only form of his novel, was a counterpoint to the narrative being spitted back to him by this Opecancanough person. Even if he was able to hack in, how could he recreate the events this fast? There was no doubt now. A new computer and an external hard drive were needed. He would drive into Spilsby now...well, in a bit. He knew he couldn't go until he finished reading. He needed to finish, to find out just how far the supposed Indian's narrative had gone.

He was literally shaking. He needed to calm down. He took some deep breaths.

What did he know of the historical Opechancanough? He went through his somewhat disorganized notes. Nowhere had he been planning on using any particular Indian by name and certainly not an Opechancanough character. Despite his panic, he knew he had to read on and then go to Spilsby to buy a computer. He read:

"I stayed…"

Opecancanough

E-MAIL ATTACHMENT

I STAYED AND watched as the Whiteman took the chest and moved back to their boat. I stood as they rowed away into the Great River. We went to our dugout and paddled to the river of the Appamatucks. Fat warriors greeted us and led us to Oppussoquionuske, my sister, the Werosqua of the Appamatucks. She seemed more an old man than woman, dressing in the fashion of a werowance with a loin cloth over her private part. Her breasts were flat, hardly more prominent then the sag of an old man's chest. Her voice was husky from the smoking of the pipe. She had a reputation for being ruthless, but she grinned at Pocahontas. "This is the child of the great Powhatan. You shall come to my yehauken, Pocahontas, and I will tell you how I killed the Werowance of the Appamatucks, my husband. But first I must have a word with your wise and ancient uncle, who knows the ways of the Whiteman that come to steal our land."

She led me apart. "Why does The Powhatan not order this scourge wiped from the earth?"

"He waits, Noonatoka." I called her by her secret name.

"He will wait until we are all dead as the great Wingina is dead." Oppussoquionuske had gone with me to Roanoke in the cold of winter with her warriors and we had wiped out the village of the *Los Ingleses*. She had kept the babies, evident by the fact that one of her warriors was white-skinned and blond and one of the squas who served her own yehauken had hair the color of carrot root.

"Apachisto, you must convince him the Whiteman have come to take our land and destroy our people. The stories you told of the Aztec are burned in my head like a mark made by a hot coal against the skin. For all Wingina's kindness he was repaid by death."

We spent five days with the Appamatuck and then moved down the Great River. We came to the bend in the river, to the sacred place of the Paspahegh. I was shaken by what I saw. The three ships of the Whiteman were tied to the trees. Bales and staves had been unloaded and men in armor, with guns, moved about the land. This was the place the Whiteman had chosen to plant, the sacred place of the Paspahegh. The choice offended me, yet I was pleased that in their stupidity they had decided to settle on this sacred land. Wowinchopunk would be incensed. The sacred place was a narrow extension of land connected to the north shore by a sand bar that, when the tide was high enough, made the strip an island. In the time before the fathers' fathers, it had been the chief town of the Paspahegh, and they had not left it, as land was often left fallow when the corn crop was poor, but because they had displeased the Kewas. They had failed to kill the sqau of the Werowance who was said to have nursed the pup of a wolf. A great illness had overtaken the Paspaheghs and many had died of the burning fever. It was the will of the gods that they must leave the place and that no man must plant upon it or the Paspahegh would be destroyed and the Werowance would be dead forever.

I heard the sound of the animal first and then I saw the beautiful white stallion. The mere sight of the powerful animal gave me joy. I knew I had to have the horse. There would be nothing the Whiteman would trade for the horse. It was like their guns which they never would let The People have. But I would have the white horse.

"Move to the other shore," I said, getting my bearings. My eyes never left the sight of the horse. "The Whiteman will plant here at the place of the Paspahegh." When darkness fell we slipped across the river and went up into the clearing near the cove. We made a fire and ate. There was silence among the warriors as they waited for me to tell them what was to be. The child, too, posed no questions, waiting for my words. "The drums will speak," I said. "Wowinchopunk will hear how the Whiteman sits upon his sacred place. Pochins and The Powhatan shall be told that the drums spoke."

Aputonok took the drum and began beating out a rhythmic message that would be heard across the night. He paused, waiting, and from the distance the beat of another drum repeated the message. And that sound would reach the ear of another drummer, and another and the message would travel from the falls to the Kecoughtan, along the Great River, to the Pamunkey, to the Mattakpoini, to the Chickahominy. The beat of the drum continued. Its echo came from all directions. But my thoughts were not on the drum. My head was filled with the white stallion.

David

RAVENSBY ABBEY

—*the present*—

THE ATTACHMENT ENDED. The horses. In his own narra‑
tive he had just unloaded the horses, one of them a white
stallion. The hacker was too close. David did not turn off
the computer or the monitor. Instead, he typed and sent a
short cryptic e‑mail. "I need to talk." Perhaps considering
the fact that he had made no attempt to get in touch with
her and left so rudely, she would not respond. He remained
online, but should he? Out the window nothing stirred
below, including the hound. He examined the packet once
again from Edward. His life seemed to be coming undone.
If he could only reach Vere. He went back to the window.
Nothing. Then the computer beeped. He sat down. An
e‑mail from themoll.

themoll: Yes, I read Opec's e-mail. Where have you been?

dsharpe: I'm a shit. Don't be angry.

themoll: Not angry. Curious. You just vanished.

dsharpe: I'm ashamed to tell you. At the moment I am alarmed by the e-mail from Opech.

themoll: Why? I thought we agreed he was just some cyber freak.

dsharpe: This time his words fit precisely into my novel.

themoll: David, he was writing about Jamestown.

dsharpe: My protagonist has reached Jamestown.

themoll: What? How?

dsharpe: I don't know. He just got there. He's fleeing events in London. I didn't plan it. It just developed. You remember Molly, I mentioned her to you, of course I did, the same name...well, she's dead.

themoll: He thinks so.

dsharpe: What do you mean he thinks so?

themoll: I just meant I understood she's dead and I guess that's why he fled.

dsharpe: Yes. The whole thing rather got out of hand. I got involved with John Smith, Gabriel Archer, George Percy, Edward Wingate, Francis Bacon and all sorts of historical figures and events simply worked out to the point that David had no choice.

themoll: Which ship was he on?

dsharpe: The Godspeed.

themoll: Gosnold's.

dsharpe: You know all this historical material? Of course, you do. I forgot.

themoll: Bacon? Why Bacon? Are you particularly interested in his philosophy?

dsharpe: Actually it was his legal expertise, his power at court that I needed.

themoll: He had a thirteen-year-old wife you know.

dsharpe: Yes, Alice. She liked dogs.

themoll: Yes. Now what exactly is the problem with Opechancanough?

dsharpe: It's as if there's someone out there who knows exactly what's in my mind or what was in my mind and is suddenly in a file on my computer. I am tempted to write the rest of the book on a typewriter or in long hand.

themoll: The story he was telling was simply the historical tale, but from a different perspective that's all. What you're writing is fiction, right?

dsharpe: Yes. Based on historical facts.

themoll: I never use the word facts when it comes to history. Historical data, records, viewpoints. Well, all he's doing is using that same historical information and giving his own twist, perspective, as you once put it, 'glorified native crap' viewpoint.

dsharpe: And that he was writing about the same moment of time in history as I was writing about, at the same time, simply coincidence?

themoll: Remember I said much of what opech was telling us that first time he came online was simply Bridenbaugh's theory. Read him, you will understand Opechancanough better. But think of all history as fiction. And in a sense it is. We don't know. We weren't there. We surmise.

dsharpe: But people were there. Wrote about events. About who was there and lived or saw those events.

themoll: And you know enough about memory to know that no two people, apparent witnesses to the same event, have the same story to tell of that event. You think the egotistical John Smith's view is entirely reliable?

dsharpe: I see your point.

themoll: So think of Opechancanough as writing fiction. Can you tell me why I didn't hear from you? What you are ashamed about?

dsharpe: It's really stupid. Really dumb. I was jealous. David Vere. Your meeting him like that. I know. It's completely irrational.

themoll: Then you aren't going to like what I have to say next. He's here with me.

dsharpe: David Vere is there? In Virginia?

themoll: Yes. We've become friends. He's here staying with me.

dsharpe: Thank God. I have been desperately trying to reach him.

themoll: David Vere? I heard you right?

dsharpe: Is he there now? May I talk with him? Tell him it's urgent.

[There was a pause. It seemed a long pause before themoll returned her message.]

themoll: He will be online directly.

dsharpe: Thank you, Moll. I am sorry I was so stupid.

themoll: It's OK, David. Read Carl Bridenbaugh.

[Before he could respond she had left, but David Vere appeared.]

verehere: David Vere. What do you need?

dsharpe: I will go through the apology bit later. For now I simply need your help.

verehere: If I can, of course.

dsharpe: Edward d'Ersby was dying of cancer, at least he implied it was cancer, here at Ravensby. I came home to find him gone. I was told by staff that he had gone to France. Now I've received an airline ticket, hotel reservation and a note asking me to come to Paris. I know it must have something to do with Tonsi a'proc ni eveneg. What is Tonsi a'proc ni eveneg?

verehere: The name means nothing, a semordnilap. Originally it was a non-public, Vatican-owned company, or some would say owned by Pius XII, himself. It was called *Et Ab Inimicis Meis Salvus Ero* and set up in Switzerland as a hedge against the political situation in Italy. Neither Pius XI nor XII were certain just how secure the Vatican state would be in Fascist Rome. Anyway there was thought that, if the papacy had to flee it could always reestablish itself in Avignon and it had some sort of arrangement to that effect with the French Republic. But soon, of course, France was no longer an independent France and Avignon was part of Vichy. It was believed that Pius XII was given huge sums of money, money probably confiscated from the Jews, in return for his willingness not to oppose Hitler. Twenty or so years after the war, John XXIII made the funds available to Jews whose property had been confiscated by the Nazis. The company was then called Hussad Geneve and headed by liberal Catholics as the Pope separated himself from ownership. It had links to the Israeli Mossad. This is when Edward must have become involved. He was working, or so rumor has it, with the MI-6 in Saudi and had connections to the Mossad. The company has continued to grow faster than it could spend its profits. It has acquired vast holdings equal to or greater than many giant public corporations. The name was changed to

Tonsi a'proc ni eveneg after a major disagreement with the Benedict papacy. Those who now own the company are said to be extremely liberal Catholics - Belgian, Dutch and American primarily, who believe in local jurisdiction of the Church with more power to the Bishops. They support married clergy, women priests and have far more liberal attitudes toward birth control and abortion than does the Vatican. And their support includes a large and open purse. Where this will all end up with the Jesuit pope is anyone's guess. Is Edward Catholic?

dsharpe: No. Church of England or no affiliation to my knowledge.

verehere: And you say he's dying.

dsharpe: Now I suspect he's not. A cover for something. I made a trip to Munich for him. A strange mission. And now he wants me to come to France.

verehere: Will you go?

dsharpe: I owe him that.

verehere: Be careful. It could be dangerous.

dsharpe: Thank you, David. I will. When are you coming back to London?

verehere: The day after tomorrow.

dsharpe: Could you meet with me? Your father has gotten me a flat in Bloomsbury, Fitzrovia actually.

verehere: *Our* father. And yes, Jane told me. I will have to report to the Minister, but in the evening perhaps.

dsharpe: Thank you. And thank Molly. It will be easier to get back to my writing now.

verehere: She is a very nice young woman, David. And quite beautiful, I might add.

dsharpe: I'm not surprised. I'll see you in London.

DAVID SIGNED OFF. He would go to France if only to get some answers. But first he would go to Spilsby and buy a new laptop and an external hard drive. He would download all his files onto the new computer. He would use his old laptop only for e-mails and online research. He would keep his novel separate from any possible online access.

Molly

JAMESTOWN

—present—

THEY HAD TAKEN the ferry across the river and then drove to the cottage. Molly made coffee as David Vere stood on the porch looking out at the expanse of the James. Molly watched him, this attractive gay man, looking impeccable in pressed jeans and a blue sweatshirt.

It was an unusual day. Molly was not alarmed by the voice of the Indian werowance. She didn't understand it, but she believed in connections. David Vere being here was a connection, part of that delicately woven web that was a mystery to her. David d'Ersby's novel had now moved to Jamestown. Another element in the web of things. David d'Ersby's novel not only fit with Opechancanough's divergent point of view, but even more tightly coalesced with the diary of Molly Dean Sharpe. To complete the cycle, must she marry David d'Ersby?

"What is that strange bird? There at the edge of water," David Vere asked. "It seems to defy the center of gravity, balancing on one skinny leg."

"It's a blue heron," she said. "The Indians called it the *shu-shu-gah* and believed it portends an impending crisis."

The heron rose up from the edge of the river, its wings expanding in a great graceful sweep into the low sky, a sweep of blue-grey against a bright blue sky.

David

DAVID RETURNED FROM Spilsby with a new laptop and external hard drive. He downloaded his documents, including the novel and his research, onto the hard drive and copied it onto the new computer. He called Jane from his cell and told her of his online chat with their brother.

"I'm meeting with him day after tomorrow, in the evening if he is free from the Ministry."

"I'll get some wine," Jane told him. She was even more ebullient than usual.

"I'd rather it were just the two of us. David and me."

"Yes," she said. "I'll leave the wine for the two of you. A nice Côtes du Rhône."

He rang off and went to work on his novel, but not before he ordered a Kindle copy of the Carl Bridenbaugh book. Thanks partially to Molly's reassurance, but also by freeing his novel from intrusion, he felt less threatened by the cyber Opechancanough. He opened up the novel on the new computer and typed: "Fools…"

The Novel

JAMESTOWN

—1607—

"Fools," Gosnold said upon returning to the *Godspeed*. "Only Martin agrees with me. Archer's Hope is the ideal place to fix for settlement."

"Where will they settle?" Archer asked.

"The long point with the deep water. They say its perfect for bringing the ships into the shore."

"Not easily defended; the area is so heavily wooded." Archer gestured with open hands.

"Martin says there is no spring water and much marsh land. Ratcliff supports Wingfield in this, and even if I could convince Kendall to support us, Martin and I would still be outvoiced." Gosnold threw up his hands. "Now we must cast anchor. We are bound for Jamestown."

"Jamestown?"

"So this dense forest is now named."

The vessels were roped to the overhanging trees. The horses were hoisted from the *Susan* and a few supplies were unloaded before dusk fell, everything left under guard for the night. David boarded the *Susan* for the night and stood at the rail. He felt flushed, as if he might have a slight fever. The moon, full and yellow, seemed stuck on the point of one of the tall black pines. It bobbled as the galleon rocked at anchor. A wolf howled. Through the dense trees, a light—firelight—was barely visible; then it disappeared only to reappear, disappear and reappear again. The water lapped against the ship. Tomorrow, David knew, they would be at the mercy of the Indians. A caw of a bird was heard. And then another. Gosnold had told him that it was probably the savages signaling each other. And then the drumbeats began, slowly but increasing in intensity. The dim vanishing light of the fire became constant and brighter. Would the Indians kill them all? David put his hand to his forehead; despite the night air, he was sweating. The sound of the beating drums continued. The moon fell below the trees and the fire seemed the brighter. The storm at sea and the seemingly endless voyage had been an ordeal for the company of men, but David suspected the worst might yet be ahead. He listened to the beat of drums, caught the fire light between the darkness of trees. The wolf cried out again. Ashore, one of the horses whinnied. The moon settled beyond the trees and the night became blacker.

A figure moved toward him in the dark. "Vileness shuns the light." The unpleasant voice was that of Sir Edward Marie Wingfield.

"Why do you hate me so?" David asked.

"Because I abjure sin…evil…you are a child of evil."

"And of what sin, Sir, am I so guilty?"

"No sin is greater. No offense so vile, no crime so heinous."

"Then, for heaven's sake, Sir, tell me of this sin, this crime which so offends you."

"Your very birth is a stench upon the sensibilities of any man, but greater upon me for vileness falls upon my name, upon my house, upon the Veres."

"Then, Sir, for my sanity, I implore you, tell me what it is of my birth that so offends you. I am, as I am led to believe, the bastard son of Mary Vere Bertie, but many a house has its bastards. Surely, Sir, that cannot be so offensive a crime."

"You think the world dense, that it does not recognize who your father was?"

"Well, I don't. No one will tell me." David cried out, "Damn it, tell me. TELL ME!"

"Devil... the world knows you are the vile seed of Mary Vere and her brother Edward." The man disappeared in the blackness.

David stood in the darkness, wishing never to show his face again to the light. He sank to the deck. They knew, the Berties, Gosnold, and all the rest knew. No wonder they should condemn him. Thank God Molly never knew. Vere had said there was a bond that separated them from the rest. But if Vere was the issue of this filthy union, why was he recognized as the offspring of Lord Willoughby and David not? But none of that mattered really. With this shame, he could face none of them now. He could face no one. There was only death.

The drums pounded in his ears. The flames burned as if to set the world afire. Lady Mary's brother put his linnet in her privates. David wanted to wail for her, yet she loved her brother. She was mad; Edward was mad; Vere was mad, and he was mad as well. He was burning with the shame and the fever. Dizziness. He could not think. But he must leave the ship, must vanish—disappear into the blackness of the night. He was certain—death at the hands of the savages or the elements awaited him. It did not matter. Molly was dead. She would not have to bear his shame. David slid down the rope ladder into the water.

He made little splash. The water was deep, but cold to the burning feeling that was enveloping him. He fought the urge to let himself be devoured by the current. He wanted to die. He would not let himself die. He fought to live when all he wanted was to wash peacefully into oblivion. He swam upstream, away from the point, and away from the horses and men ashore keeping guard. He swam, wanting not to. He swam until he was on the land. But it wasn't land, rather a murky swamp and his boots caught in the mire as he struggled to push through the mud, the water often as deep as his waist. The burning was making him delirious and at times he was out of his head. Minutes. Hours. In the darkness he pushed through reeds and grass that seemed to float. The foliage cut at his face and arms, but he didn't seem to feel it, as if it were someone else's body. The muck sank into his boots and covered his legs. Its slime wrapped about him, seemed never to end. At times he sank until the muck reached his nostrils and he spat out the brackish water. He waded ahead in the muck; didn't know why he struggled to live; didn't know if the swamp would end; didn't know if the fever would overtake him and he would drown. Yet he continued. The knowledge of his incestuous birth tore at him from the inside, the horror not diminishing as the dark mire brutalized his body. He pushed against the black wall of vegetation, a thicket on the water. The swamp subsided. He crawled up on the hard ground of a bank, felt earth beneath him, collapsed and sank into unconsciousness.

David

—*the present*—

DAVID, THE WRITER, was overcome with pain for his own protagonist. He had always known the story would come here. From the beginning it was this incestuous genealogy that formed the link with the Berties, most particularly Vere. His character's lineage had been with him from the beginning, the secret to be unveiled. This moment, however, arriving in Virginia at this place at night on the James River, had not been planned. But it was a good place. More appropriate than if he had not brought David Sharpe to Virginia.

David was exhausted. He was hungry but knew he could not eat. He made himself a bland cup of tea in a tea-stained plastic cup with hot tap water and a tea bag from among the junk on his dresser. How American we Brits have become, he thought. He sat on the floor, stretched out his long legs and leaned against the bed feeling satisfied. He would write more but not for the moment. He left a blank screen without words staring back at him.

The computer beeped, announcing an e-mail. David awoke, not realizing he had dozed, still leaning against his bed, stll holding the plastic cup. He crawled over to the old laptop without getting up off the floor and gazed up at the screen. It was from opech@earthgo.com. A copy had also been sent to themoll@wm.edu. The message was brief and exactly like the others. "For you." Was he writing to say that he was giving up, as there was no more novel on the computer? He opened the attachment. "The fire…"

Opecancanough

E-MAIL ATTACHMENT

THE FIRE DOUSED. I sat engulfed in the blackness of the pines. The moon had sunk and the stretches of trees reached to a sky pebbled with stars. The stars, unlike the sun and the moon, held no force over The People. I had found no difficulty accepting the Copernician universe, but I could not accept that individual lives were ruled by these stars as the Whiteman believed. The sun had the power of life and the moon had power over the planted seed and the rise and fall of the bay and rivers, but the stars seemed but the paint of decoration. I lowered my eyes from the sky. The shapes of the warriors sleeping on the ground were like fallen trees in the darkness. Pocahontas slept near my feet. Two guards crouched, silent, bows ready, beyond the warriors. The drums long quiet, there was only the sound of the lapping water, and now and again the whinnying of the Whiteman's horses.

The People would not have to kill the Whiteman for I knew now they would die of their own folly; they had chosen to plant at the place of death. No trees were burned to make planting fields and the woods were dense. There was no spring or clear stream from which to drink, only the swamps; and in the middle season the insects hung like buzzing fog across the swampland. The Paspahegh were forbidden to ever again live in the sacred place. The Whiteman would die and the Powhatan need do nothing. A horse whinnied again. I stood up knowing what I must do. The Whiteman would die, but the horses must not. I approached Namotock in the blackness and whispered that I was going to see the floating islands.

I moved through the trees, treading wet, dead leaves and dead brush without sound. The mast and rigging were silhouetted against the wash of stars. A lamp hung at the bow of one of the vessels, but it was the only light. Staves and bales piled back from the riverbank formed a low wall. Beyond, the horses were tethered, moving shapes in the blackness. A helmeted silhouette went from the shore side around the bales. His musket hung from his hands. He stood, turned and went back around the bales. In order to see the other side of the bales, I crawled toward the river. I could make out the figures of three soldiers. I crawled back away from the river and behind the bales. On all fours I moved to the trees where the horses were tethered and undid the ropes and led the animals the short distance into the trees. When the horses moved into the brush there was a thunder crash in the night and the soldiers came running and shouting.

I knew that I had time while they loaded their muskets. I leaped upon the white stallion and pulled the mare's rope, moving as quickly as I dared through the darkness.

The guns blasted. Shouts gave the alarm. Branches crashed in the musket fire. I kept the stallion from bolting and directed the animals between the dense trees. My warriors were on their feet. In the dark, I could not see their faces, but I could imagine their astonishment at the sight of their Werowance sitting on the beast. I reached down and lifted Pocahontas up onto the horse's back with me. There was no need to instruct the warriors; they picked up the dugout canoe, food, supplies and weapons and were ready for the cartage through the trees. The sacred ground of the Paspahegh was connected to the mainland by a narrow sandy isthmus. I led them toward the isthmus. We heard the Whiteman's cries, but none dared venture into the black of the woods in search of the horses. It was a wise choice, for the warriors were ready to kill anything that approached.

Daylight crept in, giving definitive shapes to the landscape. No warrior offered to lead the mare and I did not ask it of them, suspecting they were in terror of these creatures. It was daylight when we reached the isthmus. I sat tall on the horse. The feeling was one of immense power. Pocahontas, as if mesmerized, hardly moved. As I looked toward the swamp and the morning birds feeding, I spotted the black hair of a figure lying face down at the edge of the swamp. I brought the stallion to a halt, slipped down and walked toward the body. I was startled as I saw from the clothing that it was a Whiteman. I turned him over thinking him dead. He was alive, a youth, hardly a man in years, and out of his head. He muttered and, though I could not understand the language, I suspected it probably made little sense.

The warriors surrounded the young man. To dishonor and kill a sick man was not the way of The People. They could leave him to die or take him along. I looked at the small delirious eyes. I touched the forehead of the pale-skinned man. It was burning with fever. "We will bear him to the Powhatan," I said. With branches for poles and stretches of skin as a bearing cot, four warriors carried him. A short distance up the trail, the dugout was set in the water and the young man was laid in its bottom and covered. The warriors crowded around him in the canoe. I remained on the stallion, leading the tethered mare.

As we approached the bend in the creek where the trail split away from the water, the path was blocked by the squat figure of Wowinchopunk and his warriors. Wowinchopunk approached the horse with hesitation. "Have you become a god, part man, part beast, Opechancanough?"

"No, this is a *caballo*. I've taken it from the Whiteman."

"It is a thing of great wonder, a beast that will let a man sit upon it."

I patted the horse's flank. "You may stroke the *caballo*."

"No." Wowinchopunk circled the horse, examining it, looking under it. Raising a hand to indicate approval, he said, "The Whiteman sits upon the sacred hunting ground, the place of the Paspahegh."

"It is so."

Wowinchopunk pulled a bird claw from his hair, bent down and set it in the dirt; then with his finger made a circle in the earth about it. "I have but forty warriors," he said.

"I will send you sixty more," I told him. "The Powhatan knows the Whiteman cannot sit upon the sacred hunting place. If you kill the man who steals your totem, then you should fear no force."

The Paspahegh werowance handed me the bird claw. "Sixty?"

"Yes, I will send you sixty warriors."

He went over and looked at the young Whiteman in the bottom of the canoe, but made no mention of him. He stepped back to allow the horses by. "Will you come with them?"

"I think the gods would not be served." I didn't care if the Paspahegh or the elements killed the Whiteman. Their doom was sealed. The Powhatan must do nothing for which he might be faulted. It was too soon to become the Whiteman's obvious enemy. Pocahontas sat between my thighs, saying nothing.

The morning sun pushed its way up in the sky. Birds cawed. Drums spoke. The rowers were silent, but for the paddles cutting into the water.

"Could I sit in the canoe with the Whiteman?" Pocahontas asked.

"Are you frightened of the *caballo?*

"No, but I would like to see the coat-wearer."

"That is a good name for the Whiteman. Even in the heat they cover themselves."

I put Pocahontas into the canoe. I wanted to speed across the open field upon the beautiful white horse, but there was no clearing, there was only the woods, the mare to lead and the men and the child in my watching. The stream narrowed; it trickled shallow and clear over the rocks. White blossoms floated down as the horse brushed the flowering trees and a web of gnats stretched between branches. I decided to send the men and the child directly to Werowocomoco; I would ride upriver to where I could ford the Pamunkey. I didn't want to risk losing the mare by having the horses swim through the deep water. After we parted I was able to travel somewhat faster, but the mare kept me from galloping through any open area. The tide was out, but still the water approached the horses' necks. My moccasins were soaked and clammy. I reached one of my Pamunkey villages and, at the sight of me on the animal, though the squas stood about staring, the men prostrated themselves in my path.

My new wife brought food; she was even uglier than I had remembered. I sent warriors on to aid the Paspahegh and decided to ride directly to The Powhatan, alone but for the two animals.

The mare was slow, being ready to foal, but I entered Werowocomo feeling the power and splendor of the stallion. The squas came to touch the horses, giggling and talking in their excitement. I told them to feed the horses some corn and dead grasses. The Powhatan, flanked by warriors, ceremoniously came out of his compound, his hands evoking the sky. His voice was loud, the Werowance of Werowances, not the brother. "Your deeds arrive before you — you have seen the wonders of strange ways come among The People."

"I have seen Whiteman in the sacred place of the Paspahegh and they are doomed. And now Wowinchopunk goes to the sacred place with one hundred warriors."

We entered the palisaded compound about the yehauken of the dead where the dried corpses of the fathers of the fathers and their fathers awaited return from the dead. The Powhatan begged the dead to come again in rebirth; then led the way to the place of the Ahone, the place of sun, where he danced until he collapsed.

"You are too old for this, Wahunsonocock."

"I am too old." The Powhatan stirred at the fire with a stick. Red ash flickered up. "The Whiteman has the place of the Paspahegh. They are dead."

"So they are, but that is not to say that more will not follow."

"Yes, more will come." The Powhatan lifted the weighty chain of copper ellipses and pearls off his head. "The dance has worn me out. I had another dream. Pocahontas had the red-winged blackbird on her head and told me all her children would be born dead unless she took a husband from among the Whiteman." The Powhatan removed his soft moccasins.

"Where is the girl?" I asked.

"She sits where the Whiteman dies of the swamp sickness."

"He is dying?" I asked.

"He burns away like the fat of the bear upon the flames. He is out of his head."

"But should he live, would you spare him?"

"That is your choice, my brother whose spirit is white. He is your captive." The Powhatan lay down on the low bench. "Perhaps I will sleep."

"I brought you a present, the black horse..."

"I am too old for new ways, Apachisto."

"But I am older than you and I ride the horse."

"The way is not new to you."

I found Pocahontas sitting in the small room with the Whiteman. The young man lay buried beneath piles of skins. Papoo shook gourds and chanted. He stopped and wet the young man's lips with spring water and then held a string of acorn shells above him. "He shakes now," the priest explained. "The season of ice is upon him. It is the swamp sickness. He will die."

The tears filled Pocahontas's eyes. "I wish he would not die."

"He is but a Whiteman," the priest said. He shook the rattle again over the man.

The young man spoke, but his words meant nothing to the three.

"No man should die but in honor," Pocahontas said.

"The Whiteman has no honor." I knew better but my bitterness at *Los Ingleses* coming to the K'tchisipik brought out my anger.

"From this Whiteman I could learn to make the pictures which talk." The girl's voice was a plea.

I looked down at the miserable youth wrapped in the pile of skins, shaking with the chills. He was pitiful like a wounded deer, his small eyes staring back with the pain. Why was he alone away from the ships? Had he been accused of some crime? Could they learn anything about the men who had chosen to plant on the sacred land of the Paspahegh from this youth?

He cried out. Pocahontas said nothing, but her eyes begged me to do something.

"There is quina," I told the Papoo.

"That is for The People."

Quina was a powder of bark that cured the swamp fever. I had kept the chest of the powder that the missionaries had brought with them those years ago when they had come to convert The People. The bark came from the mountains in the land below New Spain and was brought by Father Seguara to protect the friars if they came down with the swamp fever. I had taken it for The People and though they seldom were stricken, when they had been, the quina had saved their lives. The priests respected its power.

"It is only for The People," Papoo repeated and shook the rattle over the man.

"I could make him my brother," Pocahontas said.

Any captive could be adopted into the tribe by any member of the tribe. This was the way of The People. It was not customary for children to do so, but then Matoka was not a customary child. I thought of Powhatan's dream and Pocahontas wearing the blackbird of a priest. "If you made him your brother, you could never take him for a husband." I patted her long black hair.

"I shall take no man for a husband."

In Pocahontas' eyes there was a plea for life, but in the small eyes of the figure shaking with the chills I saw a begging for death. Something tugged inside me. If this young man could teach the child the language of *Los Ingleses* then she could walk freely among the Whiteman and learn their intentions. "We will make him her brother. When he is well, he is to put his head upon the stone. Get the quina."

"I must consult The Powhatan," Papoo said.

"He sleeps. I will be responsible."

The priest was not happy, but he left to get the medicine.

I left the yehauken and walked over to where squas were building a low palisade for the horses. I got on the white horse and, when I was clear of the village, galloped across the open spaces with a feeling of power and freedom.

The messenger, an old man with the toes missing on his left foot, came from Wowinchopunk. The werowance of the Paspaheghs had failed in his first attempt. The Whiteman had built a crude abatis of boughs on the sacred place, the shape of a half moon. Wowinchopunk had first attempted to get them to lay down their arms for a feast in order to get his warriors inside the abatis. His ruse did not succeed. Outwitted, he next brought out food and mats, but one of his warriors, intrigued with a hatchet, picked it up to give it a try, and a Whiteman struck him and took it away. Then, another warrior went after a Whiteman. A struggle followed. No one was killed but Wowinchopunk stalked off to his camp nearby.

"We must council." Powhatan sent for his brothers, Opitchapan and Kecatough. His son, Nantaquaus, a handsome young warrior and the tallest of Powhatan's children, came from Uttamussack, where he was chief of The Powhatan treasury. He had the same mother, now dead, as Pocahontas. Another daughter, Matachanna, and her husband, the priest, Uttamatamakin, had come to Werocomoco. In addition to family, the priests and elder warriors gathered in the large room of the yehauken.

I spoke of what was known. "The Whiteman has settled on the sacred place of Paspahegh."

"We are many more than they," Kecatough said.

"True," the Powhatan agreed, "but they have the thundersticks and many more may come."

"Are we to do nothing?" Uttamatamakin asked.

"Opechancanough has an answer," the Powhatan said.

"While we aid Wowinchopunk in his fight for the sacred land, the Powhatan cannot be blamed for what Wowinchopunk does if others come to seek revenge. The White-man has split his numbers. The man of one hand has gone up the Great River. I will enlist the Weanocs, the Quiy-oughcahannocks, the Appamatucks and Kiskiah to see that the Whiteman on the Great River are well entertained and kept away and when they return Wowinchopunk can attack them as well." I dipped my hands in a bowl of water. "Our hands remain clean."

"And should Wowinchopunk again fail, Apachisto?" Kecatough asked.

"Then we bide our time and let the swamp sickness and starvation kill them. It is slower, but yet death. There is no fit water at the sacred place and no place for planting."

"Some will trade for the tools which cut and the beads," Nantaquaus said.

"It is true," I agreed, "but it is long until harvest and none will have but small baskets of corn for the trading. No werowance will starve his own for beads." They agreed that my words were wise. I would go to the Great River on a hunt and perhaps entertain the Whiteman. We ate and smoked the pipe.

"May I go with you, uncle," Nantaquaus asked.

"That would please you?"

"Yes." He ate and whispered to me, "And sometime might I ride upon the beast?"

"I shall teach you, Nantaquaus, but we won't take the horses on the journey to the Great River. We don't want the Whiteman to find them."

And so we traveled. I provided Wowinchopunk with warriors from the other tribes and obtained agreement of all the Werowances to entertain the Whiteman as they traveled along the river, including my reluctant sister Oppussoquionuske. At the place of hunting, I prepared a feast. I had a throne constructed of flowering trees. About the throne, I set pikes topped with carcasses of dead birds. Nautaquaus and I made a mantle of yellow flowers and for my head I made a crown from animal bones. I wished to appear outlandish. The fool is never suspected. I sat on the throne in such attire as I greeted the one-handed captain and his men in armor and helmets. I screamed out and beat my chest, the petals flying off my mantle. The Whiteman were amused. The one-handed captain announced himself as Newport and then a stocky man named Captain Smith spoke in the language of The People, which startled me. His vocabulary was not large, but he knew common words: *netoppew*-friends, *uppowoc*-tobacco, *nemarough*-man, and such. I pretended not to understand and he tried the words out on one of the warriors with success.

"You are not stupid." Smith looked directly at me when he spoke, his words in the language of The People. "We shall be the best of friends, *mawhick chammay*, or the worst of enemies, *maskapow*."

While I entertained, Wowinchopunk attacked the abatis fort with 275 warriors. It was later when my visitors had moved down river that I learned the details. The Whiteman had fired their thundersticks, but there were too many of the warriors and they broke into the makeshift fortress. A number of the Whiteman were killed, but then the great thunderblasts from the ships shot great balls into the sky and tore down the trees and Wowinchopunk and his warriors fled into the woods. I realized that the guns of the ship would not have dared fire into the fort upon their own men, and that the warriors would have been safe inside, but they did not understand. Wowinchopunk had failed again. It did not matter, the elements would not. I gathered my men and set out for Werowocomco with Nautaguaus. We reported all the events to The Powhatan, who laughed as they told of me in flowers and the crown of bones.

In the morning I walked through the mud and puddles as the spring rain fell. I stopped to rub the nose of the white stallion, which, though feisty, seemed to enjoy the attention. I reached the yehauken. A fire burned and the priest dozed. The small-eyed youth looked up; he had regained his senses. He looked frail, and though not frightened, somewhat apprehensive as I towered over him.

I turned to the priest. "Are you ill, Papoo?"

"No. No. But I miss the sun."

"You won't find much today. It rains. But it is a gentle rain. Get some air. I will see to him." I helped Papoo to his feet.

I sat close to the young man. *"Habla Espanol?"*

The young man just kept staring and then, as if realizing what I had asked, said in Latin, "No, but I can speak Latin."

Spanish had been my language; Latin the language of lessons and prayers. It came to me now with difficulty as I asked. "What is your name?"

"David." There was puzzlement on his face, and some of the apprehension seemed to have vanished. "How do you know Latin?" he asked in Latin.

"My secret. What were you doing so far from the ships across the swamp?"

The youth smiled. "My secret."

What was the Latin word for "want"? I remembered, *inopia*. "Not if you want to live."

"I am not certain I want to live." The man's small dark eyes flashed as he spoke.

I searched for the words. "Have you killed a man?"

"No."

"Then why?"

"My reasons are my own."

We were silent. The young man seemed to be measuring me up.

"*Los Ingleses* have come to take our land."

"No. That is a lie." The young man looked directly at me. "That is a lie."

"Who is Jacobus Rex?" I had seen it written on the banner.

"The King of England."

"And Regina? Elizabeth Regina?"

"Dead."

Silence.

"Have you come to kill me?" The young man pushed back the skins to his waist.

"No. I've not come to kill you."

"Is that a lie?"

"I speak the truth."

"What is the truth?" The young man seemed to speak more to himself.

I smiled. "The truth is that the world is round."

"Yes, it is, though I don't fully understand how it can be."

"And it travels around the sun. The universe is vast and endless and somewhere in the heavens is Heaven. And there is the Jesus Christ and God the Father and the Holy Ghost and there is Mohammed and Zoroaster and Zeus and…"

"There is Zeno." The young man tried to sit. "If I am not to be killed, what is to become of me?"

"That is up to you. Do you wish to return to *Los Ingleses*?"

"No. I should have been left to die."

"It was the child's wish that you live."

"The little girl?"

"Her name is Pocahontas. She is the daughter of The Powhatan."

"The werowance?"

"Yes. She would learn to read."

"Latin?"

"Ingles." I looked into the small eyes. "When you are well."

"I feel much better and I have taken food."

"But the fever will come again and you must take the quina."

I left the yehauken. The rain had stopped. I got on the stallion and rode through the clearing at a gallop. Jacobus Rex. The Queen the Spanish had so hated was dead. The horse was a powerful creature and I thought of myself as an extension of it like some mythical creature of the Greeks. I slowed to a trot and entered the trail winding through the trees. I thought of Toatoka and wondered if she had found happiness among the Nasemond.

David

RAVENSBY ABBEY

—the present—

THE DOCUMENT ENDED. David had wanted to stop reading but found he could not. He was drawn to the narrative. David had removed the novel from the old laptop but that had made no difference. It was more as if the hacker were in his head rather than his computer. David's first reaction as he read had been NO! You, whoever the fuck you are, you are usurping my story. MY story. MY fiction. Yet as he read he became more and more drawn to this narrative. He realized that he was excited. He didn't care who the hell the cyber writer of the text was. The link was made. It was as if real history — although as Molly had said, perhaps there was no *real* history — as if history and his fiction had converged. He was not simply excited. He was inspired to write and tried to organize his thoughts as he read. But as he read, the less elated he became, and at some point he became devastated. Part of what this opech related was historical, agreed with David's research, and was available to anyone. But opech had gone far beyond; he had completely taken over David's protagonist, stolen his character — a fictional character. He slumped down on the floor. Angry. Frightened. Unable to get his bearings within his own room. He would quit the novel. Give up on the story. Leave David Sharpe to the mercy of the hacker.

He left the computer, the screen still displaying the end of the attached file. He left the familiar part of the Abbey and simply wandered without direction into parts of the crumbling structure that were mostly unknown. He found a room with glassless windows, a place where the night moon appeared through a hole in the roof, big enough for an eagle to fly through, and he slumped down on the stones. It was damp and his trousers were wet, but he was indifferent. His legs extending out, he rested on his back-stretched arms. He was disoriented as he looked up into a dark sky implanted with a yellow moon. Through the glassless window's iron frames the trees shaped against the sky. He could make no sense of anything — his novel, his life. His thinking was fragmented. David Vere, the brother, was mixed with Vere the character. Edward was less real than Opechancanough the towering werowance. The papacy intermingled with rites of painted medicine men. Nothing was defined. Nothing was signified by anything. Things needed words. Words needed to define and delineate. They no longer did, having become a jumble, some aletory cluster of vowels and consonants. Words were useless. They no longer functioned. He could not write because writing had no meaning.

He began to cry and could not stop. He didn't simply cry, he wailed into the night's darkness. It was no dream, no hallucination. It was as real as life must be.

HE SAT LIKE a stone idol, his legs pulled beneath him on the wet stone. His stomach and head both hurt from lack of food, of anything to drink. Earlier, there had been the voices calling, "Mr. David. David. Master David. Sir!" Some panic in the voice. Later another: "Lad. David. Mister David. Sir." He could not respond. And then he heard no more words. Silently, he spoke in cyberwords to Molly, a young woman he had never met. But even in silence there were words. Words in the head. Words forming thoughts. Words distorting and meandering without meaning. Word, sky. And he said it out loud. Heard his voice. "Sky... moon." They must exist because he named them. The naming of the parts. The essential of life, because it was the essential of language.

His head hurt. He didn't want to think anymore. He would have no more thoughts because thoughts took words and he had no further need of words. It rained. And he said "rain." And then he slapped himself across the face hard for using a word. But it came in torrents then through the hole in the roof, both the rain and the words. And he could imagine himself as if he were looking down on himself from above, a dark shape sitting solitary in the empty hard rock space, pelted by words, in a pool of words. Water, a word. And he wondered if he were dead and envisioning his corpse. His obituary. Pelted to death by words. Heavy, weighty words.

"Molly," he screamed. But it was for the dead Molly, the fictional Molly, but could the fictional be dead? What legitimacy was there in the death of someone who never really existed? His head hurt. He had to exist because the pain within his head was real. Madness. Perhaps he was a great writer. Dostovesky was mad. Virginia Woolf was mad. Gustave Mahler was nuts. Not a writer, doesn't count. Shakespeare was. Oh shit, he was saner than all his squirrelly Timons and Gaiuses and Tituses and Tamoras. Nutsy crew those Greek and Roman folk, but Shakespeare... straight as a poke up an Elizabethan ass. Moliere maybe married his own daughter. Not too sane. Incest, and he thought of David, the son of Mary and her brother Edward. But David was fictional. He had to separate the realities and therein was the difficulty. His head pounded. Lewis Carroll and those little Alices. Not exactly unmad. Was Goethe mad? Marlowe was a homosexual street fighter, but probably not mad. Proust was not all that well. Hemingway shot himself, but Hemingway wasn't much of a writer. What of Wilde? Self-destructive. That's mad. Yeats and all that mysticism. Blake and Coleridge. There was one drug-crazy dude! And Sherlock Holmes. Shit, he wasn't real. That line again between fact and fiction and yet he had seen visitors lined up to enter Holmes's house on Baker Street. Webster had to be mad. You couldn't kill off that many characters and not be crazy. The Mad all used the tools of their trade: words. Madness was full of words, overflowing with words, and words were unaccountable.

And so it went — the night. At some point the rain stopped and came again, and he still sat. Sometimes thinking, mostly trying not to. Because it all took words. And he felt like shit and if he could have seen himself would have known he *looked* like shit as well.

And then, in the morning, the light came. An epiphany. There across the sky was a long-legged bird. Was it a crane? A stork? A heron? Blue in color, he thought. But it didn't matter what he called it because it existed, no matter what the word. He could call it a Mercedes, a clown, a toothpick. It didn't matter. The word didn't matter. It still existed. Its shape didn't change. Its movement across the sky was fleeting, but in that one short space in time, it existed. And that was the epiphany. No matter how confused, how incomprehensible life was. No matter how indefinable, how inadequate words became. None of it accounted for the fact that life was. Existence was. Fiction or real, it made no difference.

He went down to the kitchen. Bydie stared at him. "You look —"

"Like hell," he said and grinned. "Could I have a bit of porridge and some toast?"

"Yes," she said. "And a spot of hot tea. Where were you? I called to you."

"I was out." *God, was I out,* he thought.

"On such a night," she scolded. "It's a wonder you haven't a frightful something."

"Isn't it just," he said plainly, without the slightest note of sarcasm. Amazing the way words have of meaning so little.

He devoured the tea with joy. Had he ever had better tea?

He put everything on the new computer. It was wireless. Thank you, Edward. He connected to the Internet.

"I don't give a fuck, Opech. Bring it on." He spoke aloud to himself. The cyber voice no longer held terror and if this opech of the Internet wanted to provide him with words to plagiarize then so be it. Words were elusive. Be they English, Spanish, Latin or Algonquian, they held no inherent meaning. They were not threatening. But then, "An image…"

The Novel

PLACE OF THE PEOPLE

— *1607* —

An image: an ancient creature shaking a rattle above him, matching the erratic beat pounding in his chest. David trembled; slid away. A moment: his body beneath skins smelling of dead beasts. He was in the place of savages. Fade. Return: the child. A clear blue bead dripped. Sweat poured from his forehead. The soft touch of feathers; the innocent smile of a child. The moment seemed to matter; he hung on each fraction of life. The burning ceased; icy cold overtook him. Tremors. The rattle above him. Slide into darkness. Her voice, soft, incomprehensible mutterings, brought him back. The sin of Mary and Edward Vere tore at him. His burning body chilled; he shook with a freezing cold; more skins were piled on him. In times without fever or cold, in the dim light of a smoking fire, he came to know the walls and the pattern of the reed weaving. He was given cold spring water and fed sips of hot soup.

"Saupae," she said, holding an earthen bowl she had moved from his lips.

"Saupae." He hardly recognized the sound of his own weak voice. Baskets and shells hung above.

A towering shadow appeared; he suspected death was at hand. The figure crouched down beside him. "*Habla español?*"

It sounded to David as if the old man spoke in Spanish. "*Habla español?*" the man repeated.

David was jolted, and though he recognized the Spanish, he could speak none. Uncertain why, he replied in Latin. The incongruity of the savage answering him, conversing in the Latin of David's school days at Lough, no matter how disjointed, made David question whether he was really alive. The figure was of importance, a werowance perhaps. How had he come to learn Latin? To speak of Christianity? Zoraster... and Zeus? He asked why David had left the ship. Why in the marsh? David turned away, remained silent; the specter of Mary Vere, her nipples painted and her face a white-caked mask, enveloped him. These savages should have left him to die. The fever came and he slid away.

"Pocahontas." The girl moved her hand across her chest. "*Telooese* Pocahontas."

"Pocahontas," he repeated.

She pushed her finger toward him several times. "David," he told her.

"Daywud. Daywud." She brought the soup bowl to his lips.

But they called him "Ninghekekughes," two lives, he who has died and lives again. He was no longer David Sharpe or David d'Ersby. He had been consumed by fire; the fever had devoured him like a great flame, and from the ash, Ninghekekughes was formed. His recovery was gradual. Papoo, as he came to know the old creature, and Pocahontas helped him sit up. They spoke incomprehensible words of encouragement, and he found comfort in the tone. Theirs was a deliberate language with emphasis on every syllable. Pocahontas touched David near his eye, then touched near her own eye. "*M'pugikw.*"

"*M'pugikw.*" He brought his finger near his eye.

"Uuuuuhn." She made an urging sound.

"Eye." He touched his eyelid.

"Eye," she repeated. She patted her mouth with her fingers. "*Muttoon.*"

"*Muttoon.*" David put his hand over his lips. "Mouth."

"Mouth." She touched one hand on the other. "*Mipetun.*"

"*Mipetun.* Hand." And so he was taught the names of things by the girl, and he in turn taught her the English: *rout*-fire, *wooae*-egg, *poru*-bread.

From Pocahontas he learned the old man who spoke Latin was the werowance, her uncle, Opechancanough. He came infrequently, but from him David learned that he was in the village of the supreme werowance and this Powhatan was his brother and Pocahontas's father. Pocahontas stood beside him; David realized *they* were the pair, the tall old man and the child, that he had seen on the trip upriver. He spoke in Latin: "I have seen you before."

"It is so," Opechancanough said.

The wereowance left. "*Ekawiya sekisivin goci,*" Pocahontas told him." Later he asked Opechancanough what she had meant.

"When the time comes, she will protect you. It is the way," he said.

David never left the hut, nor did the crime of Mary and Edward Vere. They should have drowned the pair, he and Vere, at birth like deformed cats in a litter. It was what Vere had meant—the two of them "were alone, apart from the rest of the world." The anger he had felt toward his mirrored image dissipated. But why did Robert and Peregrine treat Vere as if old Lord Bertie were his father?

The fever came, burying the past. Through the cracks in the reed walls, he could tell day from night. Sometimes sunlight came through the seams; other times the sound of the rain.

"Today," Opechancanough said, "you will get up and go outside the *yehauken*."

"*Yehauken?*"

"A *domus*." The man wore an apron-like hide, a cloak of blue feathers, and his chest was bare. Wobbly, David leaned on Opechancanough. Pocahontas took his hand and they left the *yehauken*. The sun hurt his eyes, but warm air filled his chest; smells of spring found his nose. Death had touched him; now life enveloped him. Women in a field straightened and stood. Children stopped kicking a ball and gaped.

Opechancanough raised his arms in the air. "Ninghekekughes."

"Ninghekekughes," many of them repeated.

Over the next few days he became Ninghekekughes; he left the past as he shed his clothing and donned the breechclout. Civilization, the social order, he came to realize, was responsible for most of his pain. He came to know "The People" and among The People the strictures of his English class society were not applicable. He had once thought

London the finest place on Earth, but as he walked among The People, he recalled the filth, the starving old woman in the house at the end of the Bridge, the beggars striving to exist, the penny whores copulating to keep from dying of hunger, the palace of Southampton mirrored with the duplicity of men heavy in their jewels and garments. At Lough school, he had suffered an artificial system that created the gulf between David Sharpe and David d'Ersby.

Yet, he sensed a vacant spot in the paradise of the Powhatan. He sat alongside Pocahontas by the *sipou*, the river, after bathing with The People. She took a stick and made a letter "A" in the dirt and he began to teach her the rest of alphabet. Each day he drew words in the dirt and Pocahontas would copy them. As they squatted on such a morning, an old woman struggled up the bank by them and farted. Pocahontas held her nose. "*Piktuun.*" FART, he scratched with the stick. She copied the letters.

"*Mag lootin,*" he told her. A great wind. The child laughed.

The eagle soared against grey swirling clouds. David, embracing his freedom, wanted to tear across the clearing on the black mare, but the foal within her prevented it. Opechancanough on the white stallion waited ahead for him to catch up. David was free of the social structure where he fit in neither as the son of a lazy serf, nor as the bastard product of a great house. Rain began to fall in a gentle wash, then in torrents. The water soaked his hair, ran down his bare chest and back. He reached the edge of the dense woods. Lightning separated the sky and the crash of thunder was sharp.

Opechancanough rode up. "There is danger."

"*Matchiatchak?*" David asked.

"No. No evil spirit, but stay from the trees in a storm. Do you wish to be killed by the lightning?"

David galloped back toward the village and let the mare loose in the piked enclosure. The woman they called Face-of-Spots, the squa of Tintinoo, stood in the rain watching the horses. Her hair was brilliant red and her skin as light as David's and heavily freckled. She smiled at David and touched her bare arm. "I am like you," she said.

"Do you know your parents?"

"No. It is bad not to know who your mother and father were."

"Sometimes, it is better not to know," he said.

He slopped through the mud, back to the empty *yehauken*. The fire was smoldering coals. He wanted a book to read, something to fill his mind, some truth to search. He knew what was missing in this paradise.

Opechancanough came and stood at the entry of the *yehauken*. "Soon they will come for you. You may count the suns. It is called *pemegann*, the death dance."

Warriors came for him. Painted and dripping with shells, they chanted and led him to the center of the village. He was lashed to a stake with leather thongs. Drums pounded; the rattle shook and snake skins flew through the air; dancers stomped feet against dried earth and sped round and round until David became dizzy in the blur of movement. Squas and children and old men stood, their faces like those who gathered at Newgate wall as a cut-purse was drawn and quartered. A warrior with one ear and a scar poked a long pike in David's face, then drove the stake through a tethered animal the size of a small dog with a mask about the eyes. The animal cried out. The words of some poem came. "A

quintessence even from nothingness." Words in rhythm with
the drum. "From dull privations and lean emptiness." The
words beat. "He ruined me, and I am re-begot of absence,
darkness, death—things which are not." The drums stopped.
The dancers ceased. The bindings were removed and he was
prodded in the direction of a *yehauken*, not much wider than
the other huts of the village, but five times longer. It was
dark and smoky. Draped in pearls and pelts, the Powhatan sat
on a platform elevated above the earthen floor. His hair was
grey straggles, and his eyes, set amid wrinkles, were deep and
penetrating. There was a charismatic majesty concentrated in
those eyes. Rows of women stood behind him like sentinels.

"Ninghekekughes," he commanded.

Six chanting priests, Papoo among them, circled about
David. One grabbed him and shoved his head down on a flat
stone. He looked up to the see the warriors, their clubs raised.
They circled about him, ready to beat out his brains. Despite
the assurance, he could but think it was the end. The moment
seemed eternal, the clubs unmoving above. A seated, beautiful
Molly, with white-painted Mary Vere standing behind, hung
as a portrait in his mind. There was peace, a culmination. He
wanted it to be over; he wanted to die. His voice was quiet:
"End it."

He saw the legs of the child, her bare feet. The blue bead
pressed into him as she threw herself atop him. The clubs
were lowered. "*Odwemattin*," voices muttered. He had been
made Pocahontas' brother.

David was helped to his feet by Papoo, who turned him
about to face the four directions. A mat was brought and
he was told to sit. He faced the Powhatan and Pocahontas
sat beside him. The Powhatan yelled out. Opechancanough

translated. "Two ships of the Whiteman have gone out of the
K'tchisipik. You are the brother of Pocahontas and you know
where the Whiteman has gone."

"*Eka nag whateoog.*" I do not know. David wanted this
life as his, yet could not bring danger to Smith, to Archer,
to Gosnold. He suspected Newport had sailed for England,
but with him would have gone the protection of ships' guns.
He believed the English had no right to this land of The
People, but that did not mean they should be killed. He
remembered the lines Opechancanough had given him. "I
bear no gift to the Powhatan, no bear's teeth, nor Roanoke.
I come empty-handed."

Opechancanough translated the Powhatan's loud words
in a softer voice. "You bring a gift inside your head. Your
sister Pocahontas will tell you her secret name and you will
make for her the tongue of the Whiteman and the pictures
which speak. We will trade corn for the thundersticks. You
will show the warriors how to make them kill." David
recalled the orders read from the London Company. It was
explicit: no weapons were to be allowed the savages. There
would be no trading for guns. "I will do this."

The Powhatan smiled, made a motion with a raised hand,
and Papoo threw bits of tobacco on the fire. Food was
brought in by women. This was the lean time, David had
been told, before the harvest and when the animals birthed
and hunting was taboo. The abundance of squash, corn, fish,
roots, fowl and meat laid out on the mats indicated only
plenty in the house of the Powhatan. David thought of the
mirrored hall of Southampton House. "Those who rule do
not starve," Archer had said of the lavish feast.

Opechancanough spoke in Latin. "The Whiteman will never trade their guns."

"But I will teach Pocahontas to read and write."

David sensed eyes staring at him, and he turned around. The young warrior wore the muscular firmness of youth. He was taller than Opechancanough, with penetrating dark eyes. The skin of a grey fox was draped over his shoulder. "My brother Nantaquaus," Pocahontas said.

"*Mache, neheigh yourowgh, Orapaks.*" David didn't understand. Opechancanough explained in Latin. "He lives far at a place called Orapaks." Nantaquas spoke but David understood little. Face-of-Spots came in the *yehauken* and spoke to Opechancanough. "The mare has foaled." He arose and motioned David to follow.

The colt, as black as its dam, attempted to stand. The white stallion, which the light-skinned woman had removed from the pen, was tied some distance to a tree. Opechancanough called to Papoo, who stood in the entry of the *yehauken.* "It is not born white. That is good sign."

Pocahontas and Nantaquaus joined them at the rail. "Nantaquaus would learn to ride. Will you teach him?"

"*Nannar,*" David agreed.

Nantaquaus took the grey fox skin from his shoulder and draped it over David's.

A whippoorwill called. "*Mucko-wheese,*" Pocahontas said, pointing to the colt. "*Markate mucko-wheese.*" And so the foal was named Black Whippoorwill.

The days turned and the sun lifted in the sky. David rubbed his body with smelly oil that protected him from the burning sun and his skin became a deep bronze.

"Peas," he said. Pocahontas snapped the pod and flicked the sweet tiny peas into his mouth. "Peas," she repeated. "*Wickozowr.* Peas."

"*Wickozowr,*" he repeated and wrote the letters P-E-A-S in the dirt with a stick. She took the stick and wrote the letters. And so it went, word upon word, into sentences. Until they began to speak a mixture of English and the language of The People.

David lived alone in the earthen-floor *yehauken*. It resembled the hovel in which he had been raised in Little Muckton, except that he was able to roll up the side wall and let in the warmth. One of Papoo's wives brought him food. Sometimes he took a meal with Nantaquaus or with Opechancanough, but neither resided at Werowocomoco. Nantaquaus came to learn to ride the horse; Opechanca-nough was at his own village among the Pamunkey. Mostly David's days were spent with Pocahontas, but even she was gone occasionally. He suspected she went to the Fort, for now and again she would come out with a word he had not taught her, but he did not confront her. If she were spying upon the colonists for her father, he did not want to know. Nor did he want to know what was happening in the Fort.

"You should take a squa," Nantaquaus told him. "I will find you a wife."

David cracked the crab and sucked out the meat. "I do not want a wife."

"You need a woman to tend to your *yehauken*, Ninghek-ekughes," Opechancanough counseled.

"I had a woman once, the most beautiful. She is dead. I want no other woman."

"I understand," the older man said.

"That is why you are called Opechancanough, Uncle," Nantaquaus told him.

"It is not from the Whiteman that I learned of the singular beauty of a woman. What was your woman called, Ninghekekughes?"

"Molly Dean. She died in England."

"You are called Ninghekekughes. You must put the past away," Nantaquaus told him.

"It tears at me."

"I have seen the pain in your eyes," Opechancanough said. "I ask you not what it is. You died in the swamp. Now you must be born anew to rid you of the life before."

"*Wadchu,*" Nantaquaus said. "You must go to *Wadchu.*"

"The mountain?"

"You will sit alone atop the mountain and seek your *manitou.*"

"When your *manitou* comes to you," Opechancancough told him, "he will be your spirit, your guide. You will never sit alone again."

During the night the fever again devoured him. Soaked in sweat, the specter of Mary Vere seemed emblazoned on the walls. The white masked face and painted lips cried out to him in pain, in words of no sense. Then blood streamed from her painted nipples. He tore himself from the skins and ran out of the *yehauken* into the night. He lay on the ground shaking, and when the fit subsided, he got up and went to the river. He washed away the sweat and sat on the bank shivering in wetness. He must seek his *manitou.*

Opechancanough spoke. "Nantaquaus will guide you through the land of the Monacan to the place-of-the-rock-in-the-trail-of-the moon. It is far to the setting sun amid the

Blue Mountains. There is danger. There are tribes high in the ridges that burn men alive like heretics at an *auto da fe*."

David was startled by the man's comparison. "You learned your Latin in Spain?"

"Yes. I will speak of it to you on your return, Ninghek-ekughes." The *shu-shu-gah* shrieked. "Papoo will paint the pictures upon your body and tell you what you must do to prepare yourself. But the greatest danger is in yourself."

"The pain is driving me mad. I will risk the danger."

"Go then in quest of your guardian spirit. May your *manitou* find you."

The moon rose three times. Each night Mary Vere cried out for help, her nipples dripping blood, and he arose in soaking sweats to bathe in the river. On the fourth morning Papoo painted his body with red and black symbols representing the sun, the giver of all life, the moon, the mother of us all, *okhe*—the earth, *nootau*—the fire, and the Great Stag, the guardian of the *manitou*.

"You will sit upon the place-of-the-rock-in-the-trail-of-the-moon. You will touch no water. You will touch no food. The sun will rise and set and rise and set again." He thrust a small leather pouch into David's hand. "You will wait. You will know the time. You will eat the sacred plant. It is planted by the Great Stag in his dung when the first snow comes to the place of the shades of four trees. It will guide your *manitou* to the rock upon which you wait until your *manitou* has set you free. And he will be your guardian for all your days."

"And should the *manitou* fail to come?"

"Then may death be a comfort to you for the pain will sit in your head."

David

—the present—

HE REREAD THE chapter and was pleased. The David in his novel seemed to be adjusting to the situation, just as he found peace with himself and his writing. He was no longer angered by the words of the opech hacker. He would embrace whatever the cyber voice brought him.

He would go to France now and do whatever it was that Edward required of him, as bizarre as it might be. And he would embrace his brother, literally. Kinship was a complex word, but he would seek to find its meaning. At the moment he had the most important chapter of the novel to write: "The place..."

The Novel

THE PLACE-OF-THE-ROCK-IN-
THE-TRAIL-OF-THE MOON

— 1607 —

Lightning tore holes in the black sky—sharp rents loosening a fury of splitting thunder. David stood, anchored in the mud. He looked through the drenching water at the black sky; Zeus pissing on the world. He wore only the breechclout and the saturated moccasins, and the cold rain bit at his skin; the painted shapes on his body ran in veins of red and black, giving his flesh the appearance of striated stone. His mouth was parched and he licked the moisture from his thumb.

"You must drink nothing," Nantaquaus ordered and tugged David forward.

David had lost track of the days; no sleep and the deprivation of food and water muddled his thinking, and at times he knew neither who he was nor where he was. At the moment he was Ninghekekughes and he had traveled in a canoe up the Mattaponi until it became a trickle in a bed of rocks. They moved through the dense woods, across the open stretches, avoiding the Monacan warriors, until they reached the steep hills and tall pines. His stomach clenched in hunger and his mouth blistered; the sun burned his back and the rain came, freezing his mind. Sometimes he was in Little Muckton, and once he was standing in the carved bed at Ersby Hall, screaming for Chowder to light the fire. He tore his moccasin. He saw himself standing erect in the path ahead, wearing a yellow doublet. Or was it Vere? He saw the masts of the *Susan Constant* outlined against the sky like crosses on Calvary—Jesus come to save the savages. He saw Molly naked. He began to cry... and saw heads, only heads, a melange of faces, none of which he recognized. A blue bead dangled in the air until it became his own white pearl button ferreted out from beneath a rock by a pack of hounds on leashes in the hands of Alice Bacon. The rain ceased. The hot sun drying his lips was worse. Nantaquaus was silent. A palaver of Latin, Greek, Pocahontas's naming of things, Captain John's boasting, Hunt's sermons, screams of a burning heretic, the pleas of a dwarf, the howl of a wounded wolf and the roars of a galed sea exploded in his head. He no longer seemed to touch the ground with his feet. Still, he fell and Nantaquaus helped him up. He whirled and ran, reached out and touched the top of the trees. "*Ut puto Deus fio*," he said, and in English, "I think I am becoming a god."

"*Tet.*" Nantaquaus pointed overhead. Hanging high above the trees, a jut of rock cantilevered from the cliffs. "The place-of-the-rock-in-the-trail-of-the-moon."

Nantaquaus helped undo the pouch at David's waist. Into his mouth David smashed the dried bits of the sacred plant grown in the dung of the Great Stag. It was ugly tasting and he gagged, swallowing the bitter dried fungi. He stared at the rock. It seemed closer to the sun than the earth. "*M'bi…*Water."

"No." Nantaquaus led him to where he must climb to the place-of-the-rock-in-the-trail-of-the-moon.

"I will fly." David soared in the air, careening above the trees. But he could not seem to reach the rock and was uncertain whether his feet ever left the ground. He moved to the base of the cliff, where either fat rigid snakes or roots extended from the wall of earth. He clutched them and pulled, and with his feet, he dug his way up the mud and rock. His fingers bled, his legs bled, his feet bled through the torn moccasins, his head bled when he banged it on the rocks—the blood mingled with the red and black paint and was indistinguishable. He clutched a branch and pulled himself over onto the place-of-the-rock-in-the-trail-of-the-moon.

The sun anchored above him like a despot, burning his eyelids. He, Ninghekekughes, sat, immobile, in the center of the flat spread of rock. An ant brought him a fleck of dirt and he ate it. A soprano voice penetrated the air with music pure and haunting, its clarity driven by the roll of drums, the words Italian and meaningless. Black hares lined the edge of the rock, holding the tiniest of lutes and horns. The music, unlike the caterwauling in Southampton House, was ethereal and lulled him into joy. He did not fly but felt himself floating over the green earth, letting the warmth of the day wrap him. He floated just above clear streams, their pebbled bottoms visible, their water sparkling in dazzling runs between the pines and oaks. He dipped down and drank the spring water and was no longer thirsty. A huge grey bear, *maerraek mosq*, came to the rock with a swan's egg baked by the sun, and David felt no more hunger.

"The cruelty of the world is irrational," the bear said.

"Will you stay with me?" David asked.

"I love him who wills the creation of something beyond himself and then dies."

"Will you stay with me?" David asked.

"Man is not what he is. He is and then he IS. Nothingness is annihilation. Creation IS."

"Will you stay with me?" David asked.

"Man is alone," the *maerraek mosq* said and vanished.

The voice of the soprano pierced the air, tears in her voice; the tears reflected upon David's painted face. The sun slunk from the sky and dusk dusted the trees below. Shapes evolved, lines became indistinct, the voice of a tenor called for the end of the day, and another voice answered and the duet continued. Only darkness remained and the voices drifted off in a sudden cold wind. The sky caved in into blackness without a star of light; a pool of black swelled where the trees had been; an eddy, a tunnel, tried pulling him toward the edge of the rock, enticing him to leap, offering him rest. The blackness became a mirror and he saw his face, or perhaps Vere's, cruel and painted with destruction. The nerves of his heart shook. Another face appeared, discernible in the ebony mirror, black hair and black eyes.

"Who?" But he knew.

The voice was lilting. "'And what wul leive to your bairns, Edward, Edward? The warld is room, let them beg thrae life.' The Queen once said I danced better than any man, but she could not sing." The dark tiny eyes flashed.

"My father was a number, sixteen, and so I, too, became a number, but his crimes were his own and I would not bear the sins of the father. I loved my sister and gave her the greatest gift I owned." The face began to fade. "Let no man bear the pain of his father."

Mary Vere appeared, younger, without the painted white mask. "I will nurse thee child, for thou art but a linnet's egg." She spoke no more, but her bleeding nipples remained an imprint upon the black void. The moon rose and she washed away in the light. David sat in the place-of-the-rock-in-the-trail-of-the-moon. But the full moon was neither brilliant white nor tinged with yellow, but rather had a bluish cast and hung against the sky like icy frost. The white fox stood almost silver in its path at the edge of the rock.

"Omnia exeut in mysterium," he said. "And all is born in mystery as well. Chaos is the accoucheur of man."

"Will you stay with me?" David asked.

"I am *wobaehokus*, the white fox."

"You are wise?"

"I am cunning. Cunning is the nature of the *hokus*. Cunning is the nature of man. Even the eldest of gods, Earth, inexhaustible Earth, is mastered by man... cunning, cunning is man." The fox sniffed the rock. "Cunning, artful beyond all dreaming, for evil, for good—the invincible mind. Barbarism smolders within as well as without. The king cohabits with his mother. He is blind. Why do you choose to live among The People?"

"I am free."

"No. Freedom is the search for understanding." The *wobaehokus* vanished then reappeared behind David. His eyes were small, black and penetrating. "Freedom is language and thought as rapid as the wind. Man discovered the word for it; it made him free, to think, to write, to understand, to name, to record."

"But in that there is no certainty, no answer," David said.

"It is the search that is life, that nourishes the soul; the quest, the question becomes the answer."

"Will you stay with me?" David asked.

"The Greeks were free. The Romans were free. But man encumbers himself with answers, not questions, with gods and certainty. The logic of Zeno becomes true, because it is false as well. The infinity of the circle only poses the question. The *maerraek mosq* knows: man is not, man IS."

"And what Mary and Edward Vere have borne?"

"What man is. What Ninghekekughes IS; the verb is active; the question is David's. David is alone. He is either among the living dead, or free and alive. What creation he IS, he chooses."

"And death?"

The white fox moved toward the edge of the rock. He paced. "The ultimate freedom."

"No one can die for me. I must do this for myself."

"No one can eat, sleep, drink, fornicate, nor piss for you either. All these you must do for yourself. Is one the greater than the other? You are alone. What you create IS. David, Ninghekekughes IS."

"Will you stay with me?" David asked.

"I am cunning like a fox. Like *Das Ma*."

The *wobaehokus* lay down upon the place-of-the-rock-in-the-trail-of-the-moon. He was silent.

Only the blue heron moved. Moved across the sky as delicate, as graceful as the life of a new morning.

David

—the present—

DAVID D'ERSBY HAD written without changing a word and now he prostrated himself on the floor in his room in the ruined Abbey and cried. He cried not from pain, not from sorrow, but from joy of creation.

Then it was later. He had eaten a strange Bydie lunch of something resembling soup. But even that had not diminished his euphoria. Now he was again alone and went to the computer and found the e-mail from opech@earthgo.com and the attached file labeled truehistory4.doc:

"At the first light…"

Opecancanough

E-MAIL ATTACHMENT

AT THE FIRST light I bathed alone in the Great River. The Whiteman called it the James. They stole the land and the water and the birds and the trees and the fish and the rocks by putting upon them a name, taking away the sounds of The People. But soon the Whiteman would be silent. I sent Pocahontas to the Whiteman's Fort to play, to listen; she was my ears. Ninghekekughes had taught her the words for things, and listening at the Fort, she learned more words. She never uttered these English words for things among the Whiteman, but brought me all she had seen and heard. The werowance of the Whiteman, Wingfield, wore fancy clothes and had men to wait upon him and the Reverend Hunt had books and Wingfield hated the man named Captain John and a man died and another of the bloody flux and Captain John gave Pocahontas a small knife to cut apples into quarters and the Whiteman stank in the heat imprisoned in iron and finery and played a game of rolling balls down flattened dirt places into carved pieces of wood and lived in tents over holes in the earth and the tents were rotting and Master Hunt prayed for the sick and Pocahontas taught the boys to play football and a man died and Captain Ratcliffe accused Wingfield of hoarding food and the Whiteman never seemed to bathe and seeds were planted but the plants went untended and were left to the weeds and a man died and men complained that their rations of wheat and barley were wormy and a man died of the swelling and Captain Gosnold gave Pocahontas some cloth and told her stories of his little girl and much of the Whiteman's finery was tattered and filthy and a man died and Captain John gave Pocahontas a spoon made of metal and a man died and a man died and a man died and Captain Gosnold became ill.

The Whiteman were being killed by the brackish water and the bite of the mosquito. They died puking and emptying their bowels. They did not comprehend that they had chosen the site of death upon which to build their grand city. In the beginning there had been *necuttoughtysinough*, one hundred. Sixty were left. And if the burning summer heat did not kill them, the coming winter would, for they neither planted, nor fished, nor hunted. In the dark of night, to hide the fact from The People, the dead were taken out and buried. Still, I knew the death of every man settled there was not the end. The ships would come again. Perhaps in a cycle of seasons, perhaps five, perhaps ten, but they would come. They would bring the Whiteman's God, the Whiteman's moral absolutes. It was a paradox that the same Jesuits who poisoned the world with their restrictive morality had introduced me to Socrates, whose 'good' was the intellect, whose 'virtue' was wisdom and whose 'best society' was open and offered greater freedom than it took.

It was not yet the time of harvest, but the green corn, milky and soft, roasted and eaten from the cob, was the best of the year. I took three baskets and a gift of fresh deer meat. Only four warriors were with me as I approached the Fort; the remainder stayed in the trees. I led the way to the gate facing the water. A guard moved to challenge our entry, but I brushed him aside and barged into the Fort. I was appalled by the stench. Huts were crumbling, tents in shreds. Men stood, clothing ragged and torn, faces revealing the pallid pain of defeat. I masked my nose and mouth with my hand. The reports from Pocahontas had failed to capture how revolting the place had become. From what she had told me I recognized the four men who approached, Smith and Archer in their armor, Wingfield in his finery, and Percy like a pheasant at mating time. I offered the deer flesh as a gift. Wingfield accepted it and made a speech. I understood nothing. I showed them the baskets my men held and indicated the corn was for trade.

"*Pagatour*," Smith said. He seemed less intimidated by my arrival. I grabbed at Smith's musket, knowing full well the response, and shouted "*Pawcussocks*." Smith yanked it back. "NO! No!"

I gestured that if they could not trade the corn for guns I would leave. A casket was brought out. From it Smith took out a strand of yellow and red beads. I brushed them aside. Wingfield held out a hatchet. I would have liked the hatchet, but my purpose in coming was not to trade, but to see the Fort. Wingfield threw up his arms. Smith frowned and stood in my path, but I pushed passed the stocky man in his iron suit and moved to a hut. I ducked through a low entry. The thatched roof was collapsing on one end. The place reeked of human waste, a man sick, perhaps dying, lay on dried grass piled in a corner. I went back out into the sunlight. Attempts to plant gardens formed weed patches between the huts. There was an empty pen where an animal had been kept. Men stood, their thin bodies hinting of the affliction of diseases, their eyes containing the proof, sunken and yellow.

In the doorway of the next hovel stood Smith, but I shoved him out of the way and went inside. The walls were hung with helmets, spears, shields and guns. As I attempted to touch a musket, Smith grabbed my hand, pulled it away and shoved me out the door. I motioned to one of my warriors with a club to do nothing. I entered the largest structure in the compound; it was the church, but it lacked the gilt statues, crucifixes, lace, paintings, candles, fonts and ornate decorations of the Spanish God. Benches, a plain cross and a raised place for preaching indicated a poverty about the English God. Here was only the mildew of humid summer and remnant sweat.

In another hut, tidy, crude shelves and a table held books. I was amused at trading the corn for a book in English which I could not read. I indicated to Smith that I wanted a book. Wingfield, who appeared exasperated, came over and indicated I should have a book and get done with the business of trading. But the owner of the books shoved his way into the hut and said no books were to be traded. Wingfield argued with the man. The man lost the argument and handed me a black book with a cross on the cover. I examined the book and deliberately held it backwards and upside down. I suspected it might be a Bible and handed it back, indicating I was not interested. I pointed to a red leather-bound volume on the table. "No," the man said. Another argument with Wingfield followed. Smith and others joined and finally Wingfield prevailed. I was handed the red leather-bound volume. I smelled it. I examined it. I assumed it, too, was written in English, except for the handwritten Latin inscription inside. *Vir qui librum tibi dedit te laudavit.* A signature was scrawled beneath.

I clutched the book and gave up the three baskets of corn. Holding the book in front of me like a monk on his way to prayer, I led my men from the Fort. I felt an urgency to reach Werowocomoco, a need to be in a place of The People. I would send Pocahontas no more to the gates of the Fort. It was not just the sickness and men dying. I had sensed something else, the inability of men to seek survival, petty men who primped and argued, who existed in hovels, built a church, but did not live.

The following afternoon I traveled to Werowocomoco. Ninghekekughes was by the horses. "This is for you." I handed him the red leather book. "Tonight when the moon sits upon the river, we will talk."

My brother was alone, the side of his *yehauken* rolled up. An evening breeze came in from the river, creeping into the enclosure. "The drums spoke of your coming. I have sent the others away."

I sat down beside him. "The Whiteman is dying."

"And they have many guns?"

"Yes, and in each of the three corners of the Fort, large ones that can knock down the forest."

"How many have died?"

"Perhaps half. Many of the living are ill. Swamp sickness and rotten food and bad water."

"Ninghekekughes has come from the-place-of-the-rock-in-the-trail-of-the-moon."

"I saw him by the horses." I drew circles in the earth with my finger. "When the Whiteman are all dead, we will go to the Fort and take the big guns."

As darkness settled over Werowocomoco we sat in silence. The moon rose and the Powhatan's breath slowed; he snored softly. I slipped from the *yehauken* and found Ninghekekughes standing by the river's edge. The moonlight wrinkled across the water.

"Do you know who Plato was?"

"Yes," I told him. "The pupil of Socrates."

"The book you brought me is the writing of Plato. Thank you."

I sat down on the bank and dangled my feet in the cool water.

"It is wonderful to have a book. It was Master Hunt's."

"I traded three baskets of corn for it. You must tell me what Plato has written."

"I shall." Our conversation was a composite of Latin and the language of The People, with an occasional bit of English or Spanish. A cloud slipped over part of the moon.

"You went to the place-of-the-rock-in-the-trail-of-the-moon."

"The white fox found me there."

"And he brought you comfort."

"Yes. He showed me answers mean nothing. It is the quest that matters. Life is the search."

"The Whiteman's God has only answers and sin."

"It is true, but there are men in England who have questions; who cherish the quality of doubt."

"And you would go back to seek the questions from these men?"

"From men and from books. In time I must. But I am not certain when."

"The white fox will guide you."

Ninghekekughes sat down beside me and let his feet dip the water. "That is so. For now, I will seek the questions in the book you brought me."

"Was it the great pain of the death of the woman that drove you into the swamp at night and brought you to the place-of-the-rock-in-the-trail-of-the-moon?"

"No, the pain that sent me there was a pain for which there was no cure. I am the child of sin."

"But sin is a Whiteman's word. Here among The People there is no sin."

Ninghekekughes was silent as if weighing his words. If there was pain on his face, I could not see it in the darkness. His voice was soft when he spoke. "Even among The People it is taboo to lie with one's sister. My mother and father were of the same womb."

"But the shame is on the father and the mother, not upon the child."

"So the wise fox has shown me."

"You, too, are Wobaehokus. It is your secret name. He is your guide."

"I have spoken of the wobaehokus to none but you. I hope Nantaquaus is not offended."

"I think he understands. It is I alone with whom you could share this. I am Opechancanough."

"Yes, you and I alone have the souls of the Whiteman."

"Tomorrow we shall ride the horses. And when we are where there are no other ears, my name is Apachisto. That is my sacred name and yours is now Wobaehokus."

Molly

JAMESTOWN

—*the present*—

MOLLY HAD ALSO read the attachment. Neither David d'Ersby's fiction nor Opechancanough, if he was who he claimed to be, the voice of the past, were aware that Molly had not died in England. That Molly in her diary had another story to tell.

Molly believed that just as the Molly in the diary was to have a child, so must she. She had decided it was quite essential to have a child. Molly was well aware of her single-mindedness. She was being driven by destiny. Molly Dean's journal was not simply some relic of the past; rather, it was a determination, a direction for her to follow. She stood at the porch's edge staring at the blue heron stupidly trying to make up its mind whether to fly or stand there, looking ridiculous on one leg at river's edge. She had reached the decision to marry David d'Ersby. She had admittedly never met him, did not know him, only had a limited number of Internet conversations with him, knew that many of his qualities were not particularly admirable. But she knew, too, that she would marry him. He had reputedly respectable genes, was heterosexual, and if he looked anything like his brother, was admirably handsome. But far more important than these qualities was that David d'Ersby, fictionalized as David Sharpe, had precisely the right name, or, more correctly, names. This was not a shallow, Wilde-like consideration about the earnestness of names. This was the culmination to a series of connections, as if predetermined by history, but created almost as if it were the proper conclusion of a novel. There was a correct way for a story to end and what Molly was seeking was a tidy conclusion, a proper wrapping up and a logical dénouement. A happy ending? That was not determinable. But it would be a conclusion entirely true to the journal of Molly Dean Sharpe. What was needed was an heir to the journal, the Bible and the other valuable items in the safety deposit box.

Perhaps Inez was right in that because she was an orphan she sought a stable traditional marriage. There was nothing wrong in that. It is what the ancestral Molly achieved, an intense dedicated love that ended in a marriage whose lineage carried to this day. Molly recognized that, at the moment, she didn't actually have the intense dedicated love, but that would come. They would be wed in the Cathedral of Mary Our Queen in Baltimore, her uncle would officiate, the nuns from the College would attend and Inez Lovell would be her maid of honor. She would wear a wedding dress that the original Molly might have worn. There was a print somewhere she had seen of

Pocahontas's wedding. She must check the accuracy of the dress in that painting. The Cathedral was so grey, so dark, so cold, so stone, so appropriately reflecting the darkness in the print of Pocahontas's wedding. She would carry the Bible from the safety deposit box in the Bank in Richmond. She and David would live in this house once occupied by Pocahontas and John Rolfe. The house would need restoration, but David d'Ersby apparently had money. It might not be a perfect life, but it was the destiny they were given. The blue heron lifted off its one leg and rose oh so skillfully into the air. What was the impending crisis, she wondered. The damned *shu-shu-gah.*

She suspected David Vere would approve of her marriage plans. He had made himself at home in her cottage on the James and she had enjoyed his company. They had discussed art, world politics, American Indians of the East Coast, his family history and Sri Lankan literature. They had consumed a number of bottles of good French wine, which he had brought from Washington, and she had fed him Smithfield ham and gravy. The saltiness of the ham required the consumption of more wine. She fed him more Smithfield with eggs for breakfast while they attempted to come to grips with slight hangovers. He had taken any number of pictures of her with his phone. He said they were to show to David d'Ersby. He wanted to wade in the James and they did that before their tour to the remnants of the real Jamestown, and then they went on to Festival Park.

"They crossed the Atlantic in those dinky little boats?"

"And my ancestor, David Sharpe, in that one." She pointed out the *Godspeed*.

But now David Vere was gone and Molly was alone. She left the porch and went in and picked up the phone. Inez's response to her planned wedding was that she was being irrational.

"This coming from a woman whose last two relationships were with a TV wrestler and an Eskimo lesbian."

"At times, you are as singularly myopic as a character in a Penelope Fitzgerald novel."

"I see nothing wrong in having direction in one's life."

"But beware. While Fitzgerald's characters are single-minded, the novelist's conclusions are entirely untraditional and not given to happy endings."

"This is real life, not fiction."

"Yes, it's real life, Moll. Not historical personages. Not names in a diary, events of four hundred years ago. This is *now*. He is a man to whom you have not spoken. Only written words over an Internet connection."

"It is destiny," Molly insisted.

"Yes, destiny." Inez's voice was cautioning. "John Weston, the novelist, wrote that 'Destiny is a careless housewife.' He described her flinging us like a knotted ball of yarn into the corner with the dust and offal."

After her call to Inez, Molly returned to the journal for comfort.

The Diary

LINDFIELD

—1607—

These facts I put down upon my visit to London as it was the day upon which events did follow and reshape what had been our simple existence. Roger had been called down to meet with the Bishop of Winchester. There had been complaints that he was not dutiful in the weeding out of witches in Lindfield. Peregrine Bertie had writ Roger saying that he had learned he would be coming to London, hoped I would be accompanying him and asked that I call upon him, so that he might be amended to me for what evil he had caused. I would not have agreed, but thought he could make great harm for Roger were I not to do so.

I visited Joan Alleyn and did gossip and have a pleasant afternoon. The sign of the cardinal was gone; the house no longer a stew. She told as how both Mr. Henslowe and Mr.

Alleyn had greatly increased their fortunes. She said that I must bring the baby for her keeping when I went to see Peregrine and advised me wear my fanciest frock. I told her I was saving that for the day after when I was to be entertained by Lady Alice Bacon. I prayed she was not awful, as I heard, because we were also to spend several days at Twickenham, the great house itself, on our way returning to Lindfield.

I write this on the day next. Bertie House near Barbican Tower loomed as formidable as always. The black bunting of death was draped at the door. I was told that Master Bertie was expecting me. A fire burned in the hearth, but it didn't seem to take away the chill. Peregrine Bertie wore black and on his arm were mourning ribbons. He thanked me for coming, addressing me as Mistress Prine, and said I had no doubt been told the news. I assured him I had been told nothing. He said that David was dead. I could not hold back the tears and was glad that I had not brought David's son into this house. Peregrine Bertie stood, so tidy; his small dark beard so carefully sculptured; his clothing without a wrinkle.

I remained silent, not wiping the tears from my cheek. He told me that he had not known of David's death when he wrote asking me to call. He had at the time wished to apologize for his conduct at Southampton House and wished

me to know some facts and that as a gentleman he owed me an explanation. He told me
that what he was about to reveal were privileged
matters but without detailing them I could not
grasp Vere's motivation. He was repulsed, he
said, to tell me that their mother, Lady Mary
Vere Bertie, upon the visit to Grimsthorpe by
her brother Edward Lord Oxford, was raped by
him. He went on to say that the Earl scoffed
at the idea and assured his father that his sister was quite mad. He noted that she had been
subject to fits. Vere was born and Peregrine
said that his father never questioned that pater-
nity, although he was greatly chargrined at his
mother's screaming, wailing insistence that the
child be christened Vere. It was only to finally
stop her screaming that his father agreed. I was
struck as how Peregrine's voice had started without emotion, flat, but his voice cracked as he
continued stating that shortly after the birth,
his father went off to bring order in the Lowlands, and his mother was sent to Ersby. He
said his Uncle Edward came to Ersby to see
the new 'nephew' and he again raped his sister.
This time there were witnesses and his mother
again became pregnant even though her womb
had not yet healed. He said his brother Robert,
then in his teens, was old enough to understand
that all must be kept from their father and from
as much of the household as possible. Robert
took charge and on the day David was born

he took the baby from their mother and sent him away with a milkmaid and a field man. He went on to say that as the boy grew, the striking resemblance between David and Vere became the more apparent; they were only ten months apart. Vere was acknowledged as legitimate, and David was not acknowledged at all. Lord Willoughby died, never, to their knowledge, knowing the truth, but Vere could not escape their mother's stories. She never accused her brother of any evil, but rather ranted about his wonder, his brilliance. The Earl of Oxford was brilliant but a wastrel, and perhaps as mad as their mother. His treatment of his wife, Burghley's daughter, was public testimony to his lunacy; his treatment of their mother, a private one. Vere came to see the truth and what it generated was self-hatred. Finding David, someone with whom to share the sense of horror, became a salvation.

I told him I was more than surprised that he would reveal this private matter to me. He said that Sir Francis Bacon had informed him that if he did not, Sir Francis would tell me himself, noting that Sir Francis had the matter investigated thoroughly. The damaging papers were found in Vere's possession. He said Lord Willoughby, and himself, were both sorry for the pain it had brought me.

He said that David's death would always be a burden on his soul, telling how Sir

Edward Maria Wingfield, of mean spirit, had told David of his birth. He understood from the letter Captain Newport brought that Sir Edward had left David on the ship's deck at night, alone in the dark, after telling him. David was never seen again. It was assumed he had leapt overboard and was taken to sea by the tide. There were tears in Peregrine Bertie's eyes. He said he had been told I had a son.

I felt no pity for the man and responded coldly that the Rector and I indeed had a child. He then said that should I, or my son, ever be in grave misfortune that he felt the Berties were obliged to be of assistance and that I should avail myself of that help. I departed Bertie House.

I was not looking forward to my day with Lady Bacon, but for Roger's sake, as there was continuing trouble over the witch business, friends in high places would be essential. While I much admired Sir Francis I heard naught but that his wife was a silly girl. A footman, dressed far fancier than myself, arrived to fetch me to waiting sedan chairs. The first of the chairs was occupied by Lady Bacon, who appeared as a pretty face in a pile of pink fabric. I was helped into the second.

Lady Bacon said she liked to go fast. The chairs bounded down the cobble as the bearers ran. Lady Bacon screamed out like child. Then the bearers set us down. I looked up at the elegant structure, Bethlehem Hospital. My idea of a pleasant day was not coming to laugh at the lunatics of Bed'lam. It was cruel and demeaning entertainment. Lady Bacon attempted to straighten her hair and asked if it was fun.

"It was different, Lady Bacon."

"I'm Alice. Lady Bacon is the buttoned up old bitch, Francis's mama, who lives at Verdun and survives on Christian penance. And don't look so glum. I've not brought you to Bed'lam to giggle at loonies as do the silly ladies of Westminster. I met David once, at Twickenham, the night before he sailed." Then she pinned a small black ribbon to my gown. "Sometimes it is easier to put death to rest if it be faced openly." She took my arm, paid the visitor's admission and we went in like two young sisters bound for a lesson at the virginals.

Bed'lam had a smell unlike any other. I had been once with Benjamin Joseph who called it the smell of madness. The screams, the laughs, the incessant talking bounded off the walls. Alice spoke to a keeper and he led us through caged doors and down a corridor where snarled-haired hags shrunk against both walls as if part of the decor. A door was unlocked and I followed Alice into a cell. A man on the bed, facing the wall, wore only a long white shirt. His arms were shackled. He turned to face us. There was no mistaking Vere for David this time. The eyes were wild, but perhaps with recognition. He spoke, but made no sense. The hatred was gone. Perhaps it was the story Peregrine Bertie had told me; perhaps it was simply seeing him here caged—all the arrogance gone. He looked empty. I didn't realize at first I had said it, but I told him that David was dead. He seemed to have no control and the crying came like a bursting cask. The keeper told us he had never heard him cry.

Outside, free of the smells and the screams, I pressed Alice Bacon's hand and she said that it was something she thought I needed to see. I liked Alice Bacon greatly. As Bow-bell sounded I returned to the tavern to find Farin with David and Roger, morose, slumped in a corner. The Bishop had been informed by Sir Lindred Groom Douglas that Rector Prine had been an impediment to the prosecution of witchery. He now expected Roger to contribute to the accumulation of testimony at the quarter sessions on witchery.

Roger spoke little as we made the journey to Twickenham. The chiseled face was molded in a frown and his scar seemed more apparent. We arrived on a soft wind.

Later the wind nipped dead leaves from webs of branches and I bared my feet and stretched out in the golden long grass near the lake. David slept; a shawl pulled across poles of broken oak limbs shielded him from the brilliance of day. Alice's hounds stretched out beside him like a trio of guardian sphinxes. Barefoot Alice danced and then collapsed on the ground near me saying the affectation of freedom was wonderful. And when I asked why affectation she said it was because all freedom was an illusion. That while some were shackled by poverty, she was equally shackled by being rich. She asked me quite bluntly if I resented my husband sharing his bed with another man. There seemed no malice in Alice's question, so I told her no and that Roger Prine had taken me in when I faced the prospect of a horrid existence and that I was not demeaned by them because I was a woman. Alice looked down at the child, pronouncing he looked like a Vere and then gently sang a lullaby with the most obscene words, as the baby giggled, then slept.

The pleasant afternoon reached for a darker evening. The candles had not yet been lighted and the faces in the portraits on the wall were indistinct rectangles in the dusk. I stood in the doorway to the small drawing room. Farin spoke softly as he said it seemed Roger had but two choices, to hunt down innocent women and have them hung to the glee of the sadists of Lindfield, or suffer the persecution of the hysterical villagers and the wrath of an indifferent Bishop, too concerned with his business ventures to care about truth. I told him we could not flee to London or elsewhere because Roger would not give up the rectorage. It was then Roger appeared in the doorway, his blond hair uncombed. He asked us to bear with him and trust God. But he said we must put it aside for the moment and enjoy the hospitality of Sir Francis and his other guests. He seemed more at peace. And I was relieved.

There was entered in the side margin of the diary a note at this point: The persons I now describe were later to have influence in my life. I was not aware of it when I first put down these descriptions of those guests at Twickenham. I judged some of them not as cruelly as I might have had I known the future.

The diary proper continued:

⌈Servants in dazzling livery with the emblazoned boar's crest trailed through the house like overdressed ants.⌉ The Wests, Lord de La Warr and his Lady Cecilia, arrived with an entourage of servants. Lady Cecilia was given to giggles while his Lordship appeared sinister with long black hair, dark and deep-set eyes, dark beard and mustache. Accompanying the Wests was Captain Argall, whom Alice called Sammy and said had no wife and was a bit of a rogue. I found him pleasantly masculine with a vibrant amiability. Over whist, he announced he was seeking a new sea lane to Virginia. Cecilia West paid little attention to her cards, thinking always the knave could take the King, for, as she put it, that was the way it was at court. Alice, with a grin, told her she must not speak ill of the King in Francis's house, and Cecilia said she knew Sir Francis had his nose far up the King's bottom. Alice said it was so.

On the next day a throng of guests came at high noon for dinner in the great gallery. Not a hint of breeze; heat cut through the walls and baked through the windows. Conversation clung like perspiration in the press of bodies. Gowned women dripped jewels and fanned themselves; men smothered in colour wiped their brows on ruffled cuffs. I sweltered in Alice's borrowed gown of gold piled over heavy velvet, a strand of pearls falling to my waist. I was delighted to see Ben Jonson. He had brought a woman, Mistress Strachey, who hoped to corner Lord de La Warr on the financial plight of her husband, William Strachey. I moved through the gentleman's conversation deciding they had lives divided between fighting the Spanish in the Netherlands and proselytizing Dutch Calvinism; their discourse alternated between bravado and prattle. I sat at dinner next to Thomas Dale, who spoke of Christ, slurped his food and had much horror of the Dutch and their liberties. His wife sat across in drab brown and informed me that obedience was the first law of marriage. To my other side Thomas Gates, a loud outspoken Calvinist, was more extreme than Dale. In booming voice he spoke much on·money to be made on the commodity. His dour wife announced she had recently had a bath and found it most invigorating. There was Sir George Somers, a man of Parliament, of age about sixty, and his wife was a lady in blue. Flies seemed to light on her like bits of decoration and when she spoke of wearing an amulet to ward off wrinkles I could see the sweat in the folds of her neck. A speck of snot seemed to have settled just above her lip. The connection between all these gentlemen and their wives, beyond religious intolerance and boorishness, seemed to be a plan to go to Virginia.

David

BLOOMSBURY

—the present—

DAVID AND DAVID did not sit on the new, blue suede divan but rather stretched out on the floor and leaned against empty bookcases. They did not drink the wine that Jane had left for them but rather consumed pints of bitter. "So, why did you hate me so?" the Vere brother asked.

"I didn't really hate you," the d'Ersby brother replied.

"You did."

"An intense animosity, perhaps."

"Because I am gay."

"No, I think I was more curious about your homosexuality than put off by it." He opened another pint for each of them and handed one to his brother. "What I really resented was that you knew who you were and I didn't. I knew, down here in my gut somewhere, that you had to be my brother. But you were David Aubrey Vere, had a name and an identity. I was a fucking bastard and knew it.

I wasn't David d'Ersby. Edward wasn't my goddamn father. I didn't have either a father or a real name. I should have been David Vere as well, but I wasn't. I wasn't anybody."

David Vere took a deep drink from the bottle. "I always knew you were my brother. I never had the slightest doubt."

"You could have said something."

"No, I couldn't. You wouldn't even let me talk to you."

"That's true, isn't it?"

"Yes."

"And I am sorry." David d'Ersby slid over and put his arm around his brother's shoulder. "Really, David. I am sorry." They drank. He opened them each another bitter. "What's it like to be in love with a man?"

"I don't know," David Vere responded. "I've never been in love. Sex, lots of sex, never love. You ever been in love?"

"No. Me, too — sex, but no love."

"Do you want to see a picture of Molly?"

"All right."

David Vere handed him his cell phone. "Here."

"What's this?"

"Photos of Molly. Click there. She's pretty and nice. Very nice and very smart."

"Later. I'll look at them later. I'm too lazy to look at them now."

"I'm getting a little pissed."

"I'm getting a lot pissed." David opened another pair of pints. "What do you think? Should we give old Jane a call and ask her to join us?"

"Did you notice what big tits she has?" David Vere asked.

"I did, but is it OK for a brother to notice such things?"

"They'd be damned hard to miss, wouldn't they?"

"That is the truth. I'm going to call her."

Jane arrived and the three of them sat on the floor leaning against the empty bookcases. They went from bitters to wine, to gin. Jane asked him if he had noticed the book she found for him.

"What book?"

"Carl Bridenbaugh's *Jamestown*. You said to pick it up, if I saw it." She reached behind and took it from where it rested alone. It was used, but still with its yellow dust jacket.

"I'm indebted." David d'Ersby raised his wineglass to her. He didn't tell her that he had ordered a Kindle copy.

"I'll drink to that." David Vere downed his wine in one swig.

"Don't leave me out." Jane emptied her glass.

"I'll never win the Booker," David said.

"Why, you are a great writer," David Vere said. "Still, I've never read a word you have written, besides a note you once left for Telly Willmanhouse on the bulletin board."

"You read my private mail?"

"It was hanging on a fucking bulletin board, for Christ's sake."

Jane peered over her glass. "Why won't you win the Booker?"

"My stupid novel is too traditional, too realistic."

"The next one. You can write words mostly. Nothing too real, just words."

"Yes. Words," David Vere agreed. "I saw three ships come sailing in, come sailing in. I saw three ships come sailing in, in Jamestown, Gin in the morning. I really saw those ships, not really *those* ships, but replicas while I was in Jamestown."

"For fuck's sake." David d'Ersby poured himself a bit more.

"Dinky. Really tiny. Not much bigger than what you see punting on the River Cam."

"I knew they were small."

"But really small. There's a couple of pictures of them on my cell. I'll download those and Molly's on your laptop." He did.

They talked into the night, each with a blue pillow from the blue divan. They leaned and talked until there was no talk left. Then they faded, each passing out as the others hardly noticed.

David d'Ersby awoke with terrible cotton mouth. Jane was making tea and David Vere was mounded like a crawling snail, his back in the air. "Does he sleep like that?"

"That's his waking position. He's been doing it since he was a wee lad."

"Can I have coffee?" the snail mound asked.

"There is no coffee," Jane told him. "Tea and toast or a biscuit. That's it."

David brushed his teeth, washed his mouth, dressed in Gap clothes.

"Blue is not your colour," Jane said.

"How can you even see colour this morning?" the snail mound said. "God, I feel fuck awful." He poked around and rolled over on his back.

David was vain enough to care. "Why isn't it my colour?"

"Your dark eyes. Try browns, greys next time."

"You need beds." David Vere took a cup of tea from his sister. "Ugh, I hate Earl Grey."

"Do you want me to buy some beds, David?" Jane asked.

"Yes. But no four-poster sorts of things."

"I saw this wonderful campaign bed, glorious Napoleon sort of thing with a canopy."

"No canopies either."

"Something butch." David Vere sipped through his teeth. "These biscuits are stale."

David repacked his bag and gathered his computer. "I'm out of here."

Vere grabbed his hand. "Be careful. I mean that, David. Don't let Edward talk you into anything dangerous."

"Bye." He looked at his family and, despite the hangover, felt good. He took the tube to Heathrow, reading Bridenbaugh. A middle-aged woman plunked next to him. Her cheap scent was overpowering and did not blend well with his hangover. As he pushed his way off the train at Heathrow, he thought he saw the dwarf. It could have been only a short woman in a trench coat with greasy hair. Christ, he was getting paranoid. He waited for his plane in the blue area of Air France, conscious that blue was not his colour, and continued reading. This Opechancanough, if he did exist, as Bridenbaugh theorized, was one interesting character. On the plane he slipped open the photos David Vere had downloaded. Molly was OK. Brownish, rather nondescript hair. Weird outfit. She was pretty enough, but he preferred blondes, willowy Scandinavians. He checked out the ships. Because there were people standing near them, he could get a real sense of the scale. Damn, they were small. He opened the file on which he had been working: "Opechancanough…"

The Novel

PLACE OF THE PEOPLE

—*1607*—

Opechancanough lifted his hand, motioning to David, who released the arrow. The stag fell. A few gasps and the animal was dead. It was his first major kill; David could see the approval in the faces of the hunters. This would be food; there would be a hide. The red blood stained the snow. They made camp on the site. The circle of lean-tos was open to the fire in the center. He pulled a skin up over his head. His hair had been shaved on one side in the fashion of The People. His face bore the paint of the hunter.

In the morning, a scout returned. Opechancanough spoke with him and then raised his arms. "The Whiteman travels by boat into our place of hunting." He ordered a party ahead toward Apokant. The rest moved among the trees, invisible, silent. The wind came cold. David was torn between his loyalty to the Pamunkey and the English. This was The People's land; the English had no right. But those

English had rescued him from the hangman. A bird called. Opechancanough motioned the hunters to stop and made the same sound.

A bird replied; the scout who had first brought news of the Whiteman appeared, excited, but he spoke carefully. "The Whiteman returned to Apokant in the boat-without-a-below and tied it to a tree. Before ten, now only seven. The Werowance and two men had gone. We waited. A man came from the boat. The others yelled at him, but as he went into the brush, we grabbed him. The Whiteman on the boat let fire the thundersticks, but we did not run. We tied the Whiteman to a tree and told him to tell us where the Werowance had gone, but he would not. We cut off his toes; we cut off his fingers. With his hands without fingers he spoke that the Werowance had gone up river in a canoe. We took his scalp, set him afire and danced his death. The boat moved down river; our arrows fell to the water." David clenched his fists and closed his eyes. He knew the English at James Fort were dying of disease and were killed by ambushing Paspaheghes. He knew and accepted it. It happened beyond the wide expanse of forest. But now it was here, brutal, real and horrifying.

"We will find the Werowance," Opechancanough said. He motioned toward the river.

David stumbled behind him. David had seen the frenzied dance, the savagery, the victim symbolic, the ritual of death. But this had not been an enactment.

Opechancanough turned back to him. "It is different among the Spanish, Ninghekekughes. They tortured and burned men not for actions, but for what they thought."

"And the man afire? Of what crime was he guilty?"

"He came to take the land of the Pamunkey."

The Pamunkey hunters held a Chickahominy captive where a canoe had been pulled up on the bank. An Englishman lay dead, an arrow in his chest. David recognized him as one of Smith's men. Another lay face down, an arrow through his head. They would not be tied to trees and burned alive. David found a cloak and a writing tablet in the canoe. He felt guilty that he had such delight in finding the paper. He took both cloak and paper. "The bodies?"

"The eagle must feed as well." Opechancanough led and David followed through the brush but stopped; in the clearing the hunters had formed a half-moon about Captain John Smith, holding a Chickahominy in front as a shield. David retreated back into the brush. Smith raised his wheel lock and fired. Branches fell. A swamp was behind Smith. Opechcancanough spoke. "It is the man I hate. He is the most dangerous of the Whiteman. I can kill him."

"You must take him captive," David said. "He is an important man."

"Is he a werowance?" Aputonok asked.

"Yes." A werowance was not killed like a common warrior, by stealth, but would be executed before The People. David could at least buy Smith a little time.

"He is your friend?" Opechancanough asked.

"He is."

"He is no werowance," Opechancanough said.

"He is a werowance. One of the council."

Smith fired the wheel lock again and hit nothing. A barrage of arrows fell toward him and he inched back, still holding the Chickahominy. Moving back, as his foot slipped behind the other, he sank into the icy quagmire. He let the

Chickahominy loose and threw his wheel lock upon the dry ground. He continued sinking deeper into oozing mire. A hunter grabbed the weapon. One man, held by another, extended his arm to Smith and pulled him from the mire. Opechancanough stepped out. David shrank further back out of sight. Smith, with his usual bravado, showed no fear and in, a halting mixture of languages, expressed his importance. He took out a compass and displayed it, obviously hoping to impress the old man with his magic. David could not help but see the irony. Here was Smith on the verge of being killed, displaying the compass to a man he assumed to be childlike, while Opechancanough, who had crossed the Atlantic, feigned delight in the 'magic' needle. Smith began a pedantic rant on the sun, moon, stars and planets, on copulation as the main cause of men's failure to achieve greatness, and how the English were superior in all ways to the savages. It was a panegyric to Smith's philosophy. When Opechancanough seemingly could endure no more, he ordered the prisoner be marched toward the hunting camp at Rassawek. David remained in the rear. There was something almost silly about the parade—all those men guarding the swaggering, cocky Smith. But it was not silly. John Smith was destined to be executed. At Rassawek, the hunters danced that his crimes were great and he would be killed. Smith was taken to a *yehauken*, one of the few more permanent structures at Rassawek.

David sat in a makeshift hut with Opechancanough. "You look tired, Apachisto." The fire was low and it was dim and hazy in the small space.

"I am old, Ninghekekughes, and I have seen much and am afraid I shall live to see more that I would not wish to live to see." He sipped a bit of soup. "You never speak of the Whiteman who have brought you to the Land of The People."

"That was of the past, but the past has now come to me and I will speak. The captive is Captain John Smith. He is one of the five councilors who are in command. I think you know this."

"He is your friend?"

"Yes. He helped me escape from England when I was being accused."

"You owe him loyalty then. Will you speak falsely for him?"

"No, Apachisto—for to you, too, I owe my life."

"Why have the Whiteman come to the K'tchisipik?"

"You know why they have come. To plant a colony. To bring the Whiteman's God to The People. To find the great sea to the setting sun. To find gold and silver."

"I know all you speak is so. This is the Land of The People and we do not want the Whiteman here, nor his God who brings sin and guilt. There is no great sea to the setting sun, and if there is, it is beyond the walk of seasons. There is no gold or silver to take from us. There is only our land."

"I have gone to the mountains and have seen no great sea. I have seen no glitter of gold. This I know, but the men who come to James Fort do not know."

"And if your friend Smith were to go back to them and tell them?"

"I would speak truth. To save his life I could say he would, but he would not dare tell the others there was no gold, no sea leading to the riches of the East."

"But you would have him live. He speaks like a fool."

"It is his way."

"I cannot speak of this to the Powhatan; he cannot understand their ways. There is dissension among the werowances of Fort James. If Smith is such a fool, perhaps he can do The People more good alive, making trouble among the Whiteman. Now let us talk of Plato and you will read me more."

David took out the book, the red leather flaking. He translated into the language of The People. Opechancanough would stop David to argue a point. "We need a new book," David told him.

"We will make your friend Smith send you one."

"Plato is too ordered. Life is not ordered. We sit secure within ourselves, ordered and organized, but the exterior world over which we have no control overwhelms us. We are victims."

"We must look for new questions," Opechancanough said.

"We need a new book," David repeated.

The snow came during the night. David dreamed of red bloodstains trailed by a huge eagle carrying a man in its beak. He washed his face with snow. Opechancanough and his warriors had taken Smith. David mixed some charcoal powder, tree sap and fish oil for ink and made a point from a turkey quill. He filled the tablet pages with words—unconnected, meaningless words. And when the sun stood in the center of the sky, David walked the few miles to Orapaks. Nantaquaus knew of the White Werowance. The two alone went hunting for a raccoon or a deer. They found instead geese, turkeys and a boar. They skinned the boar and talked of killing a great bear, of spring, of going to the Bay for pearls, of the horses and going to the mountains in search of a huge cat that lived among the rocks.

"I have seen the cat," Nantaquaus said.

"And what is beyond the mountains?" David asked.

"I met a man who came from beyond the mountains. Beyond the river, the Father of All Waters, are the flat lands where herds of beasts trample the Earth. The meat feeds a *yehauken* for many suns. Someday, Ninghekekughes, you and I will go beyond the mountain and see the beasts."

David wrote all this on the writing paper and wondered if Christmas had come and gone. The air was frigid and islands of snow remained in shaded places. Two hunters came with squas leading the horses and the foal. Smith was to be taken to Werowocomoco and the animals had to be kept from sight. On the seventh day David was called to Werowocomoco. In the *yehauken* of the Powhatan old men sat stoically. David spoke. "Your son Nantaquaus stands in health. To him has come a daughter."

"The hope of The People is in its children. For as long as they are, we know the sun to follow will be there as well." He wore a formal face. "Ninghekekughes, who knows the ways, will the Whiteman, who now comes far into our land, destroy The People as the oracle and dreams have spoken?"

"He will try, Powhatan."

"How can we stop him?"

"Think as he thinks. Understand him. Learn his language. Learn from the papers which speak."

"We are all to become Opechancanough," the Powhatan said. "Ninghekekughes has come a long way. He must rest." David knew it was a polite dismissal and went from the compound to a *yehauken*. He tried to doze; he waited several hours before Opechancanough stooped through the door and sat down by the fire. There was no longer the necessity for ceremony between them. "Your friend Smith shall live. The Powhatan believes he can do more good letting the Whiteman see our strength and power."

David looked up at his ancient friend. "Why have I been brought here?" As much as he did not want to reveal that he was still alive, he did want to talk in English, especially to a friend. "Am I to place my head upon the stone for him?"

"No. He was kind to Pocahontas at the Fort. He is her friend."

David had no mirror but he knew how he must appear. His face was painted, his hair shaved on one side, decorated and falling long on the other, his body wrapped in skin. Yet, beneath the trappings of The People, his flesh, so bronzed in the hot seasons, was pale white. He approached the *yehauken* with trepidation. He went inside. Smith sat in the dim smoke by the fire, cloak wrapped around him. He didn't look up at first and, when he did, it was with indifference. Then he stared, his mouth, his eyes wide.

"I am no apparition, Captain Jack."

"Davey!" Smith got to his feet. "We thought you dead. You are a prisoner here?"

"No. I live among The People."

"You be a sight for sore eyes in that get-up."

David sat down by the fire, but the Captain moved about looking at him.

"I am treated well," David told him.

"You didn't fall overboard. You leapt, didn't you?"

"Yes."

"You'll be happy to know Wingfield's confined to the pinnace, a prisoner."

"It doesn't matter anymore. I can't be responsible for the crime of my parents."

"That's the spirit, Davey." Smith sat. "If you ain't a sight."

"You won't be killed," David said.

"I must admit it's been on my mind. I've survived the Turks, the Bulgars, Muscovites and Poles, but I did think the savages might be my end."

"How is Archer?"

"Rotten as a rat turd. I tell you, Davey, he has turned on me. He stirs trouble."

"And Captain Bart?"

"Dead, Davey. The bloody flux killed him. It was a loss that hit James Fort hard. Over half the Fort be dead. It is the stupidity of men that is their own destruction. They would starve for their laziness. They sit around waiting for Admiral Newport to sail in."

"Is he due back soon?"

"He was due afore, but you know the risks, the delays. Who's to say when he'll come, if he'll come. What's to become of me? Will I be held captive?"

"No. There will be a ceremony. You'll think they are going to bash your head in. They'll put it upon a stone and hold the clubs over you. Then Pocahontas—"

"The little girl."

"Yes. She is the Powhatan's daughter, I expect you know. She will throw herself on top of you and you will be declared her brother. It is the custom."

"Little Pocahontas. I've been teaching her English words for things."

"She already knows the English words for things."

Smith laughed. "Why, that sneaky little devil. She was a spy as much as Kendall. We hung him. He was in the pay of the Spanish King."

"I thought he was Robert Cecil's spy."

"I suspect Lord Robert thought so as well." Smith stopped talking for a moment and stared at David's hair. "And after they don't bash me brains out, what next?"

"You will be let go. To return to James Fort, I suspect."

"And you will go back with me?"

"No. I will come back, but not yet."

"I am certain the whole Vere business with Lord Henry's papers has been cleared up by now."

"I will come back in time." David stirred the fire. "Why were you so far up the Chickahominy?"

"So that's what they call this river. I was searching for the northwest passage, hoping the river's source was a lake that flowed to the other sea as well."

"Jack, it is an illusion. Beyond lies the mountains and I have been there. And beyond, I am told, are days and weeks of flat land through which flows a great river."

"The sea has to be there. Balboa found it."

"And there is no gold, no silver to be found here, either."

"I know, but you can't tell that to the men who have invested their money."

"This land belongs to The People. These are their hunting grounds."

"Archer took the law. He explains it. The land by right of discovery belongs to James Regnum to do with as he sees fit and each time we travel further up a river we extend that domain."

"Until The People's land is gone and they are destroyed."

"Reverend Hunt will bring them to God, and they will be no different than us."

"Reverend Hunt will bring them sin." He was interrupted; Papoo arrived. "It is time. If I don't see you again before you leave, remember it only looks like you are about to have your brains bashed out." He took the Captain's hand. "Someday not long off I will come to the Fort. I need go back to England."

"Is there anything else you need, Davey?"

"Writing paper. And another book. I am tired of Plato."

"The Plato was for you. Of course. That Opechancanough ain't no fool. I will send you Aristotle. Borrow it from Master Hunt."

"Aristotle would be a relief. Oh, Smith, is it Christmas yet?"

"Just come and gone. Happy Christmas, Davey."

"Happy Christmas, Captain John."

His head would be placed on the stone. The clubs would be raised and Pocahontas would intervene. David did not see Smith again before he left.

Opechancanough came to the *yehauken*. "Smith promises to send us guns."

"The English will send no guns."

"I know. Smith lies. I would that the Powhatan had bashed in his head."

"What was the real reason that he didn't?"

"A ship, a large English ship, sits at the entrance of the Bay."

"Smith didn't know this."

"No, but the Powhatan was afraid that, if he killed Smith, who he realizes is a werowance, those who come on the new ship would seek revenge."

David

CHARLES DE GAULLE Airport crawled with uniformed police holding Uzies. David sat silently in a taxi, absorbing Paris as he rode to a small hotel across the bridge from Notre Dame. In the red lobby the young woman smiled and spoke English; in return he smiled and spoke French, taking the message that a driver would arrive at ten in the morning. He squeezed into the tiny lift with a large woman under a large hat armed with a tiny yapping dog. His room was a garret with a loft and windows that looked out toward Notre Dame. The lower level in the room had a desk, but he decided not to write and left the hotel.

The water from the fountain at St. Michel had been coloured a raging pink, almost magenta, and he sat at a nearby café with a glass of *vin rouge* and watched the moving throngs. Parisians didn't simply kiss a lot of cheeks; lovers — on streets, in cafés, in taxis — seemed to prefer sticking their tongues in each other's mouths in long, enduring kisses. Evening came. Boats moved along the Seine, their sweeping flick of lights lighting the buildings on the Île de la Cité. He had more wine and *un plat de fromage et pâté*. It rained, but he moved under the awning and watched the parade of umbrellas. A tall blonde walked by and smiled from beneath a red umbrella. He was tempted to ask her to join him but was afraid of rejection. As the rain stopped, he wandered toward the Boulevard Saint-Germain in search of a restaurant, the exact name and location of which he did not remember. He stumbled on it with its checkered tablecloths just off the Rue du Fleurus. The waiter, a young man with a decidedly French nose, spiked black hair and a dangling earring, brushed David's hand whenever possible in fussing over the table, replacing an ashtray that was never used, or sweeping away crumbs that had never dropped. After the mixed fondue plate, rosemary potatoes and chocolate mousse, he went out on the street feeling admired, even if it was by another man. Up St. Michel, a herd of rollerbladers, helmeted and knee-padded, came swooping through, stopping traffic, singularly and in hand-holding couples, occasionally braking for the French kiss. Back in the hotel he did not write but stood in the dark looking out at the city of lights. He felt lonely, wishing he had been able to share the afternoon, the evening, perhaps to have stood French-kissing somewhere along the Boulevard. He would have liked to have chatted intimately with someone he loved about those passing by the table at the outdoor café near the pink fountain.

What was love like? This was a question for the city of lovers.

HE AWOKE BEFORE daylight, showered and dressed. A liveried driver, impeccably starched in a grey uniform, awaited
him. The car was a long, black Rolls Royce. A cup of tea
steamed in a cup rack. As the car pulled away, he asked
the driver in French how long the trip would be. In perfect
French the man responded that he did not speak French.
David posed the same question in English, adding that he
wanted to know their destination. In perfect English, the
man told him that he didn't speak English. He tried German and, after the same response, accepted the fact he was
to be told nothing. He caught a glimpse in the rear window of the Eiffel Tower, rising like a giant over the city.
His lunch had been packed: *pâté*, *baguette*, *fromage*, fresh
fruit, a bottle of Bordeaux. Still the driver said nothing.
They were on A6 but left it to detour around Lyon, then
on to A7. They passed through Orange and then continued south into Avignon. The old city loomed a giant fortress. A castle stuck its turret into the sky from far above.
Thick rock encircled the town in a powerful grip. The Pont
Saint-Bénezet stretched away from the wall and then, halfway across the Rhône, crumpled into the river. The driver
steered through a break in the wall and into the net of
twisting cobble. The street pressed out between medieval buildings as if never expecting cars and yet the traffic crowded the Rolls along the stones. The Place de
l'Horloge appeared and the street became even more pre-
carious as the Rolls wound its way up, nearly brushing the
encroaching sidewalk cafés. A wedding party spilled out of
the Hôtel de Ville in Provençal dress. The Place was alive
and everyone, except those on the dangerously intruding
motorcycles, seemed to be eating or drinking. Up from the

Hôtel de Ville, the grandeur of the Opera House imposed itself, dominating the Place from its proprietary position. The driver mastered his way around the carousel and at the corner stopped in front of the Mercure Pont d-Avignon.

"I have brought you here quite safely," he said in perfect English. "The hotel is expecting you. No doubt there will be a message for you at the desk." With that he carried in David's bag and computer, went back out to the Rolls and drove away.

Molly

THE CALL WAS from Syril Lovell. "Congratulations, Molly."

"For what?"

"For your engagement, of course. Inez told me."

"Well... there's no engagement. Not yet."

"That's a formality, isn't it? He's English, I understand. And your Masters?"

"At the end of May, hopefully."

"A June wedding will be wonderful. The Cathedral, certainly. And your uncle will be the celebrant. What will you wear? White, of course, but I know you and clothes."

"There is a painting of Pocahontas's wedding. The dress —"

"Perfect. Absolutely perfect for you. And all the women guests must be encouraged to wear lovely picture hats, even though you know I hate hats, but for a wedding they are essential. The Cathedral is all that dark stone. It needs some brightening. We are going to have to give some real thought to the flowers and colors. And the bridesmaids, what will we do with them?"

"I hadn't really thought…"

"The honeymoon, have you considered where?"

Molly was at loss. "Lincolnshire. He is British."

"No, you need something romantic. I have in mind Provence and the Riviera. Avignon. Now that's romantic. An absolutely excellent choice for a honeymoon."

"Money…"

"No worry about money. We will take care of the wedding and the honeymoon. You're my little girl and God only knows when Inez will marry, and God knows to what. A beautiful wedding is… well… I was cheated of that. Nuptials in a broken-down little church on the edge of nowhere in North Carolina. I am ashamed to mention the awful off-the-rack dress."

She should have told Syril the truth. But was it a possibility? If she put her mind to it. Destiny. Hermia's line, "If then true lovers have been ever crossed, it stand an edict to destiny."

Later at the college, her thoughts were on Syril Lovell's call when she heard Bill Davis stammer, "M-Molly! I was wondering. Well…" He was nice, relatively attractive, at least not totally *un*attractive, dressed in Levis rolled at his white socks, so '50s, with his hair greased back in a duck tail. "I have tickets for *Henry IV, Part 1* in D.C., the Shakespeare Theatre."

"For when?" she asked, but she knew she would not go, whatever the date.

"Next Wednesday night. It's got great reviews. And it's history, right?"

"Oh, I'd love to go, but I can't on Wednesday. Something on. Maybe some other time. I'm sorry." She was practically engaged, though it wasn't the first time she'd turned Bill down.

"Yeah. Maybe some other time." She sensed this was his final offer.

She drove up the James to the old house. She stood among the trees, leaves that never dried beneath her feet, falling and dying and rotting away, layer upon layer for centuries. She moved out from under the trees and took a stick, a bit of branch, and drew a circle about her. It was an unconscious act, but there was power in the circle, a mythic thing, Ovidian. She evoked the sun. A slight breeze filtered through her brown hair. There was the scent of the river in the air. There was such clarity in this place. She was Molly Dean Sharpe and she was extraordinary in an extraordinary place. The place where it began, a nation that stretched west, endlessly west in search of the passage to the east. But it wasn't just about the past and that Molly Dean Sharpe. It was about the now and this Molly Dean Sharpe. The story must not end. Never end.

She stepped from the circle and walked to the house. Was the journal a scholarly preoccupation or had she become obsessed by it? Preoccupation was an acceptable scholarly achievement. Obsession was dangerous. It was history, not life, not the present and without reality. Yet the journal was becoming something else and there was danger in that. She went in and continued the transcription. "As I write…"

The Diary

LINDFIELD

—*1608*—

As I write the wind howls out from the woods. The pond be frozen. The people of Lindfield go about saying witches are responsible for the terrible cold and rats which ate Minor Gavelsten's stored roots and the fire which burned Ditty Donnie's cottage. Night fires of witches been seen 'bout the woods. Justice of the Peace, Sir Joseph Joseph, choked on his phlegm, 'the work of witches for a fact.' At his funeral in the cold stone church, Roger sermonized for two hours about the evils of believing in witchcraft. Sir Joseph Joseph could not be put to ground as was too hard; he was kept frozen in his coffin in the church-yard. Farin was named Justice of the Peace, because he had been to Gray's and there was no one else, though he was much hated

in Lindfield. The Quarter Session convened
and Justice of the Peace Browne presided.
Though testimony was brought against Annakey Nobins that she had practiced wicked and
detestable acts upon the cattle of Seth Weadry
and these cows did bloat and die, and though
Nealy Henders did through sorcery and evil
means cause Boyles Clees to have pains in his
back and arms, and though Honor Truent's
supposed familiar, a striped cat with a missing
eye, was seen eating an unpeeled apple near
Mider Brooks when the fit came upon him,
Rector Prine did not bear the testimony of his
ministry against them and the new Justice did
not bind them over to the Grand Jury. Margaret Dowd rose in court and shouted that the
court was packed with devils and witches and
Master Browne ordered the constable take her
to the stocks.

Flodkin had the lightest of housekeeper's
touch. Her broom could sweep a room and
never pick up a speck of dirt. She hovered over
Davey and, in a lilt Celtic in its fancy, whispered that she would not let the fairy queen,
nor elfin king steal him off. I ordered her to
watch over the sweeping or the Rector would
have her thrashed, but in the end did do the
sweeping myself. The fish soup she made
for supper never saw the likes of a fish and
when Rector Prine demanded an explanation she told as how the fairy creature, an elf-

kin, which by name be Coolink, stole the fish, that he had come from the woods during the snow and turned the fish into gold, and Roger rapped his spoon against the table top and told her that was absolute rubbish, that the soup was no more than weed cabbage, inedible, and asked her if she could actually believe such a story and she told him no. And when asked why she made up such tales about a world that didn't exist, she told him it was better than the one what did.

February fell hard, like a rock. The swans flew away and the pond froze solid. Trees were brittle with ice. The men, the women, turned their backs to the stone church on the hill. Ash Wednesday came dead upon Lindfield and I huddled with David in the cold, hard pew and Lent entered in stillness, save the single voice of Rector Prine. We had gone on to Chelswood and Roger had gone out with the greyhounds, leaving Farin and me to the fire. When Roger returned to the house he told us that the Rollins boy, the one called Edmund, who lived in the forest with his poaching father, had been at the stables throwing rocks at the horses and that he had chased him. We took a quiet meal. Roger told us the Sussex Assize would be within the month and the Lindfield witches would be tried despite Farin not binding them over to the Grand Jury as the folk of Lindfield, the Curate and Mistress

Dowd would bring the matter to the Assize at Lewes. A cold draft stirred the fire.

Flodkin cowered in the doorway. She was bundled and shivered and when Farin poured her a cup of sack and pushed it toward her she backed away and, shaking, let it fall to the floor and screamed out to keep away. I took her off to a little anteroom and asked her what so frightened her. She said it was because Rector Prine and Justice Browne be witches. I told her stop the silliness and she told me that Edmund, the Rollins boy, was gathering bullies. And when I said there could be no plums in the middle of winter, she said there were and that they were dried and buried and frozen and Edmund were digging for them when he saw the greyhounds what belong to Master Browne and how he spotted a hare, but the dogs refused to run for it with him, so he took a switch and was going to strike the dogs to make 'em move when one of the dogs turned and stood before him as Rector Prine and the Rector offered him coin to keep quiet about what he had seen, but Edmund refused and told the Rector he be a witch. Then the Rector held a bridle over Edmund's head and turned him into a horse, and turned the other greyhound to horse as well, what he rode to the barn at Chelswood while leading Edmund by the straps. At the barn Edmund was turned into an owl and made to sit on the hay and there came to the barn Annakey Nobins, Ever Godlif, Mary Wendt and Lettice Wallon and they ate of meat and lumps of butter and por-ringers of milk what all flew about the barn. Flodkin told how they ate and did make ugly their faces and looked so fiendish that Edmund was all a fright and dirtied hisself. But while they was busy eating, he escaped and told all this to his pa.

I went to the drawing room and told the two men that I was certain they were to be charged as witches.

The snow melted, yet the wind blew cold. Roger's attempts to hold services at the church proved futile. We stayed to Chelswood and Roger left the congregation in the hands of the Curate. Bits of news drifted in from Lind-field. The Innis girl who was perhaps eleven, no more, developed a pronounced limp and whispered how at night she had been abducted by two fiends and taken to the barn at Chelswood and how the Rector and Mas-ter Justice with bridles held over their heads became white horses. She fled but was pur-sued by the familiar, a greyhound. She saw the white horses rise into the sky and demons were upon their backs and she ran and fell into a deep ditch. The greyhound stood above her barking, but in the moonlight the air crawled with ugly things; ten-year-old Wil-lie Tanx met a white horse who spoke and

told him to get upon his back and Willie did
and the horse rode to the barn at Chelswood
where Willie was beaten with bridle straps and
fed curds and turned into a greyhound and
his father displayed the welts from the beating; the Morlet twins, barely eight, told of riding greyhounds to the barn at Chelswood in
the black of night and there gathered with
Master Browne and Rector Prine were Lettice
Wallon and Annakey Nobins and Ever Godlif and Mary Wendt and Honor Truent and
they danced and drank beer and ate porridge
and all became horses and walked about in a
circle and demons with wings rode on their
backs, and the twins neither revealed, nor
seemed to know, how they got back to their
own beds. In Lindfield, it was told that Rector Prine opened the coffin of Sir Joseph and
squeezed the power from his testicles that it
might be his own. Farin explained that the
laws regarding witchcraft were in no way the
same as any other justice and that no confes-
sion was needed, no direct proof was required
and since the very concept of witchery defied
logic and the reality of nature, there was no
defense.

Rector Roger Prine of Lindfield Church
and Farin Browne of Chelswood Manor, gentleman, were arrested. Farin said I must go
to London at once and seek his cousin, Lord
Southampton. Leaving young David at Chels-

wood I rode the night, alone, not considering the possibility of attack by highwaymen. I reached London without incident and went at once to Holburn to Southampton House and was told the Earl was not there and the great door was shut on me. I went to the Mermaid in search of Ben Jonson and amid the reeking stale ale and raucous voices was told by someone that Jonson was abroad, had gone to Canterbury. It was then that young Prince Henry approached, addressing me as Molly Dean, and told me I looked exhausted. I broke down in tears; I *was* exhausted.

The words of our plight gushed from me. The Prince said quietly that there were no witches but in the minds of madmen. I told him it was to be brought before Judge Sir Lindred Groom-Douglas at Lewes. The Prince said he knew him all too well and that he was a butcher whom the King had unleashed on Sussex. A group of faces began to form about us. A man said that the Earl was to be found at Philpot Lane, at Smythe's house, and he had but saw him there. The Prince took me with him to St. James and said that he would have Southampton call upon us there.

The Prince and his entourage, along with the pageantry of Southampton, moved in train toward Lewes on the following morning, flanked by eighty-five guardsman of the Prince's house, another fifty of Southampton's, and assorted cooks, secretaries, pursers, preachers, tutors, serving men, sutlers, grooms and lawyers. The journey took three days. We crossed the Ouse, the chalk cliffs spread off from the vale of the river. The old Norman castle, or what remained of it, stood high on the bluff above the hilly city. The horses clopped up the steep streets of Lewes and the people lined the route for a glimpse of the Prince and the pageantry of his progress. At the top of the bluff near the castle keep, the bodies of Annakey Nobins, Ever Godlif, Mary Wendt, Lettice Wallon and Honor Truent had been left to swing on the gallows.

There were only two prisoners in the jail. Roger sat on the floor of the putrid smelling cell. Farin was just inside the door as we entered. I said to him I had much worried we would come too late. He told me I had for Roger but that his own trial was on the morrow. The Earl who entered behind me said there would be no trial. Roger turned about. I broke into tears. They had cut off Roger Prine's ear.

In the progress of the Prince we returned with the Earl to Southampton House. The hangings, red velvet, were apart but slightly, only a crack of light escaped from a window in need of washing. The dark oak chairs were massive. Roger sat in one, silent. He seldom spoke since Lewes. He sat staring at the wall, like a portrait on wood I had once seen of a medieval scholar, the hat covering where his ear should have been. Farin avoided the red room. He mostly went out since we had come to Southampton House from Lewes. I moved to the window and looked up into the drab sky. The sun seemed lost forever in a cloud of coal smoke. I told Roger I was going to see to Davey, but he did not respond.

I breathed lighter as I left the melancholic space. The bustle below drifted in voices up the great staircase; shadows, shapes criss-crossed as if by a loom weaving a pattern. I knelt down next to the low, small bed. David stirred and I touched his hand. What was to become of him? For Roger, there would be no position in the offing, and even if there were, Roger was in no state to preach. Farin seemed not concerned, spending his days and evenings at The Mermaid in esoteric conver-sation. I could not simply take David and go live with the Alleyns; I was under law bound to Roger Prine, his chattel.

The Countess arrived from Titchfield—her bed, her train, her son, her gowns. Liver-ied servants moved about the house like wren rabbits. I was summoned to her. The small drawing room was blue—the walls, the furni-ture, the hangings. The Countess, in contrast, stood in a gown of white. She was not laden with jewelry except for her long narrow fingers which were piled with rings. I perceived a simple beauty, blond hair pulled back from an oval face, eyes blue like the room and warm. She introduced herself as Elizabeth Wriothesley. She sat and a black and white cat, tough looking like it had crawled the streets of London, leapt into her lap. She bid me sit. She told me I was younger than she had expected and pretty and asked if I were getting on. I told her how indebted we were to her and his Lordship for their kindness in having us. She explained how dear Farin was to them. She said we be at mercy of monarchs and how in the Queen's later days, her poor Henry never knew from one day to the next whether his head was to be removed. She said they were horrible years and when Essex was killed she was certain it was over and that she cried herself to sleep near every night. She petted the cat and said he was their reminder. He had adopted his Lordship in the Tower. She said the rats were notorious, but Cat kept them at bay.

She said she wished to talk with me because she was to entertain some of those sailing to Virginia and that it would be a chance for me to get acquainted with those who would be my traveling companions on the long voyage. I am sure my face revealed how perplexed I was and I responded with the question, "To Virginia?" She said she assumed

I had been told. I said I had not. She could not imagine what my husband must be thinking and informed me we were to sail come June with the Flotilla. I explained about Rector Prine's state and that he barely spoke. She said then that Farin should have told me. She took my hand in her ringed fingers. She said that it had seemed to her Henry and the Prince the logical solution. Divines were needed in the Plantation. Her gown was spotted with cat's hair. She said that it would be a difficult voyage and not without its dangers.

In the morning I took David into the garden. Spring flowers lined gravel walkways. A boxwood maze stood near the far end. The cool gray sky hung above and the shadows cast by statuary were hardly discernible. David gripped my hand and pulled me along the walk. A raven perched on the head of Antigone, who stood forlorn, her stone white gown streaked with coal dust. I sat on a marble bench near her and David played with the gravel stones in the walk. I watched Farin come out through center doors to the garden. His gait was brisk and he threw his cloak back across his shoulder. As he reached us, he picked up David and tossed him the air. The child laughed and hugged him. He said he was sorry, that he meant to tell me of Jamestown. I told him it didn't matter; it was not as if we had a choice. He sat on the marble bench, put David on his lap and pretended to bite the child's ear. I knew I looked horrified and he stopped, realizing what he was doing.

Farin said that he was shallow and horrid, but that he couldn't stand looking at Roger without his ear. He slumped down on the bench and was silent. There were only the sounds of the morning birds and the child's noise as he played with the stones. We walked. Farin carried the boy and talked of Virginia and said that the Flotilla would be the largest colonizing venture yet attempted, some eight or nine ships, near some six hundred people. I stopped, bent and sniffed a red flower. It had no smell and I asked what it was. A tulip, Farin told me, adding that the Dutch were so tidy, they don't even allow their flowers to smell. He said that blood as red as the tulips covered the lowlands and all in the name of God. He said to hear Gates and the others at Smythe's talk, any atrocity in the name of God be acceptable. He told as to how he had been at Smythe's, preparing to endure Virginia, as he put it, the elements and the savages. He said Mr. Hariot had been teaching him the language and a good deal about the country as well. He said one John Rolfe, while a handsome man, had no interest in the poets or philosophy. He believed there was no gold and sought to find some marketable commodity in Virginia though he had no idea what. Rolfe,

Farin said, also had a massive passion for ladies and was said to quite wear his mistress out. Farin told me there in the garden that he would never marry and that he had made David his heir, and that Chelswood was his.

The preparation for Lady Elizabeth's entertainment kept Southampton House in a turmoil. I sat with David and Roger and Farin in the red room. Roger proclaimed that God had forsaken him, lashing out with his hands. It was so seldom Roger spoke, that I was taken aback. He said he could not preach to the believer, let alone the heathen, when he could not believe his own words. Farin told him that religion was mostly self-deception anyway, and announced he was going out and left. Roger said that Farin found him loathsome. I told him it was not so, but knew that to be a lie. He took off the cap, exposing his lopped off ear. I cringed, but did not look away. He said we could not go to Virginia and then spoke no more.

The day of the entertainment was hot. The mirrors of Southampton hall multiplied the mass of bodies that pressed through the huge room and out into the garden. Farin led me to a couple and stopped. The man smiled at me. He was handsome, young. The young woman at his side looked pale, sickly. Farin introduced John Rolfe and his bride. Rolfe was perhaps in his late twenties, his brown hair streaked with blond, his nose pugged; his grey eyes danced as he spoke. Mistress Rolfe was anemic, thin, a little creature who looked to faint at any moment. She had wispy blond hair.

It was determined that we had been assigned to the *Blessing*, the Rolfes to the *Sea Venture*. Rolfe, who spoke with a pronounced Norfolk accent, called for a pipe and it was lit for him by a liveried young man with red hair the colour of dead weeds. Rolfe informed me that it was good for the heart, refreshed the brain, helped the sight when let into the round balls of the eyes, cleansed the stomach and cured all sort of rheums. I was glad I had no rheums in need of curing for I found the smoke disturbing. Rolfe left us and his bride remarked that she didn't wish to go to Virginia, but that her husband said it was God's will and that Mr. Rolfe abided always under the yoke of God. She looked to faint and I asked if she was all right, to which she blushed and replied it was the often copulation to which she as a bride had not yet become accustomed.

I led Mistress Rolfe to the garden and found a place where she might sit. The Stracheys walked by, introducing themselves. The husband said he was bound to Virginia without his 'dear wife' as he was certain that it was not as yet a fit place for women. Mistress Rolfe indicated that she tended to vomit at the sight of a boat. A Captain Archer said that there was a great danger from the Indians, who are vicious creatures and refused food to the settlers though they would starve. He said there had been misrule by men like John Smith and Edward Wingfield, but now that was to be corrected with a strong governing body and a great number of colonists. He talked of safety in numbers. Because of the mention of Wingfield I was tempted to ask Captain Archer if he had known David, but I did not.

Farin said that there were some he wanted me to see. I asked whom we were to meet and he said not to meet but to see. As we moved into the hall, he pointed out two women, one to either side of another young woman. The two bore a striking resemblance to each other, and more they resembled David. The hair. The same small eyes. Farin explained that the one to the right was Elizabeth Stanley, Countess of Derby and the other her sister Bridget, Lady Norris. When I asked if they were Berties, I was told no, but the daughters of Edward de Vere, the late Earl of Oxford.

Beneath the portrait of Essex, Farin introduced me to a young woman, Temperance Flowerdew, who would be sailing to Virginia on the *Falcon*. She told me she was not to be accompanied by her parents but by her brother Stanley and although she didn't want to go was told by her father that it would be her only chance of finding a suitable husband. Temperance had pouting lips and a wart on her right nostril and a whiny voice. I thought perhaps her father be right. Sir Edwin Sandys touched his pointed beard and nodded to me. I had not seen him since the night I had been brought to this house for interrogation. A silence fell over the mirrored hall and heads turned. Standing in an entrance were Sir Francis and Lady Bacon. Young Alice looked exceedingly proper. It was a long wait as everyone stood. Then Lady Southampton went across the long room, followed by her Lord husband to greet the Bacons. I looked up at the portrait of Essex, who had caused such contention between Southampton and Sir Francis. His expression hadn't changed.

I was pinched at the waist and turned half expecting to see Lord de La Warr. It was Alice Bacon. She kissed my cheek and I said I was much surprised to see her here. She said that Francis was committed to Virginia Plantation and to the people who would be here and so asked cousin Robert to tell Elizabeth an invitation would be most welcome. Alice said she thought Francis felt left out. Cecilia West, spotting Alice, came scurrying across the room, nearly tripping on her gown as she pushed through the throng. Fawning over

Alice, she asked whatever pray was she doing in this house, turned to me and recognized me as her dearest Molly. And giggled. She wished she were going with us, for, she said, she came from a family of great adventurers and, being the Governor's lady, would have a great palace built and that she and myself could play cards from morn to midnight and in our spare time kill savages. But alas she and her Governor husband were not to go this soon. Cecilia pointed out a one-armed man, Captain Newport, and said she had just heard the most delightful gossip for when Thomas Smythe and Captain Newport stepped out into the little drawing room to have a private chat they came upon a Mr. Rolfe pounding away at his new mistress and Cecilia went into a torrent of giggles and then wondered if we had heard that Sir Walter Cope's butler did drop dead without no sickness. She told me that I must see that Captain Newport showed me every comfort on the voyage because it was long and tedious. I informed her we were not to be on the *Sea Venture* but another ship. She said that was nonsense and that she would not hear of it and that we must be on the *Sea Venture* and that Sir Thomas Gates was to be aboard as he was deputy governor, going in her Lord's place. She would remind them that I was her dearest friend. Cecilia West intermittently 'I pray'ed, giggled and rattled on about her abiding friendship with me and scattered tibits of gossip about the King's favourite until she was swooped away by Lady Somers and Mistress Gates.

On May 15 the fleet readied to sail at Woolwich. To Farin's delight, we were informed that at the Baron de La Warr's request, we were to be on the *Sea Venture*. Lord and Lady de La Warr promenaded and a preacher, a determined Puritan, intoned a lengthy prayer. Roger stood, melancholy written on his face. Alice Bacon brought me the gift of a great hound named Rufus Rex. Timbers creaked; the anchor was hoisted. Sailors in striped shirts leapt above and the sails rode rings up the masts. The *Sea Venture* slipped into the current of the Thames. I stood at the rail with Rufus Rex on one side and David in hand on the other. The frail Mistress Rolfe stood nearby. I could see the crowd gathered at the rails of the *Falcon* as its sails puffed out like bed linen hanging to air. I caught a glimpse of Temperance Flowerdew at the rail.

The River Thames was muddy dark and floated with refuse. Sir George Somers wore no hat and his white hair blew in the wind as he approached me at the rail. He rubbed the dog's head and asked if my husband were about. I told him that he remained below and was unwell. He told me that there was a matter of some delicacy that needed to be taken up with him. He said that they had a chaplain on aboard, Master Buck, and it had been expected that Rector Prine would be on the *Blessing*. He said he hoped that I might see his difficulty in that there was no duty for two chaplains. I told him Master Prine was suffering great emotional stress and that ministry at the present was extremely difficult for him and that he would be most pleased if he were not called upon to serve at the present. Sir George was most relieved to see the situation resolved. He asked politely about my son and bowed as he left.

Darkness fell and a lantern cast deep shadows and the timbers creaked with every motion of the ship. Bad winds, strong southwesterly gusts, kept the entire Flotilla waiting off Falmouth, but the winds shifted and the fleet moved into the vast sea. The coast of England disappeared. It was such a paradox. They were cramped one hundred and fifty below deck in stinking quarters with hardly room to breathe and above the sea stretched in emptiness toward the end of the Earth. The Rolfes, beneath their wrapped cloaks and a coverlet, groaned and grunted like caged bears. The voyage was long. The cramped space below seemed to shrink in proportion to the distance traveled. Rats gnawed in the darkness. The lice were communal. The grain was moldy and saturated with worms. The beer became rotten, undrinkable. There was hardly room to lie down. Mistress Rolfe grew frailer, but her belly larger. Roger, in the dark hole of the ship, found God, but it brought him no comfort. He claimed to great sin, and shrunk from Farin's attempts to comfort him. The moments of escape above deck were my best. The billowing sails of the other ships captured the wind. Flying fish were pointed out by Captain Yeardly, a young man who wore his pimples pleasantly, his eyes wide, capturing the world. Though his posture was military, for he was Captain of the Guard, there was a disarming ease in his manner. Roger had taken to not wearing his cap and Farin shrank from the sight of the missing ear. Roger was also losing his hair.

On the eve of St. James's Day, I had left David sleeping below and was standing on deck when a dead calm fell. There was no wind, the sails drooped empty. The sea ceased to move. There was silence, anticipatory and eerie, and the sailors were like statues, faces to the sky. It was as if the Earth stood still. A warm rain fell and I stood, letting the water cleanse the filth from my body. I was told by Master Strachey that I best get below as a storm was brewing, but I stood letting the rain wash me. The wind rose in a sudden torrent and the dark sky, like death, became a deep black. Sharp cracks of lightning punctuated the darkness. The cries of the sailors tore the air and the ship was tossed about by the force of turbulent waves. I was thrown to the deck and helped up by Captain Yeardly, who aided me down the ladder to the blackness below.

The roar of the howling wind was deafening. I clung to the bulkhead, holding David, and with each lurch of the ship I sensed it tearing apart. For hours the storm raged. The lanterns had gone out. There were sobs, but no screams of terror. Sailors above cried out, their voices barely audible above the crashing winds. Water dripped down from the deck. The caulking below had given way and water was filling the hold. Men with torches moved through the darkness into the hold. Each terrible thrust of the ship seemed greater than the one preceding it, each roll tilting the ship closer to the sea. I clutched David to me, expecting at any moment we would be engulfed into the vast ocean.

Men were called to pump and bail as the water below began to rise within the leaking vessel. I left David and the hound whimpering in the care of Mistress Rolfe and went on deck with the other women; we were lashed together and manned bucket brigades. Huge waves swept the deck. Even looking into the terrible black sky and hearing the screams of the wind seemed less horrible than being

cramped below in the darkness. The pumping, the bailing, the activity to maintain life
were like last rites, done not with hope, but in
despair to occupy the moments before death.
I did not mind for myself. Death was but the
end of the struggle. Benjamin Joseph and
David d'Ersby had left me empty, but my son
had not been given even the opportunity to
struggle.

There was nothing but black clouds in the
sky, save the lightning bolts, no direction to
guide them and I knew the mariners had no
inkling how far off course we had been swept.
The sails were gone, only the main mast stood.
An enormous wave swept the ship tearing
a helmsman from his post and the whipstaff
tore in both directions as if trying to beat him
to death before he could again grab the helm.
Newport stood, one arm, a visible silhouette
against the sky.

The storm raged for two days and deep
into the second night the strange light
appeared, fire that danced above on the mast,
upon the shrouds, along the rail, tiny balls of
fire appearing here and disappearing there.
Rolfe told his wife that God was lighting their
way home and she sobbed. Captain Yeardly
said it was the *corpo sancto*; he added the
Spanish called it St. Elmo's fire. The storm
had begun on a Tuesday eve. Friday morning came; the dancing fire had disappeared.

The ship tossed as if in exhaustion and sank deeper into the water as those at the pumps could no longer keep up with the water pouring through the cracks. Sir George Somers led the men from below up on the deck. The hatches were closed. The ship was thrown about but it was as if they had grown accustomed to it. I was handed a cup of aqua vitae. Farin slumped beside me, his cup in his hand. It was like final communion. David slept in my lap and the dog panted. Roger appeared, bent like an old man. Struggling, he climbed the mast. I watched horrified, not knowing, yet knowing. Something terrible was happening. There was a lapse in the storm, a momentary calm, not stillness, but the wind was less virulent. Roger reached the top of the mast, opened his arms and wrapped them around the cross piece. He hung there. No one moved, did anything but stare at the strange sight. Roger's voice, though weakened by the wind, was audible and he yelled out that he would not return to this land of darkness without order, where even the light is darkness.

There was a long terrible silence. The wind rested, the sea for the moment less terrible. Then a horrendous bolt of lightning, sharp and terrifying, hit the mast and Roger screamed out as his burning body froze against the mast. Thunder cracked. The ship rose high out of the water, carried on a huge wave.

The mast was torn free and fell with the roll of the ship and was lost to the sea.

I thought of the young man in the carriage on the road to Lindfield who had offered me marriage. Farin knelt down beside me and cried.

Molly

RICHMOND

—the present—

MOLLY CALLED THE graduate history secretary. "I'm sick," she said. "Tell Dr. Broder, I'm sick." She gave no further information and hung up. She had not cut a seminar since entering graduate school. But it was imperative now that she get to Richmond in time. She slammed the screen door and tore away from the cottage in her little purple car. She hoped she had remembered to lock the door. It was too late to worry about it. She raced north away from Jamestown. Molly Dean Prine's pain had become her own. It was not the first time she had read those passages, but now as she had transcribed the Xeroxed scrawl, the words tore at her. And it was more than mental anguish; her fingers were knotted as she finished typing. Her head ached. Jesus! Where did that car come from? She was nearly clobbered. Calm down, Molly. She had to have the real journal. Hold it. She sped through the Fan into downtown and pulled into the bank parking lot.

Her head pounded as she clutched the rolled journal to her breast, but it gave her no release from the pain. She wanted to cry, to break down in tears. But not here. Not in the bank. She took the rolled journal and went to her car. She rested it in her lap and drove up into the cemetery. Somewhere Tyler was buried and Jefferson Davis; the tall obelisk, the memorial to the Confederates reached toward the sky. She thought Monroe was buried here as well, but couldn't remember. She drove along the winding road and up. It didn't matter where Monroe was buried. Tears were beginning to cloud her eyes. She parked. Clutching the journal, she staggered and then slumped down upon the earth of graves. She let the emotion pour out of her in a torrent, gasping for breath, making no attempt to control herself. Below, the James pounded loudly over the rocks.

And then slowly the crying ceased. She was being consumed by Molly Dean. She knew that could destroy her. She should give it up, give up the journal. She clutched it to her. That was stupid. Idiotic. She could not forsake Molly Dean. Not at this point. Not until the story ended. Plus there was the practicality of finishing her graduate thesis. She held the journal, closed her eyes, and leaned against a gravestone. She promised herself she would not let the past possess her, own her. She would be her own Molly Dean Sharpe, not the ghost of history. She would be rational. She leaned forward and buried her face in her arms. She knew her resolve was not as strong as her intent, but she would try.

She sensed someone's presence. A shadow. Someone stood there. She opened her eyes. She was looking at boots, polished black high boots. She looked up to see the large figure of a Confederate soldier.

"Are you all right, miss?" His voice was deep with a pronounced southern accent that was almost too heavy for Virginia.

"Yes."

She sat there looking up at him. "My face must be a mess."

"No. You have a beautiful face."

More silence. This time he broke it. "Will you have coffee with me?"

Molly saw no reason why she should, but no reason why she shouldn't. "Yes."

"Good."

"Where?"

"Anywhere."

"Tom's," she suggested.

"Not Tom's," he said.

"Careytown, someplace?"

"Yes."

Molly got up. "That's my car over there. And yours?"

"I walked," he said.

They drove in near silence. At some point he said that there was to be an execution that night at the prison, but Molly had not known how to respond to that and so had said nothing. He was a handsome man with blond, slightly curly hair that fell down over his forehead. "There's a place. Over there on the corner."

"Have you been there before?"

"No," he replied as she found a parking space.

The waiter handed them menus. "Would you like water?"

"Please," Molly said, "and just tea."

"You wouldn't like something to eat?" the Confederate soldier asked.

"No. I'm too fat as it is."

"You're not fat." He did not look up at the waiter. "And I will have coffee."

The waiter sauntered off.

"I'm Molly," she said.

"Alexander. Alex."

"Molly Sharpe."

"Alex Carter."

"Well, that's a fine Virginia name. Any relation?"

"Yes, to the Carters, the Lees, all of them."

The waiter brought a cup of coffee and a pot of hot water and cup for Molly and then offered a box of teas from which to select. She chose the Earl Grey and he went away.

"Are you a docent?"

"No. I simply dress this way. Do you find it weird?"

"No. Look how I am dressed." He smiled. He had a nice smile.

Molly's eyes moved about the room. "Are you gay?" she asked.

"NO." He was emphatic.

"I'm sorry. It's just that I think this is a gay establishment."

He looked around. Two men held hands at a table on the far side. He laughed. It was a nice laugh. "I had no idea. I'm a bit homophobic. Guys occasionally come on to me at the gym where I work out."

"You work out?"

"Too much, probably. It becomes addictive. And you?"

"No time, but probably wouldn't anyway."

"Your job keeps you busy?"

"Grad school. William and Mary. What kind of work do you do?"

"None. Went to the Citadel a few years back. My parents were killed the day after I graduated. I haven't really gotten over it."

Molly sipped her tea. There was pain in his face, in the eyes. "You were close to them."

"No. And that ironically seems to make it more difficult. I was always carted away to some military school or another. My father was a general. They lived in Japan and around this country, but I never saw any of it. I was always in some military boarding school."

Molly sat silent for a moment and then she looked at Alex. "Were they killed in an accident?"

"No, brutally murdered. They flew in, watched me graduate. I begged them to stay overnight and celebrate with me, but they wouldn't and flew immediately back to Richmond. The next evening a deranged Vietnam vet came to the house and while Modine, the housekeeper, stood screaming hysterically, he shot both my mother and father. And your parents?"

"Were killed in a car accident when I was an infant."

"We're both orphans."

They sat silently for a while and then Alex paid the bill and they went out into the sunlight. "Can I drop you somewhere?" Molly asked.

"If you wouldn't mind. I just live over on Monument."

They drove westerly along Boulevard. "Did they get the man who killed your parents?"

"Yes. He's to be executed."

"Tonight?"

"No. That's someone different."

The house was an immense brick structure. "This one?" she asked.

"Yes."

"Impressive."

"Would you like to see inside?"

"I should probably be on my way."

"It's safe. I'm a little weird but not a loony, and there's a housekeeper."

Molly decided to go in. The place was old. Everything was clean, but the rugs and upholstered furniture were threadbare and the house itself seemed to cry out for repair. They sat in a large living room that had fireplaces at either end. The paintings and photographs in the room were all mid-nineteenth century and most were military figures of the Confederacy. Molly was not comfortable in the room and sat perched on the edge of a period divan. A large black woman appeared at the doorway. She wore the uniform of a maid and said nothing.

"Modine, this is Miss Sharpe."

"Can I get y'all anything?"

"Nothing for me," Molly said.

"We're fine," Alex told her and the woman disappeared.

"Modine? This is the room in which your parents were killed?"

"Yes. I didn't mean to make you uncomfortable. I just wanted to be with you. I think you are quite the most beautiful woman I have ever seen."

"You obviously have eye problems, but I am flattered. This room contains much history other than the most sensational aspect, I suspect. As must the house."

"Yes. Robert E. Lee was often a guest in the room. As was Jeff Davis. My great, great, great, great grandfather was governor of Virginia for a while during the War Between the States. Would you like to see the rest of the house?"

And so they toured the house. Paint peeled and turnings were missing in banisters and everywhere threadbare rugs covered darkened hardwood floors. "This is my room," he said and opened the door to a room filled with Confederate war memorabilia: swords, guns, uniforms, photos, framed documents, maps, medals, and military paraphernalia adorned the walls. Boots were rowed along one baseboard and a table was filled with a miniature battlefield of tiny soldiers and cannons. "I know the war. You are interested in history, am I right?"

"But my field is earlier," Molly told him. "Jamestown and the founding of Virginia."

"I would like to kiss you." He moved toward her.

"I am somewhat committed," she told him.

"I would still like to kiss you."

She did not make any move to reject his hands as he took her shoulders into a gentle grip and she turned her face up to accept his kiss. His tongue slid into her mouth in a long, and for Molly, exciting kiss. He wrapped his strong arms about her and she was not afraid, yet knew she ought to be. He could crush her, this strange powerful man in the Confederate uniform. She felt his erection against her thigh.

He released her.

He took off the grey coat and slipped the blousy period shirt off over his head. His chest exhibited the gym work in well-defined pecs and bulging biceps.

"I'm not going to have sex with you," she told him.

"I did not expect you would." He put on a coarse muslin shirt. It, too, was period, but not necessarily military. He smiled at her. "Though I wouldn't have objected had you been willing."

"You have quite an amazing body."

"Perhaps on another occasion I may be allowed to show you the rest of it."

"I'm committed, remember."

"Kind of committed. Here's my card in case you become less committed."

She took the card and he saw her to her car. "Call me," he said.

The housekeeper, Modine, stood in the doorway watching Alex, Molly or both of them. Her look was one of disapproval.

Molly examined the card. "Alexander Lee Carter, Captain, Army of the Confederate States of America." Perhaps he was completely mad. Perhaps she was as well.

It was too late to redeposit the rolls of the journal back in the safety deposit box. She drove home, more relaxed. She even had a beer and continued transcribing: "We waited for death…"

The Diary

We waited for death. We filled the deck and
drank aqua vitae and listened to the voice
of Master Buck entomb the ship and those
aboard in a heavy shroud of doom. The rain
fell, the lightning still tore the sky, the thunder rolled, but the raging storm seemed
tired as well. The droning voice of the minister reminded all of their sins and the ship
rolled heavy into the waves, its belly filling
with water. I clung to David. Farin's arm was
about me and the big hound lay silent at my
feet. Mistress Rolfe sobbed. John Rolfe managed somehow to keep his pipe lit. William
Strachey wrote in a soggy diary. The Deputy
Governor stood on the poop deck with Captain Newport, and Sir George Somers clung
to a rail alone in the bow. There was not a

sign of any of the vessels of the fleet in sight. Young Captain Yeardly stood, the water running from his hair; erect and immobile, like a toy soldier left out in the rain.

I looked about at the faces, resigned, without panic or terror. Some names I knew, some were only faces. Peter Martin, who had talked with Farin and John Rolfe of all things botanical he expected to explore in Virginia, stood looking more disappointed than with fear of death. Men's faces were worn from the pumping and lack of sleep. Master James Swift stood elegantly in gentleman's attire, posed as if his doublet was not torn, nor the soggy fabric clinging to his skin. Richard Frobisher, the shipwright, was examining the broken remains of the mast, as if inspecting it for repair. Much of his cargo was lost to the sea. I looked about at my companions, at the end. They was gentlemen and servants, wives, sailors, soldiers, tradesmen, craftsmen, men of learning, men who could not read, men of wealth, poor men who were aboard with hopes of fortune—now but wet men and a scattering of women, and we were all going to die together. The voice of the minister droned o'er us and I much recalled Chelmswood and laughter and the house in the shadow of St. Olave's. I touched the wet hair of my babe, remembering the cold snowy day when the

Globe be closed, and I remembered David. I would that I might take comfort in God in heaven, that I should set eyes to David again, show him his son. But I had given God away on the death of Benjamin Joseph. The timbers of the ship creaked and groaned. Rain subsided. Some daylight appeared 'neath the clouds to edge the horizon. But there be no hope, for the ship beneath us was breaking open with sea water. The drone of the preacher ceased. The thunder quieted. There was no crying, only a horrid silence and then Sir George Somers yelled out from the bow that there was land, land to the starboard.

It was no illusion.

The hatches were opened. Bailing began again. Trees were visible along the horizon. Men pumped; the *Sea Venture* stayed afloat. I heard William Strachey tell someone that the Captain said it may well be Devil's Islands, the place the Spanish called the Bermudas. The Captain maneuvered the crippled ship. The Boatswain called soundings. We were within three-quarters mile of land when the ship bottom was torn open by the reefs. Small boats were lowered, and in many trips all 150 men, women, children and a dog were brought to land. I sank into pink sand, digging my fingers into loose earth, letting it trickle down. I heard snorting, saw pigs, forty, maybe fifty.

Rufus Rex tore aft them. There would be pork to eat. Farin held David as we moved up the beach into grasses. The soil be red and there be thickets and cedars and berries weighting branches. Sun warmed my soaked body. I sat down on a rock and cried.

Molly

JAMESTOWN

—the present—

MOLLY STOPPED AT this point in her transcription. She looked back at her typed copy and at the original manuscript. The name flew out at her. Strachey—it was Strachey. She flung herself into the living room. Books were piled. She found the little red volume on the floor near the coffee table beneath a week-old *New York Times*. *The True Repertory of the Wrack and Redemption of Sir Thomas Gates*. There was the germ of a thesis here. William Strachey and Molly Dean Prine's report of the journey of the *Sea Venture*. How similar it was. Were there differences? None that she noticed. Almost identical reporting. The same duplication of names in almost the same order. Wait! Why hadn't she seen it? There was a definitive omission. Where were Farin Browne, Molly Dean Prine, little David and Roger Prine in Strachey's account? Why were these people apparently known to Strachey completely

415

ignored? Roger's death would have been a sensational event, not something Strachey would have failed to report. Farin was kin to Southampton and Molly was well known to him. Where were they?

She read all the pages of Strachey's report again, a report that had been well circulated in Jacobean London, enough that Shakespeare used it to form the basis of *The Tempest*. But from the onset of the journey, through the time on the island, there was no mention of Farin or the Prines. She looked through the photocopy of Sylvester Jourdain's *A Discovery of the Bermudas, Otherwise Called the Isle of Devils* and the Virginia Company's account in *The True Declaration of the Estate of the Colony in Virginia*. She spent the next hours pouring through all her early accounts of Jamestown, through texts, through indexes. She was struck by the fact that neither Farin Browne, nor Molly Dean Sharpe were ever listed, nor referred to, never indicated on rolls or manifests, no documentation whatsoever.

She had become so preoccupied by the journal she had failed to perform the most obvious bit of scholarship. It was a mistake that would be a problem now as she sought, beyond the transcription, to find a thesis for her study. Foucault immediately came to mind. He had written somewhere on history that it was fruitful in a certain way to describe that-which-is by making it appear as something that might-not-be, or that might-not-be as-it-is and that history could be unmade as long as we know how it was that it was made.

She went out into the dark, carrying the copied journal. She sat on a chair in the corner of the back porch and listened to the James. Somewhere a motorcycle revved its engine and then roared into the night and then there was only the lap of water. That damn *shu-shu-gah* probably stood on one leg at the edge of the river laughing at her. She took a handmade candle from a bag on the table, put it into the pewter holder and lit it. She opened the journal to where she left off and stared at the words in the candlelight. But she couldn't read.

It was useless. She blew out the candle, closed the journal, sat in the dark and listened to the river. The question of the authenticity of the journal gnawed at her. How could it not be real, the writing of Molly Dean of seventeenth-century London, Sussex and Jamestown? There was no motivation for fabrication and who would have done it. Her Bible supported the genealogy of Molly Dean Prine and David Sharpe (d'Ersby). Could that be a fake? Which was history, Molly Dean's or William Strachey's? So similar, but with essential differences. And her stupid ideas of the essential nature of the connections of herself to history — she had come to grips with that, there in the cemetery in Richmond, with the fact that she was not some reconstituted Molly Dean of Jamestown. Yet, she had not until now questioned the historical legitimacy of that Molly Dean's story. She was fully aware that history was subjective, subjectively created and subjectively interpreted. And as she completed the transcription she must bear that fully in mind.

Ringing interrupted her thoughts and she went in and picked up her cell phone.

"You've got to tell Mother soon," Inez said.

"Tell her what?"

"If there is going to be a wedding."

"A what?"

"Destiny."

"Oh shit! I didn't mean for her to go off like that and I just didn't stop her."

"Well, you'd better get yourself engaged to David d'Ersby soon," Inez told her. "Or you might tell her he died suddenly of shock. Perhaps at the thought of marriage."

"Maybe I'll go marry someone else."

"Who?"

"Would one of the Virginia Carters be acceptable to Syril?"

"Do you know a Carter?"

"No," she lied and looked down at the business card on the table.

"Shame. Mother would love a Carter as the bridegroom."

"Inez, what am I going to do?"

"About David d'Ersby?"

"No, about your mother."

"You've given up this screwy idea about marrying the Englishman because he has the right name?"

"Fuck destiny. Fuck David d'Ersby and right now fuck the historical Molly Sharpe."

"I think I better come down there. Tomorrow?"

"I have seminar in the morning. The afternoon at the cottage."

"Don't panic. I'll see you tomorrow."

It was time to grow up. Molly went in the bedroom and took off the period skirt and top and put on a pair of seldom worn jeans and a tee shirt that read "byte me." The shirt was tight and the jeans too loose. She went back out onto the porch. It was cool and she wrapped her arms across her chest and gripped her shoulders. Life had seemed so directed, planned and organized by natural events for her. That wasn't simply naive, it was self-delusional. She must treat Molly's journal in an objective fashion as a document that was probably written by a woman in the seventeenth century, whose kinship with her should have no bearing on any thesis developed out of it or that journal's relation to any other work of the period. She would continue to work on the transcription, but would also take some steps to determine authenticity. There must be rare book dealers in Washington who could determine at least that the ink and paper were of a specific period and place. She could have the Bible authenticated as well.

The James would continue to flow regardless of her findings. She went in and closed the door.

David

F R A N C E

—the present—

AT THE MERCURE, David gave his name and was handed
another envelope he assumed was from Edward. His room
had a window angling out in the direction of the Place, giving him a view of the activity below. Sounds wafted sub-
tly intrusive from both the carousel's imposing one melody
and a tape accompanying a marionette, a worn version of
"June Is Busting Out All Over." Both the marionette and
the figure controlling it looked in need of a bath, the lat-
ter in some sort of trampy-clown outfit and the marionette
costume indefinable rags.

There were bottles of wine on the dresser. He opened a
red and sat in a chair at the desk near the window, peacefully listening to the cacophony of sounds before opening
the envelope. Inside were car keys, a parking ticket to some
garage, a ticket for that evening to Bach's St. Matthew's
Passion at the Opera House and a note:

Go tomorrow at noon to the open air café in the square in front of the Palais du Papes. It is around the corner from the hotel. Sit at an empty table for four. I will find you.
Edward

He left the hotel and explored the area. Just around the corner there was a street café in the square, along with assorted souvenir shops. He bought a ticket and went into the Palais du Papes. He only had limited knowledge of the period when the papacy was in Avignon and so, as he moved from room to room, he listened attentively to the tape device he had been given to hold to his ear. In the gift shop he purchased wine from the vineyards of Chateauneuf du Papes. After a light meal he went to the Opera House. It was a splendid musical palace of gilt and scarlet velvet. He was alone in a box right over the stage, but just as the performance was to begin, a young lady came in and sat in a chair beside him. She was astoundingly beautiful; dark French without the aquiline nose; perfection save for a missing finger, the ring finger of her left hand. She smiled; the music began. The Lucerne symphony was performing with two choirs; the soloists were not known to him. His attention was torn between the beauty of the young woman and the beauty of the music. He watched the beautiful woman watch the Finn singing the role of the Evangelist with an amazingly expressive voice. They sat upstage of the conductor, a fascinating perspective, and David was aware the beautiful woman watched him as he watched the conductor. At the intermission she introduced herself as Madame Celia du Lamier and told him that she had journeyed from Geneva for this performance. He told her he was in the area on family business. He felt inadequately dressed in black turtleneck and slacks as she wore a black evening dress with thin shoulder straps. The fabric clung to her slender body. She had astounding eyes. Was she traveling alone? "Yes, I am traveling alone."

As the performance ended he asked her to join him for supper. He helped slip a thin black shawl over her shoulders and they went to a *brasserie*, ate oysters and capered salmon and discussed the performance at length. Madam Celia said she worked in public relations and traveled frequently. He told her he was a writer. They went up to his hotel room in the Mercure. She slipped away in the middle of the night while he slept.

He awoke and saw he had an e-mail from opech and started to read the attachment.

Opecancanough

E-MAIL ATTACHMENT

I LISTENED TO Ninghekekuges read. "Aristotle is greater than Plato," I told him. I sat on a log near the river. Ninghekekughes closed the book. "Plato was too much what would be, could be. Aristotle speaks of what is."

"Endlessly." Ninghekekughes picked up a stone and sailed it over the water. "Naming, organizing, cataloging." He sailed two more stones and came back and faced me. "But you are right; he confronts the reality of what is." Ninghekekughes sat down on bare earth. A butterfly lit on his shoulder.

"That is what the priests will not do, confront reality. Their divinations of doom lead The People nowhere. And it brings fear. Each warrior fears the terror of the guns and swords; the tribes fear the destruction of their *yehaukens* and crops. And the Powhatan's fear is the greatest."

"He fears the destruction of the 'nation' to use a Whiteman's word."

"But in that fear he reaps only defeat. He is afraid that if he lets the Whiteman at the fort starve, other ships will come seeking revenge. Do you think they will?"

David

F R A N C E

—the present—

DAVID STOPPED READING. So what opech-hacker added to the narrative worked. It fit his novel and he had made up his mind to live with it, to embrace what the hacker gave him as his own. A different point of view, the Opechancanough point of view. It strengthened the text. But there were times when it was enough. David Sharpe or, as he had become, Ninghekekuges, was the central character in the novel. At this moment it was his point of view that was needed in the narrative and David d'Ersby took control of his novel, writing: "Other ships will come…"

The Novel

PLACE OF THE PEOPLE

— 1609 —

"Other ships will come, that is certain. But they will not necessarily seek revenge."

Opechancanough walked to the river. "I am not sure I understand." He pushed a willow branch from his face. "The ships will come but not to avenge the deaths of the men at the Fort."

"Apachisto, they may call you, Opechancanough, but you do not always think as the Whiteman. If a son's father is killed by a Paspahegh or a Rappanhannock, then it becomes the obligation of that son to kill the man who killed his father. It is the way of The People, and I understand that, but under the English law, the man who did the killing must stand trial and be found guilty or nay. There is no personal revenge."

"There is no revenge?"

"There is still revenge among the English. I am not explaining it well. There are men who will choose to seek out and kill the slayer of their father or burn a village for the crime of one man in it, but such acts are in violation of the law, hardly the mandatory revenge required by The People."

Opechcancanough sat back on the log. "Would Smith seek revenge?"

"Not for vengeance's sake itself, not brutally, but to keep order and discipline, he might."

"Smith is an enemy. The Powhatan should have let him die."

"Better an enemy that you know. A man you know nothing of could prove worse. What, for instance, do you know of the President of the Council?"

"That he has yellow hair and is having a house built in the forest."

"Ratcliffe is doing what?"

"He is having a great house, a palace the workers call it, built off away from the Fort."

"He's a fool." He held up the book. "Shall we continue the reading?"

"No more today. I must think about what you have read already."

Ninghekekughes got up off the ground and followed Opechcancanough away from the river. "How would Aristotle class the Whiteman and The People?"

Opechcancanough thought about it a few moments before responding. "The People like wolves, wild, knowing how to seek for food. The Whiteman, like the dog Newport gave to the Powhatan—" Newport had made a present to the Powhatan of a dog, along with a red coat, a tall black hat, and a boy named Thomas Savage.

"The greyhound."

"Yes. Trained to fight, but not able to find even its own food."

"But the wolf can be tamed, can he not?"

"Perhaps I will go ride and think on it," Opechcanca-nough responded.

"And I will go find Pocahontas and give her the reading lesson."

"There will be no lessons for awhile. She is gone. To the place-of-women. To look upon the moon. The time of taboo has come upon her."

"I know it is the custom, but why are women sent away at such a time?" Ninghekekuges asked.

"To look upon a woman cursed by the moon, and worse, the first time the bleeding comes upon her, could cause a man to lose his voice, an arm or leg, or more likely his ability to father a child."

"Do you believe that?"

"It is the way of The People, the way of the moon."

"She reads well. She is smart. She must not neglect the learning."

"It is true, but I worry. She is too willing to accept the Whiteman's way." Opecancanough scratched the shaved side of his head.

"But you learned the Whiteman's ways. It has helped you understand, enabled you to know what The People must do."

"It is different for Pocahontas. When she was a child and under the great roof of her father it did not trouble me, but now she will become *wikinagen*, follow her husband, go off to another tribe."

"Why another tribe?"

"What warrior who knows her would have her? She is a bad cook, would neglect the fire, and what hunter wants a *wikinagen* that can shoot faster and better than he can? She will need a husband who does not know her. She is no more a child. She is a squa. When she returns, you must be careful, as her kin, not to touch as much as her hand."

Before the sun set upon the day, a letter was brought from Smith for Ninghekekughes, who explained the contents to Opechancanough. Smith wanted to know when he was coming back and said that Sir Edward Maria Wingfield, who was no friend, and Captain Archer, who was, had both sailed with Newport. He wrote: "The savages must stop stealing."

Later he learned another ship came. More men, more supplies. Opechancanough said they were like flies upon a carcass, for as many as died more from the maggots would appear.

Another letter from Smith came. Ninghekekughes read that "Captain Nelson has sailed the *Phoenix* back to England. I sent a letter to Robert Bertie describing 'Virginia,' but as you requested, did not tell him you were alive. The councilor Captain Martin had not been well and sailed with Nelson. I caught Maconoe, a Paspahegh, stealing guns and kept him locked up on the *Phoenix* until he admitted that the Powhatan planned to steal all the English tools and guns. When are you coming back?"

The heat of the summer became more intense. The People took from the Whiteman—saws and hatchets, pots and hoes, anything of metal, anything loose. They took swords and guns when they were able, even gunpowder. They took from the Fort whenever the Whiteman went out. When he went alone into the trees, they cut him up and threw his body on the fire. Smith was angry and sent threatening messages and the Powhatan sent him a deer. But Smith left the Fort and went up the Bay by boat. Opechancanough's spies who kept watch at the Fort said Ratcliffe did nothing but take men and guards to work on his palace in the forest. The summer illness came upon the Whiteman and sometimes the workers at the house had to be carried back to the Fort and then, if they left tools in their haste, the spies would take them. The Paspahegh burned the house in the forest. And by the time Smith returned, the summer sickness had fallen like a hatchet chopping the Whiteman to death. What food stores Smith had collected were said to have rotted in the rain. Perhaps, as the Powhatan wished, they would all die, even Smith. But a ship sailed into the Bay and Opechancanough no longer had any doubts. The Whiteman had come to stay.

The Powhatan sent for them all. Ninghekekuges stood in the hot and humid crowded *yehauken*. The Squa Werowance, Oppussoquionuske, Opechancanough's sister, arrived and spoke, not in The People's way but fast with excitement. "I saw the ship with my own eyes. I saw creatures dressed in cloth that covered their legs and their hair was long and they had covered breasts. They are squas."

Women had come to Jamestown.

Opechancnough spoke: "To breed. To multiply. To cover the Earth with their offspring."

The Powhatan raised his hands as if in some benediction. "But we are doing what we must—let them starve and die. The squas as well. We should go hunting."

It was a large hunting party. Pocahontas was no longer allowed to go with the warriors; she was angry at being left behind. Rawhunt came to them the third day. "Smith comes to council at Werowocomoco."

"Smith can wait," Opechancanough told him. "Pocahontas and the women can entertain him with the dance of the hungry women." The dance was done by women, naked except for a leaf covering. They danced about the *nootau;* the beat of the drum was intense as were the cries of the women, voices of need and anguish. When it was done the men were invited to choose a partner and end her hunger.

The Powhatan and the men left the hunting place with a boar, no deer. As they neared the Fort, Oppussoquionuske pushed past the men to Pocahontas, who was standing near Smith. "Are you yet a virgin?"

"That is a matter of my concern, not yours." Pocahontas walked off toward the river.

Ninghekekughes spoke first in the language of The People and then in English. "Captain John, the ways of The People are not the same as the English. Pocahontas is free to dispense with her maidenhood as she wishes without stigma or shame, but not to a brother. You were made her brother. This is taboo."

Smith spoke in English and Ninghekekughes translated. "Don't be silly. Do I seem so insensitive that I would deflower the favourite daughter of the chief of all the savages? Even if I were, you know my philosophy. I don't swive. It seeps away the bodily fluids, leaves a man drained and helpless."

"I don't understand the last part," the Powhatan said after David finished the translation.

Ninghekekughes explained.

Opechancanough looked at Smith with distrust. "Does he truly believe that?"

"Yes."

Opechancanough sat. "Perhaps he is right. Perhaps it is what makes him invincible." He approached Smith. "Why have you come?"

"For corn," Smith replied.

"There is no corn," Opechancanough told him.

Later, after Smith had gone, Ninghekekughes spoke to Opechcancanough of what else he had learned. "There are not good feelings between Smith and new councilors. Only two women have come. One with her husband. The other is her servant; she is to marry a man who came on the ship with me."

"One of the strong ones who did not die. Now he will bear children equally strong."

"Smith brought me a new book from London. *The Essays* of Sir Francis Bacon. I spent the night before I sailed in Sir Francis's house."

"He is not a dead Greek?"

"No. But his wisdom is the wisdom of the Greeks."

A report came that sailors of the *Margaret and Mary* would trade anything for pearls and furs. They traded shot and powder, knives and axes, cheese and buckles, chisels and hoes. They would have traded the ship itself had they not needed it to get back to England with their furs and pearls.

The Powhatan's order was given to the Weanocs, the Chickahominy, the Nansemond, to all the tribes that there was to be no corn traded to the English. There was no need to order the Paspahegh. Were any tribe to be found trading, their fields and *yehaukens* would be burned by the Powhatan, their hunters killed and their women and children taken as slaves and sold to the Susquehannocks.

David

F R A N C E

—the present—

AT FIVE MINUTES before noon, David took the lift down into the lobby, went around the corner into the square before the Palais and found an empty table. Edward approached wearing a soft black *chapeau*, the wide brim pulled down, and a sweater draped over his shoulders. He looked like a cross between Oscar Wilde and an old Truman Capote. Martin followed wearing a vibrant orange shirt and bright green shorts, his eyes hidden behind sunglasses.

"You look terribly fey," David told Edward.

"Disguise," he said and sat. Martin took the seat on the other side of David. A waiter came and they ordered lunch and 'a nice claret', as Edward was wont to call the Cabernet.

"You look well," David said sarcastically.

"I am sorry about that."

"Was it necessary?"

"Yes. Most assume I am still there and near dying."

"Most?"

"Don't ask. I need you to drive to Menton. A Riviera vacation, so to speak."

"I bet," David said. "What's the catch?"

"Stay here tonight. I have booked you a table at La Lutern, one of the finest places to eat in Provence. You could take Madam Celia if you'd like."

"Jesus. She's a whore!"

"She's in public relations."

"Shit. I thought — "

"David, don't pout. It doesn't become you. You enjoy her company, do you not?"

"A fucking whore. I thought she liked me."

"Did you not enjoy the sex?"

"I was looking for more."

"Take good sex, which I am sure it was, and be satisfied."

"I want no whore."

"Well, I shall know better than to send you one in Menton."

"Where exactly is Menton?"

"Beyond Monaco. Close to the Italian border. Tonight you will stay in Avignon. Tomorrow you will check out. That walkway leads down to a parking garage. Go to P-three level, space P-three-seventy-six; a green Peugeot with maps and hotel reservation for the Princess et Richmond. You can spend Friday and Saturday in Menton, go into Monaco, gamble at Monte Carlo. Here's an envelope with more euros. On Sunday you will leave the hotel precisely at ten-fifteen and drive straight east on the street edging the boardwalk, into Italy. There will be three tunnels. After the third you will come to a roundabout. Go through the roundabout, head back and see a car stopped as if repairing a puncture. Stop, offer to help. An old man will get out of the back seat and into the back of the Peugeot. You will drive immediately back to Menton, up the autoroute, and bring your passenger to Avignon. You will come back into the garage entrance and park the car in the same spot and bring your guest here. Martin and I will be waiting."

"What is this all about, Edward?"

"I can't tell you. It is safer for you not to know."

"At least tell me, who is the dwarf?"

"What dwarf?" The question was Martin's. He was alarmed.

"My God, Heinrich Husch," Martin said. "Did you see the giant as well?"

"Giant?"

"I call him that," Martin said. "A Bulgarian basketball player. He stands, if he didn't hunch so, about seven and half feet. Ugly big man with a bulbous nose and feet the size of skis."

"I never saw any giant, but I may have seen the dwarf again as I came off the tube."

"This changes things," Edward said. "On Sunday when you pick up the old man, go back to Menton, but don't drive directly north to the autoroute. Go through St. Martine along the coast into Monaco and then go north to the autoroute. They would not expect that."

"The dwarf!" Martin took off the dark glasses and shook his head.

"Madame Celia is staying at the Damon."

"I'm not interested." David took the money and left.

EDWARD WAS RIGHT about La Lutern; the food was exquisite. David sent an e-mail to David Vere telling him that everything was outrageously silly, but he was OK and would see him in London early in the week. In the morning, as he drove, he felt as if he was in a Cézanne painting—the light, the colour. Centuries piled on centuries in France, but not in the same way as in England. Here languages, cultures had impinged one upon another. The terrain was startling; beyond a hill lay mountains of change. The Rhône, ever present, wound wide, narrow, and seemingly in a hurry to find the Sea. The pastel vineyards quilted the rolling countryside. The Alps, if not always visible, were there, hiding behind hill and rock.

He arrived at the Sea. On the square in St. Tropez, he took a glass of wine and discovered the thin-crust Italian chorizo pizza. He drove, hugging the winding coast through the red earth of St. Raphel, but before he approached Cannes and Nice, he went back up into the edging mountains and took the autoroute. The vista below him was one of spectacular wealth and nature, intertwining the structures of man and the weathering of time. And always, the sun — the light. He found Menton charming and uncrowded. The Mediterranean sparkled at its edge. Kites lifted off from runners on the beach and sidewalk cafés lined the boardwalk. At the Princess et Richmond he changed and went out on his balcony with wine and his laptop. He watched the birds lift from the sea and waves lap toward the beach, then turned fingers to the keyboard. "David, Ninghekekuges, went to the mountain..."

The Novel

PLACE OF THE PEOPLE

— 1609 —

David, Ninghekekuges, went to the mountain. He stood listening to the sound of a falling stream, the birds and the wind in harmony. Forests, broken by an occasional meadow, stretched in the east; a glimmer of the Bay edged the horizon. There was no indication man existed, no smoke rising from a fire, no visible village, no sign of blood or butchery, no hint of the struggle between The People and the English. To the south, the mountains touched the clouds; no indication of man, but so much land, so much space. To the west, trees and land, mountains climbing beyond mountains as far as his vision could reach. Everywhere was emptiness.

"Is there but a view only of delight and not of discovery?" Bacon's words. The People needed philosophy, understanding, science, poetry and the ability to read and write that they might record their ideas and thoughts and discover the thinking of other men. "The mind is man, and knowledge mind; a man is but what he knows."

What The People did not need was the English God, the sin, the insidious litigation, the fashion, the inequities of wealth, the private possession of land, the titles, the follies of the royal court, the persecution of ideas, the poverty or the greed, beggars, whores, cheats, merchants, preachers or lawyers. The People did need tools and skills, horses, wheels, ideas, theories, books and teachers.

There was much the English could learn from The People: to hunt, to net fish, to plant and reap, to be tolerant, to be generous, to understand that so much less could be so much more. The noble savage was not noble; he was often cruel and he was savage. He believed that truth might be found in the entrails of the eagle, but he also believed in the goodness of his fellow man. Opechancanough's hatred of the Whiteman made it impossible for David to convince him that there was a way to exist in harmony.

Pocahontas had understood. As she became a woman and, by law, physically distant, she had grown closer to him in mind. She was lost among The People. "I am," she said, "like the Russian monk you told of who sat in the tub of water waiting for it to freeze. I am a victim of custom." She read Bacon; she loved not just his ideas, but the nature of English culture. With Bacon, unlike the Greeks, David continually had to explain the world of England to make the ideas clear and she devoured the world with the ideas. She wanted to go to England, to dress as the women dressed, to feast at a table and eat off silver plate, and walk in a garden of planted flowers. She wanted to experience the splendor of the masque and watch actors on a stage. She wanted to be carried in a sedan through the bustle of the city, to climb stairs, and walk in a stone house from room to room. She wanted to walk in Saint Paul's, stand in a room of mirrors.

"But there is much in England, as a woman, you could not do, be *allowed* to do."

"There is not that much time. I would have no time for what I could not do."

The summer sickness had not killed off the Whiteman. Opechancanough no longer believed starvation and sickness would rid him of James Fort. The Powhatan was growing cranky and tired of the mention of the Whiteman. The harvest came. James Fort seemed to grow out, impinging further on the Land of The People and the demands that food be provided to the Fort were constant.

After the harvest, Smith attempted to barter for corn, but the tribes under the Powhatan's edict were reluctant and few did only as Smith's threats to burn the villages became more immediate. A blizzard came in the days that followed. The Powhatan and The People of Werowocomoco departed. All the food, the trappings of his compound, anything of value was moved to Orapaks. Werowocomoco became a deserted island of empty *yehaukens*, in a sea of snow. David stood in the cold with The People at Orapaks. The Powhatan stood before them, his hands raised, his voice loud upon the wind. "I have put myself out of reach of the Whiteman. He will look upon me no more." The woods about Orapaks teemed with warriors ready to kill any intruder. Winter melted, but the hatred of the English remained frozen.

"When I go back to England I will gather many books and paper and we will write down the words, the sounds of The People, their language," David told Opechancanough.

"Perhaps you will go to England and not wish to return."

"I will return, Apachisto."

The spies had reported that a block house was erected at James Fort. Lumber was being cut and piled. The spies told of birds which did not fly, but wandered about the fort pecking in the earth. "Chickens and geese," David explained. "Their eggs are cooked." Gardens were planted. The spies tried to steal a pig, but the pigs had all been moved to a guarded island in the James. The English at the Fort flourished. Spring warmed into early summer. Heavy moist heat suffocated the days. Insects swarmed about the river. A hurricane swept in from the sea, the winds tearing apart *yehaukens*. The priests said a child must be sacrificed to pacify the wind.

"It is brutal," David told Opechancanough.

"It is the way of The People," the old Werowance responded.

David left and rode the black mare to the mountain to escape the spectre of the rite. Night fell. He sat on a flat rock edge. Moonlight illuminated the night, but it was not the light of the place-of-the-rock-in-the-trail-of-the-moon. His mind was clear, his thinking rational. The English treatment of The People and The People's right to their land had to begin in London with a decision by the men of the Virginia Company. He would have to plead The People's case. The Powhatan must be willing to sell land of his choosing to the English and let the English live in security upon the land. There was land enough, room enough. Even in the moonlight, the vastness of the land was apparent, the silhouettes of trees stretching in all directions to infinity. This was his land and these were his People. He would leave them and go to England. He would raise money and gather the wonders of the Greeks and the skills of the English craftsman and he would return to teach the children. The moon vanished as dark clouds clumped in the sky and he made his way down the mountain. A gentle mist wet his face and bare torso. The rain came heavier and daylight encroached upon the night. He rode in wetness back to his *yehauken*. Two days later the white fox appeared. David went to Opechancanough. "The *wobaehokus* has come for me."

"Then you must go, Ninghekekughes."

"I will return within the cycle of the five seasons. May I bring you something special?"

"Yes, Ninghekekughes, you may bring me some chocolate to drink."

At the edge of the woods he spotted the white fox, moving onto the trail. Keeping a distance, David followed. Occasionally the *wobaehokus* would disappear into the brush and reappear further along the trail. The ground cover was damp from morning dew and the sunlight reflected off outstretched leaves of foliage like bits of mica. He carried his bow and arrow but took no aim at the turkeys feeding in a clearing. Far inland from the river, the fox still leading him, he saw a bear and her two cubs playing amid some fallen trees. But the fox gave him little time to loiter and he ran so as not to lose sight of the *wobaehokus*. The fox disappeared as two Paspahegh hunters approached.

"I am Ninghekekughes," he told them.

"Yes," one of the men responded. He had a blue fish painted on his cheek and one of his teeth hung over his lip. "You are the Whiteman who died and was born again among the Pamunkey."

The other, who carried a dead skunk, asked, "Why have you come to the place of the Paspahegh?"

"I go to the Fort of the English."

"Be careful," the fang-tooth man warned him. "The Whiteman is treacherous and may not know you once were a Whiteman. They kill us with their thundersticks and then ask the name of our corpse."

The *wobaehokus* reappeared. The morning dragged into afternoon. Insects murmured the heat. He ate some dried fish and meal and drank cold water from the skin he carried. Brow sweat ran down his face and his bare torso glistened from bear grease. He followed the *wobaehokus* along the trail toward the peninsula. From the woods he saw the soldiers, their armour shining in the hot sun. One man, who appeared to be a captain from his dress, was not a familiar face. David watched the men as they talked, one cleaning his gun, another pointing to a diving hawk.

Leaving the white fox in the trees, David moved into the clearing.

"Who the devil?" The Captain grabbed his pistol.

"I am a friend. I am called Ninghekekughes."

"You speak damn good English. Are you alone?" "I am alone."

The Captain examined him. "My God, you are English. What are you doing... like that?"

"I live among The People."

"Are you one of the children of Raleigh's Lost Colony?"

"No. My name is David d'Ersby."

"David d'Ersby is dead."

"David d'Ersby is quite alive." He pushed his long hair back over his shoulder. "And you are?"

"Captain Samuel Argall. But I don't understand. Peregrine Bertie is quite certain you drowned."

"You know Perri then?"

"I know your brother well. Distant kin by marriage. Your kin, too, I guess."

"Peregrine and Lord Willoughby do not admit me as their brother."

"They do now."

Argall's men crowded about, staring at David. "Leave us," the Captain ordered. "This is not your business." The men moved back. He lowered his voice. "They will be damn glad to set eyes upon you. Peregrine particularly has been greatly upset by the wrong he did you. I know the story, the documents, the miniatures, and how you were sent to Virginia and Molly to Lindfield—"

"Molly is dead."

"No." Sam Argall moved back and sat down on a large protruding rock. "Molly is alive."

"She... she drowned in the Thames."

"The story she let them tell you so as to save your neck. She was 'feared you try to follow her."

"I would have." Molly alive! His world in a moment had changed completely. He looked back. The *wobaehokus* had vanished. "I was coming to the Fort so as to go back to England. Now I must go."

"Molly Dean is married now. She has married the Rector of Lindfield. She is Molly Prine."

David turned away and faced the trees, his emotions tearing at him. He wanted to shout with joy that Molly lived; he wanted to scream in anguish because she was another man's wife.

"I saw Molly and her husband, the Rector, at Twickenham. She is content, David."

"I will go back to England."

"I am to sail within the fortnight—the next ship to go
back. I am certain Captain Smith will grant you passport to
travel back with me." Argall stood up. "Shall we go to James
Fort then?"

Pocahontas had talked of the Fort. He had listened to the
spies, the messengers. He had been interested but had never
experienced a desire to see it, but now as he approached
from the blockhouse and saw the triangular palisades, a few
drifts of smoke rising up, thatched roofs and men in armour
near the open gates, he had to suppress an urge to run. A
pinnace, a barge and a ship were moored to the trees.

"Look what we have captured," said Captain Argall.

John Smith stepped forward. "Davey, you've come home."

"I would go all the way to England, Captain John."

There were not many faces from the past in the men that
crowded about. To most, he was a curiosity, but he saw the
grand figure come from the doorway of the crude house.
Green and purple and plumes and pearls, George Percy
was bedecked as if for Whitehall. "Scalp my soul," he said.
"David d'Ersby be reincarnated as a savage princeling."

He put aside his bow and arrows. He slept on a crude
bed in a crude dwelling with a dirt floor, no worse, no
better, than his *yehauken*. But he found books and read.
From Argall he learned his name had been cleared through
Bacon's efforts, that Vere was in Bed'lam, and that Molly and

her husband had a son. A son, as well as a husband. He must accept that. There was no future for them together. But he would see her. He spent the days reading. His hair began growing out on the shaved side of his scalp and he cut the hair on the other. He found the clothes he was given constrictive and mostly went without a shirt, covering his torso with bear grease. He knew he must appear half savage, but return meant that he had given up the great freedom of life among the people and he was perhaps clinging to that freedom.

Argall told of a great fleet that should have already sailed with more than five hundred settlers, eight, maybe nine ships. A new government was to be formed. Lord de La Warr was to be the Governor General and Sir Thomas Gates his deputy. John Smith seemed neither upset nor delighted about being relieved of his command. He went about strengthening the defenses, attempting to see there were food stores, keeping order and discipline. David was questioned by those he knew and those he did not about life among the 'Indians'. He did his best to convince them that The People were not beasts but had a culture, though different to their own. The moist heat was oppressive. He wanted to see Opechancanough before he sailed and sent a messenger asking him to ride in four days to the place of the eight fallen trees. He asked for use of a horse and took his bow and arrow with him. He waited. A doe came to the clearing with her fawn and he watched. Beavers felled another tree.

Opechancanough came on the white stallion. He was alone. "You look like an Englishman."

"Only for a time."

"Perhaps you will not return."

"I will return. But there is much I must do in England. Smith soon may not be the President. A governor will arrive from England, an important man. Eight or nine ships and five hundred new settlers."

"Perhaps the oracle is right." Opechancanough patted the horse. "We are doomed; we are to be eradicated."

"No. I will speak with the men who are the power behind the Virginia Company, the important men in London. The English must come in harmony, but they must buy the land they need. The Powhatan will sell them land, and The People and the English can live side by side in peace."

"Ninghekekughes, you have a head filled with *toosa*. The Whiteman will not buy land he can take without trade and the Powhatan would never trade away the land of The People."

"The Powhatan must sell and the English must pay. Else there will be bloodshed."

"The rivers will run with blood and the leaves turn red long before the season of the harvest. The Powhatan will go to the den like the fox and keep from the predator's eye, but I will go among the Whiteman like the wolf in the hungry season."

"Be patient. I will return and there shall be peace."

"There will be peace only when the Whiteman is gone or all The People are dead."

The sky was blue. The sea was blue. David stood aft. The wake of white foam fanned away in a ripple of waves. Virginia lay days behind the wake. The sea stretched in all directions in boundless peace. Before David sailed with

Captain Argall on the *Treasurer*, the *Blessing*, the *Lion*, the *Falcon*, the *Unity*, battered and beaten, their masts toppled, their sails torn or gone, came like wounded soldiers up the James. There were men, women and children. They came ashore like refugees of war, gaunt and in shock, without emotion. Smith was told that Sir Thomas Gates, the Deputy Governor to Lord de La Warr, was in sole command.

"And where be Sir Thomas?" Smith asked.

"Aboard the *Sea Venture*," he was told.

"We haven't laid an eye upon the *Sea Venture* for nigh two weeks," another told Smith. "We were hit by a terrifying hurricane. Who's to say what be afloat and what be at the bottom of the deep. We've either dumped or lost most of our supplies to the sea. The passengers are all sick. Many died."

"Who besides Sir Thomas bears the orders?" Smith asked.

"Sir George Somers and Captain Newport, but they be with Gates aboard the *Venture*."

"I will wait upon the *Sea Venture*, step aside when the order is presented. For the time I need see the Fort remains strong and plenished for winter ahead. You have brought more mouths and no victuals."

David learned Prince Henry was well and to be named Prince of Wales, and that many were to be dubbed knights at investiture, including Peregrine. As David had readied to sail, a girl came to see him. Her clothing tattered rags, she was less than pretty and wore sadness as if a cloak. She had pouting lips and a wart on her right nostril; her blond hair was cropped short, most likely, David suspected, to rid it of the lice from the journey. Her eyes were slightly yellow, a sickness of the urine, no doubt. "Could you get this letter to my father, Esquire Flowerdew?"

"Of course. You are?"

"Temperance Flowerdew, Heathersett, Wymondham Parish in Norfolk."

"I will send word that I have seen you and that you are well. Are you here alone?"

"No. I am with my brother." She never smiled. "I would that I were home."

David had stood at the rail as the ship moved out with the tide and reached the wide mouth of the Bay. He heard the screech of the blue heron. He was granted a place of rank. His brother was Lord Willoughby, so he shared a cabin with the ship's master and took table with Captain Argall. The voyage was quiet and he found time for contemplation. Tolerance and freedom were the abstractions occupying his thinking. But in the less abstract realm, he knew he must achieve some education. He had to put Molly into the past. He must be happy that she was alive. And he must make his peace with Vere.

London came—not a glittering city in the sunlight, but a drab grey monument to a cloud-weighted morning. A thin fog mingled with black smoke and hung like a canopy, shutting out the light.

"Will you go to Bertie House?" Argall asked. "I can have a man accompany you."

"No. The Berties may well be in Lincolnshire, and even if they be in London, I shan't wish to scare 'em half to death. Better I put it to pen first and prepare them that I be alive." With the loan of a small purse from Argall he found lodgings at the Devil Tavern in Fleet Street. He sent a letter off with a boy to Bertie House. He sat in the public room and devoured beef pie and pork cakes and dark bread and beer. It was a divine feast. As he finished eating, he was approached by a young man, a tutor who was to be off to Greece with his pupil. The fellow, one Thomas Hobbes, declaimed about the sorry state of Oxford, government and England and was anxious to hear David's report of the natives of Virginia. He listened, he talked, he drank and he left. David had another beer.

Peregrine Bertie stood just in the door, slight, unimposing in brown with a few pearls indicative of careful wealth, his small Vere eyes searching the room. His slight beard was tidy and he wore the same small earring. David stood up.

Peregrine came across the room to him. "You are my brother. And you are alive."

"I am."

"May I embrace you, David?" His arms were stiff. "I am not good at this sort of thing. And I am still in shock… excited, and thankful, ashamed, sorry, confused—"

"It is behind us." David held his hands open. "I have a room to myself above."

They went to the room, where Peregrine related the blunt details of David's and Vere's births.

David said he wanted to see Vere and that he knew Molly was wed, but he simply wished to see her.

"Molly has sailed," Peregrine said.

"Sailed?"

"In the great flotilla, ironically bound for Virginia, while you were bound for home."

"Some of the ships arrived; five actually. She wasn't on any of them."

"She and her husband, the Rector Prine, were aboard the flagship, the *Sea Venture*."

"It is lost at sea. Hit by a tremendous hurricane. Of the ships that arrived, most of the supplies were lost, placing a greater burden on the limited stores of the Fort."

"Sir Thomas Gates, the Deputy Governor... Sir George Somers were..."

David nodded. "And Captain Newport. It's possible the *Sea Venture* is still afloat, off course."

"This is a mortal wound to the Virginia Company." Peregrine shook his head in despair. "Will you come home now, David? To Bertie House?"

"Yes. I was told you are to be knighted."

"Yes. Of the Bath and wed as well. I barely know her, but it is a good match and has Robert's approval. She is virtue and kindness, I am told. The daughter of Nicholas Saunderson, the Viscount Castleton."

As they went home to Bertie House, David told his brother about Virginia and his life among The People. In the morning David went with Peregrine to Smythe House. Lord Southampton and Edwin Sandys were there and, after formalities, David was presented to a dark man who was the Governor, Lord de La Warr, and they were all seated at a big table.

Sir Thomas Smythe addressed David directly. "Captain Argall testified to us yesterday on the condition of the fleet and the failure of the flagship to appear. Is there anything you would add? This is a terrible loss to the investors. And there are many investors."

"I can only emphasize the difficulty this will cause the Fort in the winter months ahead," David replied. "Food is the problem. President Smith's policy is: no work, no eat. He strengthened the structures for the coming winter, planted crops and accumulated what he could from The People, the natives. But this did not take into account the new mouths, many women and children, who arrived. Their supplies were lost in the hurricane. The winter ahead will be difficult."

"Will the savages help?" Smythe asked.

"Not willingly. They see no reason to feed men who have invaded and stolen their land."

"This is Smith's policy that has brought them to this," Smythe said.

"No." David looked directly at the man at the head of the table. "Smith has dealt firmly with The People of the Powhatan. If any be at fault, it is the Virginia Company itself. The People own the land; there is no attempt to acquire the land by purchase, to fairly—"

"You would have us buy the savages' land?" Lord de La Warr asked. "We would be brought to bankruptcy even the sooner. The land is ours by conquest. In compliance with the accord."

"The accord—an edict set down by the Pope?" David did not take his eyes from those of Sir Thomas glaring at him. "Since when does England recognize the jurisdiction of Rome?"

"You have the mind of a lawyer." Southampton smiled. "Robert best see you to the Inns."

Sir Edwin Sandys spoke. "We are not inhumane like the Spanish. We don't wish to submit the natives to slavery; to the contrary, we wish them to be Christian children—"

"They do not want the Englishmen's God."

"He is hardly the God of the English." Sir Edwin choked on his wine.

"What David meant, Sir Edwin," Peregrine explained, "is that is the natives' view."

"Damn what the savages want," Sir Thomas said.

Sandys took another sip of wine and coughed. "Their souls shall be saved."

"You feel Smith's policy is effective?" the Earl asked.

"When done without interference."

"Captain Archer and Captain Ratcliffe have reported to us that Captain Smith was overbearing and heavy handed, a tyrant, if you will," Lord de La Warr said.

"With all due respect to those gentlemen, and Captain Archer is my friend, he is also one for stirring trouble. His nose has been out of joint since the Company first passed him over for the Council in place of John Smith. As for Ratcliffe, I don't know the gentleman well, but when Smith left him in command of the Fort he went out into the forest, taking labor, to have a mansion built for himself."

They spent hours eating and discussing. In the end there seemed little resolution and little change and they cautioned David as to what he said publicly about the true nature of conditions at the Fort.

The next day David went out seeking Ben Jonson at the Mermaid.

"You are dead," Jonson said and stood up, tipping over his beer.

"I arose like Lazarus." He was introduced to Will Shakespeare and the playwright George Chapman.

"Rumour has it the *Sea Venture* has gone down at sea," Shakespeare said.

"No certainty. But it hadn't reached Virginia before I left. A terrifying hurricane."

"A real tempest," Shakespeare said. "Perhaps it went aground on some deserted island."

"One full of fairies as you would likely have it. You are such a romantic, Will," Jonson said.

"Will you take me to Sir Francis, Ben?" David asked "To thank him, but also to seek his advice."

"Best down to Twickenham. No use trying to see him at Westminster."

David spent an hour listening to the philosophy of the poets and took his leave for Bethlehem Hospital. It was stately, quiet on the outside. Inside was Bed'lam—cursing, groaning, singing, dancing, preaching, screaming, sobbing, laughing—human sounds in an ensemble of disharmony. There was an insidious smell, a mixture of the ammonia of urine and strong herbs. He was led to a locked room, a cell with a barred window in the door. Vere lay crumpled on the floor. The table and chair were overturned and a wooden feeding bowl was tipped over into gruel. The keeper scrutinized David. "You are brothers?" David put some coins in the man's hand.

"He does not talk." The keeper left David, the door unlocked.

"Vere." David's voice was soft.

Vere rose to kneel and stared silently at David. Then he began to cry and his weeping turned to heavy sobs. David helped him up and took him over to the bed; he cradled Vere's torso in his arms and rocked him as if Vere were an infant. "David," Vere sobbed. "Yes. It is David." Peregrine had also said that Vere couldn't talk. "David," Vere repeated.

David continued to hold him, to rock him for over an hour. His arm turned numb and he moved it from beneath the weight of Vere's body.

"Home." Vere voice was clear and coherent.

"Yes, I am home."

"Home," Vere repeated. David understood. "Perhaps soon, Vere. When you are better."

"Home!" Vere continued to scream in a piercing, incoherent rage.

David called for the keeper and left.

Over a supper of fish and pudding, David told Peregrine of his visit to Bed'lam.

"He actually spoke?"

"Yes, he said 'David', 'home', but I could hardly keep from crying myself, seeing him like that."

"But he spoke? That is a good sign. This is the first he has spoken."

David spent a quiet day reading until an invitation came from the Prince. David was to be presented to the King at Whitehall. Peregrine rushed him out to the Tailor of City Ditch.

"The man is the best fast tailor in all London," Peregrine told him. The red doublet was accented with black velvet and hung with pearls, and the tailor pinched the fabric here and poked it there and the apprentices all nodded their approval. In black hose, a shirt of weighty pink fabric and shiny black shoes with silver tassels, David thought he might die from sweating in the weight of all the cloth.

David met Prince Henry, whose auburn hair was in disarray from tennis. In entourage David was led by the Prince through a literal tour of Whitehall, finding it an architecturally ugly place. He was presented to the King, heavy under piles of oversized clothes but with skinny crooked legs. He talked briefly to David in a heavy Scottish accent about the muscled and painted natives that had been brought to his court. The audience was cut short by the entrance of the Queen, who slurred words in a Danish accent and admonished the King when he said she was drunk. She announced she was off to Greenwich for a go of hide and seek among quality persons. It was not an auspicious occasion.

He spent time with the Prince in the Privy Garden and told the sixteen-year-old of his wish to bring education to The People, and of the English taking away the land that rightly belonged to them.

"The Company is not going to pay for land they can take and the King is not going to support buying the land. Utopia cannot be achieved by force. But it can be achieved under the law."

"The law?"

The Prince snapped a dying rose from a thorny branch. "The law is primary. If you want to change England's policy of taking the native's land from them, then you must change the law and appropriate the funds for your purchase of it."

"The King makes the law."

"No. The King *thinks* he makes the laws. The inherent nature of English law is that it rests with the people. The people are more and more asserting that right. Parliament is the law, a house of lawyers who make the laws, and now, through men like my father's nemesis, Edward Coke, interpret the law as well. The King will have to come to understand that he only has as much power as Parliament grants him."

"The King is a king. I still don't see how Parliament can stop him from doing as he would."

"Money. Power is not but money, David. Parliament holds the purse through its rights of taxation and the King can only have as much money as the Parliament provides him." They started walking.

"And how does this relate to lands being taken from Virginia's native People?"

"You're going to have to seek either direct laws from Parliament establishing the natives' ownership of their land or you are going to have to litigate through the courts for it."

"You're saying I have to become a lawyer."

"I am saying that you have to get your butt end to the Inns and learn the law." The Prince grinned. "Of course, you still can take time enough to learn tennis."

David went with Ben Jonson to Twickenham. A book still served as a doorstop in Bacon's room. David wondered if it was still the same book. "Go to Gray's, David. Learn the law." Sir Francis stuttered slightly and his eyes fluttered as he spoke. "But Utopia does not exist. Neither Plato's nor More's."

"I do not seek Utopia. As I explained, I only seek to keep The People from being annihilated."

"That can best be served by finding a champion in Parliament, or becoming that champion of the natives yourself, a watchdog for the rights of your 'People' as you call them."

"But I don't want to stay in England. I want to go back and bring The People learning. I speak of the need to educate The People, but my own education is sorely lacking. I know little of the arts. I dislike music. I need to learn the practicalities of science. I even have a need to know the most simple crafts that can be taught The People. How does a weaver make cloth? And for my own need, I have a thirst for the greater philosophy. I met a man, an educated man, in the tavern in Fleet Street. He told me any new ideas were to be found on the continent. Do I set off on the grand tour?"

Bacon pinched some dried herbs from a bowl. A scent of basil sifted on the air. "If you found Kepler, would he see you, could you speak his language? Could you carry on a conversation with Galileo? Scour Fleet Street and find their writings in translation. Read, devour. Music flourishes in England. Learn an instrument. The poets gather at the Mermaid. Gather with them and listen. The crafts of all the world abound in London. Make friends of the cooper's apprentice, the printer's, the iron monger's. But above it all, learn the law. I can recommend you to Gray's Inn. I maintain chambers there. I am a powerful man with equally powerful influence. Much of that comes from Gray's, the law I learned there and the valuable acquaintances encountered. It gave me my voice in Parliament and more power and more friends and power breeds more power."

"I am not seeking power."

"Yes, you are. You are seeking ways to maintain an entire nation, the Powhatans. To control the greater events of history, as it were. To turn back the tide of England's present conquest and redirect it. To force powerful men like Smythe to accept your view of the natives. Only through power can you achieve that and power is an accumulation. Your friendship with young Henry, a man who's to become King, is a foundation for power. Human knowledge and human power are basically one; when the cause is unknown, the

457

effect cannot be produced. But knowing the root cause bears fruition. Knowledge of the law is essential to manipulate the law to your ends. At Gray's you will accumulate that knowledge."

"Along with a few powerful friends," Jonson added.

"Lord Robert will be my patron if I choose the Inns. I am too old for the university."

A servant entered, stood inside the door. "The architect is here, Sir Francis."

"David, we'll talk again shortly. I need Ben to hear what this fellow wants to do."

David found Alice Bacon in the garden with a man. She dismissed him as David approached. "He is handsomer than Francis, don't you think?"

"Who?"

"My usher."

"Alice, you're still at war with the world."

"Society and all its silly conventions." Alice skipped along beside him. "You are as copper-coloured as a statue. It becomes you."

"I've lived under the sun." He stopped walking. "I've been told you've seen Vere."

"What you really want to ask about is Molly, isn't it?"

"Yes."

"You know, of course, about the *Sea Venture*. It is likely it has gone down at sea."

"No. The *Diamond* was given up as well, but it arrived, battered and barely afloat. It survived and the *Sea Venture* could as well." David moved along beside her. Leaves of fall floated down from the trees. Fall was a time of dying. David tried to remember the poet who had written that. "Was she happy, Alice?"

"I took her to see Vere. She needed to put that behind her. The anger. You understand." Alice stopped, sat on a bench and motioned for David to sit beside her. "She is not *un*happy, David. Her marriage is one of convenience for both her and the Rector. She is fond of Rector Prine and in all respects his friend, but he has a lover, a gentleman well-connected and kin of my Lord Southampton."

"A pervert."

"No, David. Your anger is ill spent. Molly is protected by the arrangement. She lives in comfort, or did, and is well cared for and about by both men. But the marriage has never been consummated."

"She has a son."

"The child is yours, David. Your son's name is David."

He stood from the bench. He said nothing. He stared down at Alice. It was beyond words. There was nothing he could say. The news was overpowering. It changed everything. It changed nothing. Alice reached up and took his hand; his vision was blurred by tears.

Fall came. There was no word as to the fate of the *Sea Venture*.

Sara Smythe's entertainment on her husband's birthday was an immense crowding of the regaled and rose-watered in the long gallery of Smythe House. David entered with Lord Robert and Lady Willoughby, who swept about and complained of the drafts and the strong taste of the salmon tart which she put back on the tray. Mistress Gates, layered in black, wept profusely whenever *Sea Venture* was mentioned, but she ate well and belched loudly. A man in a hat with the eyes of some animal on its ribbon pointed his finger into the face of a tallow-cheeked fellow with huge ears that fell like a bloodhound's. "No, the Earl of Dorset is dead. You lie; he could not have writ you saying he would amend your debt to me. I should call you out, but me wife, your bloody sister, would no doubt poison me for it."

Lady de La Warr grabbed David's arm. "I am told, pray, I hope it true, you lived with the savages. Tell me everything there is to tell." But giving David no chance to tell, she explained how Lord de La Warr planned to bring those savages to heel and told him that the nature of curing warts was not accomplished with ground beetles—pray, never! —and giggled and prayed that Ben Jonson's masque for Prince Henry's Twelfth Night would be intellectually stimulating, entertaining and certainly naughty, and giggled and prayed that Princess Elizabeth would wed that gloriously handsome young Protestant from Hanover and posed the question as to whether or not Christopher Newport, now that he was in Heaven, would have his arm restored. "A stimulating hypothetical theological speculation, don't you find it?" She giggled and was whisked off to dance with a young man sporting masses of pimples.

The music never seemed to vary. A man spilled wine on his green ruff and spoke in a scraping voice to a woman whose wig sat askew. "'Tis no wonder Smythe be as rich as the Pope's mistress. At Dartmouth a ship were unloaded, a hundred tons were it if an ounce, all clove from the Indee. He can cry poor all he would over Virginia and serve stinkin' salmon, but he could get the King out of debt. I calculate…"

"I'm bothered by the rheums." A fat woman leaned on a narrow woman with billowing masses of red hair. "Mind that Doctor Flaggart tells me to give up comfits. I would rather give me up the doctor and I will. Don't take one of those salmons, Seantra, 'tis spoiled, but reach me a marchy-pane."

David escaped to the end of the long gallery.

"David," a woman pressed his arm. "Did you know a Vere married the Conqueror's sister?"

"No, Lady Norris, I did not."

Her small dark eyes flashed. "My name is Bridget. The Veres go back to Denmark, to Zeeland, to Ver in Normandy and hence crossed with the Conqueror and we have arrived to this. Edward was only twelve when he inherited and bore the Queen's great sword as Lord Chamberlain in Westminster. He should have been nicer. He was at Cambridge at fourteen and a master of Oxford at sixteen. He was three years at Gray's and in all the learning never achieved the art of kindness. He wore a gold ring in his ear which I dare never touch and was deaf to Mother's pleas. They talk yet of his wit, his skill at falconry, his poesy, fencing, horsemanship and cunning as a hunter, but never of his humanity. He had no duplicity for feigned kindness. He spent lavishly his son's inheritance, had the Queen's ear, but never heard the cries of his daughters. He was made lame in a duel and cut other men to shreds with his tongue. He fled the plague, but it caught him at Hackney. He was fifty-four; the Cecils never shed a tear, and his daughters put on black, but it meant nothing, and remembered that he had never spoke an unkind word to them, never demanded obedience and never sought a daughter's affection. His legacy to me is the same as to them, the same as to Henry, the same as to you. We knew him not. You are not alone, David d'Ersby."

Lord Norris came over and grabbed his wife's arm. "It is unseemly, lady, that you converse intimately with this person. You know the talk, and in such a gathering as this. Voices whispering, old gossips dredge from rivers that should have run dry." He glared at David. "By Jesu, the two of you look enough alike to be disgusting." He pulled her by the arm. "Stay from her d'Ersby!"

"We cannot escape the sins of Edward Vere," Bridget Norris shouted back.

"*Veronihil Verius,*" David said.

"Oh blessed St. Bertram! The salmon is rotten. I am mortified." Sara Smythe fell to the floor in a swoon.

"She sunk like the *Sea Venture,*" the man with animals' eyes on his hat ribbon said.

Mistress Gates burst into sobbing.

The next morning in the crisp autumn sunrise David had his first game of tennis and was trounced by the Prince. Later, he went to Westminister Abbey and stood staring at the stone. "Edward de Vere, Oxen XVII" it read and a boy asked him for a penny for some bread. He found a translation of Galileo in Fleet Street and kept an appointment at the weavers where women clicked with their feet, pulled with their hands and carried the tonnage of their drudgery in their eyes and yet, before him the weave of cloth, the magic of fabric was created. He tennised with the Earl of Southampton and was trounced, and the Earl's Lady with a cat in her lap spoke of Molly, Rector and the sadness of the *Sea Venture,* and the Earl gave him a book on brick making and a slim collection of equations by Master Hariot, and he went with Prince Henry to the Tower and met with *the* Sir Walter, who questioned David about the Indians, and David played tennis and lost to the Prince and David went to Bed'lam and, amidst the screams and ranting, listened to Vere speak in disjunctive words and cry when David left; and near midnight, when Morgant the papermaker's apprentice had finished work, David fed him a heavy supper and beer and the young apprentice told him how the making of paper was a great art learned from the 'Chinee' and that it was a secret and, in the morning after tennis, David met Princess Elizabeth and understood why her brother so liked her and found in the afternoon at the bookseller a slender volume on the cultivation and grafting of berry trees and a folio of Mister Shakespeare's *Romeo and Juliet*, and he was certain the *Sea Venture* would yet appear and at Bed'lam, Vere spoke in short fragments and rubbed David's arm and begged to go home, and Lady Willoughby gave David a copy of Erondell's *The French Garden* and Prince Henry had to forgo tennis because of the rain and he talked to David of his investiture to be held in June and promised him after Gray's that he would be made part of his own household and that when he became King, David would have a place in the government and could help the Prince bring the Court to financial stability and David would be rewarded with a barony and together they would work with Parliament and bring England again to the glory of the Virgin Queen and invoke laws of toleration and end the persecution of witches and Papists and Puritans, and David did not remind him that it was his intent to return to The People, and David received books from Peregrine: Erasmus and Virgil and Ovid, all in Latin, and he took Mongard on a Sunday up the Thames, though they told the paper-maker it was to hear a fiery preacher, and David brought Chowder to attend them loaded with baskets of food and beer and Mongard on the grassy river bank told him of vats, and hammermills and the pounding of fibers and the hanging of sheets and how a man could make paper with a simple frame, if he knew his business, and the papermaker beamed when they returned and told David more of the gentry should concern themselves with the salvation of the simple folk and that David would surely die and go to Heaven, and David went home and made notes on making paper, and in the morning Princess Elizabeth stopped on her morning walk at the tennis court and gave David a copy Spenser's *Fairie Queene* and told David that her mother was opposed to the marriage to the handsome young German and Elizabeth said she was destined to marry whomever the King would chose and Prince Charlie came up and whined and wanted to play tennis and Prince Henry told him to 'butt-off' and Charlie pouted and said that he hoped Henry would die soon and then he would become King and he would make Lizzie marry a heathen blackmoor and go live in heathenland.

In November the *Falcon* arrived from Virginia and John Smith was aboard and David met him at the Mermaid. He said there was no word of the *Sea Venture* and thought after so long there could be little hope. He detailed the trials and tribulations of Jamestown and its upheavals. David listened and asked many questions, but if truth be known his mind was more on The People than the problems of the Fort.

David made his first pieces of paper and wrote a letter to Prince Henry.

David was ushered to Gray's in no less than the company of Sir Francis Bacon. The Reader and the Utter Barrister were most impressed. David was given quarters with a young gentleman from Essex. "This room," Martin Garrister of Essex told him, "was not in too many years past the room of an Earl."

"Which Earl?" David asked and settled on the hard bed.

"Oxford. Edward Vere, they tell it."

David

FRANCE

—the present—

DAVID SHUT DOWN his computer and went down to dinner. He had veal and listened to voices. So many speaking Italian. The boardwalk was strung with lights and he
watched from across the street — lovers, families, roller
bladers, skateboarders, a man with a large gut who pulled
up his shirt and rubbed his belly, dogs, so many dogs on
leashes tugged by owners whose expressions matched the
dogs, and the young women, some pretty, some not. David
looked out at the sea. The sea was blue. The sky was blue.

He walked along the boardwalk, feeling pleased with
what he had written but weary. The air was warm and a
slight breeze brushed in off the sea. Walking east from the
hotel, in the distance, he could see Italian hills pushing out
into the sea. He saw an enormously tall man, seated, but
he could well be seven and half feet. Was it Martin's giant

who was Bulgarian and played basketball in Italy? The man didn't give David the slightest look. David walked back and passed him again. Once more the man didn't even glance up. He settled in a hanging basket chair and ordered a French beer. He kept the giant in his vision, but the man seemed intent on talking with those at his table. Finally he stood up. He was indeed at least seven and half feet tall. He took notice of David but walked off in the other direction. David ordered another beer.

In the morning David arose, showered, dressed and went down to the lobby for breakfast. He yearned for some English fried eggs and toast to dip in the yolks, but he settled for a single hard-boiled egg, a bit of cold ham and a croissant. He checked out of the hotel and examined his watch as he threw his bag and computer case in the boot and left the hotel parking lot precisely on schedule. Flowers lined the boulevard on the sea side and seemed to be self-illuminated. He could imagine the Peugeot in a painting, a sort of moving green dot on an impressionistic landscape of colour. After a few short kilometers he was in Italy. The border was unattended. A tunnel, cool darkness, and then the sun and another tunnel, shorter but darker, and then sun and the third tunnel, and a short distance to the roundabout. He saw an old black Mercedes parked on the opposite side as he approached the circle. He slowly made his way on the roundabout, headed back and pulled ahead of the black vehicle. He swore the driver was less than ten years old. An elderly man, all in black, with hair the color of old white vinegar, banged out of the back seat of the black sedan carrying an open red umbrella and seemed to

skip as he moved into the back of the Peugeot. David nodded to the overly young driver but was given no recognition.
He waited for a white Mercedes with tinted glass to pass
and then pulled away. He was conscious now of the traffic
and behind him was a Volvo, white with a rusted roof.

The elderly man said in English with an Italian accent.
"You may kiss my ring now."

"Pardon me?"

"You may kiss my ring." The man shoved his hand over
David's shoulder.

David didn't know quite what to do with it, so, trying to
keep his eyes as best he could on the road, he lightly kissed
the man's ring. Jesus, what in hell had he been asked to
chauffeur? The man began a rapid series of prayers quite
loudly in Latin. At least David assumed he was praying
and he recognized enough words to assume it was Latin.
And did the language matter? It was essentially surreal. A
bishop. One kissed Roman Catholic bishops' rings. Or
maybe a cardinal. Certainly not the Pope. He knew from
pictures what the Pope looked like. Or maybe he was none
of these things, and what the fuck was the red umbrella
for?

The man said in French and then repeated in English:
"It was all Pius the Eleventh's doing. The Twelfth was a
work, that one, but he only carried on."

David moved along with the traffic down the water's
edge back into Menton. The Mercedes stayed ahead and
the rusty-roofed Volvo just behind. "I have a tendency
to pass gas," the elderly man said. "Please excuse me if I
should. It's my age. Martin Luther had the same problem.
Maybe it's something clerical."

"Certainly, sir."

"You may call me Your Excellency."

"Your Excellency." Jesus, did he need a farting, pretentious cleric all the way to Avignon? He followed the given directions along the coast through Cape St. Martine to Monaco.

"The Twelfth thought even his defecation sacred. What a sanctimonious shark that one was. 'I was young then. Amazingly handsome and skilled at the crossbow.' Strange that."

You said it, but David kept the words in his head. There were bicyclists around every curve. He followed the Mercedes, not attempting to pass on the narrow two-lane road. Elegant houses and gates lined both sides. He wound in through Monaco, found signs pointing the direction of the autoroute and turned north.

"I have a weak bladder... always having to piss."

He was on the right road and pleased with himself, and then traffic came to a stop. It started again and then came to a complete halt.

"There must be an accident ahead, Your Excellency."

"I will pray for the victims. How many?"

"I haven't the slightest notion, Your Excellency."

"A general prayer for victims everywhere then."

The same white Mercedes was ahead of him and the same white Volvo behind him. David got out of the Peugeot and looked ahead. Traffic was backed up as far as he could see, which wasn't all that far as there was a curve ahead. David got back in the car. The old man was praying.

Suddenly two men leaped from the Mercedes, another man from the Volvo. The Volvo man was dressed in military fatigues and carried a weapon. Instantaneously, David was pulled out of the driver's seat and shoved in the back of the Peugeot as the old guy was yanked out and pushed into the back seat of the Volvo. The man in the fatigues got in beside David, his weapon at the ready. The Volvo made a U turn. The Peugeot sat there.

"I speak English," Fatigues said. He was dark, not French-looking, and spoke English with an accent David did not recognize. Late twenties, perhaps. Dark curls crept from beneath a blue beret tilted jauntily to one side. They sat and then traffic moved, as if it had never been stopped. The silent driver was a squat man dressed like a French resistance fighter of World War II movies. The scenery was spectacular. Late morning light washed the landscape. David felt he should be more frightened than he was. Perhaps it was the smiling face of his gun-toting guard. David smiled back. The guard seemed pleased. The car left the autoroute and moved on to a narrow, old, less maintained cobble road that wound steeply up into the mountains. The light of the day seemed to get brighter and brighter. Then, with a slight screech of the Peugeot's tires, they stopped before iron gates, which shortly opened, and they drove through a maze of flowering plants to a villa that clung to the mountainside. Stucco, with many tile roofs, it seemed to meander with balconies out over the edge of a cliff. The car chugged up behind the house and stopped.

The bereted guard held David by the arm and directed him over a terrazzo terrace into a large room with twenty-foot ceilings, heavily carved wooden furniture and large burgundy-suede chairs and sofas. Huge expanses of wall were given over to large works of surrealist art, reminiscent of Remedios Varo. The windows, doors actually, opened to one of the balconies. David was gently pushed through the room to a hallway and finally through a doorway into a dark room. His eyes were adjusting to the darkness when the light switch was clicked on by his armed companion.

He was almost immediately aware that it was a suite of rooms, and plush, as if in a luxury hotel. The door closed and he was left alone. He explored. The windows were without glass, only tightly bolted wooden shutters. The sitting room had a large sofa, overstuffed chairs, a desk and tables. There was a predominance of blue and grey, but all the walls were white stucco. The bedroom had a large bed and heavy wooden chests; the bathroom was marble, with a sunken Jacuzzi and separate shower, WC and bidet. He sat on the sofa. He had nothing to read and didn't have his computer. The whole damn novel was on that laptop, all of it backed up on the external hard drive — where were they? Through a crack in the shutter he could make out some sort of shaded terrace and beyond, greenery and mountains. He sat down again. He could hear music, American pop music; there were no other sounds. No conversation or voices.

The door opened. The guard came in with a tray, but no weapon. David supposed he could have overpowered him — and then what? The man, who was relatively handsome without the beret, looked to be about David's own age, maybe as much as thirty. Hard to say. He was swarthy with dark hair on his arms and poking through the top of his shirt at the neck. His dark penetrating eyes didn't threaten, appear angry or display any animosity.

"Madame LaFrontan is a marvelous cook." He set the tray on the desk. "I am Yossef Ben Nather."

"You're an Israeli soldier?"

"I was. Now I am but hired security."

"May I ask for whom?"

"No," he said, but he laughed when he said it.

"Can you tell me why I am being held?"

"I frankly don't know. We will be here by ourselves."

"Madame, the chef?"

"She brings and leaves."

"And the driver?"

"He has gone."

"And my car?"

"It is well."

"And to whom does the house belong?"

"This is the first I have been here, but it's quite comfortable. We shall be fine here."

"For how long?"

"I cannot say. You should eat your lunch. I will go have mine."

"Why not bring it here?" He didn't know why he asked.

"Yes." He left and came back with another tray.

Both trays were the same: pumpkin or squash blossom soup, sliced melon, a country pâte, baguette and a bottle of blanc vin. The music changed to Mozart and drifted in as if seeping through the walls.

"Were you in the army long?" David asked.

"Long enough. And you, are you an undercover agent of some sort?"

"Jesus! No. A writer."

"What were you doing taking Cardinal Belodiosi out of Italy to Avignon?"

"Is that who he was? I was asked to do it. Why is this cardinal wanted in Avignon?"

"I haven't the slightest," he said. "Do you always do whatever is asked of you?"

"No." David should have felt uncomfortable the way the man was staring at him. He was not certain it was sexual, but thought it so. Oddly, he didn't find it threatening. "Is it beautiful out now?"

"Yes, but I think it must always be beautiful out here."

"Can the shutters be opened?"

"You could walk out. There is no glass. Perhaps tomorrow for a time, if I stay with you, I will open them." He looked intently at David, picked up both trays and said, "You are very fair." He went out, manipulating the trays and locking the door.

David's dark hair and dark eyes were not fair. Yossef could have meant nothing else by fair than exactly what he said. Mozart had evolved to some indefinable rock and then to Britten. Obviously Yossef's taste was eclectic. Even though David could not see the landscape he could smell the greenness and the blossoms, unfamiliar but interesting scents.

Yossef came in with David's bag. "Do you want me to knock before I come in?"

"It's not necessary," he said. "Any possibility of having my computer?"

"That might be dangerous. Let me think on it."

"I just want to write. You can keep the phone jack."

"Maybe you are able to get some sort of wireless signal up here. Or activate some sort of honing device with it."

"Yeah, me, the big spy."

"I'll think about it."

"Is there anything to read in the house?"

"Do you read French?"

"Not too well."

"I've got a Penelope Fitzgerald in my bag. Do you like her?"

"Love her. Which one?"

"*The Beginning of Spring.*"

"May I?"

Yossef brought him the book and he read the afternoon away quite comfortably. He had read the novel before, but that didn't spoil his enjoyment. Yossef came in later with a bottle of *vin rouge* and a couple of wineglasses. After they killed two bottles of wine and a lovely fish and pasta dish prepared by Madame, they talked about writers and writing, of music and films, but nothing of family or friends, or of life away from this strange prison.

"Would you think about my computer?"

"I'll think first about opening the shutters for you, tomorrow." Yossef got up and took the trays to a cart outside the door. "We can talk in the morning. I will leave you now and say good night."

"Aren't you going to kiss me good night?" David asked.

"Is it that obvious?"

"It seemed apparent."

"You're straight, aren't you?"

"Yes."

"Then I'll say good night."

"Good night, Yossef. I didn't mean to offend you."

"You didn't." The door closed.

MORNING CAME AND with it, Yossef with a real English breakfast of fried eggs, a banger of sorts, and beans and potatoes. And the coffee was hot and strong. "How did you manage this?" David asked.

"I had Madame bring the ingredients and fixed it for us myself."

"I love you," David said, not realizing at the moment quite what he said.

"That's exciting. I don't make you uncomfortable, do I?"

"No." And for the first time he was really able to say, "My brother is gay."

Later in the morning, Yossef opened the shutters. David stayed within the confines of the room but was enraptured with the light and the air, the sun and the shade, and Yossef, in skimpy bathing trunks, stretched on a lounge in the sun on the edge of the arbored terrace just beyond the windows. He was, David realized, a well-built, handsome man. From a distance they exchanged words about innocuous world events or celebrities.

Later David went in the bathroom and soaked in the Jacuzzi. Yossef appeared above him and announced he was going for their lunch but would be gone only moments and though the shutters were open, David should not attempt an escape.

"Hardly dressed for it. I'm bare-ass naked."

"Yes, you are, and amazingly beautiful," he said and left.

One day wore into the next and then the next. They were always alone. David never saw Madame, the vanishing chef. Yossef now left the shutters open at night. David wondered if Yossef stood guard on the terrace through the night. They came to talk of personal things and David told him about Edward and Vere and his mother and the Baron and Alice. Yossef talked about his days growing up in Israel. He had gone to college in the United States at Stanford and then returned to serve in the military. This was an interim gig, as he put it. He was hired by an agency and knew as much about what they did as David apparently did about Edward's business. He thought the dwarf business was an exaggeration of the truth.

"The truth, I swear," David said.

Then one morning he brought David his computer. But there was no wireless accessibility. So David could not check his e-mail.

Opecancanough

E - M A I L   A T T A C H M E N T

I RODE THE horse along the river. The trees were bare, sharp branches snapping in the cold wind, the earth stiff with frost. It would be a cruel winter. The council at James Fort told The People that Smith was dead, but my spies had seen Smith board the ship for England. Smith was gone and they would starve. Snow fell on a second day and then a third. Pocahontas, bundled in heavy skins, came to Manapucunt with Face-of-Spots, Kopokopo and his squa Noolockma. "My father will not let me speak his name."

"What have you done?"

"The Powhatan invited the Whiteman of James Fort to Werowocomoco to trade. I sent Face-of-Spots to the Fort to warn Percy. The Powhatan sent Rappaton after her and brought her back."

"You should not have gone against the Powhatan's command."

"He would have killed all the Whiteman when they came to Werowocomoco."

"That is as it must be." Pocahontas and I went inside out of hearing of the others. Pocahontas looked about my disorderly *yehauken*. "Where is your squa?"

"Gone off."

She found some corn in a basket and began to pound it in the stone bowl.

"Do you not see? They are destroying us by taking our land. Like the creeping vine they wend out from the root." I sat down beside her. It was cold and I pulled the skin wrap tighter about me. "You must promise me, Matoaka, that you will not go to the Whiteman, nor send Face-of-Spots."

"I will do as you bid, Uncle. Even if I wished, I could not move from this place. Kopokopo and Noolockma are sent by father to watch me like the vulture eyes the carcass."

The wind whined and men with their squas and children huddled in their *yehaukens*. Pocahontas made me a warm soup and, though cooking was not among her skills, it tasted good. She stirred the fire and we sat in the glow from the flames and talked of philosophers. The weather turned bitter cold. The Powhatan came from Orapaks with two hundred warriors and their squas. They left a great swath in the snow leading from the forest. The squas dragged litters piled with skins beneath which were food and clothing; the men walked before them.

"This is the time, my brother, to sit by the heat of the fire," I said.

"I go to Werowocomoco to trade with the Whiteman."

"I will gather my warriors and go with you." The snow blew in my face as I spoke.

"You go to kill the Whiteman," Pocahontas said.

"The voice that calls out I do not hear. It is like the wind; it makes sounds that have no meaning."

The wind swirled the snow in drifts. Seldom had I seen the snow so deep, nor a winter so cold. It was good the harvest had been bountiful, for the budding of trees was a long, cold time yet to come. Tracks of the deer were seen, but we did not stop to hunt. At Werowocomoco, the women started fires in the *yehauken*, but the warriors remained out in the cold, hidden behind the leafless trees of the forest. I sat beside my brother near the fire. He said, "They have killed the animals on whose backs they rode and have eaten the flesh." The Powhatan held up his bowl for the woman to put more steaming soup inside. "They have eaten their dogs and even their moccasins." I thought of the horses being eaten with sadness.

Captain Ratcliffe with thirty men came up the near-frozen river in the small ship; the pinnace, Ninghekekughes had called it. The Captain held two hostages, Mormako and his squa, whom he referred to as the Powhatan's son and daughter. They were actually my spies. The soldiers drifted off throughout the *yehaukens* of Werowocomo, the women enticing them in with bowls of corn and roasted venison. The Whiteman sat by fires and gorged. The small ship was left unattended, but for a couple of men who yelled that some food should be brought them, too. Captain Archer attempted trading in halting language of the People, but the Powhatan began a tirade about the nature of trees, the great hunt of his grandfather, the necessity of washing the body every day even in the cold of winter. While he talked, outside about the stake, the snow was cleared. Food was brought for Ratcliffe and Archer. As the Powhatan continued to rant, both men chawed roasted deer, stuffed boiled roots in their mouths, and the Powhatan's prattle never ceased and Marmako and his squa drifted off from their captors and the Powhatan excused himself and went out. Men slipped slipped from the trees into *yehaukens* and butchered the eating soldiers. Ratcliffe and Archer were lashed to the stakes and squas came and scraped away their flesh with shells and threw the flesh into the fire. Their screams were carried away on the wind.

The Powhatan returned to Orapaks with his People. I went back to Manapucunt with my men.

"Are they dead?" Pocahontas asked.

"Yes." I made notches in a long pole. I was keeping count. There had been approximately five hundred Whiteman when the leaves had first fallen. I sent a rabbit to the fort with the old man Aputonak; he returned. He drank soup by the fire and spoke of what he had seen at the place of the Whiteman. The men, the women, the children looked like walking corpses, with their bones sticking out, their clothing rags hanging on their bodies. They burned the houses of those who died to keep from freezing. They fed on soup made from dried weeds dug from beneath the snow; they ate shoes and chewed on leather bindings. He saw stiff corpses on the ground in the woods beyond the Fort where many had fled and either were killed by the Paspahegh or froze to death. I made notches on the pole.

The snow melted but it became colder. Werowance Percy had little control. Captain West had fled with the pinnace, their only means of escape. The Whiteman could not hide the death blanket hanging over the settlement. It was told they ate the corpses and Percy could not stop them and that one man killed and ate his wife and Percy had him burned alive. Percy walked thin and sickly in a pile of rags. The nasty little animals that had come on the ships, the rats, were all that was left to eat, along with what few roots they could find to boil with their melted snow. I made many notches in my pole.

Yet the Whiteman clung to life and then on a day when the last snow had melted and the wind had died, a bud appeared on a tree. In days to follow purple and yellow flowers appeared and the trees were full of pink and white blossoms and the sweet smell of new life was carried on a breeze. Grasses spouted green and the black bear was seen. The squas readied the earth for the corn planting.

Amid the life of the new year, the Fort stood, a reminder of death. It was warmer, but the Whiteman still had no food, save a few bird eggs and green twigs pulled from trees and new grass to chew. My pole now counted no more than sixty of the near five hundred were left and they near death. I took the pole and rode the white stallion to Orapaks. The day was chilly, but the smell of the planting season was everywhere. I saw the blue heron by the river's edge, standing on one foot in the mud, but the *shu-shu-gah* was silent and I felt the danger of the Whiteman coming to an end.

The Powhatan was not well. "The bad food of the dead season has killed me. I shall die."

"We will live to see all the Whiteman dead. We must attack the Fort now and kill the rest."

"They still have the big guns."

"But no strength to use them. They are dying."

"Then let them die of hunger and when more ships come we can speak that we had no part in it and they will not send guns to attack us."

"We should rid ourselves of the menace now. They are weak and there are few of them."

"They will die tomorrow, Apachisto, the time of plenty will come too late for them. They have no food, nowhere to get food, no boats to escape. If they leave the Fort, the Paspagegh will kill them. We need exert no effort, lose no lives. It is but a little while. You must have patience."

I returned to Manapucunt. "Shall I teach you to ride, Matoaka?"

Pocahontas did not smile. "I must work in the planting earth."

"You are the daughter of the Powhatan. You need not work in the earth like the others."

"I am a squa." She went off with Face-of-Spots to where the women were bent over, putting the kernels of corn into the soil. Pocahontas worked in the fields and the new corn sprouted and the trees lost their blossoms and small fruit wrapped the end of branches. Men talked of diving for pearls and the squas and children gathered early berries and the eggs of birds. "A warrior has come from Kecoughtan," Pocahontas told me as I leaped from the horse and tethered it to a tree. There was a flash of vengeful glee in her eyes and her voice held the hint of defiance. "Two ships of the English have entered the Bay."

Molly

THE TRAIN

—the present—

MOLLY READ THE e-mail from Opechancangouh as she waited for the train to pull out. And then she closed her laptop, put it in the case and stashed it on the shelf above the seat. Staring out at the platform, she realized she would be riding backward out of Richmond and was about to move when an elderly African-American man with large ears and a German shepherd sat down opposite her. She couldn't move now; it would appear racist. The dog sat in the aisle alongside the man. The man's ears were like carved handles attached to a mop of tight grey wires of hair. "I didn't know they allowed dogs on the train," Molly told him.

"A seeing-eye dog." The man had very white, even, quite beautiful teeth. His enunciation of words was that of a highly educated man.

"I'm sorry, I — "

"It's not for me. My sight is perfect. It's my daughter's."

Why he was with his daughter's seeing-eye dog and why they allowed it on the train made little sense to Molly, but she wasn't about to pose questions.

The train pulled out from the station. Molly was decidedly not comfortable riding backward. They rode in silence with the dog as a sentry on the aisle. The conductor came and took their tickets. The elderly man had a ticket for the dog as well. "We'll be arriving in Washington on time," the conductor said and moved off. Molly got her bag from the overhead; carefully placed alongside it was the mailing tube containing the original journal. Molly slipped the printout back into her bag.

"I have the power," the elderly man said, as she sat back down in her seat. "I don't know why. A gift from God, I do suppose."

"Yes," Molly replied, not knowing what to say. She looked directly at the man. His ears were ridiculous, but his eyes kind.

"Was it a friend or relative who lost her husband?"

"Pardon?"

"The man struck by lightning."

"I'm not certain I understand."

"The woman with the small child… left a widow. He was a preacher, I believe. Hung there on the ship's mast like Christ, himself, on the cross. And a dog. There was a dog, wasn't there?"

"A relative. The woman," Molly stammered, quite taken aback by the man's words, so precisely articulate, so melodic.

"Was it recent?"

"No. A very long time ago."

"You must put it behind you."

"Yes."

IN WASHINGTON, SHE went to two rare books dealers. Their responses were nearly identical. The journal and most certainly the Bible were early seventeenth century. Both paper and ink confirmed that. "Do you want to sell?"

"No."

"They are quite valuable." The similar appraisals differed only by a few hundred dollars. One of the two suggested if she still had concerns she might have a museum do carbon analysis, but he felt it unnecessary. She was relieved. The fact that Strachey had ignored reporting on Molly, Roger and Farin provided an historical challenge for her. She caught the train for Richmond. She was in the quiet car and this time she had the sense to sit facing the direction in which the train would be moving. The table was up and open between the seats and no one sat opposite. She took out her laptop and begain transcribing the next section of the journal — from the photocopies, despite the fact that she had the original with her. "We came with such great expectations…"

The Diary

JAMESTOWN

— 1610 —

We came with such great expectations. But
despite the flowering trees, as we moved into
the river, the hostility of Virginia seemed to
engulf us. There was so little sound and when
we at last came to Jamestown, those lining
the rails were silent. Below on the dock, waiting like some London beggar, stood George
Percy in his rags. He seemed decrepit beyond
his years, and as we moved slowing down the
plank, Sir Thomas Gates introduced himself
to Percy. Then Percy, with horror, related the
terrors of the winter past. Those that moved
about him, the survivors of the winter, were
like phantoms in emaciated bodily form.

Many of us had left the nine months in
Bermuda with reluctance, others under threat
of execution if they persisted in determination to stay. Bermuda had been idyllic. Food

seemed to be there for the taking without effort—hogs running wild, inlets massed with fish, sweet berries, tortoises and bushels of bird eggs. Cedars and palm leaves for thatch. But it bred laziness. Gates had toiled to set an example. Laborer and gentlemen alike felled trees, sawed and shaped them for the building of the ships. Shipwright Richard Frobisher oversaw the construction as the pounding of hammers reverberated through the cedars. One of the *Sea Venture*'s long boats was rigged with a mast and, at Gates's instruction, set sail for Virginia with Master's Mate Henry Ravens, the Cape Merchant Whittingham and six sailors. A watch fire was built on a high point to aid their return. They were never seen nor heard from again.

Mistress Rolfe gave birth; a sickly girl baptized Bermuda by Reverend Buck. Sir George Somers gathered a crew and began the building of a second pinnace. I worked with the food gatherers, carrying David in a sling on my back, while the hound ran behind. Mistress Rolfe became more frail and could no longer walk. I dove in the clear water and collected oysters and pearls, but no pearl was as precious as the one I had kept from David's doublet. Bermuda Rolfe died and Mistress Rolfe was unable to stand with the others at the grave and John Rolfe erected a cross on the small pink sandy mound.

I stood every morning and evening at prayers and calling of the roll. Failure to attend was punished by whipping. Mistress Rolfe died and John Rolfe put another cross on another mound and asked me to wed him and I refused. A plot was uncovered to break into storehouses and seize the arms and kill Gates, so Captain Yeardly strengthened the guard and John Rolfe again asked me to wed him and I refused. He gave me one of Mistress Rolfe's dresses. As spring came the pinnace was caulked and was launched, though unrigged as yet, and it floated and some cheered and some plotted to remain behind and Captain Yeardly paraded his guard. Farin suggested that when we reached Virginia it would be best for us, and David, if I became Mistress Browne. John Rolfe asked me to wed and Farin informed him that I was engaged to marry him. Rolfe publicly made aspersions about Farin's manhood and Reverend Buck reminded Rolfe that Farin Browne was a close kinsman of the Earl of Southampton, and Rolfe apologized and gave me another of Mistress Rolfe's gowns.

Sir George erected a monument to commemorate our salvation and the watch fire was let to die. Both new pinnaces were rigged from tackle taken from the *Sea Venture*. Some fled to other islands and hid, but most boarded the *Patience* and *Deliverance* and we set sail for Virginia.

And so it is we are here. It reeked—the odor of corruption, the filth of human excrement. Gaunt figures stood silent in rags at the openings in hovels. I saw Temperance Flowerdew, barefoot, her bones nearly protruding through her yellowed flesh, a rag hanging on her body. Captain Yeardly approached her and called her name and she crumpled to the earth and began to sob. I stayed with Miss Flowerdew as she whispered the horrors of her brother's death in the snow. Governor Gates attempted to bring order to Jamestown. The stockade was repaired and the church roof propped up. Guards escorted cadres of men who went to saw down trees or net fish and at the sight of any Indians shots were fired. The roll was called. Those who had lasted the starving time stood and answered in voices without emotion. They were hollow people, men and women who had lost the human spirit, the core of their being. I gave Temperance a dress that had been Mistress Rolfe's and pearls and combed her hair; she did not smile. She put on the dress and went with Captain Yeardly and four guards and picked dandelions and made a garland.

Farin came from felling trees. He told me that it was no use, that there was not enough food to feed us all until a harvest or until supplies might arrive. He said Sir Thomas talked among them and they had agreed that Jamestown was to be abandoned. We were to sail for England and though the ships were small they were seaworthy. He suggested we be married aboard by Preacher Buck to prevent the vicious tongues against himself and the threats of marriage I would be forced to endure. He said without Roger it would be easier for us now in England, and that he would most likely be knighted and that we could live in both London and Chelswood. Farin assured me the trip back would be easier because of the prevailing winds and that we would be taking the faster northern route. And so it seemed settled.

It was with difficulty that Sir Thomas persuaded us not to burn the Fort as we loaded what possessions we had salvaged and prepared to board the small ships. I comforted Temperance Flowerdew as she wailed at water's edge. I was soothing her with words of going home when Farin came and told me they would be boarding soon. I asked of David and Farin told me he thought he was with me and that he had come running to me. I heard the hound bark and then I was torn with panic as I saw David with Rufus Rex at the edge of the trees beyond the Fort. The child seemed to be chasing a butterfly.

I ran toward the dog and boy screaming, "David," as Captain Yeardly yelled to me about savages. Farin started to follow and I urged him to go back, that I would get my child. David disappeared into the trees. I heard the bark of the dog and moved into the shade. I tore my skirt and nearly fell over a log. I kept yelling for David. The dog responded. I saw my son and then the line of natives, tall, painted. They stood beyond the boy. David moved up to an erect ancient figure who held his hand out to him and placed it on his shoulder as the boy came to him. The hound stood back with me, barking, and I screamed repeatedly at the painted creatures not to hurt my son. I tried to make them understand. The line of creatures looked at me. The old man kept his hand on the boy's shoulder. The hound stopped barking and stayed at my heels. I could hear Farin calling for me, but dared not answer for fear the savages would harm David. My boy, I repeated and then tried *mein kinder...mon fils...mi hijo.*

The ancient Indian responded with *El nino es muy bonito. Habla Espanol?* I stared at the old man. "*Si.*" The hound growled; I quieted him. Farin was still calling out my name. And the old Indian asked me in Spanish where the English at the Fort were going. I said in Spanish back to England. I asked for my son. He responded by asking if I read. I asked if he meant Spanish. The old creature was tall and intimidating but I was not as frightened once I was able to communicate. English? I said yes and asked for my son. He reached and ripped the front of my dress and tore away a section of the fabric and told me I would stay and read to him. I knelt down; the fright returned. I clutched at David and begged them not to harm the boy. *El muchacho*. The old man told me that neither I nor the boy would be harmed. He took David's cap from his head and gave it and the piece of my dress to another Indian. The man cut his finger and smeared blood on the cap and the piece of fabric. He stepped to the edge of the trees and put the cloth on an arrow and sent it whizzing through the air. He then did the same with David's cap. He told me that now they would not wait for me or look for me and told me again no harm would come to us, but that I must be quiet or the next arrow would contain a piece of my flesh. I heard Farin crying out my name and for David. Then I heard President Percy tell them it was too late and to come away from the trees.

I heard the roll of the drums. With the Indians, I moved closer to the edge of the trees. I watched the English board the two ships. Farin knelt down. He buried his face in his hands. I wished that I could reassure him, to tell him I was not dead. Captain

Yeardly helped him up the plank. The plank was raised and the ships drifted back from the shore and began to move downriver. I was left behind in this strange land with these strange people. But I had my son, David's son.

An army of other Indians appeared from the woods and ran toward the Fort. Their screams were incoherent and frightening. I asked what was to become of me and the old Indian said that I was to read him Aristotle. I was startled to see the white horse brought to him. He mounted it and we moved off. The hound stayed close at my heels. We camped the night at some sort of village. I was not frightened by the Indians, only of the unknown, the prospects of what the morning might bring and the mornings to follow. I was given food and fed David and I asked the old man where he learned to speak Spanish and he told me from the Jesuits and I told him a Jesuit had taught me as well, only they burned him and he told me that in Spain it was the Jesuits that did the burning. When I questioned him he told me he had been to Spain when he was young. The next morning, the old man, who I realized was the chief, put David and me on the horse. I had not ridden since Chelswood and yearned to let the horse gallop beneath me, but held him to the slow walk. The old Indian seemed to sense what I was thinking and told me the horse loved to run. We reached a village, a collection of oval houses woven of reed and thatch. Inside there were skins piled on a low bed-like platform and I put Davey down on it to sleep.

A young woman came into the hut. Hardly more than a girl, tall with dark skin, clear except for patches of red and black designs, she wore a large blue stone, dangling between her exposed breasts. She had white perfect teeth. She told me in English that she was Pocahontas. I told her my name. She repeated "Molly" and said that the Werow-ance, her uncle, was called Opechancanough and that he was wise and old and hated the English. She said he would have sent me and the boy back had he not discovered I could read, for it was not the way of The People to hurt a child. She told me that she could read but "not good" and that Ninghekekughes showed her. She said this had been his *yehauken* and these his books and went over to a corner and from a wicker basket took out three books and handed them to me. I examined them: the compiled works of Aristotle and Plato and the essays of Francis Bacon. I asked who Ninghekekughes was and she said he was her brother and that he was English. She went on to tell that he had nearly died of swamp fever and that they had made him well and that he had lived with The People. She told how his *manitou* came to him and took him back to England, but he would return and live again among The People and teach them to read and have philosophy and how to make guns and paper and make a garden of flowers and play the lute and how The People and the English could live in peace. She said she wanted to go to England and funerals and weddings and masques and disputations and lectures and sermons and arsenals and fencing and churches and exchanges and hangings and all such things of which Bacon writes and go to the place Twickenham and see the great Bacon.

I was startled and asked if Ninghekekughes went to Twickenham and she said yes and that it is a place that abounds in gardens and a place of water like a pond and men dressed in fancy clothes with pictures of boars on them. I told the young woman that Lady Bacon, the wife of Sir Francis, had given me this dog and that his name was Rufus Rex. Pocahontas begged to be told more of Twickenham and I did.

The few days there fell into a routine. I began to learn the names of things in the language of The People. David played with the children and, though he asked for Farin, seemed happy. I learned to grind corn in a stone bowl. There was a boy called Kemadakun, nearly a man, I suspected. He had lighter skin and blue eyes. I asked Pocahontas about him. She told me his mother lay down with the wind spirit, but Pocahontas laughed and said the wind spirit was more likely a Spanish sailor, one of those who came and went before the English. He was a tall graceful youth. She said the Pamunkey maids would all have him, but he none of them and added that perhaps he would become a squaman. I needed no interpretation.

Pocahontas came later to say that Opechancanough was angry. He had heard the *shu-shu-gah*, a thing of whose identity I had no notion, cry three times and so knew of the danger before the messenger came from Pochins, who was her brother. As the two ships of the English left the Fort down the Great River and waited at dawn for the tide to change, there in the Bay came other ships of the English and they all returned to James Fort and the Paspaheghs camped there fled. The new governor wore more clothes and baubles than President Percy and was of the name Delaware. I asked if it were Lord de La Warr and she said yes and that she knew this because she heard Opechancanough's spies talking.

It did not now occur to me to return to the Fort. I was content. I was learning the language; I read to Opechancanough and translated easily for him into Spanish. I learned to cook over the fire and weave rushes and reeds and how to make a fire from stones. I bathed with The People in the river and David played and learned the language easier than I. I met Face-of-Spots, who was white, but had been raised from infancy among The People and Pocahontas translated.

Contrary to having assumed Ninghekekughes was an old man, I discovered that he was young. I wondered what he looked liked, where he was from, how he knew the Bacons. He was apparently well-schooled, obviously gentry, unlikely to be of the nobility and his conversations with Opechancanough were in Latin. He did not speak Spanish. He was proficient in the use of the bow and arrow, dressed as The People and, if all told were true, found the lifestyle preferable to that of James Fort. I, myself, felt comfortable and at peace at this place called Manapucunt. There was no tyranny of the church to force me or my son to kneel in prayer twice daily, or to profess beliefs I could not hold. I was allowed to ride the mare, as had Ninghekekughes. I was content among The People and did not feel like a prisoner. Kemadakun often came to the *yehauken* where I taught him the English names for things and continued to learn the meaning of the words in the language of The People.

Pocahontas kept me informed of James Fort. Life there seemed to hold no great joy; still she yearned to go there but was forbidden. Lord de La Warr ruled with an iron fist, punishing with severity all infractions. Men lost limbs and ears for disobedience. The People refused to trade. Sir George Somers sailed to Bermuda in the *Patience* in search of more food. Opechancanough's spies seemed to miss nothing. Tension continued to grow. The English burned villages and fields of corn not yet ripe and The People moved deeper into the woodland. When the Governor and his party attempted to reach the falls, the Paspaheghs attacked. The Governor escaped but most of his party was killed. Wowinchopunk was hunted down and killed.

Rufus Rex kept Opechancanough company and followed him when he rode the white stallion. The harvest came and The People stored their food away from the English. Lord de La Warr burned more villages. Nantaquaus, who was Pocahontas's brother, came from Orapaks with his wife Toatoka and daughter and he talked of Ninghekekughes, his friend, and his little girl piled rocks with David in the dirt by the river. I collected nuts and helped with the harvest; Pocahontas said Sir George Somers never came back from Bermuda and was thought dead. The river began to form ice. Lord de La Warr ordered Gates to attack the Kecoughtan and he did, killing many and senselessly burning the stores of food. Pochins and some of his warriors and

squas and children escaped to the deep wood-
lands near the mountains.

The spring came and the river thawed
and I helped plant the corn. Gates and Newport sailed for England. Pocahontas went to
Orapaks and I made soup for Opechancanough. He asked me if longed to be among
the English and I told him seldom. He asked
if I had no family or friends. I told him only
one friend, a man called Farin Browne, and
I would like to know if he were well or not.
Opechancanough said he would make questions about him.

Pocahontas taught me how to cook *saks-
kolaas*, scallops, and said that if she could not
go to the Fort, she could not get to London.
She told me she would take a husband from
the Accomac or even Susquehannock to free
herself from the Powhatan and then leave her
husband and go to James Fort. I looked up as
Pocahontas was talking. A shadow appeared
in the entrance, then a figure bent and moved
into the *yehauken*. I leaped up. It was Farin. I
hugged him and asked how he knew to find
me. He said an old Indian named Rawhunt
was sent by Opechancanough and told that I
was alive and here. I introduced him to Pocahontas and he said there was no man, woman
or child who had not heard of the Princess. I
asked of his news and he said that most was
horrible and that Lord de La Warr was a

tyrant and while the church got colored windows, and they marched and prayed, he ran-
domly ordered the killing of more Indians,
foolishly burned crops on which they could
all survive and hanged men for little or no reason. He said they were but slaves to the great
Baron. The hope was that de La Warr was
not well and had taken all his cronies, more
than fifty fawning hangers-on, and gone off
to Nevis to take hot baths and Farin said he
would not be too surprised if they all didn't
simply go on to England from there.

I fed Farin some cooked squash and dried
venison. He said he was much out of favour
as he had taken a young laborer to his bed, a
fine young lad by the name of Allen Plomb,
but that John Rolfe had made certain the
matter had become common gossip. He also
said the lecherous Master Rolfe had decided
tobacco was the way to his fortune. He admitted the local stuff was bad, bitter tasting, but
somehow had managed to get some seeds
from some Spaniards in the Indies Islands.
Farin said he stole some of Rolfe's precious
seeds because there did seem to be a growing
demand for the weed in London.

David came running into the *yehauken*
and leaped at Farin who hugged him and
tossed him in the air. Farin stayed for three
days. It was agreed that no one among the
English should know I had survived.

A Patowmak warrior came to trade. Pocahontas told me that she would become his squa and go live in the place of the Patowmak where the Powhatan had no voice. She said the warrior had the face of a dead sturgeon. Pocahontas packed her pots. Her uncle told her that she was cutting off her finger to punish her hand. She told the warrior Kocoum that she would be his squa and bid us goodbye. She was now the warrior's wife, no longer her father's daughter.

It was perhaps May, maybe early June. There was no calendar to tell the days more than clocks to tell the hour. Farin Browne arrived at my *yehauken* in the middle of the night. He said that Marshal Dale had burned Alan Plomb at the stake and that he had barely escaped, being saved by an Indian, Gohundta, who cut him loose and helped him reach here. I asked about Dale. He said Lord de La Warr had apparently reached London and the Company sent him out as Marshal to take command. He came with 250 passengers, 12 cows, 20 goats and Farin added that no doubt with a goodly supply of whips, shackles, stocks and hanging rope. I remembered Dale as the awful creature I sat next to at Alice Bacon's feast. Farin said he was all God and cruel orders and that he made Lord de La Warr seem lax in discipline by comparison. Hanging had replaced the chopping off

of limbs. Any lapse in devotion was punish-
able by death and for sleeping in church he
put one to the stake for beatings. He allowed
houses built outside the walls, but all were
forced inside for prayers and the gates were
locked and the church was locked and none
could escape. Chastity and celibacy was mandatory for those without wives at the Fort and
sodomites were to be burned. Farin told me
all he had managed to bring with him was his
tobacco seeds.

Molly

RICHMOND

—the present—

MOLLY PUT THE marked up copy back into her bag as the train approached Richmond station. As she did so, Alex's card fell out. An omen, perhaps, she thought, and dialed his number on her cell phone. "Molly Sharpe, perhaps you remember me."

"Such beauty I don't forget." The accent was honeyed Virginia.

"You are so full of it. I was wondering if I could take you to dinner."

"No."

"No?"

"No, but I will take you."

"And why can't I take you?"

"Because I am a Southern gentleman with antebellum mores."

"And attire."

"Yes, that, too."

"All right, you may take me to dinner. May I, despite your being a Southern gentleman, come pick you up when I get in?"

"Allowed."

"I will see you within the hour then."

When she arrived at the brick house, Modine stood in the doorway as if blocking it but moved back as Alex came out. He was dashing, Molly thought, in his confederate grey. He wore a sword which he had not been wearing on their previous meeting. My God! He was handsome.

"I thought the Jefferson," he said. "I made a reservation."

"Look at me. No Jefferson Hotel. I'm in jeans."

"Why are you not dressed like a Jamestown settler?"

She didn't want to go into detail. "Washington business."

"There are some period dresses in the house. They're museum pieces, a little old, but —"

"I'm much afraid I could never squeeze into one. They had waists like mice."

"Then Tom's," he said.

"Fine with me, but is there any particular reason?" She put the car in gear.

"I used to go in there all the time. Loved the place. Then one night I overheard a couple of the waitresses telling a girl I had been talking to at the bar that I was a madman and believed I was a Confederate officer."

"I can relate," Molly told him.

"Yes. I was sure of it. I wish you weren't so nearly committed."

"Well, I'm less committed from when I last saw you."

"Ah, how sweet that sounds." He leaned over and kissed her. It was another wet, passionate, long, tongue-probing kiss.

Molly looked over her shoulder to see Modine, arms folded across her chest, still standing in the doorway.

The Novel

LONDON

—1612—

David was consumed by moots, bolts, putting cases, reading, exercises. Dinner was at noon; the law was argued; cases were put. Supper was at six; the law was argued; cases were put. 'Law is a babblative art,' he was told repeatedly. 'Learn to babble.' The Utter Barristers taught incessantly. 'Speak out.' The Readers talked incessantly. Gray's Inn was no place for the reticent. The only time he was allowed to be quiet was at prayers. Preachers orated incessantly. Dogma tinged with theological politics. The King's divine right was disputed in the name of the Lord. Salvation was Parliament and Heaven the exercise of power over the Sovereign. Sir Francis Bacon was offended by the tone and the great respect in which Edward Coke's genius was held by Gray's, but the Inns were sacrosanct, independent of King and Commons, and Bacon would in no way interfere in the independence of his beloved Gray's.

Coke and the Court of Common Pleas, the Puritans in their pulpits and Sandys in Parliament undermined the divinity of James's rule. Bacon saw there must be Parliament, but it must be subservient to a strong monarchy. It was not a matter of divine right to Bacon, but a matter of practicality. David listened to Sir Francis and kept his mouth shut, but he believed the Prince and Parliament to be right except in the matter of religion. When it came to theology he kept his own council.

He had a social position now, friend to the Prince of Wales. He attended a play given for Princess Elizabeth and her betrothed, the Elector of Hanover. "As you from crimes would pardon be, let your indulgence set me free." The applause released Prospero. Like Miranda and Ferdinand, the Princess Elizabeth and Frederick rose, imbued with innocence, the beautiful Princess and the curly-haired youth. David watched Elizabeth, so like Miranda in some ways, reared at Combe Abbey in Warwickshire away from James's corrupt court and Queen Anne's Catholicism. Elizabeth smiled at David and touched Frederick, whom she called her 'Elector Charming.'

The players mingled with the guests. Miranda shed her gown and became Alexie, the young man David had met so long ago.

"You are no innocent," David told him.

"Do I know you, sir?"

"You and your Romeo gave up your bed to Molly Dean and me. I am David d'Ersby."

Alexie asked of Molly. How strange it was to talk of her this way. David had been so elated when he first learned she had been on the *Sea Venture*, but it was lost... then found and then later, from those returning from Jamestown, came the news about Molly being killed by The People. The People would not kill a child. That was not their way. Perhaps his son lived.

David went to the Mermaid. Chapman was arguing the nature of Christ's divinity with Jonson.

"Caution, George," David warned. "They'll burn you for heresy."

"I hope we've put that behind us in this enlightened age."

"I wouldn't be too certain," Shakespeare cautioned.

"You should feel safe," Jonson said. "You believe in everything, Willie. There are no more things in Heaven and Earth, Horatio, than are dreamt of in your philosophy."

"Yes," Chapman said. "The King accursed the spirits, witches all. Will glories in them."

"I but saw *The Tempest*," David said. "I think you be right, George."

"David's Molly was aboard the *Sea Venture*," Jonson said.

"How came you the details of the storm?" David asked Shakespeare.

"Strachey wrote a long letter on it, and of Bermuda, to Thomas Smythe's lady. Lord Southampton arranged the reading of it for me. John Florio's translation of Montaigne gave me Gonzalo's ideal state."

"Montaigne is like Ben," David said. "He stayed Catholic long after he ceased being a Christian."

"Our David is becoming a wit," Chapman said.

David returned to Gray's. At supper the arguments over the banning of *The Interpreter* raged. The Archbishop had placed his seal to the law dictionary which declared the

King above the law. The Commons banned the book. That argument brought on further arguments about the 'great contract' —the King's demand for monies to pay his horrendous debt and the Parliament's demand against the King's imposition. And so the meal went. He was reprimanded for his reticence. "Learn to babble. A mute has no place at the bar." David went to play tennis with the Prince.

After, he walked back to Gray's. At supper they argued the legalities of the confrontation. David, when stared at by the Utter Barrister, raised the contention of Coke's ruling that James could not make laws through proclamation. "The King will make proclamations," someone said. "It is not legal," David responded. "The King loves to make proclamations," another retorted. There was laughter.

"Seriousness," the Reader shouted. "There is no laughter at the bar."

David went with Sir Peregrine Bertie, newly knighted, and his bride, Margaret, to Verdun, the Bacons' country house. David's new sister-in-law was a beautiful woman who buried her beauty in layers of morality. In the garden at Verdun, David walked alone with Thomas Hariot. "I am glad we have this chance to talk," Hariot said. "You are one of the few who understands The People. You seem aware that they have much in their culture to commend it. They are not encumbered by our silly vanities."

"They will be annihilated," David said. "They will not willingly see their land taken from them and the English will overpower and destroy them."

"I know that."

"What can be done?"

"What I am told you are doing. You must champion their rights at the bar and in Parliament. The Prince will become King. You and Raleigh, who believes as you do, have his ear."

"I am faced with a dilemma, Master Hariot."

"What is it?"

"The Prince believes The People must be brought to the English God. That culture which you find commendable is so because it is not burdened with guilt, nor laden with sin, divine grace or fear of Hell."

"I know that. But the Prince supports toleration. He understands the irrationality of witchcraft and that horrid Hell. It is not a long leap from tolerating Puritans and Catholics in a joint existence, to tolerating Deists, and the Indians are Deists, in a sense. Where do you stand with God?"

"I don't know."

"I am a good friend of Chapman, David. You may speak openly with me. Do you believe in Hell?"

"No. Nor in sin. I accept the goodness of Christian charity and love, but rebel against the theological subjugation of new ideas, new discoveries, and I sincerely doubt there be a Heaven."

"It is with me the same, and Raleigh. The Prince has great respect for Sir Walter. He will be rational in his enforcement of a policy of religion for The People."

"There is hope?"

"There is hope for us all in the eventual reign of Henry Stuart."

It was a month later that Robert Cecil took ill. "A tumor far bigger than the Treasury has got Lord Salisbury,"

Northampton was reputed to have said. At Marlborough but days later, age forty-eight, the King's secretary expired. The court was not abject with grief. Limericks about the hunchback scrivener were repeated in soft voices. The Howards openly rejoiced. The King beamed, David was told, as if his shackles had been removed. "God save England," Edwin Sandys said at the burial.

David looked down at the wooden coffin. It was so small.

Alice Bacon, buried in layers of black fabric, brought her hounds to the gravesite.

A veiled Mary Vere was helped by Peregrine to the rectangular hole in the ground. David stood beside her, Lord and Lady Willoughby at her other side. "You're David. I remember you," the voice beneath the veil said. It was an old voice. "Though not without some pain. I once dined with the Danish Ambassador. The man drank like a dry slop pit."

Margaret Bertie prayed louder than the rest. Lord Norris did not attend. "These are the sisters," Bridget Norris told David. "Susan and Elizabeth."

David bowed.

"The Countess Montgomery," Susan said, throwing open her hand.

"The Countess Derby," Elizabeth said. "As you note, Bridgie married beneath us."

"And you have not married at all, d'Ersby," Susan said. "We'll find you a spare countess. Elizabeth keeps lists of widows and eligibles."

Alice, holding her hounds on leashes, shook her head. "No, I will get David a rich merchant's daughter, common as pork rind, but suffocating in riches."

"David, I must be off," Lady Mary said. "I have an appointment, but I don't remember whom it is with, though I think it might be with the Queen—not the new one but the dead one."

David walked her to their carriage, helped her in and stood beside it.

Sir Francis did not grieve at the death of his powerful first cousin. "How is it at Gray's?"

"Too much law. From morning 'til bed. England, it seems to me, Sir Francis, is binding itself into knots of litigation. A man sues because another's horse peed on his new slippers. I do not exaggerate."

"There can never be enough law. Understand what the alternative is—personal war. Dukes had armies; earls had armies; barons had armies; even knights had little armies. They scourged the countryside with their personal griev- ances. Civilization cannot exist without laws."

"But so many?"

"The more law, the more civilized we are. Dueling will be prevented only when laws are upheld."

"Maybe it is bloodless, but I wonder if the pain is less." David climbed into the carriage.

"Robert Cecil was never a nice boy, that back of his and all." Lady Mary took off her veil, her face a mask of pow- dered eggshell. "I don't think Lord Burghley ever cared for his son; the Lord Keeper didn't like him at all. 'Little weasel,' he called him. I don't think the Lord keeper looked a bit well today."

"That was his son, Mother," Peregrine told her. "Francis Bacon. Not Lord Nicholas."

"Francis was a hound lapping at the Queen's behind. The Queen is dead and the Scot with the ugly little legs is the monarch. Your father, Perri, was kin to that Bloody Mary, but I married him anyway. It's what makes you Berties so stiff-necked. Robert's the same, not enough laughter. It's all that Spanish religiosity stuck in your veins." The carriage bounced her about. "Are you Spanish, Margaret?"

"No, Lady Mary," Peregrine's wife said. "I have no Catholic blood in these veins."

"You must be dead then, Margaret. You're so stiff. Anthony Bacon must be dead. I didn't see him at the burial. Sweet boy. Lame, though. Everywhere I go, everyone is dead these days. Be glad, David, you have none of that Bertie blood to you. You are still alive."

"Mother," Peregrine scolded, "could we change the topic of conversation?"

"Look over there." She pointed across the field. A stallion was humping a mare.

The morning sun never appeared. David beat the Prince at tennis for the first time. "You're not well."

"Just a headache. Salisbury's death means disaster for the Treasury. What are you doing today?"

"What else? Reciting the law. Babbling."

"Go with me to the shipyard. We've no Navy left. I don't know what, but I must do something."

"Give me a royal command. I will do anything to escape hearing the plea of another litigant."

"I command you attend me to Woolwich." Prince Henry dried his forehead with a towel. "There will be chaos. The King has no idea of the value of money. His debt is sending

England to ruin. It worries me. I have seen the King stand alone in the Presence Chamber while a crowd gathers about me. There is a look on his face as if he were Henry Two and wanted to yell out 'will no one rid me of this curse.' He hates me. Mother and her Catholic friends hate me. The Howards would poison me if I weren't careful of my meals. I wish I could be like Elizabeth with her handsome Elector and be in love and know I would soon be gone from the Stuart Court. She will be free and I in chains."

"I am not given to flattery, my Lord Prince. You know me well enough. But you will be England's great king. You will bring divisiveness to an end."

They walked toward the stables. "But the Treasury can't wait for my turn."

Six days later the Prince fell ill. Doom hung over London. David was not allowed to see him.

The case at supper caused turmoil, spiced with anger and rage. Without the knowledge of Coke, or the Court of Common Pleas, a man was brought before James from the Ecclesiastic Courts. He told the King he did not accept the divinity of Christ. He was ordered by James to be taken to Smithfield and burned. The uproar was not limited to Gray's—the Inner Temple, Lincoln's and Middle Temple were infuriated as well. The Temples were united in their anger with the King. It was not the intolerance of the burning; it was that the King had no jurisdiction to act. It was the mandate of the Common Pleas.

The Prince got up from his sickbed. David was sent for and the Prince beat him at tennis.

George Percy came from Virginia. Wrapped in a cocoon of melancholy, he was no longer the dandy. He told of the starving time and the horrors of James Fort, gave a litany of the dead.

Elizabeth sent for David. "Henry collapsed at Richmond. The physicians do not tell me what is wrong, David. It is said to be contagious. He has a terrible fever, and they report his lips are black and his eyes so bad he cannot look at a lighted candle. He suffers convulsions. I am forbidden to see him."

"The King?" David asked.

"He has fled to Theobalds. Father is terrified of death and must believe Henry is dying. Mother has taken Charles and locked herself in Denmark House. Poor Henry has no one with him. I tried to disguise myself and sneak in but was found out. The physician said I might ask one of Henry's house to represent me. I asked his Secretary, but he said the danger was too great. None of Henry's house consent."

"I will go, of course, Princess."

"Der be many risk," the Elector told him.

"He is my friend."

Near the chamber entrance the Earl of Southampton stood with the Earls of Montgomery and Pembroke. Southampton took David aside. "I know what you do, you do in kindness for the Princess, but there is a great danger to your person, David. The Prince is stricken with typhoid."

"What I do, I do for myself, my Lord. He is my friend."

A crier came through the corridor announcing that boiled sene and rhubarb had brought forth a great store of putrefied choler. David was taken into the bed chamber. It reeked of death. Soft candlelight flickered as physicians hovered over the youth. An old man plastered freshly killed roosters and pigeons to the Prince's skull. The youth's beautiful auburn hair had been shaved off. David sat for hours. The physicians spoke mostly in Latin and David listened to them mumble. A man entered and stood for awhile. He came over to David. "Who are you?"

"David d'Ersby. I am his friend."

"I am John Florio. I informed him in French and Italian, but I taught him Montaigne." John Florio stayed for a time. The Prince shook the bed, overcome with convulsions. John Florio wiped tears from his eyes and left. An assistant reported that an application of powdered unicorn horns and pearl mixed with bone of stag's heart was given to the prince.

The Prince had a moment of lucidity. "Elizabeth. My sister, Elizabeth."

"She sent me," David said.

The Prince made no reply.

The Archbishop of Canterbury sent a hooded representative. "Sir, hear you me, hear you me, hear you me. If you hear me in certain sign of your faith and hope of the blessed resurrection, give us for our comfort a sign, lifting your hands." The Prince's hand moved slightly. "Yet another sign, lift with your eyes." The Prince seemed to raise his eyes. The cleric administered the benediction and left.

The Prince lay silent. The convulsions had ended. The physicians did little but stand and wait. They waited the afternoon and David sat and the evening came and the physicians waited and David sat, and as darkness cast over the windows, the Prince of Wales, Duke of Cornwall, died at age nineteen.

The hope of England was dead.

Molly

JAMESTOWN

—the present—

MOLLY WENT SEARCHING the papers scattered across her floor for the earliest Virginia census records. They were somewhere amid the piles of books and papers. And there were Sharpes from her Bible listed on those rolls. Where are those damn papers?

She picked up the copy of *Mrs. Dalloway.* Ah Clarissa, my dear, you thought it was about connections. Fuck connections. Connections were to be found in fiction. What she needed to find was the focus of a thesis, something upon which to hang all this work, this transcription, this journal. Woolf's connections were not what this was about. Life did not emulate fiction. Fiction had a neat dénouement. Fiction would have her wed David d'Ersby. Oh, there was something so right in at least the idea of it. The completion of a narrative begun four centuries earlier.

And utterly insane, unreal. Reality was sitting on the floor in only a long tee shirt, searching for a piece of paper. Not about fucking connection. And speaking about fuck…the word "fuck" was now in the OED. Yes, she had found it there in the online edition. Ah, David d'Ersby, who never even bothers to come online anymore, put that in your Anglo pipe and smoke it. She touched the shift key on her computer and it left its standby mode. She went online — e-mail to dsharpe: Fuck now in the OED. Molly.

There was another e-mail from opech@earthgo.com addressed directly to her: dsharpe has not indicated that he read my last e-mail. I have attached another document.

She really should be finding that census, but instead she opened the attachment:

Opecancanough

E-MAIL ATTACHMENT

I WATCHED MOLLY as she closed the book. I noticed how calloused her hands had become. "Aristotle — is wrong, Molly." The People had named her *Anumwitsqua,* the woman with the dog. I could sense her discomfort with the name and always called her Molly, just as Pocahontas had done.

The dog was stretched out beside her. "Not making Plato right, I hope. Human nature would sink to the level of the beast in a Platonic society. Aristotle respects the individual, privacy, liberty…"

A broken branch slipped beneath the drinking willows. "Ownership, possession, division of labor — these lead men to quarrel. There is no inherent wickedness. Evil arises out of the idea of possession."

"Plato's communal society collapses because there is no incentive for superior ability."

"If an individual doesn't contribute, what does it matter? The evil comes from accumulation."

"The Powhatan accumulates," she said.

I thought about it. "But only as a symbol of power. The People of the Powhatan is assured by that tribute — from other tribes within the Powhatan and from outside that would invade."

"There is still the necessity of labor. Women must work in the fields; men must hunt."

"Not must. No one is forced to work. No woman will starve because she does not go to the fields. A warrior who does not hunt may still eat of the kill. No one has to live in the village of his family. A woman may choose any man for a husband and a man any woman or none at all. If a squa tires of her husband she leaves. We choose to live together and share food because we are companions and sometimes kin. When it no longer suits us we leave, as Pocahontas has chosen to do. We can go off and live alone in the woods as your friend —"

"Farin."

"Yes. We can build a *yehauken* off by ourselves and hope the *abooksiguin* doesn't come from the mountain and make us his feast. Could we have any more liberty in Artistotle's complex society?"

"And I am free to go if I wish?"

"Yes."

"And who would read you the Greeks?"

"Perhaps I have had all the philosophy I can take. Or maybe I have memorized it all."

"Liberty here is greater than in England, I concede, but your world is not as perfect as you would make it out to be. The Kecoughtans who refused to recognize the Powhatan were burned."

"No. It is not perfect. But it is better than Aristotle's Athens must have been."

"Is Face-of-Spots, who must have come as a captive like myself, free to leave?"

"She is not held by any bindings. Let her go where she would. But where could she go? Her ways are not the ways of the Whiteman. Would you wish to return to the Whiteman's Fort?"

"You know I would not, particularly with Marshal Dale in command."

"Perhaps join your friend in the woods?"

"I would worry about the mountain lion eating my young son."

"Go back to England?"

"Pocahontas would. I prefer it here."

"You believe Pocahontas really would go to England?"

"If she could."

"You should go see her. Kemadakun is your friend," I teased. "Have him take you to the land of the Patowmak."

She kicked my foot. "You gossip like the squas. Kemadakun is but a boy who wants to learn the language of the Whiteman."

"And when he comes and lays wampum at my feet as if I were your father?"

"He will not do that. You are only worried there will be no one to cook for you."

"What little I eat, would it matter?"

"That is true. You should eat more. The land is important. Is that not a possession?" she asked.

"Yes. Perhaps, we place too much significance on certain land. Pochins has been driven off from Kecoughtan, yet his people are as content in their new place. They complain that the weirs bring fewer and smaller fish and go further for oysters, but they are content. Land perhaps is only land."

Molly petted the dog's neck. "You know, it's ironic. All you claim right with The People's way of life fits the Platonic ideal; mostly what is wrong with James Fort is the Platonic communal lifestyle. It doesn't work for them. The gentlemen will not work and the laborers tire working for them and they would all starve before lifting a finger for the common good."

I stood up, brushing the dirt from my legs. "Perhaps you are right." I started to walk away.

"Where are you going?"

"To Orapaks."

I assembled thirty warriors. This was not a private visit to my brother. This was the visit of the Werowance of the Pamunkey to the Powhatan. I did not ride the white stallion, but walked before the warriors. Spies could no longer get into the Fort. The People were kept out, but I was aware that the English kept coming in the ships. Gates had returned with six ships, perhaps three hundred men, women, children and more cattle and hogs. More mouths open for food. The animals also needed feed. The Whiteman encroached upon the land like the locust. From the falls, across and down to the mouth of the Pamunkey, they drove off The People. They burned the *yehaukens* and the corn and took the land.

The drums had spoken of my march and the Powhatan greeted me, wearing ceremonial robes. Nantaquaus stood beside his father. I greeted him formally and then followed into the long *yehauken*.

"How are you, Wahunsonocock?"

"Dying."

"We are all dying," I told him.

"None of us will live to die," Nantaquaus said. "The Whiteman will kill us all first."

"It is why I've come."

"Many ships have come," Nantaquaus said. "Ninghek-ekughes has not returned."

"Perhaps he will not come back." I gestured with open hands.

"He will come back." Nantaquaus's eyes reflected the firmness of his voice.

It was a dreary day and smoke from a small fire found its way up through the hole in the roof. "It is not the season for a fire," I said.

"*Nijirdakotze*, I am cold," the Powhatan answered.

Papoo stepped from the darkness. "*Paalsu*, but he will not go to the sweat lodge."

"You must make yourself well, Wahunsonocock, for I would have you assemble the Werowances for counsel. We must stop the annihilation. My idea to starve the White-man has failed."

"It is my doing...I should have destroyed the survivors of the winter famine when you urged me."

"More would have come." The smoke bothered me. It was stifling in the closed *yehauken*.

Nantaquaus wiped sweat from his brow. "The boy called Henry —"

"The one given the Powhatan that ran away to the Fort and then ran back to The People?"

"Yes. He is with Pochins and says the sailors say that in the London place there is much talk of Dale and how he is a tyrant and the Whiteman do not want to come any more to James Fort."

"They will empty their jails to get Whiteman to fill our land if they must."

"Jails?" Nantaquaus asked.

"Yes. Where they lock up their bad people. Ninghek-ekughes told me," I explained.

The Powhatan gestured for silence. "You came with a purpose, Apachisto."

"Yes, Wahunsonocock, we cannot let any more of The People be killed. We must make peace."

"Peace with the Whiteman means they take all our food and we starve," the Powhatan told me. "I will not sit with them and talk the peace. I will make no bargain. I will not give them our food."

"Not that kind of peace, brother. But we will stop kill-ing, let them build their forts, let more come, let them see we are peaceful, trade only when we must and give little as possible, stop taking their guns and tools; let them believe we are their friends. We will go among them, be welcome into their forts and *yehaukens*; then on a certain day, when the sun sits at a certain point in the sky, we will kill them all."

"When will be the day?" Nantaquaus asked.

"A cycle of the seasons, two, perhaps even five *cohunks*. We will know when the time is best."

"We kill them all," the Powhatan said. He coughed.

"All but the children, the babies," Nantaquaus said.

"All but the children," I repeated. "It must be thorough, but for those Whiteman who live with us as we live, all must be killed. There will be none left."

The Powhatan coughed again. "We stop killing them. We stop taking their tools and guns. We do all this. We make the peace. What is to stop them from killing us, burning our *yehaukens* and corn?"

"We let them take a hostage, an important hostage."

"You, Uncle?" Nantaquaus asked.

"Me they'd kill. It must be somebody they admire, someone they trust, someone…"

"Matoaka," the Powhatan said.

"Yes, Pocahontas."

The werowances were sent for. The Powhatan went to the sweathouse. Inside, hot coals smoldered beneath a pot and he sat for hours, sweating away the disease, and when he could bear no more he ran from the sweathouse and plunged into the river. Seven suns and the werowances gathered at the stake in the circle at Orapaks, squatted, their hands in their laps. We spoke in soft voices, words slow and deliberate as was the way of The People. We awaited the Powhatan.

The Werowance of the Accohannoc wore many beads of the Whiteman's. The fierce wereosqua of the Appamatack, Oppussoquionuske, her hanging breasts bare except for the necklace of Whiteman scalps, sat next to him. The Chickahominy, the Moraughtacund, the Kiskiack, the Mattaponi, the Onawamanient, the Secacowoni, the Wighcocomoco, the Quiyoughcohanncock, the Youghtanund, the Tauxent, the Rappahannock, the Warrasqueoc, the Nansemond, the Pissaseck, the Weanoc, the Onawmanient, and the Nantaughtacund were all represented by their werowances, their priests sitting behind in the circle. Kictopeake and his brother Debedeavon, the laughing werowance of

the Accomac, had come from across the bay. The werowance of the K'tchisipik had sent his son. Pochins sat for
the Kecoughtan and his brother the Tanx Powhatan, Parahunt, had come from the Falls. Japazaros of the Patowmak
came from the North. The new werowance of the Paspahegh was the son of the slaughtered Wowinchopunk's sister. I, as wereowance of the largest tribe, the Pamunkey, sat
among them.

Flanked by priests, Nantaquaus escorted The Powhatan
from his *yehauken*. He wore a coat of yellow feathers and
the eagle feathers on his head, and when he raised his arms
there was silence. The pipe was passed. The Powhatan
spoke in deliberate words about the killing of The People
and how the Whiteman moved like a creeping vine grasp-
ing the forests and the hunting places. He spoke of how
more ships came bringing more of the invaders. He spoke
of how he had forbidden trading and had urged the taking of guns and tools and how this had failed and all the
Whiteman did was kill more and more of The People until
soon there would be none left in the land.

"The eagle spoke," the Wereowance of the Pissaseck said.
"Nothing we do will save The People."

"Nothing we do will save us if we do nothing." My voice
was loud and firm.

The Powhatan again raised his arms. There was silence.
"We must save The People and save our place upon which
they live. But it will take five seasons or five of five seasons; we must wait our time and rid us of this pestilence
that comes like a locust to the Powhatan. We will make a
peace, but a peace not made with promises and the smok-

ing of a pipe and a giving up of more of our corn and land. We will let the Whiteman force us to a peace, let him take a hostage of importance, and we will be forced to stop killing the Whiteman, and he us, yet we will trade only as little as we must. We will walk at the place of forts and be the friend like the wolf who lies down with the hare. When the certain day comes and the sun sits in its place in the sky, we will strike. We will kill them all until, like the Whiteman who came among the Roanoke, there is not a bone to be found."

"*Tarokeouesou*, the wolf howls," Debedeavon of the Accomac yelled, "and kills the hare."

"It shall be kept in silence," the Powhatan said. "We must not speak of this among The People, not to our warriors, not to our wives. When the day of revenge comes, the Whiteman must have no warning. Like the unsuspecting hare, he must lay in the warmth of the wolf's breath."

"The hostage must be a werowance," the nephew of Wowinchopunk said. "Important enough that the Whiteman would believe the Powhatan would order the peace to protect him. Opechancanough, Opitchapan, Kecatough or Oppussoquionuske, those of the Powhatan's family."

"Or I," Pochins said.

"Is the hostage to be me?" Parahunt asked.

"It must be one the Whiteman would not kill, yet who they believe important to me."

Oppussoquionuske spoke, "It is to be Pocahontas."

"Yes," the Powhatan said.

"She is with the Patowmak," Japazaros said.

"You trade with the Whiteman, Japazaros?" I asked.

"I must. For if I have no tool and beads for the Susque-hannas, these giants will burn our corn and steal our women and children."

"I am not accusing you, Japazaros. I am asking."

"I have trade with the Whiteman."

"The boy Henry, is he still with you, Pochins?" I asked.

"Yes. He is afraid to go back to the Fort, afraid of the Captain Dale."

The Powhatan held his hand for silence. "You suggest to the boy Henry, if Pocahontas were taken captive, how much grieved the Powhatan would be and how he would forbid the killing of the Whiteman for fear they would kill his daughter; how there would be peace and how it is a good thing for The People that the Whiteman does not know where Pocahontas is. You must give Henry to Japaz-aros."

"I will do all this," Pochins agreed.

"Japazaros, you must let the Henry see Pocahontas when the Whiteman comes to trade. Henry, who talks much, will tell how Pocahontas should be a captive and how he knows where she is." The Powhatan's words were deliberate. "You, Japazaros, must see that the husband of Pocahontas does not interfere when she is being taken hostage."

"She has left the *yehauken* of Kocoum and is no longer his squa."

"So much the better," I said.

The Powhatan rose. "We must be patient. The *cohunk* will pass and pass and pass again. But the day will come and on that day all the Whiteman will die." He left them.

The werowances smoked the pipe and danced and ate and slept and left Orapaks, but I remained. What I had suggested to the Powhatan seemed the only logical solution. The People had only one weapon left — cunning. At the morning bathing, Nantaquaus spoke of the return of Ninghekekughes and said it would be soon. He had seen great cat on the rock-that-moves-where-the-river-bends, but had been unable to raise his bow before it was gone. Ninghekekughes would bring them the secrets of the Whiteman and they would make guns and powder and learn to make bells like the one that rang out at James Fort.

Japazaros's messenger came during the failing of the moon. He ate roasted pig, stolen from the island of pigs, and in slow words told of the Captain Argall who had come to the land of the Patowmaks and how Japazaros left the Henry with him. The Captain Argall came to Japazaros with much deviousness. He told Japazaros that he had the copper kettle that Japazaros had much wanted and that he should bring his wife and Pocahontas aboard the ship named the *Treasurer*. But Japazaros said he knew nothing about Pocahontas and Captain Argall said he knew her to be living in the place of the Patowmak and Japazaros said yes that was true but that he would never betray the trust of the Powhatan. The Captain Argall said there would be peace in the land if Pocahontas were taken to Jamestown, where she was much loved and would be given honor and friendship, and he gave Japazaros a cutting knife and three spoons and so Japazaros agreed. He went to Pocahontas and explained how she must pretend to be abducted and be hesitant about boarding the ship and how she should say she was ill once aboard and let them take her to a place to lie down. And so all was done by Japazaros as the Powhatan had told it must be.

I returned to Manapucunt. Kemadakun stood by a canoe and Molly was loading a bundle and held the boy's hand. "Where are you going?" I asked. "Is Kemadakun making you his squa?"

"No. You told me I could go where I would choose. I chose the Patowmaks. A short visit."

"Your trip is for nothing. Pocahontas is no longer there. She has been taken hostage by the English and is at Jamestown."

Molly said nothing. She set the boy on the ground.

"There will be peace now in the Powhatan. The killing will stop," I said.

David

FRANCE

—the present—

THEY FINISHED THE wine and the talk and Yossef stood up. The CDs still delivered Schubert in the background. They had eaten in the dining room and then moved to the suede sofas, leaving the dishes on the table with their wineglasses. The aromatic night air came in through the open doors. David felt so thoroughly content. Being here alone with Yossef, basking in the sun and writing, was fulfilling. Perhaps he never had felt happier.

"I will go to bed. Don't run away," Yossef said.

"Kiss me good night," David told him.

"Yeah," Yossef laughed.

"I'm serious." David looked up at the bronze-skinned, dark-haired man.

Yossef bent down and kissed him, mouth open, and David returned the kiss, felt Yossef's tongue with his tongue. Then Yossef pulled away. "I'm in love with you, you know."

"I know... Good night, Yossef."

Yossef went off toward his room and David watched his back as he moved slowly away. He was a nice man, this Yossef Ben Nather. David got up and went to his own rooms and turned on the computer and began writing.

The Novel

LONDON

— 1612 —

James Wiley babbled on the case of Goodwin Harnoid, master, who ran away so as not to have to support his indentured servants. David ate his pudding. The others argued. "D'Ersby, have you nothing to dispute on this case?" The Utter Barrister pushed aside the pudding.

David stood up. "Sir Edward Coke has declared the Court of Chancery has no jurisdiction in—"

"That is not the case!" The Utter Barrister stood up. "That is not the case before us."

"That is the matter we *should* be arguing. A week ago in the Star Chamber the King proclaimed that the 'mystery of the King's power is not lawful to be disputed—'"

"That is not the business of our argument!"

"That is at the root of the law. That should be our business." David did not sit.

Fists were rapped on the tables. Feet were stomped. "Hear! Hear!" A chorus rose. The Utter Barrister slumped down on the bench. David read from his notes. "The King has said, 'the absolute prerogative of the Crown is not subject for the tongue of a lawyer, nor is it lawful to be disputed. It is atheism and blasphemy to dispute what God can do; good Christians content themselves with His will. It is presumption and high contempt in a subject to dispute what a king can do, or say that kings cannot do this or that, but rest in that which is the king's will revealed in law.'"

The tables reverberated.

The Utter Barrister arose. He yelled above the clamour. "You are hung by your own words."

David ignored him. "Yesterday Sir Edward Coke was removed from the Privy Council, removed from the bench and told to go home and employ his leisure in looking over his reports and to correct his extravagant and exorbitant opinion. The law is dead!"

The uproar increased. The Utter Barrister screamed above the din. "It is your patron, your Sir Francis Bacon, who brought the King's judgment against Coke—your Sir Francis…"

The hall of 'lawyers to be' became a mob. David pushed his way from the huge chamber. The Utter Barrister was still screaming at him. "Your Sir Francis…"

The day was cold, wet; the sky a black blanket. He moved away from the Inns. He could still hear the clamour in the hall. All was accumulation. Life in England was nothing more than accumulation, possessions. He had wasted years babbling at Gray's. There would be no pleading the rights of The People. Justice was dead and there was no

Parliament. The King refused to call a Parliament. He sold Dutch cities and no longer was content to sell little baronetcies. Corruption was the law. The law was naught but buying and selling—a great parasite, feeding on all the little parasites and growing the fattest because it made the rules, subject only to the interference of the King, the grand corruptor. The Prince was dead and England had become like a Webster play, all about evil and corruption.

Charles, Duke of York, whiney Prince Charlie with the speech impediment, was about to be invested Prince of Wales. George Villiers looked to be the main player in the third act. The Archbishop fawned over him, the Queen seemed forced to as well, and the gossips said Sir Francis was not above it.

David found Ben Jonson at the tavern. He was alone. "You look horrid," Jonson said. "I'll buy ye wine. I'm celebrating. I've been given a court pension. A hundred pounds a year."

"Jesu. I thought you alone uncorruptable."

"It's not the money. You know me—one mouth away from starvation. Money and power have never interested me. It's recognition. I am the greatest poet England has ever known, perhaps will know, and the hundred pounds but attests to it. But you're glum."

"The law, the greed, the corruption. I don't want it any more. I need out of Gray's, out of London." David lowered his voice. "It's the King. He's destroying England. Prince Henry—"

"Is dead, David."

"Parliament—"

"A ranting gang of Puritans. Do you know about men like Sandys? You think him the defender of the law. His brother George, the poet one, the bad poet one, twice has been caught red-handed as a highwayman. Now a third time and again he escapes going to the clink. Sandys uses influence and money to rig the trial. There is no ideal, no Utopia. Men are all corrupt. All but me, who doesn't care, and you with your ideals. Sir Francis Bacon be the star ascending and will be named to the Privy Council, but it does not end there. Villiers, the King's toy, will soon be named Earl of Buckingham."

"That is nonsense, George Vil—"

"He will be made Buckingham and Sir Francis, kissing his buttocks, will be made Lord Keeper. Francis is power hungry. All he has ever wanted was the title his father held. He hated the Queen for depriving him of what he felt was rightfully his. But now he flatters James and Villiers and will, as well, flatter the Prince of Wales and will be made Lord Keeper. No one knows how to give a bribe or how to take a bribe better than Francis. He prosecuted Essex to gain favor with Queen Elizabeth. He let Raleigh languish in the Tower to appease James. He prosecuted Carr to win Villiers's favour—"

"He is your friend."

"Best, and one of the most astute minds living. But I know him. David, reality is that men are base."

"Are all men either Volpone or his victims?"

"Yes. It saves them from having to labour. The wealth of the Berties keeps you, my friend, from having to work as a cooper's apprentice or scullery boy. At some point in man's social climb from savagery, accumulation becomes a habit." Jonson poured David more wine.

David emptied the cup and stood up. "I want to go back to Virginia."

"Go to Guiana with Raleigh. They have but let him out the Tower. He walks London like a mummy. He's an old man and doesn't know it's finished. The glorious England he knew is gone."

"It died, didn't it? It mostly died with the Queen, before I even knew it existed."

"If it ever did exist."

David wandered toward the door. He ran head-on into John Smith.

"I thought you at Plymouth." His words were slightly slurred.

"And I thought you at Gray's. Where are you off to in midday?"

"Virginia. Are there any ships sailing?"

"None that I know of. I'll be bound again for New England if I raise the capital. Come with me to the North. There are ships to be had in Plymouth."

"I want to go back to The People."

"To the old fox Opechancanough. There is something about that old Indian I never understood. I always had the sense he was laughing at me." He grabbed David's arm. "Things change. Jamestown is a jail with Dale as its keeper. Pocahontas is a Christian and now called Rebecca. She up and married some yeoman stock from Norfolk. The—"

"It was her dream."

"And that weed, tobacco, is the gold Martin couldn't find. It all changes, Davey. It's all a muddle."

"Not among The People. It is not Jamestown I go back to."

"Think on New England, lad." Smith released the grip on is arm. "I be off to Lincolnshire. The French won't yet give me my share of the booty taken from the pirates. Your brother is to Lincoln?"

"Lord Robert and his Lady are to Grimesthorpe. They've taken Vere to be with Lady Mary."

"'Tis a bedlam then."

"He's improving. He doesn't always make sense, but he's getting better."

"Let's hope he doesn't improve too much or I'll find Lincolnshire in a shambles. If the French won't part with my money I'll have to see to my shares, lest I starve."

"I'm sorry Sir Francis never responded about your book dedication. I brought it to his attention."

"'Twas my fault. They tell me he does naught without a bribe."

"Surely…"

"It was for the better. The Prince named the places on me map for the book and—"

"Charles?"

"I know he not be Henry, but he is the heir and, with his name in dedication, books will sell."

"It's all accumulation."

"It's all what, Davey?"

"Never mind." David left the Mermaid.

Molly

JAMESTOWN

—the present—

THE PHONE RANG. She found her cell phone in the bed-room. Oh God, it was Syril. Now is the time to tell her. She took a deep breath. "I've been meaning to call. But I've been so shook up," she lied. But a lie was better. She hes-itated and then weakly added in a voice that seeped with deep distress, "The engagement is off."

"Oh, my poor Molly. How dare he? Who does he think he is? And after all the plans you have made. Leaving you like that. Money reaches. We can have revenge."

That wouldn't do. "Oh, no. It was me. I met someone else."

"Someone else?"

Molly hesitated a moment and then decided what the hell. "A Carter. A *Virginia* Carter." It was not totally a lie. She had met him.

"A Carter! What a catch. Something far grander than what I planned would be in order for a wedding to a Carter, a Virginia Carter."

"Syril, I've only had a couple of dates."

"Of course, my dear."

"It probably will go nowhere."

"But you did break off your engagement for him. What's his full name?"

"Alexander Lee Carter."

There was silence and Molly wondered if she had been cut off. Then Syril came back on the phone. "He's in the register. Don't let him get away."

"I'll keep that in mind."

"A Carter. A Virginia Carter. Goodbye, my dear."

She sat on the edge of her bed in her long tee shirt. She should go out. Yes, get dressed and go for a walk along the James. Clear her head. Her muddled head. Instead she went to her computer in the cluttered room, picked up the journal and continued work on the transcription.

The Diary

AMONG THE PEOPLE

— 1612 —

Opechancanough was of course wrong about Kemadakun wanting me to be his squa. The young warrior had picked up his *attawap* and gone off to live with Farin and his tobacco garden. I was not surprised.

Peace had come to the Powhatan, not gentle in a soft voice, but in abduction and loud demands. For Pocahontas, the Governor had demanded the release of all the English held by the Powhatan and all the tools and weapons taken over the years. The Powhatan sent him seven settlers, including a Dutchman and a Pole, and returned a dull whipsaw and a hoe with a broken handle. But The People had become passive and I didn't understand it. The People no longer killed the English; the English no longer killed The People.

But the land of the Powhatan was still being eaten away by the encroaching English settlers. While the bellicose Oppussoquionuske ruled her Appamatuck, Dale staked out a town and called it the Bermuda One Hundred. Below Jamestown, Elizabeth City sprouted in the wilderness. The *yehaukens* of Parahunt became Henrico. The English built their houses and The People moved deeper into the forests. Though Orapaks was far removed in a dense wooded area between the Pamunkey and Chickahominy rivers, the English were creeping ever closer.

I remained content at Manapucunt. My son thrived. Opechancanough was my friend. To the English I remained dead. On the day Pocahontas married, I wished to stand in the church at Jamestown with Parahunt and Pochins and Opitchapan, but I remained nearby in the woods with Opechancanough. I caught sight of the bride buried in layers of English cloth, looking more the English lady than the daughter of the Powhatan. Jamestown extended beyond the palisades. Two-storey houses rowed out in streets away from the Fort. Gardens, planted fields, a wharf, fenced cattle and horses affirmed the permanence of the English presence. In the reports from Jamestown I perceived there was no longer communal property, each settler had been given acres to farm and raise food for the family. But the cruel laws and Calvinism of Gates and Dale were equally apparent in the reports.

Pocahontas had been taken by Dale to Henrico to be instructed in religion and taught English by the Reverend Whitaker. I wondered what devises Pocahontas had used to disguise the fact that she could already read. And what was her real reaction to the Puritan teaching? Whatever it was, the spies of Opechancanough told she had been doused with water and named Rebecca.

I called my son from football. He was seven and more one of The People than English, though his face was a Vere, his small eyes. Opechancanough had named him *Oolode*, joy. It was an apt name. Rufus Rex came running after him as he arrived home. He did not object to having to do his lessons while the other children played. He seemed to find *oolode* in pleasing me and he copied the letter I scrawled with a quill dipped in the homemade ink on the precious paper left by Ninghekekughes.

The People came and went freely at Jamestown, at Elizabeth City, at Fort Henry on the Cape, at Henrico near the Falls, and at the Bermuda One Hundred. And they reported all to the werowance of their tribe, who then reported to Opechancanough. His interest in the doings of the English was insatiable. It was how I had first learned of Pocahontas's mar-

riage. I was stunned to learn that John Rolfe
was to be her husband and it was written on
my face for Opechancanough said I did not
look pleased. Did I not like the man? I told
him I very much did not like the man and
that he was a lecherous hypocrite with great
Puritan prohibitions. I took David and went
to Farin to bear the news. He was not as surprised and said Rolfe would have a wife and
none else seemed inclined to have him. I sat
with David at the fire and ate partridge and
crab and rice and walnut cakes. I asked Farin
if he had made the cakes and said they were
quite good. No, he told me, but Kemadakun
did. Kemadakun smiled and told me he was
learning to read better. I gave them new moccasins and shirts and caps from some cloth
Pochins had gotten from Pocahontas.

Farin said that perhaps when Dale and
Gates were gone, he would be free to walk
among the English and sell his tobacco. He
said that because of Alan Plomb his hatred for
Rolfe knew no bounds.

David slept. I sat alone with Farin as
Kemadakun had gone outside into the air. I
told him that something about the peace disturbed me, something I could feel, and he
said he thought the same. There was something wrong in it. In the morning I returned
to Manapucunt.

During the year I often went to the place where Farin and Kemadakun lived apart, in the clearing near where the beaver made the dam. Kemadakun had showed Farin how to burn the trees to clear more land and more tobacco was planted. Farin had no market and stored the dried leaves. He waited for Dale to be gone so he could ship them to England. Farin and Kemadakun built a house of wood and daub and had a real floor and a door and windows with wooden shutters to keep out the cold and rain. They had a table and stools and a loft and a fireplace built of stone. Farin stole a pig and a cow from Henrico and hoped it was Dale's and milked the cow himself, but David made a face and hated the taste of the milk.

Nantaquaus came to Manapucunt. He told me Pocahontas had come to Orapaks, that it was her time. I left David in Face-of-Spots's care and rode the black mare to Orapaks. Nantaquaus, who rode with me, hung on at my waist and let out a whoop and told me he had ridden with Ninghekekughes.

At Orapaks, Tootoaw pointed off toward what she called the special place by the tree that cries in the wind. Pocahontas wore a maroon and gold damask gown, and despite her large belly, a farthingale, and her breasts were pushed up and girdled beneath a starched ruff. She was sprawled against a log, her legs spread apart. I approached and made a deep curtsy and called her Lady Rebecca, ma'am. Pocahontas picked up a pebble and threw it at me and called me a savage. She attempted to sit up and I helped her stand up and get out of the clothing. I asked why all the priests were there and she told me it was the custom and I asked if they delivered the baby and she told me no, the woman standing by the trees did that. I asked why she left her husband Kecoum and she said he was not only ugly but bad at *kisea*. She sighed with great relief when freed from the whalebone. She said Rolfe was at the *kisea* morning and night and when the sun sits high and low and when the sun sits not at all. I told her I knew that and that it killed his first wife and she said it wouldn't kill her and that she liked it much. A woman came with a deerskin apron to tie about the naked Pocahontas. All the while she talked, complained of praying, had a table and silver cups and plates and candles, a horn book and a pig. And a bed and lots of *kisea*. I told her she was about to have its reward. She asked if the pain would be bad and I told her it would, but that she could scream a lot and she said no, that a woman of The People makes no sound during the birthing. Pocahontas moved toward the hut that was under a tall willow standing in a clearing not far from the small stream. She told me Mister Rolfe would be angry with her and had forbade her to come and engage in pagan ways, but she said she had to come, it was the sacred time. I was allowed into the hut and Pocahontas endured the hours of labour without a sound. The child was a boy and the cord was cut by Papoo. Part of it was burned and the afterbirth was gathered by the priests and taken to a small platform on a post. The eagle appeared. Pocahontas was taken to bathe. She said that before she returned to Varina and her husband, she wished to see her father.

The Powhatan sat on a perch in the long *yehauken*. His breathing was heavy as he pulled the skin covering back and examined the infant's genitals. He told Pocahontas that daughters were better but more trouble. He sent his wives away. The three of us sat. The old Wereowance, still holding the baby, looked at me and asked if I was the one called Anumwitsqua. I told him I was she. The Powhatan handed the child back to Pocahontas and said he had something for me and from a skin pouch took out an ivory comb and gave it to me. It was so like the one Benjamin Joseph had given me for my birthday. He told me that when Ninghekekughes returned I would be his squa and that Ninghekekughes needed a woman. I voiced no opinion, but suspected that after so long a time this Ninghekekughes about whom they spoke so often would not return. From the pouch he removed a silver cross inlaid with turquoise stones and handed it to Pocahontas for the child. The Powhatan told his daughter that the annihilation of The People had ceased. She told him she would go to England. He told her he was old and dying, would not see her more.

Opechancanough arrived to see the child and the Powhatan handed the baby up to him. He told her it was a fine son and opened the baby's mouth and rubbed its gums. He told her she would see Ninghekekughes in England and that she must tell him that perhaps it was not good for The People to learn from the books for it created a knowledge which bred greed. I said nothing. Perhaps Opechancanough was right. Yet, the English were in Virginia to stay and unless The People learned their ways, they would be devoured. I went part of the way to Varina with Pocahontas, sometimes carrying the baby. I helped her into the maroon damask gown and asked when she was to go to England and she said within the year. I told her she would not be back to have another baby before she went. She said it was not the way of having another baby while one suckled and that the child would be at her breast for three years. I reminded her of all the *kisea*. She said she would take bark ground from the tree of the dying. She slipped into the ruff as I fastened it for her. She asked me to come to Varina. I told her that I could not, but asked when she got to England if she would tell Lady Bacon that Molly, Rufus Rex and young David be well. Pocahontas took a blue stone from her bag. She said it was the colour of the *shu-shu-gah* and would keep me safe. I took it. It was only blue glass, but I knew it meant much to her. I loosed the string at my neck and told her the pearl had been David's. She said I must not give it away, but I pressed it in her hand and kissed her goodbye. Alone, carrying her newborn son, Pocahontas moved off into the trees. She was bound for England. I wondered if I would ever see her again.

Molly

JAMESTOWN

—*the present*—

MOLLY DECIDED SHE would take that walk along the James. She went back in the bedroom and pulled the tee shirt off and was standing naked when the phone rang.

"What are you wearing?" Alex Carter asked.

"If I told you, you wouldn't believe me."

"Try me."

"I'm stark raving naked."

"And I'm sitting here in my boots with a raging hard on."

"You are not."

"But I could be if you keep talking about being stark raving naked."

"I was just going to put something else on and take a walk along the river."

"Put something period on."

"Why is that important to you? Why do you dress the way you do?"

"It gives me somewhere to belong. Don't you sense that?"

"I don't know."

"We are orphans, you and I. We are in need of some-where to belong."

"But you have only been an orphan as an adult."

"I've always been an orphan, even when I had parents."

"So I will find something period in which to walk in the dark of night. No one to see me."

"It's not being seen. It is about how you feel in the clothes. Which brings me to why I called. The Dixie Ball is in a month. It's Richmond's big social event of the year. I always go in my dress uniform. Would you be my lady?"

"I'm of another period."

"You had folk in antebellum Virginia. Will you accompany me to the ball, Miss Sharpe?"

"Well, Mister Alexander Lee Carter, I would be most happy to be your partner at the Dixie Ball." Molly dropped the southern drawl and added, "I will whip up a gown they will think came straight from the Smithsonian. Unless they look closely at the waist."

"You do me great honor. I wish I was there to walk along the river with you."

After she hung up Molly dug around a chest and dragged out a hide Indian outfit that she hadn't worn in more than a year, found some moccasins, got dressed and went out and walked down toward the sound of the lapping water. It came to her as she stood in the moonlight. The focus of her work didn't have to be about the accuracy of the journal or how it related to other works of the period. There was a search for utopia underlying Molly's journal that was reinforced by the online attachments of the phantom Opechancanough. How would one go about the citation of something which could possibly not exist? An interesting academic question. What fabric should she choose for her gown for the Dixie Ball? And what color? It would have to be spectacular if she was to march in on the arm of Alexander Lee Carter.

Molly was dragged from her thoughts by the sound of Inez's car. She walked in the blackness back toward the house and Inez's white blouse, shining in the dark.

"Sorry, I didn't mean to frighten you by suddenly appearing in the night."

"I heard your car."

"I may not have it much longer. I'm sinking into poverty and may have to drive some little used Plymouth. You won't have to worry about Syril hounding you about your wedding."

"I just talked to her. I couldn't tell her it was completely off and I lied. I told her I would probably be wedding a Carter."

"You're not, are you?" Inez slumped down into a porch chair.

"No. But you know Syril. I just couldn't tell her the truth and dash all those plans."

"She was being brave. Too ashamed to give it to you straight. There probably won't be any money for a wedding, at least not the kind of bridal memorial Syril would insist upon."

"What happened?" Molly found another chair and they sat in the darkness.

Inez picked up the brown paper bag that she had set on the floor of the porch and, without taking out the bottle, twisted the cap, took a slug and handed the bag to Molly.

"What is it?"

"Irish. Jameson's."

Molly took a drink. "Right tasty. Do we plan on getting drunk?"

"Yes."

"And the occasion?"

"Tonsi a'proc ni eveneg. Dear Papa has been ousted. No more CEO, no more high-flying income. And his prospects don't look too good because of it."

"He wasn't caught dipping into the till?"

"*Au contraire.* Turns out dear Daddy's too moral, too Catholic. A large group of folk, important folk, at Tonsi a'proc ni eveneg hatched a coup d'etat to overthrow the pope."

"You've got to be kidding. In this day and age? And who gives a fuck?"

"A great many, apparently. Anyway these plotters had convinced some liberal Italian Cardinal, if that's not an oxymoron, to be the pope and move the papacy to Avignon."

"And your father?"

"Got wind of it." Inez took another swig from the bottle and handed to Molly. "He apparently had visions of women priests, gays in the church and, God forbid, birth control. He notified Rome, rounded up some Vatican operatives and squashed the plot even as Cardinal whoever was being secreted out of Italy."

"Shouldn't that have made him a hero?"

"Not at Tonsi a'proc ni eveneg. This is a powerful force of liberals within the church. They are the only real bastion for change, I suppose, and Daddy was labeled a traitor and given the boot in a big way."

Molly took a drink from the bagged bottle. "What's going to happen now?"

"Daddy is home in D.C. and Mother calls him stupid and wants a divorce."

"Your parents will never divorce. They can't. They are the perfect couple."

"They won't divorce because Daddy, the good Catholic, would never allow it. Syril's stuck with him. But life is going to be hell at home."

"And you, Inez, how will your life be?"

"Probably saner. At least simplified. Mother can't just buy shit for me."

"Surely there are investments."

"Yes. We aren't ready for food stamps and poverty programs, but most of what Daddy had was tied to the corporation and they have stripped him of it all." A distant airplane sounded from somewhere overhead. "And you, Molly... what is your destiny?"

"Fuck destiny. There are no connections." She took a large swig of the whiskey. "Life is a random bunch of shit and I can live with that."

David

FRANCE

—the present—

DAVID CLOSED OUT the file and went to bed. In the morning, after breakfast, he stretched out, nude, on a low wall at the edge of the terrace. Yossef came out on to the flagstone. David looked over at him, but mainly saw only his legs and feet. He had nicely shaped calves, hairy, and the hair came down over his ankles. His feet were bare. "You're going to burn," Yossef said. "You want me to put some oil on you?" The oil was cool but Yossef's hands were warm on his back, his arms, his thighs, his calves and then moved up on his buttocks.

"Roll over," Yossef told him.

"I can't."

"Why not?"

"I have an erection."

"Is there something you would like me to do about it?"

"Yes," David said.

Yossef kissed him at length and blew him, there on the terrace.

In the afternoon, David wrote.

The Novel

LONDON

— 1612 —

David felt as if he were being suffocated under a blanket of greed. On the Bridge, the air was no better. Hucksters tried to sell him scraps of London. He moved through Southwark. The Mermaid's wine had made him light headed. He stopped to rest at the Globe. The old building, where he had first seen Molly, had burned. "With the firing of cannons in Henry the Eighth," the old man guarding the gate told him. "The new'ens better... bigger 'tis." And the Bear Pit was gone. Henslowe had put up another theatre in its spot, but Henslowe was dead. He crossed the little bridge to the Alleyn house. It was boarded up. The shutters from the house beyond slammed open. A woman in a yellow cap yelled out, "The whores is all gone. Go away!"

"I was looking for Mistress Alleyn."

"Gone. Two years gone. All that money... the likes of 'em couldn't afford to live in a slum be this 'en. Poked their noses to the air and packed it off for Dulwich where they say none but rich folk be livin'."

It was all accumulation.

David went to Bertie House. He was surprised to find Peregrine in town.

"Like old times." Peregrine seemed delighted to see him. "We can sup together."

The candles cast their silhouettes against the tapestries. David, eating cold mutton, became a shadow on Diana and the Hunt. "Your Mistress does not like London?"

"She says it be but depravity and greed."

"I think she might be right."

"Are you becoming a Puritan, too? Is that what Gray's does? You and Mistress Bertie hold that Parliament is God and the King must answer to it."

"I only want a Parliament so that it might rule fairly for the Indians."

"And you think a Parliament would? Illusion, my brother. The next Parliament—"

"There will be a next Parliament?"

"Eventually. There has to be. It will be a tool of the Calvinists, the Puritans, the Separatists, the Lutherans, all the dissenters; instead of a greater liberty, it will stifle the freedoms we do hold."

"Why? How can you be sure?" David fixed a plate of herring with orange sauce and a dollop of prune larded with chopped capon.

"The men of fortune are assembling power, those who find the court of James depraved."

"Isn't it?"

"Yes. But to combat the licentiousness of the courtiers, the Parliament of these men will bring the tyranny of morality down upon us all. Puritanism is incurably political. The great moral tyrant. Listen to its sermons. Read the tracts. It would tolerate no theatre, no art, no critical writing nor poetry and certainly no lapses into the scientific probing of the universe." Perri raised his cup. "But cheers. The monarchy is not dead. The Star Chamber becomes each day more abusive."

"The judicial abuses of that body be not fit topic for a digestible meal. Are you telling me the only choice might be between the tyranny of Parliament and the tyranny of the Star Chamber?"

"Yes."

"Well, I choose neither. I've already made up my mind. I'm going back."

"I am little surprised. Your pleading the cause of the Indians' has been constant."

"To no result. But the Company is the only alternative I have."

"The Company is broke. It couldn't buy a bottle of good Canary to give one of your tribe's chiefs. Investors are screaming for a return. No new pledges. The loss in revenues continues."

"So I have been told in repetition."

Peregrine poured them more wine. "When do you plan to go to Virginia?"

"On the next ship."

"That could be some time. What will you do in the mean?"

"Not Gray's. I will gather books and materials to take back with me. Go to Ersby and see Vere."

"And Mother?"

"Yes, Lady Mary as well."

"You never call her Mother."

"No."

Peregrine picked at his herring, removing a bone. "I am certain Lord Robert will continue your allowance. Sir Francis will be disappointed that you're not staying to the Inns."

"I am disappointed in Sir Francis."

"I warned you on that many years ago."

"An opportunist you called him and you warned me of London as well."

"I am much afraid, brother David, you are an idealist in a pragmatic world."

"I'm but scrubbed linen that got dropped in a full chamber pot." David drank his wine.

The next day he played tennis with the Earl of Southampton. The Earl's long blond hair was streaked with grey and flew about his head as he ran the court. He was thin and untiring, and David puffed to keep up, having lost the edge of the warrior with recent overindulgence. He also lost the tennis game.

The Earl sat on a bench near a statute of Antigone. He pushed the hair back from his shoulder. "I have some news for you, young d'Ersby. The *Treasurer* has sailed into Plymouth."

"Captain Argall?"

"Yes. But my news is not so much of Argall. Aboard the *Treasurer* is the Deputy Governor, Marshal Dale, and his guest Lady Rebecca and her husband Wolfe, or whatever his name is."

David stood up. "Pocahontas is in England! Perhaps I should ride to Plymouth."

"By this time they are on the road to London. To stay at the Belle Savage. Who of the Virginia Company had the audacity to quarter them in an Inn of that name, I know not, though it is said to be a fit place. There will be a reception at Smythe House for the Marshal and his guests come week ending."

"It was her dream."

At Smythe House, David stood in the doorway of the big hall taking in the tableau. Pocahontas and the titled were flanked by ten of The People in native garb. Next to Pocahontas stood a squat man with a pugged nose, who had to be Rolfe. In line with them were Marshal Dale and his wife, The Earl and Lady Southampton and Lord and Lady de La Warr. Cecilia was giggling. Pocahontas wore a grey dress and an auburn wig topped with a small grey hat. A strand of pearls fell from her neck. She looked radiant.

He approached and whispered. "Matoaka."

"Ninghekekughes!" She looked ready to cry.

"Were it not taboo I would hug you." He took her hand.

"I am English. It is no longer taboo."

David embraced her. Pocahontas laughed.

"Sir!" Rolfe had a sour look and his hand moved nervously.

"I am her brother, Master Rolfe. Ninghekekughes. David d'Ersby." David extended his hand. Rolfe ignored the hand.

"Opechancanough. How is he?" David asked.

It was Uttamatamakin who answered in the language of The People. "He awaits the return of Ninghekekughes."

"He does," Pocahontas said in English.

"I am going back on the next ship." David was being hurried by those behind him waiting to be presented. "We must have a long, long talk."

"Yes," she said in the language of The People. David moved out of the way.

Later, David watched as Pocahontas moved from the dignitaries with the grace of a queen and swept across the room toward him. Her dark eyes sparkled at him. "Where is Captain John?"

"He did not know of your coming and has gone to Lincoln."

"I like it here. I shall never return."

"Perhaps you will be disappointed. I am. I can no longer endure the greed and corruption. And now I worry about bringing education to The People. I don't want to carry the corruption with it."

"Opechancanough speaks of this, too."

"Does Rolfe treat you well?"

"Yes, except for the praying. Have you found a squa?"

"I shall not take a wife. There was only one for me."

"I have a wife for you—" But Pocahontas was interrupted as Sir Thomas Dale came and swept her away. "You must take me to meet Sir Francis," she said back over her shoulder.

There was no opportunity to take her to see the Bacons in the days ahead. Her time was fully occupied. David went to see Vere and Lady Mary before the time came to sail. The timbers of Ersby looked more sunken. The house seemed weighted by its own massiveness. But it was home. The gatekeeper nodded from his nap. "Master David." He said it as if David had been gone but for a morning walk and had returned. Chowder, who had accompanied him, rang the post bell.

"It ain't Master Vere, cuz he's to in," the old man said from the window. "So's must be Master David come from London, bless me bottom." He came down and opened the door, grunting and coughing, and gave Chowder a slap on the back. It was near noon and and a place was set for him for dinner in the hall. Despite the warmth of the day a fire roared in the hearth and the long hall seemed to perspire in the heat. "They knows you're here. They be dressing, so as to be fit to eat," the old man said.

David remembered the first time he had stood in the room and looked into the next and into the mirror, still where it had been. He saw his reflection and realized that more than eleven years had passed. He was no longer the ignorant boy. He had been halfway around the world and never fell off.

A door was ceremoniously opened. Above, a servant played a sputtering, grating flourish on a long trumpet. Another voice cried out, "The Baroness Dowager of Willoughby, Lady Mary and Sir Vere Bertie."

The 'sir' was obviously self-acquired knighthood. Lady Mary flew into the room. Clad in piles of yellow fabric, faded and wrinkled, her face was veiled in yellow net and her nipples decorously hidden. Vere wore a suit of mail obviously taken off the wall, and he clinked and creaked as he walked.

"The Baroness Dowager welcomes her son David Edward Robert Richard de Vere," Vere announced then bowed deeply and leaped, clanging, onto the middle of the table.

"Where did I get all the names?" David asked.

Lady Mary threw the veil back off her face. "You were christened by an anti-Lutheran in the cow barn." David wondered if it were true. "You must sit beside me at dinner. You are my favourite."

"It is true and nothing is truer than truth." Vere clanged as he sunk down in the middle of the table. "She likes you best because I am so rotten and Robert and Perri walk like Calvinists."

David sat beside her. Vere stayed in the center of the table like an ornament at a feast. A dish of larded grouse and raspberries was scooped out onto silver plates for them. Vere ate with his hands.

"I was never Queen of the May until yesterday when Vere crowned me. Vere set a wreath of straw flowers on my head." David did not remind her that May had long since passed.

Vere spooned raspberries out of the bowl and rattled as he moved. "London is a sewer of greed. Gold runs in the streets like piss and men like dogs lap it up."

"Your father's imagery was better," Lady Mary said and picked raspberry seeds from her teeth. "He was not given to coarseness and vulgarity, but then this is the age of the Jacobean, when a King with tiny legs and bad teeth sits in a chair made too big for him by the Queen Gloriana."

"I came home," David said, "because I have decided to go back to Virginia."

"Pope Boniface said there was no salvation, nor remission of sins outside the holy catholic and apostlic church: *Unam Sanctam.*"

"That was in thirteen o-two," Vere said. "I think the pope was in Avignon."

"Times've changed, I admit," Lady Mary said. "I hope the savages aren't Papists."

"They are corrupted by neither the law of Moses, nor Christian doctrine," David answered.

"You will take them God like John the Baptist on a platter." Vere tossed an egg as a stewed nest of boiled egg and herring with basiled walnut creme was served, along with heavy dark bread.

"I will take them language and knowledge."

Lady Mary clapped her hands. "We shall have music now."

The servants came in carrying tambourines, a drum, a recorder, and a horn. They created a discordant racket. "That was horrid," David said when they had finished and had left the hall.

"Yes," Lady Mary said. "Perhaps by tomorrow they will be better. You will leave me and go to Virginia beyond the edge of the Earth?" There were tears in her eyes and she dried them with her sleeve.

"I must. There is no place for me in England. I do not find peace in so much accumulation. A well-ordered society is not enough. An understanding of why it is well-ordered is essential."

"Madness is often but like Vere's chain mail, a protection against the barbs."

"I understand, Mother," he said. It was the first time that he had called her that.

A week later, as he left Ersby Hall, he thought he saw the white fox at the edge of the woods just beyond the River Steeping. The *wobaehokus*. He was uncertain, but it is the questions that count. He thought of the place-of-the-rock-in-the-trail-of-the-moon. The question becomes the answer. He was glad he had come home. He was glad he was going back to Virginia.

He found Smith in the white house in Willoughby Village and told him that Pocahontas was in London. Smith agreed to travel back with him. Pocahontas was still inned at the Belle Savage, but David waited for Rolfe to go off to Norfolk on business before calling on her. They talked in the language of The People and she told him of the peace brought about by her abduction and marriage, and how Opechancanough watched without raising either his voice or his arm in battle as the English took more and more of the land. She told him how Pochins had been forced from Kecoughtan, Parahunt from the Falls, even Oppussoquio-nuske was driven from the place of her *yehaukens*. As The People were pushed deeper into the woods and would soon be pressed against the land of the Monacan, the English went across the bay to the land of Accomac and Choptank. David was saddened, but such pacifistic behavior was not in Opechancanough's nature.

The wet foul weather of fall gave her a cough, but she bore herself in the fashion of a lady. Smith, in a letter to the Queen, had described her as the 'nonpareil of Virginia', and David thought it an apt description. She doted on her son Thomas and played with him, like any squa would, and nursed him and sang him English songs, mostly hymns. She seemed content and happy with Rolfe. David had taken an instant dislike to the man, a bore who talked of making a fortune in tobacco and little else. He asked Pocahontas if she was going back.

"No. I will never go back. I could not endure it. I must stay in London. There is much to see and do and then talk about."

Pocahontas's cough grew worse and the Virginia Company moved her and Rolfe to Brantford beyond Westminster, near Syon, house of the Earl of Northampton. The Company began a new lottery. This one was much more successful due to the arrival of the 'Indian Princess'. She was their testament to the success of the venture. Raleigh called upon her. Smith visited her at Brentford. Lord and Lady de La Warr presented her to the King. When David went to Brentford to see her, George Percy was there, dressed in red velvet cut in the latest London fashion. His slippers were decorated in pearls and bows, as were his hose.

"Dale is not going back. So much the better for Virginia," Percy said.

"Who's to be the deputy?" David asked.

"Argall. Sam is to return on the *George*."

"I will be with him then."

"And I will not," Pocahontas said. "We are to live in Heachem."

John Rolfe arrived from London and David said, "I really must get back to Bertie House."

"Argall has been given twenty-four hundred acres," Rolfe announced. David did not say that it was The People's land. Rolfe was handed a filled pipe by a servant and had it lit for him. "And I am honoured by being named the new Secretary of the Colony."

"How could you be?" Pocahontas asked. "We are going to Heachem, to live in England."

"No. I have spoken with my brother. He is in agreement. My fortune is in Virginia."

"No," she said.

"We are going to Virginia." There was finality in his voice.

David readied for the journey. He put his books in barrels and found more books and more barrels to put them into and though he had learned to make paper, he collected a good supply. He found chocolate for Opechancanough at a shop near the wharfs. He purchased a shirt of cambric for the Powhatan, a dress for Face-of-Spots, a knife with an inlaid handle for Nantaquas, a shawl for Toatoka, toys for their child, and a gilded mirror for Papoo. He was given books by Sir Edwin and Lord Henry.

He escorted the Rolfes to Twickenham. Leaving them to be entertained by Alice, he sought Sir Francis in his room. The book still held the door open.

"I am leaving Gray's and going back to Virginia," he said.

"So I am told. You desert the law."

"The law has deserted me." They argued. The same argument. "You are perhaps the most brilliant man in England, maybe the world—"

"And the most vain... to hear you talk. I am, David, much too human, too bifurcated to be the ingenious philosopher commanding myself to isolation and thinking, and too driven to be as my father was, a man of great power. I am the product of the old Lord Keeper." Bacon sat back in his chair. "I am ranting." He paused. "Will you give some further thought to Gray's? Speak to me later on it?"

David smiled. "As the philospher or the politician?"

"You jest, but no theory of politics can be sound unless based on the study of man."

"We are all the spiritual heirs of Plato."

"We are indeed, David." Bacon played with a pen on his desk. "Think on Gray's, and in the mean you must introduce me to this Indian Princess."

"She is an admirer of Philosopher Bacon. I taught her to read; she would have none but the *Essays*."

"You are puffing up the vanity again."

"But her husband is a bore. Talks of naught but tobacco."

"Then I shall make you a bargain. I will show him my herb garden while you have a word with Alice and the Princess. Then you and Alice can run the bore with the hounds and I will have a word with Pocahontas. For Alice's sake, I hope the Princess is bizarre. Alice thrives on the bizarre."

"She is more English than most English ladies."

Pocahontas and Rolfe were presented to Sir Francis in the golden drawing room. At the window David looked out across the pond, the afternoon sun resting its reflection in the water. At times England could be beautiful. Rolfe was flattered to be in the company of the great man and was even polite to David. "Since you are interested in horticulture, Mister Rolfe, you must let me show you my prize herbs."

"I don't wish to go back, Lady Bacon. I love England." Pocahontas spoke breathlessly of all she had seen and done.

"All this in such a short time," David said.

"If I stayed I could see more."

"And I would show it to you," Alice said. "David says you are an admirer of my husband."

"Yes, the great philosopher."

"When he returns from his garden we will leave him with you and take a run with the dogs."

"You have dogs?"

"Huge hounds. They drag me about," Alice said. The dogs were brought in as they spoke.

"Anumwitsqua has a dog like that."

"Anumwitsqua," David translated for Alice, "means the woman who has a dog."

Pocahontas didn't take her eyes from the dogs. "She said you gave her the dog, Lady Bacon."

"To take to Virginia? No. The only one I ever gave a dog to...was...MY GOD...MOLLY?"

David stared at Alice and then at Pocahontas.

"Her name is Molly," Pocahontas said.

David sunk to his knees.

"She has a son?" Alice asked.

"Yes," Pocahontas said. "His name is David...the same as yours, Ninghekekughes."

"But The People..." David found it impossible to believe as true.

"...would not kill a child..."

Alice threw open her arms. "David, she is alive. Molly is alive!"

"Opechancanough discovered she could speak the language of the Spanish. He needed someone to read Plato to him and tell him in words he could understand. Ninghekekughes was gone."

David stayed on his knees, afraid his legs would not hold him. "Molly spoke Spanish."

"But the dress, the blood?" Alice asked.

"A trick of Opechancanough's to make them think her dead."

"But did no one ever see her?" David got up. "All this time, surely, from the Fort… Sam?

"She kept from them. She was afraid of Dale. Farin was her only friend at Jamestown and he left."

"I know that story," Alice said. "Farin was charged with sodomy and escaped, but the young man charged with him was found guilty and burned. Is Farin alive and well?"

"Yes," Pocahontas said.

"It was through Farin that I knew Molly, David. Sir Francis saw to Farin's will. He left his estate in Chelswood in Sussex to your son, whom Francis assumed was dead. This is a wonderful day."

"For me, glorious," David said. "But Matoaka, I often talked to you of Molly."

"She spoke of a David. I sometimes thought…but then no. I thought it could not be."

"You never spoke of me to her?"

"Yes, constantly. But your name is Ninghekekughes and she would not have known."

"Alice!" David picked her up and turned her about. "Alice! She is alive!"

The hounds barked.

Sir Francis and John Rolfe came in the drawing room.

"She is alive. Molly Dean is alive."

"Molly Prine," Alice added. "Pocahontas knows her well. She lives among the Indians."

"I see I will not have to await your decision as to Gray's then, David."

"I will swim to Virginia, Sir Francis."

Charles Stuart was invested Prince of Wales. The *George* was not yet ready to sail. Pocahontas's cough seemed worse as the weather turned colder. Christmas came, but David did not go to Grimesthorpe where the Berties gathered. He entertained the Rolfes at Bertie House, where Pocahontas continued to cough. For Christmas, Cecilia West gave her a brown mare and saddle. The *George* was still not ready to sail. Princess Pocahontas in heavy brocade and full ruff went to Court to see Jonson's *Twelfth Night* masque.

"We must sail soon," Rolfe insisted.

Within the month, the *George* and her companion vessels lifted anchor. "Sails to the yards!" the Master yelled out. The ship moved down the Thames.

Pocahontas stood at the rail and coughed. It was a deep hack and her voice had become hoarse.

"A distemper," Rolfe said and hung on to his young son's hand.

The ships moved through the reaches—Busby, Woolwich, Barking—and to where the shores were marshy. At the bend they passed Erith. Pocahontas had been taken to Captain Argall's quarters and the barber was ordered to her. She was spitting blood. Rolfe was called to the cabin. The Thames grew wider and the chalk cliffs towered. Beyond lay Gravesend. David went with Captain Argall and John Rolfe in the small boat that carried Pocahontas from the ship. She was delirious with fever. She was taken to an Inn and the physician of Gravesend came to attend her. David waited in the public room with the Captain. In a room above, Pocahontas lay, attended by the physician, Rolfe at her bedside.

The hours slipped away and Captain Argall and David sat silently. Rolfe came down.

"How is she?" Argall asked.

"She asks for you," Rolfe said to David.

David went up the narrow steps. She was pale and coughed, but she looked up at David and spoke, her voice barely audible. "I said I would not leave England."

"You will get better." He remembered the death of Prince Henry.

She motioned for him to take the single pearl that was on a strand about her neck.

David removed it. It was not a good pearl, not like the many he'd seen taken from the beds in the Bay. It was small and imperfect. "Yours." Her voice broke. "Molly...fell... your doublet..."

All those years ago at Joan's. He tightened his fist around the pearl. It was the most perfect pearl he had ever seen.

"I am in England." Her voice was clear, and she died.

John Rolfe did not seem upset that he had not been with her at the end. At Plymouth he left his son with the Vice Admiral of Devon that he might be delivered to his brother Henry Rolfe of Heachem. David thought Pocahontas would be happy to know that her son was staying in England.

David

FRANCE

—the present—

FOR SEVERAL NIGHTS David slept in the smaller room, in a bed Yossef shared with him. And in the morning before breakfast, he would go back to his own room and write. Then he spent the rest of the day with Yossef. They moved about the house, sometimes hand-in-hand, sometimes just looking, smiling, laughing. They listened to music and sat leaning against the wall of the house on the terrace and were still, as if putting time into memory. They had sex and ate and drank wine and for a brief moment danced together on the terrace. David made no attempt to analyze his feelings. He simply enjoyed where he was and what he was in the moment. When he went to sleep, his head rested on Yossef's arm. In the morning he awoke and wrote.

The phone rang while he was writing. Yossef came in and put his hand on his shoulder. David looked up into eyes that now were sad.

"You are free," Yossef said.

"Free?"

"Free to go. It has ended. I am told you have an e-mail from Edward with instructions."

"I have no Internet." David smiled and stroked Yossef's arm.

"Your Peugeot is in the garage... just below." Yossef held a wireless modem out and plugged it in.

"All this time... I could simply have driven away."

"You could have driven away."

David opened his e-mail. He had messages from themoll, several from opech, one from David Vere and a message from an Internet name he assumed must be Edward.

It read: David, the plan to bring the papacy back to Avignon on the death of the Pope has been thwarted by traitors within the corporation. I thank you for your help and was relieved to find you well and unharmed, although I was always promised you would be. Your mother and I were both worried. I have made arrangements for you to return the car in Nice and fly from there. There will be a ticket for you at the British Airways counter that will take you into Gatwick. I will not see you immediately upon your return as I am off to Oslo. Again my deepest thanks and know you have my love, Edward.

And that was the full, albeit parsimonious explanation. Damn him. Still David was sorry to see the end of his captivity.

"Will you leave immediately?" Yossef asked.

"Tomorrow's soon enough. Would you mind calling British Airways and see if you can locate a reservation for me on a flight out of Nice to Gatwick. Apparently, I have a ticket."

"Yes. When Madame gets here where shall we dine, the final meal?"

"The terrace. Romantic. By candlelight, if you can grouse up some candles."

Later Yossef handed him a slip of paper with the next afternoon's flight information to London on BA. "I knew it would have to end," he said.

David agreed.

He opened the e-mail from David Vere, asking about his whereabouts. He replied that he was well and leaving tomorrow for Gatwick, the time of the flight and would David like to meet him? The e-mail from themoll and those from opech he could open in London. In fact, he had no further need for the e-mail attachments from opech at all.

He went out and had wine on the terrace with Yossef. They dined by candlelight, listened to music and talked as if there would be night after night like this and yet both knew it was the end. They went to bed much later that night.

The morning light was more awkward. There seemed finality.

"We will never see each other again, will we?" Yossef asked.

"No."

When at last he was at the car, his bag and computer stowed, Yossef embraced him, kissed him and said, "I love you, David."

As the Peugeot pulled away, David called back, "And I love you, Yossef."

He drove the winding cobblestones down from the mountain villa. A memory.

In the Nice airport he waited for his flight to be called and wrote on the laptop, hoping he had enough battery power to finish.

The Novel

THE LAST CHAPTER

— *1 6 1 2* —

The journey was uneventful, but despite the good speed, David was impatient. Off Cape Cod, the fog surrounded them, and down the coast, visibility was minimal, yet Argall's skill kept the ships on course. They arrived in the Bay. He had come home, really home. He wanted to leap off and run to Molly. They moved up the Great River and docked. Argall was upset. What Dale had left in such a state of order was, under Yeardly, 'a damnable mess', as Argall put it. The wharf was in pieces. Tobacco was growing everywhere—in the streets, beyond the broken palisades, in stretches to the river. Yeardly greeted them with a parade. Argall was furious but held his temper.

"Bad weather," Yeardly said of the wharf and relinquished his command.

A pinnace looking to be rotting away banged against the broken wharf, but the settlers of Jamestown looked well fed and happy.

"May I borrow the horse Lady Bacon gave Pocahontas?" David asked Rolfe.

"Yes, but make certain I get it back."

"May I have your leave," David asked Captain Argall, the new Deputy Governor.

"You may fly, David. Tell Molly we shall have a game of whist later."

David rode to Manapucunt. Although the ride seemed as long as the sea voyage, in less than a day he reached the encircled *yehaukens*. It was dark. He was impatient to see Molly, but he went first to the *yehauken* of Opechancanough, as he must. The old man sat alone.

He looked up, tears in his eyes. "Ninghekekughes, you have come back to us."

David spoke in the language of The People. "I have. And I would call you Father."

"And I, you, my son. Yet you are dressed as an Englishman."

"I have not had time to change."

"You have been gone so long, yet would rush to be here?"

"Molly, the woman of whom I spoke so often as dead, is here, Apachisto. Her son is my son."

"She reads me Plato. She hates Plato."

"I have brought many books. And we will discuss many things. I have left behind greed and accumulation. It must stay from the people."

"And Pocahontas?"

"She will never be able to leave England."

"A fever?"

"A disease of the lungs." David put his hands to his lips. "She did not want to leave England."

"It was well she was happy." The old Werowance stood up. "I will take you to Molly."

They moved out of the *yehauken*. Despite the evening darkness, The People began gathering about him.

David went to the horse and from a bag took a box and handed it to Opechancanough.

"Is it chocolate?"

"It is chocolate."

Opechancanough, holding the box of chocolate, led the way toward a *yehauken* on the far side of the cluster.

"Tell me," David asked as they walked slowly in the open area. "Why do the English take so much of your land, yet you do nothing?"

"There is a time for peace…a time for killing. Now is the time for peace."

David suspected there was to be a blood bath.

Opechancanough stuck his head inside the *yehauken*. "Ninghekekughes has returned. He would speak to you." Opechancanough moved back out and David went in.

Molly stared across the dim firelight. She began to shake and sob without control. He reached over to her but she shrank away. "It…it will…be taken…taken from me."

"Not this time." He took her hand and pulled her into his arms. She was shaking. "Not this time."

They stood silently. She ceased crying. Her breathing eased. He kissed her. She clung to him. "Sometimes," she said, "I sensed Ninghekekughes was you, but I could not let myself believe it."

"I am Ninghekekughes."

"And you are David and alive."

"My son?"

She moved from his arms and bent down in the corner of the *yehauken*. She pulled back a bearskin. Only the boy's head was visible. "He sleeps," she said. "But I assure you, he has your eyes."

"The Vere beady eyes." He touched the sleeping child's small hand. He turned and kissed Molly again. "It was a long journey for both of us, but we are home."

"Yes, we are home."

They lay together beneath the skin of the bear. The smells of The People engulfed him.

David heard the distant single shriek of the *shu-shu-gah*.

David

LONDON

—the present—

THE END. DAVID sat staring at the screen. He was done. Traditional endings and endings that didn't have to be. Perhaps in his next novel he would be more daring.

At Gatwick he was met by not just David Vere, but Jane as well. She carried one bag and his brother the other and he walked between them, an arm thrown around each of them. He turned and kissed Jane on the mouth.

"Are you supposed to kiss a sister like that?" she said when he released her.

"Only if she has big tits."

He turned then and kissed David Vere on the mouth in the same way.

"Jesus," David Vere said, "where did they have you, in Russia?"

"Tell you all about it sometime, my brother." He felt happy, truly happy, walking through the airport with his brother and sister. As they went outside, he looked at the very tall Scandinavian flight attendant. Her blond hair swung in the wind. "Look at the legs on that," he said.

"Nothing for me," his brother said.

"And certainly nothing for me," his sister said.

Late that night after consumption of pints, David Vere asleep in one of the new beds in the flat and Jane gone back to her own flat, David went online.

---

themoll: You are alive?

dsharpe: But a bit draggy at the moment.

themoll: I was wondering if you would like to come to Virginia. The novel. In the way of research.

dsharpe: The novel is finished.

themoll: You're finished, as in done?

dsharpe: Yes. My David has his Molly.

themoll: Yes. And that would mean my Molly has her David, I suppose.

dsharpe: Yes.

themoll: Historical fact I guess. And Opechancanough?

dsharpe: Well, he has his Ninghekekughes back.

themoll: And the online Opechancanough?

dsharpe: The hacker?

themoll: If that's what is? Yes.

dsharpe: I can't say I'm not indebted to him. But if he chose to give away his story, well...

themoll: His narrative.

dsharpe: Well he made no claims. Perhaps he was just a figure from a different time lost in cyber space.

themoll: And you chose to belief that?

dsharpe: Plausible as any other answer. And I am finished with it. A chapter of my life, I suppose, as well. I've been thinking of going to Norway. A new novel idea, less traditional, about the Norse and their migration into England.

themoll: The Vikings, that sort of thing.

dsharpe: Weren't they supposed to have gotten to America before Jamestown existed?

themoll: Some theory like that, yes. I was thinking it would be fun to get together.

dsharpe: Well you are always welcome at Bloomsbury. My brother thinks a lot of you and I am sure my sister would like to meet you.

themoll: Perhaps sometime. Plans. Involved in something to do with the Civil War.

dsharpe: I understand. Things get kind of screwed up sometimes.

themoll: Screw. A twist or turn of.

dsharpe: A cylindrical rod incised with helical spiral threads.

themoll: To cheat.

dsharpe: To fasten tight to.

themoll: To become attached to.

dsharpe: A jail guard.

themoll: To shrewdly bargain.

dsharpe: To use force.

themoll: To penetrate.

dsharpe: Don't even go there.

She suddenly vanished offline. She'd seemed a little strange. Well, he was done with the novel, perhaps her interest in him had waned.

Acknowledgments

A crucial part of *The Blue Heron* is the Opechcancanough narrative, which would not have been possible without the scholarship of Carl Bridenbaugh. Dr. Bridenbaugh's theory and support for the contention that the youthful Indian prince was taken to Spain and New Spain before being returned to the Chesapeake area underlie my efforts to breathe life into this historical character. I'm grateful to Dr. Bridenbaugh for providing this foundation.

In my research I was aided by the staffs at the Virginia State Library, the Richmond Public Library and the Virginia Historical Society. I would also like to acknowledge the support of George Sands, former head librarian of the Caroline County Library in Denton, Maryland. And the good people of Lincolnshire in the U.K. directed and guided me over the wolds and through the villages and towns of this historical shire, so essential to place in the novel.

And finally, special thanks to my daughter Mary for her professional proofreading skills.

About the Author

GENE FARRINGTON was one of perhaps thirteen people born in North Dakota. Growing up he lived with his seven siblings in towns in South Dakota, Minnesota, Wisconsin and Iowa. The varius loci perhaps enhanced the potential to produce a writer. At Monona High in Iowa, he wrote only one poem, confiscated as the English teacher assumed it had been plagiarized because of its brilliance. He joined the Marines and was shipped off to Korea. There was a war on, although they didn't call it that. Whatever it was it provided fodder for a novel presently in process entitled *The Accoucher Comes*. After the USMC he enrolled at Kent State, married, moved to Los Angeles to escape the Ohio winters, divorced, managed an in-house advertising ad agency and, in his spare time, wrote bad fiction. He discovered creative writing at Cal State L.A. and, under the tutelage of novelist John Weston, learned to write. He completed his B.A. and M.A. and had his first play produced. Liz Trupin of JET Literary Associates became his agent and remains his agent eons later; she sold his tenth-century novel, *Breath of Kings*, to Doubleday. He went off to University of California, Santa Barbara and got his Ph.D. Another play was produced — *Halek*, in which Shakespeare speaks only words he had written. It won the Corwin Metropolitan Theatre award. He taught at Cal State, L.A., University of San Diego and Cal State San Bernardino before arriving at Notre Dame of Maryland University where he teaches literature, theatre courses and creative writing.

Readers' Guide

1. The structure of *The Blue Heron* is best described as post-modern. Farrington plays with time and place and character until, ultimately, the characters in David's novel, Molly's ancestral diary and Opechancanough's narrative all intermingle and become one story. Does this aspect of the novel work for you? Why or why not?

2. The contemporary Molly and David are meant to be sympathetic characters. Do you identify with them and/or recognize their situations as realistic?

3. Opechancanough had an interesting life, having been to Spain and New Spain in his youth. Does Farrington's fictionalized characterization of this historical figure work for you? How? If not, why?

4. The relationship between Pocahontas and Captain John Smith has often been pictured as a romantic one. How do you feel about Farrington's depiction? Were you surprised to find out she married John Rolfe and died in England?

5. Do you believe Farrington is successful in presenting the Powhatan people, not only the structure of their society but the complexity of their relationship with the white colonists who arrived on their shores? Did anything you read in this novel change your perceptions about them or their culture?

6. The founding of Jamestown was not easy for the English, and life in the colony was often brutal. Do you feel Farrington is fair in his presentation of it? Did it change your perceptions about the culture of the colony?

7. How well does Farrington capture a sense of place, of period and lifestyle of Jacobean England in terms of both the noble and lower classes? Did anything you read in this novel change your perceptions about their culture?

8. Jacobean attitudes toward Catholics, witchcraft, the poor, prostitution, the theatre, public punishment and women, while sometimes varied, were more often extreme and cruelly intense. How successful was Farrington in addressing these attitudes in the novel? Were you surprised by anything?

9. Were you already familiar with the historical Prince Henry, the oldest son of James I? Now that you know something about him, do you think English history after King James might have been different had he lived?

10. While the novel has a few fictional characters, it is laden with historical figures. How successful is Farrington in breathing life into those historical figures? Are they believable? Do you have favorites?

11. Farrington interweaves many themes throughout *The Blue Heron*: the importance of family, the importance of culture, the importance of words, the transcendence of love and loyalty, to name just a few. What resonates most with you? Why?

12. Do you find the title evocative?

OTHER BOOKS FROM WATER STREET PRESS

Virgins & Martyrs
A NOVEL

Hugh Mahoney

New Yorkers open their Sunday morning paper to find a photo of Virgil Quinn, teacher of history at St. Lucy's School for Boys, splashed all over the front page. How did he get there? Scandal, of course. Virgil has made enemies—the Cardinal of New York not the least among them. The Cardinal's research reveals that Virgil has lived many lives, all of them scandalous. Was he really a ranking nun in the Sisters of Mercy of Baton Rouge? Did he really walk the ramps of Seventh Avenue as the city's highest paid supermodel? Just how did he come to know all those men whose names appear in his notorious (and deadly convenient) Black Books? *Virgins & Martyrs* is shrewd and malicious fun, a wicked commentary on love, life, gender and the history of our nation, a work in which the peripatetic and intrepid—yet all-too-human—Virgil Quinn lets no one off the hook.

Stalking Carlos Castaneda
NON-FICTION

Joan Wulfsohn

In 1972, professional dancer Joan Wulfsohn underwent a double mastectomy. And her soon-to-be-ex-husband abducted their three children and spirited them away to a foreign country. "I should have died," Joan writes. But she didn't. *Stalking Carlos Castaneda* chronicles her journey back to life by way of lessons learned from stunning transvestites and music hall dancers, teen porn stars, a brain-damaged boy, Eastern holy men, Western supermodels and a certain aging sorcerer. It is the story of how one woman learned to live a magical life—bound not by spells and hexes but rather filled with wonder and transcendence.

The Happy Party of Honorable Women

FICTION

Cate Quintara

Jill's daughter is getting married. The two women with whom Jill has been best friends since they were little girls—Deanie, a successful novelist, and Trick, who struggles with bipolar disorder—arrive to help celebrate the happy event. The bride, however, has a bigger role than "wedding guest" in mind for them all—she has decided she will make up her wedding party by honoring the women who raised and nurtured her.

Throughout the week of pre-nuptial parties, Jill and Deanie and Trick relive the events that have shaped their lifelong friendship—their marriages and relationships, the births and losses of their children, the tragedies and joys that have forged their bond. The women discover the true depths of this bond—and how the wish of one unconventional young bride has transformed them all.

Cate Quintara invites you to be a guest at a unique and wonderful wedding, and to celebrate a jubilant life milestone—one made possible only because of the lifetimes of ordinary, everyday love that have preceded it.

Creole Son

FICTION

Michael Llewellyn

In 1872, French painter Edgar Degas is disillusioned by a lackluster career and haunted by the Prussian siege of Paris and the bloodbath of the Commune. Seeking personal and professional rebirth, he journeys to New Orleans, birthplace of his Creole mother. He is horrified to learn he has exchanged one city in crisis for another—post-Civil War New Orleans is a corrupt town occupied by hostile Union troops and suffering under the heavy hand of Reconstruction. He is further shocked to find his family deeply involved in the violent struggle to reclaim political power at all costs.

Despite the chaos swirling around him, Degas sketches and paints with fervor and manages to reinvent himself and transition his style from neoclassical into the emerging world of Impressionism. He ultimately became one of the masters of the new movement, but how did New Orleans empower Degas to fulfill this destiny?

The answer may be found in the impeccably researched, richly imagined historical novel, *Creole Son*.

Tradition

FICTION

Marci Blackman

At the age of 21, Gus Weesfree witnessed a brutal crime in his hometown of Tradition, Ohio, and fled. Now an old man, exhausted by a life on the run, he is compelled to confront his past only to find most of his memories buried by urban sprawl. He seeks solace in Mabel, the sister he abandoned, a lifelong alcoholic who presumed him dead.

As the surviving Weesfree family exhumes their history, Gus finds that not all was as it seemed in Tradition. The love and betrayal of his youth ran far deeper than he ever imagined.

Moving seamlessly between present-day and the 1930s and '40s, award-winning author Marci Blackman reveals the powerful force exerted by the past on the present. *Tradition* gracefully uncovers the Weesfree family secrets—and how race, family, and loyalty can shape a life.

Made in the USA
Lexington, KY
06 April 2014